EVERYONE LOVES

Today Tonight Tomorrow

Named a Best Book of the Year by
The New York Public Library • *Kirkus Reviews* • *BuzzFeed*

"Swoony, steamy." —*Entertainment Weekly*

"Brilliant, hilarious, and oh-so-romantic." —*BuzzFeed*

"A sweet YA novel that fans of *Nick and Norah's Infinite Playlist* will love."
—*HelloGiggles*

★ "A dizzying, intimate romance."
 —*Kirkus Reviews*, starred review

★ "Funny, tender, and romantic."
 —*Publishers Weekly*, starred review

★ "A breezy, one-sitting read that wraps the immediacy of a single day with outstanding layers of nostalgia, empowerment, and self-acceptance."
—*BookPage*, starred review

"A thoughtful and current story, and a fun summer read." —*SLJ*

"*Today Tonight Tomorrow* is romance done right." —Tamara Ireland Stone, *New York Times* bestselling author of *Every Last Word*

"Fun, flirty, and downright adorable." —Deb Caletti, award-winning author of *A Heart in a Body in the World* and *Girl, Unframed*

"I fell head over heels for this smart, swoony, hilarious story."
—Jennifer Dugan, author of *Hot Dog Girl*

"[A] pitch-perfect romance." —Emily Wibberley and Austin Siegemund-Broka, authors of *Always Never Yours* and *If I'm Being Honest*

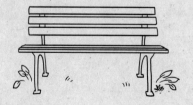

Also by
RACHEL LYNN SOLOMON

You'll Miss Me When I'm Gone
Our Year of Maybe
We Can't Keep Meeting Like This

Today
Tonight
Tomorrow

RACHEL LYNN SOLOMON

SIMON & SCHUSTER BFYR
New York   London   Toronto   Sydney   New Delhi

SIMON & SCHUSTER BFYR

An imprint of Simon & Schuster Children's Publishing Division
1230 Avenue of the Americas, New York, New York 10020
This book is a work of fiction. Any references to historical events, real people, or real places are used fictitiously. Other names, characters, places, and events are products of the author's imagination, and any resemblance to actual events or places or persons, living or dead, is entirely coincidental.
Text © 2020 by Rachel Lynn Solomon
Cover illustration © 2020 by Laura Breiling
Illustrations on pages i, vii, 9, 23, 33, 43, 61, 101, 113, 126, 138, 157, 169, 213, 221, 233, 252, 266, 329, 336, 346, 352, 359, and 365 © 2020 by Laura Breiling
Confidential stamp on page 69 by Zerbor/iStock
Emojis on pages 98, 127, 144, 222, 224, and 360 by denisgorelkin/iStock
Wolf illustration on pages 86, 150, 199, and 292 by Omar Mouhib/iStock
Cover design by Laura Eckes © 2020 by Simon & Schuster, Inc.
All rights reserved, including the right of reproduction in whole or in part in any form.
SIMON & SCHUSTER BOOKS FOR YOUNG READERS and related marks are trademarks of Simon & Schuster, Inc.
For information about special discounts for bulk purchases, please contact Simon & Schuster Special Sales at 1-866-506-1949 or business@simonandschuster.com.
The Simon & Schuster Speakers Bureau can bring authors to your live event. For more information or to book an event, contact the Simon & Schuster Speakers Bureau at 1-866-248-3049 or visit our website at www.simonspeakers.com.
Also available in a SIMON & SCHUSTER BFYR hardcover edition
Interior design by Laura Eckes
The text for this book was set in Adobe Garamond Pro.
Manufactured in the United States of America
First SIMON & SCHUSTER BFYR paperback edition June 2021
20 19 18 17 16 15 14 13 12 11
The Library of Congress has cataloged the hardcover edition as follows:
Names: Solomon, Rachel Lynn, author.
Title: Today tonight tomorrow / by Rachel Lynn Solomon.
Description: Hardcover. | New York : Simon Pulse, 2020. | Audience: Ages 12 and Up. | Audience: Grades 10-12. | Summary: "Throughout the years both Rowan and Neil have been at competition with one another on everything from who has the best ideas for school functions to which one will be their graduating class's valedictorian. However, in the twenty-four hours left they have as high school students, the two learn they share something much deeper than a rivalry"—Provided by publisher.
Identifiers: LCCN 2019029488 (print) | LCCN 2019029489 (eBook) | ISBN 9781534440241 (hardcover) | ISBN 9781534440258 (pbk) | ISBN 9781534440265 (eBook)
Subjects: CYAC: High schools—Fiction. | Schools—Fiction. | Competition (Psychology)—Fiction. | Love—Fiction. | Jews—United States—Fiction.
Classification: LCC PZ7.1.S6695 Tod 2020 (print) | LCC PZ7.1.S6695 (eBook) | DDC [Fic]—dc23
LC record available at https://lccn.loc.gov/2019029488
LC eBook record available at https://lccn.loc.gov/2019029489

For Kelsey Rodkey,
who loved this book first

MESSENGER

I see, lady, the gentleman is not in your books.

BEATRICE

No; an he were, I would burn my study.

—*Much Ado about Nothing* by William Shakespeare

I used to dream of you nightly
I would wake up screaming
—"Make Good Choices" by Sean Nelson

5:54 a.m.

McNIGHTMARE
Good morning!
This is a friendly reminder that you have three (3) hours and counting before suffering a humiliating defeat at the hands of your future valedictorian.
Bring tissues. I know you're a crier.

The text jolts me from sleep a minute before my 5:55 alarm, three quick pulses to let me know my least favorite person is already awake. Neil McNair—"McNightmare" in my phone—is annoyingly punctual. It's one of his only good traits.

We've been text-taunting since we were sophomores, after a series of morning threats made both of us late for homeroom. For a while last year, I decided to be the mature one, vowed to make my room a McNair-free zone. I'd put my phone on silent before slipping into bed, but beneath the pillow, my fingers twitched with combative responses. I couldn't sleep thinking he might be texting me. Baiting me. *Waiting*.

Neil McNair has become my alarm clock, if alarm clocks had freckles and knew all your insecurities.

I fling back the sheets, ready for battle.

> oh, I didn't realize we still thought crying was a sign of weakness

> in the interest of accuracy, I'd like to point out that you've only seen me cry once, and I'm not sure that necessarily makes me "a crier"

> Over a book!

> You were inconsolable.

> it's called an emotion

> I highly recommend feeling one (1) sometime

In his mind, the only thing you're supposed to feel while reading a book is a sense of superiority. He's the kind of person who believes all Real Literature has already been written by dead white men. If he could, he'd bring Hemingway back to life for one last cocktail, smoke a cigar with Fitzgerald, dissect the nature of human existence with Steinbeck.

Our rivalry dates back to freshman year, when a (small) panel of judges declared his essay the winner of a school-wide contest about the book that had impacted us the most. I came in second. McNair, in all his originality, picked *The Great Gatsby*. I picked *Vision in White*, my favorite Nora Roberts, a choice he scoffed at even after he'd won, insinuating I shouldn't have gotten second place for picking a *romance novel*. This was clearly a really valid stance for someone who'd likely never read one.

I've despised him ever since, but I can't deny he's been a worthy antagonist. That essay contest made me determined to beat him the next chance I got, whatever it happened to be—and I did, in an election for freshman-class rep. He turned around and narrowly edged me in a history-class debate. So I collected more cans than he did for environmental club, further cementing us as competitors. We've compared test scores and GPAs and clashed on everything from school projects to gym-class pull-up contests. We can't seem to stop trying to one-up each other . . . until now.

After graduation this weekend, I'll never have to see him again. No more morning texts, no more sleepless nights.

I am almost free.

I drop my phone back onto the nightstand next to my writing journal. It's open to a sentence I scribbled in the middle of the night. I flip on the lamp to take a closer look, to see if my two a.m. nonsense makes sense in the daylight—but the room stays dark.

Frowning, I toggle the switch a few more times before getting out of bed and trying the ceiling light. Nothing. It rained all night, a June storm tossing twigs and pine needles at our house, and the wind must have snapped a power line.

I grab my phone again. Twelve percent battery.

(And no reply from McNair.)

"Mom?" I call, racing out of my room and down the stairs. Anxiety pitches my voice an octave higher than usual. "Dad?"

My mom pokes her head out of the office. Orange glasses lie crooked across the bridge of her nose, and her long dark curls—the ones I inherited—are wilder than usual. We've never been able to tame them. My two great nemeses in life: Neil McNair and my hair.

"Rowan?" my mom says. "What are you doing up?"

"It's . . . morning?"

She straightens her glasses and peers down at her watch. "I guess we've been in here awhile."

The windowless office is dark, except for a few candles in the middle of their massive desk, illuminating stacks of pages slashed with red ink.

"Are you working by candlelight?" I ask.

"We had to. Power's out on the whole street, and we're on deadline."

My parents, author-illustrator duo Jared Roth and Ilana García Roth, have written more than thirty books together, from picture books about unlikely animal friendships to a chapter book series about a tween paleontologist named Riley Rodriguez. My mom was born in Mexico City to a Russian-Jewish mother and a Mexican father. She was thirteen when her mother remarried a Texan and moved the family north. Until she went to college and met my Jewish father, she spent summers in Mexico with her father's family, and when they started writing (words: Mom, pictures: Dad), they wanted to explore how a child might embrace both cultures.

My dad appears behind her, yawning. The book they're working on is a spin-off about Riley's younger sister, an aspiring pastry chef. Pastel cakes and pies and French macarons leap off the pages.

"Hey, Ro-Ro," he says, his usual nickname for me. When I was a kid, he used to sing "row, row, Rowan your boat," and I was devastated when I learned those weren't the real lyrics. "Happy last day of school."

"I can't believe it's finally here." I stare at the carpet, suddenly gripped by nerves. I've already cleaned out my locker and taken my finals breakdown-free. I have too much to do today—as student council copresident, I'm leading the senior farewell assembly—to get nervous now.

"Oh!" my mom exclaims, as though suddenly waking up. "We need a picture with the unicorn!"

I groan. I was hoping they'd forgotten. "Can it wait until later? I don't want to be late."

"Ten seconds. And aren't you signing yearbooks and playing games today?" My mom cups my shoulder and gently shakes me back and forth. "You're almost done. Don't stress so much."

She always says I carry too much tension in my shoulders. By the time I'm thirty, my shoulders will probably touch my earlobes.

My mom rummages around in the hall closet, returning with the unicorn-shaped backpack I wore on my first day of kindergarten. In that first first-day photo, I am all sunshine and optimism. When they snapped a picture on the last day of kindergarten, I looked like I wanted to set that backpack on fire. They were so amused, they've taken photos on the first and last days of school ever since. It was the inspiration for their bestselling picture book, *Unicorn Goes to School*. It's odd, sometimes, to think about how many kids grew up knowing me without really knowing me.

Despite my reluctance, the backpack always makes me smile. The unicorn's poor horn is hanging on by a thread, and one hoof is missing. I stretch the straps as far as they'll go and strike a tortured pose for my parents.

"Perfect," my mom says, laughing. "You really look like you're in agony."

This moment with my parents makes me wonder if today will be a day of lasts. Last day of school, last morning text from McNair, last photo with this aging backpack.

I'm not sure I'm ready to say goodbye to everything yet.

My dad taps his watch. "We should get back to it." He tosses me a flashlight. "So you don't have to shower in the dark."

Last shower of high school.

Maybe that's the definition of nostalgia: getting sappy about things that are supposed to be insignificant.

After showering, I wrestle my hair into a damp bun, not trusting it to air-dry into a flattering shape. On my first try, I draw a flawless cat-eye with liquid liner, but I have to settle for a mediocre little flick on the left side. My kingdom for the ability to apply a symmetrical face of makeup.

Last cat-eye of high school, I think, and then I stop myself because if I get weepy about eyeliner, I have no chance of making it through the day.

McNair, with his punctuation and capital letters, pops back up like the world's worst game of Whac-A-Mole.

> Aren't you in that neighborhood without power?
>
> I'd hate to mark you late . . . or have you lose the perfect attendance award.
>
> Have they ever had a student council (co) president win zero awards?

The outfit I planned days ago waits in my closet: my favorite sleeveless blue dress with a Peter Pan collar, the one I found in the vintage section at Red Light. When I tried it on and dipped my hands into the pockets, I knew it had to be mine. My friend Kirby once described my style as hipster librarian meets 1950s housewife. My body is what women's magazines call "pear shaped," with a large chest and larger hips, and I don't have to struggle with vintage clothes the way I do with modern ones. I finish the look with knee socks, ballet flats, and a cream cardigan.

I'm poking a simple gold stud through one earlobe when the envelope catches my eye. Of course—I set it out at the beginning of the week, and I've been staring at it every day since, a mix of dread and excitement warring in my stomach. Most of the time, the dread is winning.

In my fourteen-year-old handwriting, which is a little larger and loopier than it is now, it says OPEN ON LAST DAY OF HIGH SCHOOL. A time capsule of sorts, in the sense that I sealed it four years ago and have only fleetingly thought about it since. I'm only half certain what's inside it.

I don't have time to read it now, so I slide it into my navy JanSport, along with my yearbook and journal.

> how have you not run out of ways to mock me after four years?

> What can I say, you're an endless source of inspiration.

> and you are an endless source of migraines

"I'm leaving, love you, good luck!" I call to my parents before shutting the front door, realizing, with a twinge of my heart, that I won't be able to do this next year.

> Excedrin and Kleenex, DON'T FORGET.

My car is parked around the block, since most Seattle garages are barely big enough for our Halloween decorations. Once inside, I plug my phone into the charger, pluck a bobby pin from the cup holder, and plunge it into my mountain of hair, imagining I'm jabbing it into the space between McNightmare's eyebrows instead.

I'm so close to valedictorian. Three more hours, like his first message so helpfully reminded me. During the farewell assembly, the Westview High School principal will call one of our names, and in my perfect-last-day fantasy, it's mine. I've only been dreaming of it for years: the rivalry to end all rivalries. The velvet bow wrapped around my high school experience.

At first, McNair will be so devastated he won't be able to look at me. His shoulders will hunch and he'll stare down at his tie because he always dresses up on assembly days. He'll feel so embarrassed, this loser in a suit. Beneath his freckles, his pale skin will flush to match his fiery red hair. He has more freckles than he has face. He'll cycle through five stages of grief before arriving at acceptance of the fact that after all these years, I have finally bested him. I have *won*.

Then he'll glance up at me with an expression of utmost respect. He'll dip his head in deference. "You've earned this," he'll say. "Congratulations, Rowan."

And he'll mean it.

Meet Delilah Park TONIGHT in Seattle!

 Delilah Park Publicity <updates@delilahpark.com>
to undisclosed-recipients
June 12, 6:35 a.m.

Good morning, lovers of love!

Internationally bestselling author Delilah Park's *Scandal at Sunset* tour continues this evening with a stop at Seattle's Books & More at 8:00 p.m. Don't miss your chance to meet her in person and take your photo with a ten-foot replica of the Sugar Lake gazebo!

And be sure to grab Delilah's new book, *Scandal at Sunset*, on sale now!

X's and O's,
Delilah Park's publicity team

6:37 a.m.

McNIGHTMARE
Ticktock.

Gray skies rumble with the threat of rain, cedar trees shuddering against the wind. Coffee is my first priority, and Two Birds One Scone is on my way to school. I've been working there since I turned sixteen, when my parents made it clear there was no way we could afford out-of-state tuition. While I've spent my entire life in Seattle, I always wanted to leave for college if I could. Scholarships will cover most of my first semester at a small liberal arts school in Boston called Emerson. My Two Birds money will cover everything else.

The café is decorated like an aviary, plastic ravens and hawks watching you from every angle. They're famous not for their scones but for their cinnamon rolls, which are about the size of a small baby, slathered with cream cheese icing, and served warm.

Mercedes, a recent Seattle U grad who works mornings so she can play in her all-female Van Halen cover band, Anne Halen, at night, waves at me from behind the counter.

"Hey, hey," she says in her too-chipper-before-seven-a.m. voice, already reaching for a compostable cup. "Hazelnut latte with extra whip?"

"You're wonderful. Thank you." Two Birds is small, a staff of about eight with two working per shift. Mercedes is my favorite, mainly because she plays better music than anyone else.

My phone buzzes while I'm waiting, Mercedes humming along to Heart's *Greatest Hits*. I'm positive it's McNair—but it's something much more exciting.

Delilah Park's book signing has been on my calendar for months, but in the midst of my last-day-of-school-isms, I somehow forgot that tonight I am going to meet my favorite author. I even stashed a few paperbacks in my bag earlier this week. Delilah Park writes romances with feminist heroines and shy, sweet heroes. I devoured *These Guarded Hearts* and *Lay It on Me* and *Sweet as Sugar Lake*, for which she won the country's highest romance-novel award when she was twenty.

Delilah Park is the person who makes me think my journal scribbles could be something someday. But going to a book signing where the books being signed are romance novels means admitting I am someone who loves romance novels, which I stopped doing after that fateful ninth-grade essay contest.

And maybe admitting I am someone who is writing a romance novel too.

Here is my dilemma: my passion is, at best, someone else's guilty pleasure. Most of the world takes any opportunity to belittle this thing that centers women in a way most other media doesn't. Romance novels are a punch line, despite being a million-dollar industry. Even my parents can't find respect for them. My mom has called them "trash" more than once, and my dad tried to take a box of them to Goodwill last year, simply because I'd run out of space on my bookshelf and he thought I wouldn't miss them. Fortunately, I caught him on his way out the door.

These days, I have to hide most of my reading. I started writing my novel in secret, assuming I'd tell my parents at some point. But I'm a few chapters from the end, and they still don't know.

"The finest hazelnut latte in all of Seattle," Mercedes says as she presents it to me. The light catches the six piercings in her face, none of which I could pull off. "You working today?"

I shake my head. "Last day of school."

She holds a hand to her heart in mock nostalgia. "Ah, school. I remember it fondly. Or, at the very least, I remember what the bleachers looked like when I was behind them sneaking joints with my friends."

Mercedes won't charge me, but I drop a dollar bill into the tip jar anyway. I pass the kitchen as I leave, calling out a quick hello/goodbye to Colleen, the owner and head baker.

The traffic lights are out all along Forty-Fifth, making every intersection a four-way stop. School starts at 7:05. I'll be cutting it close, a fact that delights McNair, based on how often he's lighting up my phone. While I'm stopped, I voice-text Kirby and Mara to let them know I'm stuck in traffic, and I sing along with my rainy-day soundtrack: the Smiths, always the Smiths. I have a new-wave-obsessed aunt who plays them nonstop when we spend Hanukkahs and Passovers at her house down in Portland. Nothing goes better with gloomy weather than Morrissey's lyrics.

I wonder how they'll sound in Boston, beating against my eardrums as I stroll through a snow-dusted campus in a peacoat, my hair tucked into a knit hat.

The red SUV in front of me inches forward. I inch forward. Tonight unfolds in my mind. I glide into the bookstore, head held high, none of that shoulder-scrunching my mom is always scolding me about. When I approach Delilah at the signing table, we trade compliments about each other's dresses, and I tell her how her books changed my life. By the end of our conversation, she finds me brimming with so much talent, she asks if she can mentor me.

I don't realize the car in front of me has slammed on its brakes until I'm crashing into it, hot coffee splashing down the front of my dress.

"Oh, *shit*." I take a few deep breaths after recovering from the shock of being thrown backward, trying to process what happened when my brain is stuck at an exclusive authors-only after-party Delilah invited me to. The harsh metal-on-metal sound is ringing in my ears, and cars behind me are honking. *I'm a good driver!* I want to tell them. I've never been in an accident, and I always go the speed limit. Maybe I can't parallel park, but despite present evidence to the contrary, I am a *good driver*. "Shit, shit, shit."

The honking continues. The SUV's driver sticks an arm out the window and motions me to follow them onto a residential street, so I do.

I fumble with my seat belt, coffee dripping down my chest and pooling in my lap. The driver stalks toward the back of his car, and the knot of dread in my stomach tightens.

I rear-ended the boy who dumped me a week before prom.

"I am so sorry," I say as I stumble out of my car, and then, because I didn't recognize it: "Um. Did you get a new car?"

Spencer Sugiyama scowls at me. "Last week."

I inspect Spencer inspecting the damage. With longish black hair obscuring half his face, he kneels next to his car, which is barely scratched. Mine has a mangled front bumper and a bent license plate. It's a used Honda Accord, gray and completely uninteresting, with an odd interior smell I've never been able to get rid of. But it's *mine*, paid for in full with my Two Birds One Scone money last summer.

"What the hell, Rowan?" Spencer, a second-chair clarinetist I partnered with on a history project earlier this year, used to look at me like I had all the answers. Like he was awed by me. Now his dark eyes seem filled with a mix of frustration—and relief, maybe, that we're no longer together. It gives me a surge of pleasure that he never got first chair. (And oh yes, he tried.)

"You think I did this on purpose?" Needless to say, the breakup was not a cordial one. "You stopped really abruptly!"

"It's a four-way stop! Why were you going so fast?"

Obviously, I don't mention Delilah. It's possible the accident was mostly my fault.

Spencer wasn't my first relationship, but he was my longest. I had a couple one-week boyfriends freshman and sophomore year, the kind of relationships that end over text because you're too awkward to make eye contact at school. At the end of junior year, I dated Luke Barrows, a tennis player who could make anyone laugh and liked partying a little too much. I thought I loved him, but I think what I really loved was how I felt around him: fun and wild and beautiful, a girl who liked five-paragraph essays and also fooling around in the back seat of a car. By the time school started in the fall, we'd broken up. He wanted to focus on tennis, and I was glad to have the extra time to spend on my college apps. We still say hi when we see each other in the halls.

Spencer, though—Spencer was complicated. I wanted him to be my perfect high school boyfriend, the guy I'd one day reminisce about with my friends over cocktails with scandalous names. I dreamed of that boyfriend all through middle school, assuming I'd get to high school and he'd be sitting behind me in English, tapping my shoulder and shyly asking to borrow a pen.

I was running out of time to find that boyfriend, and I thought if we spent enough time together, Spencer and I could get to that point. But he acted withdrawn, and it made me clingy. If I liked who I was with Luke, I hated who I was with Spencer. I hated feeling so insecure. The obvious solution was *break up with him*, but I hung on, hoping things would change.

Spencer pulls his insurance card out of his wallet. "We're supposed to swap info, right?"

I vaguely remember that from driver's ed. "Right. Yeah."

It wasn't always terrible with Spencer. The first time we had sex, he held me for so long afterward, convinced me I was a precious, special thing. "Maybe we can still be friends," he said when he broke up with me. A coward's breakup. He wanted to get rid of me, but he didn't want me to be mad at him. He did it at school, right before a student council meeting. Said he didn't want to start college with a girlfriend. "Spencer and I just broke up," I told McNair before we called the meeting to order. "So if you could not be vile to me for the next forty minutes, I would appreciate it."

I'm not sure what I expected—that he'd congratulate Spencer? Tell me I deserved it? But his features softened into an expression I hadn't ever seen and couldn't name. "Okay," he said. "I—I'm sorry."

The apology sounded so foreign in his voice, but we started the meeting before I could linger on it.

"I really did hope we could stay friends," Spencer says after we take photos of each other's insurance cards.

"We are on Facebook."

He rolls his eyes. "Not what I meant."

"What does that even mean, though?" I lean against my car, wondering if now I'll finally get closure. "Are we going to text each other our college class schedules? See a movie together when we're home on break?"

A pause. "Probably not," he admits.

So that's a no on closure.

"We should get to school," Spencer says when I'm silent a beat too long. "We're already late, but they probably won't care on the last day."

Late. I don't even want to think about the McMessages waiting for me on my phone.

I give a little wave of my insurance card before tucking it back into my wallet. "I guess your people will call my people. Or whatever."

He speeds off before I can start my engine. My parents don't need to know about this yet, not while they're on deadline. Still shaky—from the impact or the conversation, I'm not sure—I try to relax my shoulders. There really is a lot of tension there.

If I were in a romance novel, I'd have gotten into a fender bender with the cute guy who owns a bar and also works part-time in construction, the kind of guy who's good with his hands. Most of the heroes in romance novels are good with their hands.

I convinced myself if I just waited long enough with Spencer, he would turn into that guy and what we had would turn into love. While I love romance, I've never believed in the concept of soul mates, which has always seemed a little like men's rights activism: not a real thing. Love isn't immediate or automatic; it takes effort and time and patience.

The truth of it was that I'd probably never have the kind of luck with love the women who live in fictional seaside towns do. But sometimes I get this strange feeling, an ache not for something I miss, but for something I've never known.

It starts raining again as I approach Westview High School because Seattle. Homeroom's already started, and I'll admit, my vanity is stronger than my need to be on time. I'm already late. A few more minutes won't matter.

When I reach the bathroom and get a clear view of myself in the mirror, I nearly gasp. The stain fully covers one and a half boobs. I run some soap and water on my dress, scrubbing at it with all the strength I can muster, but after five minutes, the stain is still very brown and all I've accomplished is groping myself in the first-floor bathroom.

It's not my perfect last-day outfit anymore, but it's all I have. I blot at the dampness with a paper towel so it looks a little less like I'm lactating and adjust my sweater so it hides the stain as best as possible. I mess with my bangs, finger-combing them to the right and then to the left. I can never decide whether to grow them out or keep them short. Right now they skim my eyebrows, just long enough for me to fidget with. Maybe I'll trim them for college, try a Bettie Page kind of look.

I'm almost done fidgeting when something catches my eye behind me in the mirror: a red poster with block letters.

> **HOWL**
>
> **JUNE 12**
>
> **NOON**
>
> **GRAND PRIZE TBA**

Another thing that slipped my mind in the morning rush. Howl is a Westview High tradition for graduating seniors. It's a game that's part Assassin, part scavenger hunt. Players chase each other down while trying to decipher riddles that lead them all over Seattle. The first to complete the clues wins a cash prize. It's put on by the student council juniors every year as a send-off to that year's graduates, and last year McNair and I nearly murdered each other trying to organize it. Of course I'll play, but I can't think about it until after the assembly.

As I exit the bathroom, Ms. Grable, my sophomore and junior English teacher, hurries out of the teachers' lounge across the hall.

"Rowan!" she says, eyes lighting up. "I can't believe you're leaving us!"

Ms. Grable, who must only be in her late twenties, ensured our reading list was majority women and authors of color. I loved her.

"All good things must come to an end," I say. "Even high school."

She laughs. "You are maybe one of five students of mine who's ever felt that way. I shouldn't tell you this, but"—she leans in, cups a conspiratorial hand over her mouth—"you and Neil were my favorite students."

That is when my heart plummets to my toes. At Westview, I've always been packaged with McNair. We are never not mentioned in the same breath, Rowan versus Neil and Neil versus Rowan, year after year after year. I've observed everything from terror to sheer joy pass over a teacher's face at the beginning of the year upon realizing they have both of us in their class. Most find our rivalry entertaining, pitting us against each other in debates and partnering us on projects. Part of the reason I want valedictorian so badly is that I want to end high school as myself, not half of a warring pair.

I force myself to smile at Ms. Grable. "Thanks."

"You're going to Emerson, right?" she asks, and I nod. "Your essays were always so insightful. Planning to follow in your parents' footsteps?"

How difficult would it be to say yes?

While of course I'm worried about how people respond to romance novels, there's another fear that pulls my shoulders into a shrug when people ask what I want to be when I grow up. As long as being a writer is a dream that stays in my head, I don't have to face the reality of potentially not being good enough. In my head, I'm my only critic. Out there, everyone is.

As soon as I declare myself a writer, there will be expectations that come with being Ilana and Jared's daughter. And if I somehow fail to meet them, if I'm messy and imperfect and still learning, the judgment would be harsher than if my parents were podiatrists or chefs or statisticians. Telling people means I think I might be okay at this—be *good* at this—and while I desperately want that to be true, I'm terrified of the possibility that I'm not.

At least no one expects me to know my major yet, so while I picked Emerson largely because of its great creative writing program, I've been telling people "I'm not sure yet" when they ask what I'm going to study. I never expected to want to follow in my parents' footsteps, but here I am, dreaming of running a finger along my name on a cover. Ideally in a glossy raised font.

"Maybe," I concede at last, which feels like a half-confession, but I justify it with the fact that I won't see Ms. Grable again after graduation. For someone who loves words, I'm occasionally not great at speaking them.

"If anyone could publish a book, it would be you! Unless Neil manages to beat you to it."

"I should get to class," I say as gently as I can.

"Of course, of course," she says, and wraps me in a hug before heading down the hall.

Today is full of so many lasts, and maybe most important is that it's the last day I can one-up McNair once and for all. As valedictorian, I'll end our academic tug-of-war. I will be Rowan Luisa

Roth, valedictorian of Westview High School, with a period at the end. No comma, no "and." Just me.

My inner rule-follower guides me to the main office instead of homeroom. I'll feel worse walking into class without a late pass, even on the last day. When I reach the office, I push open the door, square my shoulders—and come face-to-face with Neil McNair.

Rowan Roth versus Neil McNair: A Brief History

SEPTEMBER, FRESHMAN YEAR

The essay contest that started it all. It's announced the first week of school to welcome us back from summer break. I am used to being the best writer in class. It's who I've been all through middle school, the same way, I imagine, this skinny redhead with too many freckles has been at his school. First place, McNair and his beloved Fitzgerald, second place, Roth. I vow to beat him at whatever comes next.

NOVEMBER, FRESHMAN YEAR

The student council president visits homerooms to ask for volunteers for freshman-class rep. Leadership will look good on my future college apps, and I need scholarships, so I volunteer. So does McNair. I'm not sure if he actually wants it or if he just wants to further ruffle me. Nevertheless, I win by three votes.

FEBRUARY, SOPHOMORE YEAR

We are both forced to take gym for a physical education requirement, despite the hour we spend trying to convince the counselor we need the space in our schedules for our advanced classes instead. Neither of us can touch our toes, but McNair can do three pull-ups, while I can only do one and a half. His arms have no definition whatsoever, so I don't understand how this is possible.

MAY, SOPHOMORE YEAR

McNair scores a perfect 1600 on the SAT, and I score a 1560. I retake it the next month and score 1520. I do not tell a soul.

JANUARY, JUNIOR YEAR

Our AP Chemistry teacher makes us lab partners. After a handful of arguments, chemical spills, and a (small) fire, which was maybe mostly my fault but I'll carry that with me to the grave, he separates us.

JUNE, JUNIOR YEAR

In the election for student council president, the vote is sliced perfectly down the middle. Neither of us concedes. Reluctantly, we become copresidents.

APRIL, SENIOR YEAR

Before college acceptances start rolling in, I challenge him to see who can rack up the most yeses. McNair suggests we compare percentages instead. Assuming we're both casting wide nets, I agree. I get into 7 of 10 schools I apply to. It's only after all the deadlines have passed that I learn McNair, crafty and overconfident as he is, applied to just one school.

He gets in.

7:21 a.m.

"ROWAN ROTH," MY worst nightmare says from behind the front desk. "I got you something."

My heart rate spikes, the way it always does before a sparring match with McNair. I'd forgotten he's an office assistant (aka Suck-Up 101—please, even I'm better than that) during homeroom. I'd been hoping to keep him confined to my phone until the assembly.

With his hands clasped in front of him, he looks like an evil king sitting on a throne made from the bones of his enemies. His auburn hair is damp from a morning shower, or maybe from the rain, and as predicted, he's in one of his assembly-day suits: black jacket, white shirt, blue patterned tie with the crispest, tightest knot I've ever seen. Still, I manage to spot his flaws right away: his pants a half-inch too short, his sleeves a half-inch too long. A fingerprint smudge on the left lens of his glasses, one stubborn piece of hair behind his ear that won't lie flat.

His face, though—his face is the worst part, his lips bent in a smirk he perfected after winning that ninth-grade essay contest.

Before I can respond, he reaches inside his jacket pocket and tosses me a travel pack of Kleenex. Thank God I catch it, despite a serious lack of hand-eye coordination.

"You shouldn't have," I deadpan.

"Just looking out for my copresident on the last day of our term. What brings you to the office on this stormy morning?"

"You know why I'm here. Just give me a pass. Please."

He furrows his brow. "What kind of pass, exactly, do you want?"

"You know what kind of pass." When he shrugs, continuing to feign ignorance, I lower myself into a deep, dramatic bow. "O McNair, lord of the main office," I say in a voice that oozes melodrama, intent on answering his question as obnoxiously as possible. If he's going to turn this into a production, I'll play along. After all, I only have a few more chances to mess with him. Might as well be ridiculous while I still can. "I humbly ask that you grant me one final request: a fucking late pass."

He swivels his chair to grab a stack of green late slips from the desk drawer, moving at the pace of maple syrup on a thirty-degree day. Until I met McNair, I didn't know patience could feel like a physical piece of me, something he stretches and twists whenever he has a chance.

"Was that your impression of Princess Leia in the first twenty-five minutes of *A New Hope*, before she realized she wasn't actually British?" he asks. When I give him a puzzled look, he clucks his tongue, like my not getting the reference pains him on a molecular level. "I keep forgetting my great vintage *Star Wars* lines are wasted on you, Artoo."

Because of my alliterative name, he nicknamed me Artoo, after R2-D2, and while I've never seen the movies, I get that R2-D2 is some kind of robot. It's clearly an insult, and his obsessive interest in the franchise has killed any desire I might have once had to watch it.

"Seems only fair when so many things are wasted on you," I say. "Like my time. By all means, go as slow as humanly possible."

Sabotage has been part of our rivalry nearly since the beginning, though it's never been malicious. There was the time he left his thumb drive plugged into a library computer and I filled it with dubstep music, the time he spilled the cafeteria's mystery chili on my extra-credit math assignment. And my personal favorite: the time I bribed the janitor with a signed set of my parents' books for her kids in exchange for McNair's locker combination. Watching him struggle with it after I changed it was priceless.

"Don't test me. I can go much slower." As though to prove it, he takes a full ten seconds to uncap a ballpoint pen. It's a real performance, and it takes all my willpower not to dive across the desk and snatch it from him. "I guess this means no perfect attendance award," he says as he writes my name.

Even his hands are dotted with freckles. Once when I was bored during a student council meeting, I tried to count every freckle on his face. The meeting ended when I hit one hundred, and I wasn't even done counting.

"All I want is valedictorian," I say, forcing what I hope is a sweet smile. "We both know the lesser awards don't really mean anything. But it'll be a nice consolation prize for you. You can put the certificate on your wall next to the dartboard with my face on it."

"How do you know what my room looks like?"

"Hidden cameras. Everywhere."

He snorts. I crane my neck to see what he's writing next to "reason for tardiness."

Attempted to dye her dress brown. Failed spectacularly.

"Is that really necessary?" I ask, pulling my cardigan tight across my dress and the latte stain that shouts *here's where my boobs are!* "I was stuck in traffic. All the lights in my neighborhood were out." I don't tell him about the fender bender.

He checks the box marked UNEXCUSED and tears the pass from the pad—ripping it down the middle. "Oops," he says in a tone that suggests he doesn't feel bad at all. "Guess I have to write another one."

"Cool. I don't have anywhere to be."

"Artoo, it's our last day," he says, holding a hand to his heart. "We should cherish these precious moments we have together. In fact"—he reaches inside his jacket pocket for a fancy pen—"this would be a great time to practice my calligraphy."

"You're not serious."

Unblinking, he peers at me over the top of his thin oval glasses. "Like Ben Solo, I never joke about calligraphy."

Surely this is my villain origin story. He presses the pen's tip to the paper and begins forming the letters of my name again, his glasses slipping down the bridge of his nose. McNair's Concentration Face is half hilarious, half terrifying: teeth gritted and jaw tight, mouth scrunched slightly to one side. The suit makes him look so rigid, so stiff, like an accountant or an insurance salesman or a low-level manager at a company that makes software for other companies. I've never seen him at a party. I can't imagine him relaxing enough to watch a movie. Not even *Star Wars*.

"Really impressive. Great job." I say it sarcastically, but my name actually does look good in that delicate black ink. I could picture it on a book cover.

He passes the slip to me but holds it tight, preventing me from escaping. "Wait a second. I want to show you something."

He lets go of the slip so suddenly that I stumble backward, then hops off his chair and heads out of the office. I'm annoyed but curious, so I follow him. He stops in front of the school trophy case, gives it a theatrical wave of his arm.

"I've been here for four years, so I have, in fact, seen this trophy case before," I say.

But he's pointing at one particular plaque, engraved with names and graduation dates. With his index finger, he taps the glass. "Donna Wilson, 1986. Westview's first valedictorian. Do you know what she ended up doing?"

"Saved herself four years of agony by graduating three decades before you enrolled here?"

"Close. She became the US ambassador to Thailand."

"How is that close?"

He waves his hand. "Steven Padilla, 1991. Won a Nobel Prize for physics. Swati Joshi, 2006. Olympic gold medalist for pole vault."

"If you're trying to impress me with your knowledge of past valedictorians, it's working." I step closer to him, batting my lashes. "I am so turned on right now."

It's over the top, I know, but this has always been the easiest way to ruffle this seemingly unruffle-able guy. He and his last girlfriend, Bailey, didn't even acknowledge each other at school, and I wondered what they were like outside of it. When I thought about him shedding his stony exterior long enough for a make-out session, I felt a strange little tremor in my belly. That was how horrific I found the idea of someone kissing Neil McNair.

Just as I hoped, he blushes. His skin is so fair beneath his freckles that he's never able to hide how he really feels.

"What I'm trying to say," he says after clearing his throat, "is Westview High has a history of successful valedictorians. What would it say for you—Rowan Roth, romance-novel critic? It's not quite at the same level as the others, is it?"

I've told Kirby and Mara I don't really read them anymore, but McNair brings up my romance novels whenever he can. His derogatory tone is the reason I keep them to myself these days.

"Or maybe you'd graduate to writing one of your own," he continues. "More romance novels—exactly what the world needs."

His words push me backward until his freckles blur together. I don't want him to know how much this infuriates me. Even if I get to the point where "romance author" is attached to my name, people like McNair won't hesitate to tear me down. To laugh at the thing I love.

"It must be sad," I say, "to despise romance so much that the thought of someone else finding joy in it is so repulsive to you."

"I thought you and Sugiyama broke up."

"I—what?"

"The joy you find in romance. I assumed that was Spencer Sugiyama."

I feel my face heat up. That is . . . not where I thought this was going.

"No. Not Spencer." Then I go for a low blow: "You look different today, McNair. Did your freckles multiply overnight?"

"You're the one with the hidden cameras."

"Alas, they're not HD." I refrain from making a dirty joke I really, really want to make. I flash the green slip in front of his face. "Since you were kind enough to write me a late pass, I should probably, you know, use it."

Last homeroom. I hope the walk to class is enough to get my blood flowing normally again. My adrenaline always works overtime when I'm talking to McNair. The stress he's caused me has probably sliced a half-decade off my life span.

With a nod, he says, "End of an era. You and me, I mean." He wags his index finger between the two of us, his voice softer than it was ten seconds ago.

I'm quiet for a moment, wondering if today carries the same

sense of finality for him that it does for me. "Yeah," I say. "I guess so."

Then he makes a shooing motion with one hand, snapping me out of my nostalgia and replacing it with the contempt that's been both a warm blanket and a bed of nails. A comfort and a curse.

Goodbye, goodbye, goodbye.

OVERDUE NOTICE

Westview High School Library
<westviewlib@seattleschools.org>
to r.roth@seattleschools.org
June 10, 2:04 p.m.

This is an automated message from the WESTVIEW HIGH SCHOOL LIBRARY.

Library records show the following item(s) are overdue. Please either renew them or return them to the library immediately to avoid accruing a fine.

- *Your Guide to a 5: AP Calculus* / Griffin, Rhoda
- *Conquering the AP Government Exam* / Wagner, Carlyn
- *Love Notes: Romance Novels through the Ages* / Smith, Sonia, and Tilley, Annette
- *Analyzing Austen* / Ramirez, Marisa
- *What Now: Life After Senior Year* / Holbrook, Tara

8:02 a.m.

FIFTEEN MINUTES WITH him, and I already feel a McMigraine coming on. I rub the space between my eyes as I hurry to homeroom.

"Our future valedictorian," Mrs. Kozlowski says with a smile when I hand her my late pass, and I hope she's right.

Our homerooms are mixed to foster camaraderie between the grades. McNair proposed it two years ago in student council, and the principal ate it up. It wasn't the worst idea, I guess, if you ignored every single one of our other, more pressing issues: rampant plagiarism among the freshman class, the need for an expanded cafeteria menu to accommodate dietary restrictions, reducing our carbon footprint.

Before I make my way to Kirby and Mara, a trio of junior girls pounces on me.

"Hi, Rowan!" says Olivia Sweeney.

"We were worried you weren't going to be here!" says her friend Harper Chen.

"Well . . . I'm here," I say.

"Thank God," Nisha Deshpande says, and the three of them giggle.

We're all in student council, where they've unanimously thrown their support to me instead of McNair, which I've always been grateful for. They compliment my clothes and worked on my campaigns and brought me cupcakes when I got into Emerson. Kirby and Mara call them my fan club. Truly, they're very sweet, if a little overeager.

"Is everything ready for Howl?" I ask.

The three of them exchange wicked grins.

"We've been ready for weeks," Nisha says. "I don't want to say it's going to be the best Howl the school has ever seen, but it just might be."

"We're not giving you any hints," Harper adds.

"As much as we might want to." Olivia reaches down to tug up one of her knee socks, which are eerily similar to the pair I'm wearing.

"No hints," I agree. McNair and I organized the game last year, but none of the previous year's locations can be reused.

"Will you sign our yearbooks?" Nisha asks. "Since it's your last day?"

Three arms thrust Sharpies in my direction. I sign all of them with slightly different messages, and after a chorus of thank-yous, I turn toward Kirby and Mara, who are waving at me from a corner of the room. My mom was right; all we're doing is signing yearbooks. We have an extended homeroom, then the assembly, and then shortened classes for everyone who still goes here.

"There you are," Kirby says. Her black hair is braided in a

crown around her head. The three of us spent hours teaching ourselves how to Dutch braid last year, but Kirby is the only one who mastered it. "What happened this morning?"

I recount the day so far, from the power outage to my Spencer bender. "And then I was McNaired in the front office," I finish. "So yeah, it's been a day and a half, and it's only eight o'clock."

Mara places a hand on my arm. She's quieter, gentler than Kirby, rarely the first to speak in a group conversation. The only time she steps into the spotlight is when she's dancing a solo onstage. "Are you okay?"

"I'm fine. McNair was just being his usual troll self. Can you believe he wrote my late pass in calligraphy? It was like last fall when he downloaded all those dog videos in the library to mess with the internet when I was researching my Jane Austen paper. He'll do anything to slow me down."

She arcs a pale eyebrow. "I meant the accident."

"Oh. Right. A little shaken up, but I'm okay. I've never hit anyone before." I'm not sure why my mind went immediately to McNair when the accident was clearly the more traumatic event.

"Mara," Kirby says, pointing to a yearbook photo of the two of them dancing in the winter talent show earlier this year. "Look how cute we are."

Kirby Taing and I became friends first, when we were grouped together for a fourth-grade rite of passage: the volcano experiment. Kirby wanted to add more baking soda, create a bigger eruption. We made a mess. We got a B. She met Mara Pompetti in a ballet class a couple years later, though Mara's always been the more serious dancer.

We wound up at the same middle school and have been a unit ever since, and while I love them both, for years I felt a tiny bit closer to Kirby. She got me through my grandpa's funeral in seventh grade, and I was the first person she came out to in ninth grade, when she said she'd only ever liked girls. The following year, Mara told both of us that she was bisexual and wanted to start using that label for herself. For a while, she and Kirby used me as a go-between, trying to figure out how each felt about the other. They went to homecoming together last year, which has cemented them as a couple.

They laugh at an unfortunate hair situation in someone's senior photo while I flip through the book, though as editor in chief, I've seen each page hundreds of times. For the senior superlatives, the photo editor made McNair and me pose with our backs pressed up against each other, our arms crossed. Above us are the words MOST LIKELY TO SUCCEED. In the photo and in real life, we are exactly the same height: five-five. After the photo was taken, he sprang away from me, as though the back of his shirt touching the back of mine was too much physical contact for rivals to have.

"Pleeeease can we leave the classroom?" star quarterback Brady Becker is begging Mrs. Kozlowski. Brady Becker is the kind of guy who got Bs because teachers loved it when our football team was good, and they couldn't be good if Brady Becker got Ds. "All the other homerooms are."

Mrs. Kozlowski holds up her hands. "Okay, okay. Go ahead. Just be sure to make your way over to the auditorium after—"

We're already out the door.

Mara and I lean against the bank of lockers we claimed back in freshman year, sharing a cheesy pretzel and a bag of chips from the student store. The combinations will be changed next week, after we're gone. We were supposed to clean out our lockers earlier this week. Kirby is doing it now, which is kind of Kirby in a nutshell.

"Should I keep this?" She holds up her WHS gym T-shirt. We had to stage an intervention to get her to wash it sophomore year because she kept forgetting to bring it home.

"No!" Mara and I say in unison. Mara aims her phone at Kirby, who poses as though she's waltzing with the T-shirt.

"Sophomore gym was a special kind of torture," I say. "I can't believe they wouldn't let us waive it."

"*You* wanted to waive it," Kirby corrects. "I for one enjoyed discovering my hidden talent for badminton."

Oh. Huh. I must have assumed because I remember hating it, that they did too. But I guess it was only McNair and me making a case to the counselor about changing our schedules.

If I used to be better friends with Kirby, it's faded a little since she and Mara became a couple. But that's natural. While they spend plenty of time alone, for the most part, we're just as close as we were in middle school.

Across the hall is that trophy case with the plaque of valedictorian names. It says something about our school that this is what's front and center—not the football or basketball trophies, but our academic achievements. At Westview, it's frowned upon if you don't take at least one AP, and not Music Theory, since everyone knows Mr. Davidson uses it as an excuse to play his shitty jam band's records. He offers extra credit for going to one of his shows. Kirby and I went sophomore year when she took the class, and let me just say I could have gone my entire life without seeing a middle-aged teacher rip off his sweaty T-shirt onstage and fling it into the audience.

Mara turns the phone on me, and I hug my sweater as tightly as I can. "This boob stain doesn't need to be immortalized on Instagram."

Kirby waves the T-shirt at me. "Hello, perfectly good T-shirt right here. I won a lot of games of badminton in this shirt."

"You can barely see the stain." Mara says it so sweetly, it almost doesn't sound like a lie. Then her jaw falls open. "Kirby Kunthea Taing. Is that a condom?"

"From health class last year!" she says, holding up what is definitely a condom. "They were giving them out, and I didn't want to be rude. . . ."

Mara hides a laugh behind a curtain of wavy blond hair. "I'm pretty sure neither of us needs it."

"You want it?" Kirby asks me. "It has spermicide."

"No, Kirby, I don't want your old health-class condom." If I need one anytime soon, I keep a box in my dresser, tucked behind my period underwear. "Besides, it's probably expired."

She peers at it. "Not until September." She unzips my backpack and drops it inside, patting the backpack once she zips it up again. "You've got three months to find a worthy suitor."

With a roll of my eyes, I offer Mara the last chip in the bag, but she shakes her head. Kirby tosses her gym shirt and some other tchotchkes into a nearby trash can. Every so often, a group races down the hall and shouts, "SENIORS!" and we whoop back at them. We trade fist bumps with Lily Gulati, high fives with Derek Price, and whistles with the Kristens (Tanaka and Williams, best friends since the first day of freshman year and virtually inseparable ever since).

Even Luke Barrows stops by with his girlfriend, Anna Ocampo—ranked number one on girls' varsity tennis—so we can swap yearbooks.

"I've been counting down the days until they let us out of here," Luke says.

"Since freshman year?" Anna volleys back. Turning to me, she says, "I'll miss your Wednesday-morning announcements. You and Neil always cracked me up."

"Glad to have provided some entertainment."

They both got tennis scholarships to Division I schools, and I'm genuinely happy for them. I hope they can make it work long-distance.

"Kirby, oh my God," Anna says, muffling a laugh when a pile of papers tumbles out of Kirby's locker.

"I know," she says with a small moan.

Yearbooks are returned to their owners, and Luke crushes me into a hug with arms made muscular from a killer backhand.

"Good luck," he says, and why can't all breakups be like this? Drama-free, no lingering awkwardness.

While Mara uploads an Instagram video of Kirby extricating an eight-foot-long scarf from her locker, complete with creepy horror-movie soundtrack, I reach into my backpack for my journal. But my fingers skim something else: the envelope I shoved in there this morning.

I know what it is—or at least, I have a general idea. But I don't remember the exact details, and that makes me a little twitchy. Carefully, I run my finger along the envelope flap and pull out the sheet of folded paper.

Rowan Roth's Guide to High School Success, it says across the top, followed by ten numbered items, and the words drag me back to the summer before high school. I added number ten a month into freshman year. Naturally, I'd been inspired by something I read in a book. I'd been so excited about high school, half in love with the person I imagined I'd be by the end of it. Really, it's more a list of goals than an actual guide.

I've accomplished none of them.

"What about this?" Kirby asks. "One hundred percent. On a math test!"

"Recycling, Kirby." But Mara takes a photo of it anyway.

"Our little paparazzo," Kirby says.

I'm still in the world of the success guide—particularly, item number seven. *Go to prom with boyfriend and Kirby and Mara.* Since Spencer and I broke up right before, prom didn't happen. I would have gone without a date, but I worried I'd end up being

Kirby and Mara's third wheel, and I didn't want to ruin the night for them.

It shouldn't hit me as hard as it does that my life didn't go quite according to plan. And yet here's the physical proof of it. High school is ending, and it's only today that I'm realizing everything I didn't do.

It's a relief when the clock hits 8:15. I spring to my feet, throwing the list into my backpack and my backpack over my shoulder. Time for the final test of my high school career.

"I have to prep for the assembly," I say.

Kirby tears open a Snickers she found in her locker abyss. "Whatever happens, you're a winner to us," she says in a tone that's probably meant to be encouraging, but from her, it comes out sounding sarcastic. She must hear it, because she winces. "Sorry. That sounded nicer in my head."

I try to smile. "I believe you."

"Go, go," Mara says. "I'll make sure Kirby disposes of any other potentially hazardous materials."

As I head for the auditorium, their laughter takes a while to fade.

I'm leaving Seattle at the end of the summer, but Kirby and Mara are going to the University of Washington. Together. Mara wants to study dance, and Kirby plans to take one class in each discipline before deciding on her major. I'll see them on breaks, of course, but I wonder if the distance will push me farther away. If this friendship is another thing I can't take with me to college.

<u>Rowan Roth's Guide to High School Success</u>
By Rowan Luisa Roth, age 14
To be opened only by Rowan Luisa Roth, age 18

1. Figure out what to do with your bangs.

2. Obtain the Perfect High School Boyfriend (heretofore known as PHSB), ideally by the middle of 10th grade, summer after 11th grade at the latest. Minimum requirements:
    - Loves reading
    - Respectable taste in music
    - Vegetarian

3. Hang out with Kirby and Mara EVERY WEEKEND! (As much as you love books, please don't forget about the outside world.)

4. Make out with PHSB under the bleachers during a football game.

5. Become fluent in Spanish.

6. <u>Never</u> tell anyone you like romance novels unless you're 100 percent sure they won't be royally awful about it.

7. Go to prom with your PHSB and Kirby and Mara. Find a fantastic dress, rent a limo, eat at a fancy restaurant. The whole John Hughes experience, minus the toxic masculinity. The night will culminate in a hotel room, where you and PHSB will declare your love for each other and lose your virginities in a tender, romantic way that you'll remember for the rest of your life.

8. Get into a college with a great secondary education program to fulfill your lifelong dream of becoming an English teacher to MOLD YOUNG MINDS!!!

9. Become Westview valedictorian.

10. Destroy Neil McNair. Make him regret ever writing that <u>Great Gatsby</u> essay and everything he's done since then.

9:07 a.m.

"... SCREAM IT LOUD *for the blue and white—*
Westview Wolf Pack, time to fight!"

At the end of our school's fight song, we all throw back our heads and howl. My first Wolf Pack experience at a football game freshman year, I was embarrassed and intimidated, but now I love the noise, the energy. The way, just for a moment, we all forget to be self-conscious.

It's the last time I'll howl with this exact mix of people.

Backstage, I hand over student council secretary Chantal Okafor's yearbook, and she passes me mine.

"I think I used up the last of your space," Chantal says. "I hope it's you. For valedictorian, I mean."

The high school success guide burns in my backpack. I try to focus on the fact that I have three months with Mara and Kirby ahead of me. We can have a perfect last summer before college: music festivals, days at the beach, nights complaining how cold the water at the beach was.

But that doesn't account for everything else. Sure, it was a semi-joke, but I haven't even accomplished the most basic item on the list: figuring out my bangs. If I can't figure out my bangs, how could I have expected to become valedictorian? Logically, I know those things aren't linked, but I've had four freaking years. My hair should make more sense than my future.

The line about becoming an English teacher struck me too. In middle school, I had a phase where I pretended to grade papers and dreamed up a reading list or two. My fourteen-year-old self called it a "lifelong dream," but I can barely remember it. I picture myself at fourteen, brimming with optimism, wanting to get that guide exactly right. My favorite books got happily-ever-afters—why couldn't I?

I cling to number nine on the list. Valedictorian is still possible. It's nearly mine.

I smile at Chantal and tuck my yearbook into my backpack. "Thank you. Are you excited for Spelman?"

"Oh yeah. I can't wait to leave all the high school drama behind." Chantal's braids twirl as she jerks her head in McNair's direction. He's reviewing his index cards, his lips forming the words. Amateur—I don't need index cards. His head is bent in concentration, and his glasses are slipping down his nose. If I didn't despise him, I'd march over there and shove them up. Maybe superglue them to the backs of his ears. "You've got to be excited too, right? No more Neil?"

"No more Neil," I agree, fluttering my bangs across my forehead, to one side and then the other, wishing they'd lie flat. "I can't wait."

"I'll never forget that student council meeting last year that lasted until midnight. Mr. Travers couldn't get you two to wrap it up. I thought he was going to cry."

"I forgot about that." We'd been trying to reach a conclusion about allocating funds for the upcoming year. McNair insisted the English department needed new copies of *A White Man in Peril* (okay, the books have real titles, but that's what they're all about), while I argued we should use the money for books by women and authors of color. *They're not classics*, McNair had said. I might have lazily fired back "your face isn't a classic." In my defense, it was late. Needless to say, it got a little out of hand.

"At least you made high school memorable."

"Memorable. Right." With a twinge of guilt, I realize I barely know Chantal. I knew she was going to Spelman only because she passed me a marker when all the seniors wrote our schools on a sheet of butcher paper hanging in front of the school. I assumed when I joined student council that I'd make friends with everyone, but it's possible I was so focused on besting McNair that I never got the chance.

McNair must catch us staring, because he strides over until he and I are face-to-face. I wish, not for the first time, that I had at least an inch on him.

"Best of luck," he says curtly, dusting imaginary lint off his lapels. His hair is no longer damp.

I match his tone. "You as well."

We don't break eye contact, as though the winner of this staring contest gets a Jet Ski, a puppy, and a brand-new car.

From the stage, Principal Meadows takes the mic. "Simmer down, simmer down," she says, and the auditorium grows quiet.

"Nervous, Artoo?" McNair asks.

"Not a bit." I straighten my cardigan. "You?"

"Sure, a little."

"Admitting that doesn't make you better than me."

"No, but it makes me more honest." He glances toward the curtain, then back at me. "It was thoughtful of you to make that stain large enough for people in the last row to see."

I motion to his too-short pants. "They've got to have something to distract from that scandalous bit of ankle you're showing."

"I hate it when my mom and dad fight," Chantal says.

McNair and I whirl to face her. My mouth drops open, my expression of horror surely mirroring his. But before we can say anything, Principal Meadows continues.

"To kick things off," she says, "please join me in welcoming your copresidents, Rowan Roth and Neil McNair!"

I relish the applause and the small but not insignificant joy of my name being uttered before his. McNair pulls back the velvet stage curtain and gestures for me to step through first. Normally I'd call him out for this—chivalry is outdated and I am not a fan—but today I just roll my eyes.

We grab wireless mics from the stands in the center of the stage. The lights are bright and the auditorium is thick with an antsy, pulsing energy, but I haven't been nervous up here in years—it's home.

"I know everyone's eager to get out of here and play Howl," McNair says, "so we'll keep this as brief as possible."

"But not too brief," I add. "We want to make sure you all get the recognition you deserve."

McNair's brows knit together. "Right. Of course."

Laughter ripples through the auditorium. Our classmates have come to expect this from us.

"It's been a pleasure serving as your president this year," McNair says.

"*Co*president."

He fiddles with something on his mic, sending a warped wave of feedback through the speakers. Hands clutch ears and the audience groans in unison.

"Guess that's how everyone feels about your presidency," I say. McNair has annoyed them, but I will win them back.

He turns crimson. "I'm sorry about that, Wolf Pack."

"Not sure if everyone heard that. You might have permanently damaged some eardrums."

"Moving on," he says firmly, with a glance down at his note cards, "we'd like to start with this montage that Ms. Murakami's film class put together to remind everyone of all the great times we had this year. The soundtrack is provided by Mr. Davidson's band"—another squint at his notes—"the Pure Funk Project."

Literally two people cheer. I'm pretty sure one of them is Mr. Davidson.

The lights dim, and the video is projected onto a screen behind us. We laugh along with everyone else at the ridiculous moments captured on camera, but I can't ignore the anxiety brewing inside me. There are shots from football games and spirit assemblies and drama club productions. From prom. A few seniors in the front row of the auditorium are crying, and though I'd never admit it, I'm grateful for McNair's pack of tissues in my pocket. Maybe I didn't love every single one of these people, but we were a *unit*. No one else would understand how perfectly in sync the Kristens are, to the point where they showed up with their dates at homecoming in the same dress, or the hilarity of Javier Ramos attending every home basketball game wearing a carrot costume.

Deep breaths. *Keep it together.*

After McNair and I rattle off more highlights from the past year, Principal Meadows takes the microphone back. We retreat to a couple chairs on the side of the stage while she announces the departmental awards, presenting trophies with molded plastic wolves to the top students in each academic discipline. It stings when McNair wins not just for English but for French and Spanish, too, the latter of which makes me a little salty. I stopped taking Spanish junior year to make room for more English electives. I'd wanted to one day be able to talk to my mom's side of the family, and I guess that "one day" isn't here yet. Number five on the success guide—another goal unaccomplished.

"Next up is the perfect attendance award," Principal Meadows says. "Of course, it's not academic in nature, but we always think it's fun to recognize the students who managed to make it all 180 days without a single tardy or unexcused absence. This year we're pleased to honor Minh Pham, Savannah Bell, Pradeep Choudhary, Neil McNair, and Rowan Roth."

That has to be a mistake.

"Rowan?" she calls again when I'm the only one who doesn't stand up, so I scramble to retrieve the certificate with my punctual peers.

Back in our seats, I stab McNair's leg with the edge of the paper certificate.

"I, uh, didn't end up turning in your late slip," he mutters. "Figured I'd let you have this one. Since it's the last day and all."

"So charitable of you," I say, but I don't actually mean the sarcasm. I'm confused, more than anything. McNair and I don't give each other any freebies.

There's no time to dwell on it because Principal Meadows is gesturing to us, preparing for the only honor that really matters. "It's been stiff competition for valedictorian this year," she says. "Never before have we had two students so equally matched in their grades, extracurriculars, and devotion to this school."

I grip the certificate tighter. This is it. Our last battle.

"You're already well acquainted with these two, but what's most astounding about them is that they care not only about their own accomplishments, but so deeply about Westview High School as an institution. They've both done incredible work to ensure future Westview students will have the best experience here imaginable.

"Let me start with Neil. He'll be going to NYU in the fall to study linguistics. He had a perfect SAT score and achieved all fives on the AP Spanish, French, and Latin exams. He was the creator and head of the student-faculty book club, and during his student council leadership, he established an activities fund to generate money to support club activities on campus, which I know a lot of students are going to benefit from for years to come!"

Polite applause. I join in half-heartedly. A flush and his freckles fight for control of McNair's face.

"And then we have Rowan." I swear, she smiles more when she says my name. "She'll be an undecided freshman at Emerson College in Boston. Here at Westview, she's been captain of our quiz bowl team, editor of the yearbook, taken a total of twelve AP classes, and served on student council all four years. As copresident, she campaigned for all-gender restrooms, and she was also responsible for helping the school become a little greener. We now compost and have a trash sorting system, thanks to Rowan."

I wish she hadn't concluded with that. My legacy: garbage.

Mentally, I consider my odds for the hundredth time over the past few months. AP classes were weighted with some complicated math, so I can't accurately predict how his GPA compares to mine.

"Artoo," McNair whispers as Principal Meadows goes on about prominent valedictorians in our school's history and what they've accomplished, rounding out his earlier lesson.

I ignore him. Everyone can see us when we're sitting up here. He should know by now not to talk.

Gently, he knocks my knee with his. "Artoo," he repeats, and

I'm certain he's going to remind me of the latte stain. "I just wanted to say . . . it's been a good four years. Competing with you has really kept me on my toes."

His words are slow to sink in. When I steal a glance at him, his eyes are soft, not sharp, behind his glasses, and he's doing something weird with his mouth. It takes me a split second to realize it's a smile, a genuine one. I've grown so accustomed to his smirk that I figured it was his only expression.

I have no idea how to respond. I'm not even positive it's a compliment. Should I thank him, or tell him "you're welcome"? Or maybe just smile back?

At this point, I've been staring too long, so I direct my attention back to Principal Meadows. For four years, I've dreamed of this moment. Now it'll be the one item I can cross off my list, the proof I did something right. I can practically see my name on the principal's lips, hear it through the speakers.

"Without further ado, I'm thrilled to introduce your valedictorian: Neil McNair!"

10:08 a.m.

THE REST OF the assembly blurs by. In a symbolic gesture, McNair and I pass the microphone to next year's student council president, Logan Perez, though I am so numb I drop it. Then it's my turn to wince at the distorted sound.

Principal Meadows informs the underclassmen that while the seniors are done for the day, everyone else needs to be back in class by ten o'clock sharp. When she dismisses us, the auditorium turns thunderous, and I allow myself to get lost in the storm. I can't find Kirby and Mara, but our group text fills with weeping emojis from Kirby and encouragement from Mara. The two of them are still there when I exit out of my messaging app. My phone background is a photo of the three of us last summer at Bumbershoot, a music festival we've gone to every year since middle school. In this photo, we'd pushed our way to the main stage; Kirby has her hands in the air, Mara's hand is over her mouth, muffling a laugh, and I'm staring straight into the camera.

All of this is over—Seattle, my McWar, high school.

I don't go here anymore, but I can't bring myself to leave.

I roam the hall for a while. Seniors celebrate and teachers

attempt to lasso underclassmen back into classrooms. Finally, I find a long bench in a deserted hallway near the art classrooms, crushing myself into a corner against the wall. I dig my journal out of my backpack. Kirby and Mara and I made plans to meet at our favorite Indian restaurant before Howl, but I need to collect myself first. Writing has always calmed me down.

I open my journal to the line I scribbled in the middle of the night, half hoping it'll be some great inspiration that enables me to get through the rest of the day.

And of course, it's not even legible.

The guide taunts me from the depths of my backpack. Perfect high school boyfriend, nope; prom, nope; valedictorian—and by extension, McNair's destruction—nope. Every dream dashed, every plan foiled, some by time and some by circumstance and some just because I wasn't good enough.

This was the person I wanted to be by the end of high school.

A person I am now so clearly not.

"Artoo?"

I glance up from my notebook, though of course it's McNair, ruining my period of contemplative self-doubt, as though he hadn't already ruined everything else. Jittery, I shove my journal into my backpack.

He stands on the opposite side of the hall, tie loosened and hair slightly mussed, maybe from so many congratulatory hugs. When he lifts one hand in a wave, I sit up straighter, hoping my eyes communicate that I would rather eat the pages of my yearbook one by one than talk to him. He heads toward me, not getting the message.

"When are they fashioning a bust of your head to appear in the entryway of the school?" I ask.

"Just got done with the measurements. I insisted on marble, not bronze. Looks classier."

"That's . . . good," I say, slipping. Usually we keep pace with each other, but this past hour has thrown me. I'm off my game.

After a few moments' hesitation, he slides onto the bench next to me. Well—there's two feet of space between us, but given we are the only two people on the bench, I suppose he is still technically next to me. He pushes up a sleeve to check his watch. It's not digital, and it can't do anything except tell time. It's old and silver, with Roman numerals instead of numbers. He wears it every day, and I've always wondered if it's a family heirloom.

"I meant what I said earlier. About competing with you all these years. You've been a truly formidable opponent." Only Neil McNair would say something like "formidable opponent." "You've pushed me to do better. I don't mean this in an asshole way, but . . . I couldn't have become valedictorian without you."

My temper flares—I can't help it. Maybe he's trying to be genuine, but it sounds like he's mocking me. "You couldn't have become valedictorian without me? What is this, your fucking Oscars speech? It's *over*, McNair. You won. Go celebrate." I flick my hand in a shooing motion, mimicking the one he made by the trophy case earlier.

"Come on. I'm giving you an olive branch here."

"If I can't smack you with it, what's the point?" I heave out a sigh and rake my fingers through my bangs. "Sorry. It's all just hitting me. Everything ending. It's . . . a weird feeling." But "weird" is much too tame a word for how I stack up against Rowan Roth's Guide to High School Success.

What it really feels like is failure.

He exhales, his shoulders visibly softening, as though he's been tensing them all day or maybe even all year. Evidently, we are both doomed to dreadful posture.

"Yeah," he says, tugging on his tie to loosen it some more. In another odd display of humanity, he adds: "I don't know if it's sunk in yet for me. I'm half convinced I'll show up at school on Monday."

"Strange to think about it all going on without us."

"I know. Like, does Westview exist without us here? If a tree falls in a forest and no one's around to hear it and all that?"

"Who's going to torment Mr. O'Brien in AP Chemistry?"

McNair snorts. "I think he was the only teacher who hated us."

"Honestly, I don't blame him. And that fire was your fault." It wasn't, but this balance between us is unsettling, and I'm dying to poke at him some more. "You're the one who added the wrong chemicals."

"That's because you wrote them down wrong," he says, widening his eyes in an expression of innocence. "I was just following your instructions."

"At least Principal Meadows will miss us."

He holds up an invisible microphone. "Rowan Roth, who

revolutionized garbage collection at Westview High School."

"Shut up!" I say, but I'm laughing. I can't believe he noticed that too. "Rowan Roth, literal trash-can emoji."

"You are not a trash-can emoji. You're, like, the emoji of the girl holding her hand out like this." He demonstrates, flattening his hand like he's carrying an invisible tray. Apparently, the emoji is supposed to represent an information desk, but I don't see it.

"She's flicking her hair, and no one will convince me otherwise."

"I pity the person who tries."

It's an unusual moment of accord between us.

"According to Principal Meadows, you speak about a hundred languages," I continue. "So emojis might not be advanced enough to describe you."

"True," he says, "but I'm shocked you'd pass up the opportunity to tell me I'm the poop emoji."

"If you feel that's the emoji that captures the essence of Neil McNair, who am I to disagree?"

A chirp from his jacket pocket ends our emoji debate. He pulls out his phone, frowns.

"Did you get a notification that you actually flunked AP Lit and you're not valedictorian after all?"

"Oh, I still am." He sends a quick message before sliding the phone back into his pocket, but the frown doesn't leave his face.

If he were anyone else, I'd ask if something's wrong.

But he is Neil McNair, and I'm not sure how.

I'm not sure what we are.

A silence falls over us, a strange and anxious one that makes me stare at my flats, cross and uncross my ankles, tap my nails against my backpack. McNair and I don't do silences. We are arguments and threats. Fireworks and flames.

Not anymore, you aren't, a voice in the back of my head reminds me. Number ten on my success guide, the final chapter in my book o' failures.

He drums his knuckles on his yearbook, which I realize he's carrying, and clears his throat. "So—um. I was wondering. If you'd maybe sign my yearbook?"

I gape at him, convinced it's a joke. Except I have no clue what the punch line is. The words "Sure, why not?" dangle on the tip of my tongue.

What comes out instead is the single word right in the middle: *"Why?"* I manage to utter it in the most obnoxious voice imaginable. And I regret it instantly.

His eyebrows crease together. It's an expression I've never seen on his face, not in the four years I've sparred with him.

It's something a little like *hurt*.

"Never mind," he says, pushing his glasses back up without looking at me. "I understand."

"Neil," I start, but again, the words tangle behind my teeth. If I insisted on signing his yearbook, what would I write? That he's been a formidable opponent too? Freaking *HAGS*, like an amateur? I'll do it, if that's what he wants. Anything to make this less awkward, to restore the balance between us.

"Rowan. It's fine. Really." He stands and dusts off his too-short suit pants. "See you at graduation. I'll be the one whose speech comes after yours."

The use of my real name startles me, pulls my heart into a strange rhythm. *Rowan* sounds soft in his voice. Uncertain.

I guess this is one of the last times I'll hear it.

*Text conversation between Rowan Roth and Neil McNair
February of freshman year*

UNKNOWN NUMBER
This is Neil McNair's number.

I love group projects designed to give two people the same grade even when one of them *clearly* does more of the work

UNKNOWN NUMBER
Hi Rowan.

just meet me in the library after school so we can get this over with

UNKNOWN NUMBER
Near the section of vastly inferior literature with shirtless men on the covers, or closer to the real books?

Contact saved as McNightmare.

11:14 a.m.

GARLIC NAAN LIFTS my spirits the way only bread can.

"Are you sure you're okay?" Mara asks for the tenth time.

I nod, dragging a hunk of naan through tamarind chutney.

Apparently not believing me, she continues: "This should be an exciting day. Let's focus on the positives. We're graduating, Howl's starting soon—"

"This samosa exists," Kirby finishes, holding one up. "I'm going back for more."

But Mara's pale-blue eyes won't leave mine. She reaches across the table, grazing my wrist with a few fingertips. "Rowan . . ."

"I guess I'm having trouble accepting that all of this is over," I manage to say.

"It's not like we don't have an entire summer ahead of us. It's not *over*, over. And salutatorian in a class of five hundred is an incredible accomplishment."

I don't know how to explain it. It's not about valedictorian or the fact that as salutatorian, I'll have to introduce McNair as part of my speech. It's about everything valedictorian represents, a whole mess of things I'm not sure I'm ready to say out loud. Even in my head, they don't quite feel real. What McNair said, about showing up at school on Monday . . . That burrowed somewhere deep inside me. There are no more high school Mondays. No more spirit days or student council meetings. No 5:55 alarms or even earlier McNightmare wake-up calls. And it's not that I'll miss the wake-up calls specifically—they were just wrapped up in my whole high school experience.

The bottom line is this: every time I pictured today, I felt a whole lot better than I do right now.

Kirby crashes back into the table with samosas and a welcome change of subject. "I can't believe we're finally going to be playing Howl."

"Oh, I've been ready for years," Mara says with a sly smile. She snaps a photo of Kirby's artfully arranged plate of food.

"Are we going to see Competitive Mara?" Kirby asks, and Mara rolls her eyes. "She terrifies me, but I love her."

While I'm competitive about academics, Mara is cutthroat when it comes to sports and games. Because she's sweet and small, it's totally unexpected. Last year, we played a round of Ticket to Ride that lasted three hours and left Kirby on the verge of tears.

"I just want to see McNair lose. Preferably before I do," I say, surprised by how much this perks me up. I take a sip of mango lassi. It tastes sweeter than it did a few minutes ago.

An idea begins to take shape. There's still Howl, which means there's still a way to beat McNair. It's one more battle between the two of us—and the rest of the school, but if the past four years have been any indication, they've never stood a chance.

"I really am going to miss hating him next year," I say as my mental gears kick into overdrive. I defeat McNair, and I'll have accomplished something on that success guide, arguably the biggest, grandest something. A perfect ten.

Kirby and Mara exchange a glance. "Don't you guys text each other 'good morning' every day?" Mara asks, tentative.

"We tell each other to have a shitty day," I explain, because I imagine it's easy even for my closest friends to misinterpret the relationship I have (had?) with my rival. "It's different."

"You're going to miss him telling you to have a shitty day?" Kirby asks, and shakes her head. "Straights, I swear." She tucks a wisp of hair back into her crown braid. "If we're all dead by tonight, we should have a sleepover. It's been forever."

"Definitely," Mara agrees. We used to have a sleepover every last day of school. In fact, there used to be a time we slept over at someone's house once a month before surrendering to the stress of senior year.

"I—um . . ." I stumble, because tonight is Delilah's signing.

I can go to the signing and still best McNair, but if Howl hasn't ended by then, I'll have to sneak away from it. While I'm not worried I'll see any of my competitors there, I don't know if I can explain the signing to Kirby and Mara. I can't tell them how badly I want to see Delilah's signature rubber stamp, the one made from a mold of her lips that she presses into crimson ink so it looks like she's kissed every book.

The fantasy: my friends love Delilah Park's books as much as I do.

The reality: my friends think my favorite books are trash.

Once at the mall, we passed a bookstore display of romance novels, and Mara scoffed at it. The way she tore them down with a single sound made me ashamed I'd read every book on that display. Another time, Kirby noticed the romance novels on my bookshelf. "They're my mom's," I lied. Kirby proceeded to pull them out one by one, laughing at the titles. My face flamed, and I didn't know how to ask her to stop.

Once upon a Guy: that one distracted me in the hospital waiting room freshman year when my dad needed an emergency appendectomy.

Lucky in Lust: that one made me realize women could make the first move in a relationship.

The Duke's Dirty Secret: well, that one just made me *happy*.

"Let's see how Howl goes?" I finish.

The bell on the restaurant's door dings, and I glance over on instinct, not expecting to see McNair's three closest friends: Adrian Quinlan, Sean Yee, and Cyrus Grant-Hayes, presidents of the chess club, the robotics club, and the Anime Appreciation Society, respectively. McNair is notably absent, which immediately raises alarm.

I used to go to school with these guys, I think, because after today, it will be true. Seattle will be full of used-to-be's.

"I'm going to get more food," I say, pushing out my chair and getting in the buffet line behind them.

"'Sup, Rowan?" Adrian says, scooping basmati rice onto his plate.

"Hey, Adrian. Where's McNair?" I ask as casually as I can.

Individually, his friends are decent humans. As a group, they've assisted him with the Roth-McNair war on a number of occasions. There was the time he stacked student council with them to swing the vote his way, and once they did, they immediately dropped out. Then there was the time they teamed up to mess with the curve on a calculus test. Most of the time, though, they just shake their heads and smile, like we're a show they're not that invested in but that entertains them just enough to keep it on.

Cyrus goes for the saag paneer. "Already missing your other half?"

The question throws me. *Other half.* I've always hated being paired with McNair, but there's something about the way Cyrus says it that makes me hate it less than usual. Almost like it's not necessarily a bad thing.

"Miss him? I just want to make sure he's ready for Howl. I don't miss him. I saw him a couple hours ago," I say, forcing a laugh at the sheer ridiculousness of Cyrus's suggestion. "And I'll probably see him again in another hour. I definitely don't miss him."

"Chill," Adrian says. "Dude's not here. There was some emergency, and he had to pick his sister up from school."

"Oh." *An emergency?* "Is everything . . . okay?"

I should have just sucked it up and signed his yearbook. We've exchanged so many jabs over the years, and yet it's only now that I managed to hurt him with a single word. That hallway version of McNair seemed oddly vulnerable, a word I've never associated with him simply because he's never shown any vulnerability. No cracks in his armor.

Sean shrugs, adding a couple samosas to his plate. "He didn't say much about it. He's . . . not the most forthcoming about his personal life."

"Come to think of it, I can't remember the last time I was at his house," Cyrus says.

Adrian gives him a pointed look I can't interpret. "He doesn't really have people over much."

I take stock of what I know about McNair's personal life. He must live near Westview, but I'm not sure where. Evidently, he has a sister, but until Adrian said that, I would have guessed he was an only child like me because he's never mentioned siblings. *Not the most forthcoming about his personal life.* What could be so, well, *personal*, that he wouldn't share it with his friends?

Even confronted with this emergency, it's impossible to picture McNair in any role except capital-*R* Rival.

"But he's still playing, right?" I ask.

"Oh yeah." Sean flicks black hair out of his eyes. It's doing this swoopy thing I've always found cute. McNair's hair could never achieve that kind of effortless swoop. "He said he wouldn't miss this."

That helps me relax. The emergency can't have been that serious. I won't let it distract me from my new goal, the one that fills me with a familiar rush of confidence.

I'm going to destroy McNair one last time.

Maybe then I'll feel like myself again.

HOWL: Official Game Rules
Property of the junior class of Westview High School

TOP SECRET
DO NOT SHARE.
DO NOT DUPLICATE.
DO NOT LEAVE UNATTENDED
ON THE COMPUTER WHILE YOU GET
A CHEESY PRETZEL FROM THE STUDENT STORE
EVEN THOUGH YOU'RE "PRETTY SURE" YOU SAVED IT.
(THAT MEANS YOU, JEFF.)

HOWL is a citywide scavenger hunt with a twist: you're being hunted by your classmates.

OBJECTIVES
1. Find and photograph 15 scavenger-hunt clues located around the city.
2. Send to the junior class for verification.
3. Don't die.

At the beginning of the game, you will be given the name of your first target. You can only eliminate your target by removing their blue armband. Once you eliminate your target, you will assume their target.

Anyone using real weapons will be immediately disqualified and reported to the police.

Once you've found all 15 clues, you must be the first person back at the Westview gym to win.

GRAND PRIZE: $5,000
GOOD LUCK . . . YOU'LL NEED IT.

11:52 a.m.

BY THE TIME we reach the football field, nearly the entire senior class is here. Kirby and Mara drift toward their dance friends for selfies and yearbook swaps. It's finally starting to warm up, so I slip off my cardigan and fold it into my backpack. I feel much better now that I have a plan. Destroy McNair. Regain confidence. Meet Delilah and hope she loves me.

Just as his friends assured me, McNair's here, standing by the bleachers and rummaging through his backpack. The sun on his fiery hair is nothing short of an ocular hazard. If I look directly at it, it'll probably fry my corneas. Total eclipse of McNair. I hold a hand to my forehead and wrench my gaze downward. He's changed into a black T-shirt with a Latin phrase scribbled across it, and his dark jeans have a hole in one knee. Below them: scuffed Adidas, the laces chewed and frayed at the ends. I wonder if he has a dog. For once, he looks like a teenage boy, not a tax attorney or middle school assistant principal.

The T-shirt is the real mystery. Usually he wears sweaters or button-downs, the occasional grandpa cardigan with elbow patches. For all I know, this is his summer uniform; we're only ever around each other the nine gloomy months school is in session. Freckles up and down his pale arms disappear into his sleeves, and I think he has *biceps*. In sophomore-year gym class, he was a scrawny little thing, twig arms poking out of the boxy Westview gym shirt that fit exactly no one. This T-shirt, though—it definitely fits him.

"Are you okay, Artoo?"

I blink. He's turned to face me, eyebrows lifted, a half-smile on his lips.

"What?"

"You look all squinty," he says.

I'm not sure what he's insinuating, but I wasn't staring at him. He just happened to be in my line of vision, looking different from how he usually does. It was natural for my gaze to linger.

Standing up straighter, I gesture to his T-shirt and jeans. "Casual clothes? Did the robot that controls your body get overheated in the suit?"

"Nah, we've mastered temperature regulation. It's just not worth it to have a robot without that ability these days."

"And here I was looking forward to watching you run around Seattle in twelve cubic feet of polyester." It's a relief to spar like this after the yearbook debacle.

He crosses his arms over his chest, as though self-conscious about how much of him is on display. It makes his upper arms appear even more muscular. God, does he lift weights? How else would he achieve that kind of definition?

"Don't insult me," he says. "That suit is a cotton-wool blend."

We've inched close enough for me to read the Latin on his chest: QUIDQUID LATINE DICTUM, ALTUM VIDETUR. He's probably dying for someone to ask him what it means. I plan to google it later.

He zips his backpack and swings it over one shoulder. There's a pin on it, a shiny enamel basket of corgis and the words FREE PUPPIES! I have no idea what this means either, only that I'm 98 percent sure he isn't running an underground dog-breeding operation.

"Is everything . . . ?" I wave my hand to indicate the word "okay," unsure if finishing the sentence would indicate some kind of closeness we've never had.

"Curvy?" he asks. He taps his chin. "Twisted? My charades skills are a little rusty. How many syllables does it have?"

"No, I—I ran into your friends at lunch. They said you had an emergency?"

The tips of his ears turn scarlet. "Oh. No. I mean, yes, but everything's okay now."

"Good," I say quickly, because if his friends don't know much about his personal life, I know even less. I've always imagined he does homework in his suits, eats dinner in his suits, sleeps in his suits. Then wakes up and does it all again. This T-shirt and the revelation about his arms have poked holes in my McTheories. "That it wasn't serious, I mean. I'm glad you can still play. Then I don't have to feel bad when I beat you."

"Even though you won't deign to sign my yearbook?" He says

this with a lift of his brows, like he knows exactly how shitty I feel about it.

Now it's my turn to blush. If my bangs were longer, I could hide behind them. "I wasn't—I mean—"

He holds up a hand to indicate it's fine, though his remark makes me uneasy. "I'm going to find the rest of the Quad."

McNair and his friends call themselves the Quadrilateral, abbreviated as the Quad, and yes, it is the nerdiest thing I've ever heard. But it does make what they said about his personal life even stranger. Almost like the Quad is more of a triangle with an extra appendage hanging off it. They're splitting up next year too, Neil to NYU, Adrian to one of the UCs, Cyrus to Western, and Sean to the UW.

Kirby and Mara wander back to me. Mara is frowning down at her phone. "It's 12:02. Are we sure we're in the right place?"

"Unlikely that all three hundred of us got it wrong," Kirby says.

Another few minutes pass, and a nervous energy pulses through the crowd. I can't help wondering if one of the juniors made a mistake. The game is different every year; the juniors spend most of their last quarter in student council planning it. Despite all our behind-the-scenes bickering, McNair and I executed a flawless Howl last year. Our clues, when connected on a map, formed the outline of a wolf.

"It said noon sharp," Justin Banks yells.

"Did they forget about us?" Iris Zhou asks.

From a few yards away, McNair's eyes snag mine, asking a silent question: *Should we do anything?* And I'm not entirely sure. We're not presidents anymore, but we're used to taking the lead. . . .

"This is bullshit," Justin says. "I'm out."

As he stomps off the field, nearly three hundred phones buzz, chime, and ding at once. A text blast from an unknown number.

> WELCOME, SENIOR WOLF PACK
>
> Surprised yet? We're just getting started. Only the first 50 players who make it to our secret location will remain in the game.
>
> Here's your riddle:
>
> 2001
>
> 1968
>
> 70
>
> 2.5

"2001, 2001 . . . ," Kirby says. "That was before we were born. What was going on in 2001? Besides some really questionable fashion choices?"

Google isn't off-limits, but the clues are always designed in a way that makes them difficult to find online.

"Oh!" Mara exclaims. "Maybe it's a reference to that old movie? *2001: A Space Odyssey?*"

"Say it a little louder," Kirby says.

"Sorry. Got excited."

We decide to head for my car, since I'm the only one of us who drives to school. Kirby and Mara live close enough to walk. The rest of the seniors seem to have the same idea. Most people split into groups, some racing toward the parking lot and others to the bus.

"I think Mara's right about the movie," I say as our shoes hit concrete, willing my mobile browser to work faster. "I watched it with my dad once. Or more accurately, he watched it, and I fell asleep. And . . . it came out in 1968!"

"There has to be some link to Seattle," Kirby says. "Maybe it was shot here. . . . Nope, Wikipedia says England."

"You've been in AP classes for three years and you're still using Wikipedia?" Mara sounds horrified. Before Kirby can defend herself, we arrive at my Accord and its mangled front bumper. "Rowan! Oh my God, your poor car."

"It still drives," I say, a little sheepish. "Get in."

"If it's movie-related, maybe 'seventy' is referring to seventy-millimeter film," Mara says, sliding into the back after Kirby claims the front passenger seat. "Are there any theaters in Seattle that still use seventy millimeter?"

"My guess would be Cinerama," I say. It's one of Seattle's oldest theaters. Some more frantic googling. "One sec . . . There!" I turn my phone to show them, filled with the rush that comes with being pretty sure you have the right answer to a problem. "Cinerama showed the movie in seventy millimeter for two and a half years."

"To Cinerama!" Kirby says, slapping my dashboard.

While we cruise toward downtown, Kirby scrolls through my

music, blatantly ignoring the unspoken driver's choice rule.

"I knew Howl would fix things. You're already significantly peppier," Mara says. She leans her head against the window. "But would it kill Seattle to give us more than ten minutes of sun?"

The clouds have shifted again, the sky a tranquil gray.

"You know what they say," Kirby says without looking up from my playlists. "Summer doesn't start in Seattle until after the Fourth of July. Why do you have Electric Light Orchestra on here?"

I grab for my phone, but she holds it out of reach. "Because 'Don't Bring Me Down' is timeless."

"We might even get rained out in Lake Chelan," Mara says.

Kirby freezes, turning her head to glance back at Mara.

"What's happening in Lake Chelan?" I exit 99 North onto Denny Way, landing in the middle of Seattle's downtown lunch rush.

A pause. Kirby becomes invested in peeling old parking stickers off my window.

"Shit," Mara mutters.

"We were going to tell you," Kirby says. "Mara's parents are going to Lake Chelan for the Fourth, and they invited me to go with them."

"They invited you," I say, my stomach dropping. "Just you."

"Yeah."

"For the weekend?"

"For, uh, for two weeks."

Two whole weeks. It's not that we've always spent every day of every summer together. Every other year, Kirby's family visits relatives in Cambodia, and twice, Mara went to a dance camp in New York. But this summer is our last one, and I thought that meant something.

I had it all planned out in my head. Sand between our toes at Alki and Golden Gardens, daring each other to touch the fountain at Seattle Center like we're twelve, portabello burgers at Plum Bistro, molten chocolate lava cakes at Hot Cakes, cinnamon rolls at Two Birds One Scone . . .

"We can still go to Bumbershoot together," Mara says softly.

I tighten my grip on the steering wheel. "I can't go to Bumbershoot. I leave for Boston at the end of August."

"Oh."

"I just—I thought we had all these plans."

"We haven't really talked about it," Kirby says as traffic crawls forward.

I open my mouth to insist that of course we have—except I can't actually remember it. We had AP tests and graduation prep and final exams, and now it's *here*, our last day on the cusp of our last summer, and I'm losing my best friends much sooner than I thought I'd be.

3. Hang out with Kirby and Mara EVERY WEEKEND!

"Parking spot!" Mara practically shouts, then holds a hand to her mouth like she's surprised by her outburst. "I mean, there's a good parking spot. Right there."

Silently, I pull into it.

The theater takes up nearly an entire square block, despite

having only one massive screen, and costumes from various film franchises are on display in the lobby. But my favorite thing about Cinerama has always been—

"Chocolate popcorn," Mara says, still trying to play peacemaker. "Do you want some, Rowan?"

I shake my head, declining it for possibly the first time in my life.

Student council juniors Nisha Deshpande and Olivia Sweeney are waiting at the entrance to the auditorium. "Rowan, hi!" Nisha says as she scribbles my name on her clipboard. "I'm so glad you made it."

Fan club, Kirby mouths.

We're within the first ten to have arrived. With the exception of some hushed conversations, the auditorium is quiet. We grab three aisle seats near each other so we can make an easy escape.

And then we wait.

Our classmates show up mostly in small groups but occasionally solo, and I crouch down low in my seat when Spencer ambles up the aisle. I spot McNair hair—a homing beacon, as always—and a mix of relief and pride rushes through me. He made it, but I beat him.

It's almost twelve thirty when the last person arrives.

"Lucky number fifty!" Brady Becker shouts, tearing down the aisle with an outstretched hand. A few people reach out to high-five him.

The moment he slides into a second-row seat, the auditorium door shuts with a *whoosh* and the lights go completely dark.

12:26 p.m.

A FILM STARTS to play. *Welcome*, a title card says, white letters on a black background. *You've passed the first test.*

The juniors modeled it on a silent film, black-and-white stills interspersed with written dialogue and scored by a jazz piece. They act out game play and demonstrate both proper kills and unsportsmanlike conduct, including an over-the-top chase sequence that ends with a player diving into Green Lake.

"Lights!" someone calls when it ends, but the room stays dark. "*Lights*," they say again, more forcefully.

As my eyes readjust, a group of student council juniors takes the stage: incoming president Logan Perez and VP Matt Schreiber, plus Nisha and Olivia. They're all wearing blue T-shirts, though Nisha and Olivia are weighed down with clipboards and papers and boxes filled with armbands. It's clear they're the minions in this operation.

"Congratulations, class of 2020!" Logan shouts, her voice so controlled that she doesn't need a microphone. She's led Westview to two basketball championships already, and she'll probably do it again her senior year, though I won't be around to see it. "You're all officially playing Howl."

Whoops go up from the crowd, and it's impossible not to feel amped. Last year, I couldn't wait until it was my turn. You're not done with WHS until you play Howl. Right now, I'm clinging to that pretty tightly.

"As far as you know, *everyone* is an enemy," Logan continues, pacing the stage. "Your best friend, your boyfriend, your girlfriend. Trust no one."

Mara and Kirby exchange a worried glance as Matt takes the mic.

"The basic game structure is the same as past years," he says. "Before you leave this room, you'll receive a blue armband and a slip of paper with your target's name on it. In order to make a kill, you have to pull off your target's armband. Then you'll assume their target, so *do not lose your slip of paper*." He cups a hand over his ear. "What was that?"

"Do not lose your slip of paper," the auditorium echoes, and he flashes us a thumbs-up.

"You also need to message us when you make a kill so we can keep track," Logan adds. "You all have the number from earlier."

"But, Logan," Matt says, "how do you win?"

"Great question, Matt. You'll receive all fifteen scavenger-hunt clues as soon as you leave this room. You'll need to capture photographic evidence for each clue. Some of them might refer to very specific landmarks, while others are more general. You can get them in any order, but keep in mind that there might be a lot of other people at those specific landmarks, people who might be hunting you. You'll send your photos to us, and we'll verify them for you. While you can share photos with your friends at your discretion, we'll be running them through a reverse image search to make sure you're not cheating.

"To win, you have to be the first person with all fifteen clues who makes it back to the Westview gym. The game will end one hour before graduation on Sunday if we don't have a winner."

"So what you're saying is this game goes all night?" Matt says. "And tomorrow, too?"

Logan nods. "Yep! And you all raised a ton of money this year, so we have a really exciting game in store for you." Logan pauses for dramatic effect, then grins. "The grand prize is five thousand dollars."

A low whistle rolls through the crowd. Five thousand dollars—that's more than double our prize from last year. It would cover the first-year tuition my scholarships didn't.

I could buy so many books.

"Okay, okay," Logan says, holding up a hand to regain control. "Should we talk about the safe zones, Matt?"

"Let's talk about the safe zones, Logan!"

I have to admire how they've choreographed this, how well they work together. They've always been friends, partnered up on projects in leadership, and as demonstrated by their nearly landslide votes, are pretty universally well liked among the student body. It'll probably be a much more peaceful student council.

"Throughout the day, you'll get text blasts from us instructing you to meet at certain safe zones, and showing up at those safe zones *will* be mandatory. We want to make sure you're not just hiding out somewhere, but we also want to give you a chance to rest and spend time with your friends. You can hang out at the safe zone if you're killed, too. This is your last day! The last time you're going to see all these people! We want you to have fun with them—"

"—when you're not trying to murder them," Matt finishes. "Any questions?"

A freckled hand shoots into the air.

"Are we to assume we have geographical limitations?" McNair asks in his overly formal way.

Logan points at him. "Yes. Good question. No farther north than Eighty-Fifth Street, no farther south than Yesler, no farther east than Lake Washington, and no farther west than Puget Sound."

They answer a few more questions—"What happens if you lose your armband?" (don't do it), "Can you double up on photos?" (no: one clue, one landmark). Text blasts will keep us updated on the game standings.

"We won't take any more of your time," Logan says. "Nisha has armbands, and Olivia has your targets. Be sure to collect one of each. Your armband should be tied only once around, not in a knot. And obviously, don't let anyone see the name you have. We know some of you will decide to work together on the scavenger hunt, but be careful. You never know if someone will sacrifice your friendship to win a big pot o' cash."

That's what happened last year: two best friends worked through the entire scavenger hunt together, and at the end, one of them killed the other, who'd been her target.

"You have five minutes before there's a target on your back," Logan says. "Same with the safe zones: five minutes of safety before your enemies are free to take you down."

"Good luck, Wolf Pack!" Matt says, and the auditorium erupts into a loud, anxious howl before we jump to our feet and race to the auditorium doors.

In the lobby, Nisha ties the blue bandanna around my upper arm. "Good luck," she whispers as I get my slip of paper from Olivia.

My stomach plummets when I see my first target: *Spencer Sugiyama.*

Outside the theater, everyone splits off in different directions, some in clusters, some alone. The list of clues is daunting. A handful of them are obvious, but I'm stumped on at least a couple.

Kirby, Mara, and I linger at Cinerama's Lenora Street entrance. Now that we're alone again, the car conversation feels like a physical barrier between us.

"Our five minutes are almost up," I say, staring at my phone before sliding it back into my dress pocket.

"Right." Kirby toes a dent in the sidewalk with her sandal. "And any one of us could have the other."

I do a quick mental calculation. "There's a two percent chance."

"No math. School's over," Kirby says with a groan. "I'd tell you if I had you."

"Really? Because I wouldn't." Mara tucks a strand of blond hair behind one ear, smiling innocently.

"Oh my God, I don't trust either of you!" Kirby says when I don't volunteer my target either.

There's a stiltedness that's never cloaked our interactions before. I tug on my bangs, my perennial nervous habit. The street is busy, downtown corporate types heading back to their offices after lunch.

My phone buzzes. "That's five minutes," I say quietly, unsure where to go from here. Both literally and figuratively. "I guess we should split up until the first safe zone?"

I didn't think we'd become Howl enemies so quickly, but I need some time on my own to figure out how I feel about all of this.

Mara nods, her mouth threatening to slide into a devious grin. Competitive mode. "If you guys last that long."

They already apologized. They shouldn't feel bad about wanting to go on vacation together. It's that they didn't tell me. They'll have this entire year to be together, whereas my days with them are, quite literally, numbered on the calendar in my room, my end-of-August Boston move-in date circled in red.

"Good luck," Kirby says. Mara stands on her toes to kiss Kirby, and they squeeze each other's hands, a small gesture that communicates one thing: *you are loved*.

"See you guys at the safe zone," I say.

Then I take a deep breath, tighten my armband, and start running.

HOWL CLUES

- ☾ A place you can buy Nirvana's first album
- ☾ A place that's red from floor to ceiling
- ☾ A place you can find Chiroptera
- ☾ A rainbow crosswalk
- ☾ Ice cream fit for Sasquatch
- ☾ The big guy at the center of the universe
- ☾ Something local, organic, and sustainable
- ☾ A floppy disk
- ☾ A coffee cup with someone else's name (or your own name, wildly misspelled)
- ☾ A car with a parking ticket
- ☾ A view from up high
- ☾ The best pizza in the city (your choice)
- ☾ A tourist doing something a local would be ashamed of doing
- ☾ An umbrella (we all know real Seattleites don't use them)
- ☾ A tribute to the mysterious Mr. Cooper

12:57 p.m.

A FEW MOMENTS later, I stop running. Seattle has too many hills.

It's not that I dislike exercise. It's just that it's frowned upon to read books on the soccer field . . . which is what I did when I was eleven and my parents stuck me on a team called the Geoducks. I tucked a paperback in my waistband and, when the ball was on the other side of the field, pulled it out to read. I always put it away before the other team headed our way, but needless to say, it was my first and last season of soccer.

I check the clues again to assess what's in my immediate vicinity. If I go to the coffee shop across the street, I could get the cup with someone else's name on it and devise a strategy for the rest. Most people likely ventured much farther, so I'm probably safe here.

The coffee shop is playing folk music with airy female vocals, and I inhale the scent of chocolate and coffee beans. My vision of a Real Writer is someone who haunts coffee shops and wears chunky sweaters and says things like, "I can't; I'm on deadline." Most of my writing happens late at night, sitting in bed with my laptop warming my thighs.

"Riley," I tell the barista when I order my second latte of the day.

After I pick it up, I grab a table and swipe over to Delilah's Twitter instead of the list of Howl clues.

Delilah Park @delilahshouldbewriting
I'm coming for you, Seattle! And yet somehow it's not raining? I feel betrayed. #ScandalatSunsetTour

I've rehearsed a hundred times how to tell her what romance novels mean to me, and yet I'm still worried I'll get tongue-tied. I found my first one, a Nora Roberts, at a yard sale when I was ten, a bit too young to understand what was really happening in some of the scenes. After speeding through everything the school librarian recommended, I wanted something a little more adult. And this . . . definitely was.

My parents humored me, letting me get that book. They thought it was funny, and they encouraged me to ask if I had any questions. I had a lot of questions, but I wasn't sure where to start. Over the years, romance novels became both escapist and empowering. Especially as I got older, my heart would race during the sex scenes, most of which I read in bed with my door locked, after I'd said good night to my parents and was sure I wouldn't be interrupted. They were thrilling and educational, if occasionally unrealistic. (Can a guy really have five orgasms in a single night? I'm still not sure.) Not all romance novels had sex scenes, but they made me comfortable talking about sex and consent and birth control with my parents and with my friends. I hoped they'd make me confident with my boyfriends, too, but Spencer and I clearly had communication issues, and with Luke, everything was so new that I didn't know how to articulate what I wanted.

But then my parents started asking questions like, "You're still reading those?" and "Wouldn't you rather read something with a little more substance?" Most movies and shows I watched with my friends showed me that women were sex objects, accessories, plot points. The books I read proved they were wrong.

It's a comfort knowing each book will end tied up with a neat bow. More than that, the characters burrowed into my heart. I got invested in their stories, followed them across series as they flirted and fought and fell in love. I swooned when they wound up at a hotel with only one room, which of course contained only one bed. I learned to love love in all its forms, and I wanted it desperately for myself: to write about it, to *live it*.

I am sick of being alone in my love for romance novels. This is why I want—*need*—to meet Delilah tonight. Other people read and love these books too, and I have to see them in real life to believe it. Maybe some of their confidence will rub off on me.

"Are you hiding out in here?" someone asks, interrupting my thoughts.

Spencer Sugiyama is standing in front of me, coffee in hand. *Spensur*, it says on the cup.

"Jesus Christ. You scared me half to death."

"Sorry." He eyes the chair at my table. "Can I—" he asks, but doesn't wait for a response before sliding into it. Even McNair would have waited, I'm pretty sure. "I'm actually glad to see you. I've been thinking a lot, and . . . I don't want to end on such bad terms."

"It's fine." The slip of paper with his name on it feels red-hot in my dress pocket. His armband is right there. I could reach across the table and pull it off. "Really."

But a small part of me I'm extremely not proud of wants to hear what he has to say first. I want to know why my longest high school relationship was such a failure, turned me into someone I wasn't happy with, someone incapable of accomplishing items one through ten on my success guide.

"No," he says. "It's not. I need to say something." He makes a pained face, and there's something vulnerable there that must have initially drawn me to him.

That's what always gets me in romance novels: when the love interest reveals a tragic past, or the reason he's never home on Friday nights isn't because he's cheating—it's because he's playing bridge with his sick grandmother. When someone displays that kind of softness, I can't help wanting to know more. I want them to open up, and I want it to be to me.

If this were a romance novel, he'd confess he hasn't been able to stop thinking about me since our breakup. That it was the worst decision of his life, and he's been thrown overboard in a sea of regret without a life jacket. Somehow, I get the feeling that's not what's about to happen. Spencer is not that eloquent.

"Then say it."

He sips his coffee, then wipes his mouth with the back of his hand. "Do you remember our first date?"

The question throws me.

"Yes," I say quietly, my heart betraying me in my chest, because of course I remember.

We'd been flirting in AP Government for months, to the point where romance-novel heroes had started to take his face. Like most modern relationships, it started over social media. *Your color-coded study guides are so cute*, he typed, and I responded, *So are you*. It was easier to be brave when you couldn't see someone's face.

Then he asked if I was free on Saturday. It was October, so we went to a pumpkin patch, got lost in a corn maze, and sipped hot chocolate from the same cup. After dinner at a restaurant so nice it had a dress code, we made out in his car. I felt drunk on him, drunk on the way he ran his hands down my body and kissed the tip of my nose. It was more than the *omg a boy likes me* relationships from earlier in high school. This felt serious. Adult. Like something out of one of my books.

It felt like he could love me.

My face must be turning red because I'm suddenly warm all over.

Evidently, the memory doesn't trigger the same response in him. He's still calm, collected. "Okay. Do you remember our second date? Third? Seventh?"

"I mean, no, but I don't understand what you're trying to say."

"Exactly. I think you want the entire relationship to be like that first date."

"That's ridiculous," I say, but he holds up a finger to indicate he's not finished. I slump back in my seat, fully aware I could do it now. Grab the bandanna and shut him up.

"I could tell you were disappointed when we just hung out and did homework or watched a movie. I felt this weird expectation with you. Like I was never going to measure up to the guys in your books."

Of all the regrets I have about Spencer, at the top of the list is that I told him about my reading preferences. He took it better than most, but in retrospect, maybe it was because he just wanted to sleep with me.

"I wasn't disappointed," I say, but I'm not sure I trust my memory. "It felt like you just . . . stopped caring."

It was more than that, though. It was how I wanted to hold hands in public and he'd keep his in his pockets. It was how I wanted to lean my head on his shoulder in a movie theater and he'd wiggle his shoulder until I moved. I tried to get close, but he kept pushing.

I planned romantic dates too: ice-skating, a picnic, a boat ride. Most of the time, he stared at his phone so much that I wondered if I really was that uninteresting.

"Maybe I did," he admits. "It started to feel like an obligation, I guess. Okay, that sounds bad, but . . . high school relationships aren't really meant to last."

It's clear now that Spencer and I were never going to have a happily-ever-after. The best parts of our relationship happened in a bed when our parents weren't home, and maybe that's okay. It's okay that he wasn't the perfect boyfriend.

What's not okay is that he's still sitting here, making me doubt something that's never let me down.

"I'm sorry our relationship was such a terrible seven months for you."

"That's not what I meant." He grimaces, staring down at his coffee cup. "Rowan . . ." Then he does something perplexing: he stretches his hand across the table as though he wants me to hold it. When it becomes clear that I won't, he draws it back.

I think about Kirby and Mara. Their hand squeezes never seem compulsory. My parents, too—they still have major heart eyes for each other after twenty-five years.

"Look, I'm not sure what you wanted from this, but if your goal was to make me feel like shit, congratulations?"

It felt like an obligation. You *felt like an obligation* is how my mind warps it. I want so badly to be stronger than this. Luke and I even signed each other's yearbooks. But Spencer has never not been complicated, and maybe it's because I'm the complicated one.

Maybe I'm too difficult to love.

With a sigh, he scrubs a hand through his hair. "I'm just trying to explain what happened, at least on my side. You want this idealized romance, and I don't think that's real life. I'm pretty sure all relationships get boring after a while."

It's in that moment that pity is the overwhelming thing I feel. I feel *sorry* for this troglodyte because he has no idea that love doesn't have to sour over time. I don't need to be whisked away in a horse-drawn carriage, and I fully believe both partners are responsible for making a relationship romantic, if that's what they want. Not whatever heteronormative bullshit that tells us guys are supposed to make the first move and pay for dinner and get down on one knee.

But I do want something big and wild, something that fills my heart completely. I want a fraction of what Emma and Charlie or Lindley and Josef or Trisha and Rose have, even though they're fictional. I'm convinced that when you're with the right person, every date, every *day* feels that way.

"I'm gonna go," he says, getting up and turning away from the table.

"Spencer?"

He glances back at me, and with a sweet smile, I dive forward to yank off his armband.

1:33 p.m.

I'M STILL BUZZING with Howl adrenaline by the time I hop a bus heading down Third Avenue. It wasn't until Spencer grumbled about being out of the game so early and surrendered his target (Madison Winters, who wrote a lot of stories about shape-shifting foxes in my creative writing class—one or two, fine, but seven?) that it hit me, zipping through my veins like some wild drug. If it feels this good to kill Spencer, I can only imagine how it'll feel to beat McNair.

After Spencer left, I sent the juniors a photo of my coffee cup, was rewarded with a green check-mark emoji almost instantaneously, and then scrutinized the list of clues. The ones referring to specific landmarks stood out right away—the *big guy at the center of the universe* has to be the Fremont Troll, a statue under the Aurora Bridge in a neighborhood nicknamed the "Center of the Universe."

It makes the most sense to get what I can downtown before going north. Pike Place Market is only a few bus stops away, not worth giving up my parking spot. It's probably one of the top three things people associate with Seattle, with the Space Needle being number one and Amazon-Microsoft-Boeing-Starbucks being a combined number two. It's one of the country's oldest year-round farmers markets, but it's also a living, breathing piece of Seattle history. And it's always packed with tourists, even on rainy days.

"Rowan!" a voice calls after I swipe my ORCA card. Savannah Bell waves at me from the middle of the bus, and at first I hesitate, worried she has my name. But she holds up her hands to indicate she doesn't, and I wave back to confirm the same while groaning inwardly. Bus law dictates that if you run into someone you know on public transit, you are obligated to sit by them.

"Hey, Savannah," I say as I slide into the seat across from her.

She pushes her black hair behind one ear, revealing chandelier earrings made entirely from recycled materials. Last year she opened an Etsy shop to sell them. I don't have strong feelings about Savannah Bell, though I know I'm not her favorite person. In every class ranking, she comes in at number three, right behind McNair and me. Though she joked about it sometimes—"Guess I'll never catch up to you guys!"—I could sense there was some hostility there.

I attempt some small talk. "Good last day?"

"Not bad." When she laughs, it sounds forced. "I never really stood a chance against you and Neil, did I?"

"It's possible we were a little intense."

Savannah reaches into her pocket and flashes a familiar slip of paper. Her Howl target. "I can be content with some revenge."

Neil McNair, it says.

My stomach drops, which might be the bus's sudden lurch

forward. We've only been playing an hour, and the look in Savannah's eyes is raw determination. Maybe it was arrogant to assume Howl would end with McNair and me, but it's not enough to simply survive longer than he does. I want to be the one ripping off his bandanna.

If Savannah kills him, I won't see him until Sunday, his fiery hair sticking out from beneath a graduation cap.

"Good luck," I offer, though my voice sounds scratchy.

Savannah looks down at her phone, the universal sign for it being okay for you to look down at your own phone, so I do the same.

I'm typing out the message before I have a chance to give it a second thought.

> savannah bell has your name, and she's out for blood

If he ends up dead before I have a chance to take him down, then I don't know what I'm playing for. I'd have no way to accomplish number ten.

His reply is almost immediate.

McNIGHTMARE
> Why should I believe you?

> because you want to win this as badly as I do

> I suppose you have a point there. 🙍

> she's across the aisle from me on a bus right now, heading south from cinerama

"I worked my ass off, you know?" Savannah says. "I can't remember the last time I went to sleep before midnight. But I never got the kind of attention you and Neil did. All our teachers thought you two were so cute with your little rivalry."

"Believe me, it wasn't cute."

A muscle in her jaw twitches. "Oh, I believe you. It's just—I could have gotten into Stanford . . . but I was wait-listed."

"I'm sorry," I tell her. "Seattle U is a great school." And I mean it, but Savannah scoffs.

"Pike Street!" the driver calls, and Savannah beats me to pulling the cord.

Reluctantly, I follow her off the bus and down another hill.

There's the light-up sign that says PUBLIC MARKET CENTER. The streets here are rougher, bricked, which is common in the older parts of the city. Inside the market, vendors hawk local produce, flowers, and crafts. Down the street is the first Starbucks, which always has a line out the door despite having literally the same menu as every other Starbucks. And up ahead are the world-famous fishmongers who toss halibut and salmon around all day. I'm a vegetarian, and every year in elementary school, we took field trips here, and every time, I hid my face in my coat, mildly disturbed by the fish-throwing.

"See you," I say to Savannah, who's already started toward the first Starbucks. Not a bad idea for the cliché tourist photo, but I had something else in mind.

I turn left, following a cobbled path lined with street art down into Post Alley and my reason for coming here: the gum wall.

Thousands of tourists stick their gum here every day. Gum drips from windows and doorways, strung from brick to brick, holding up brochures and business cards. It's only been cleaned a few times in its more-than-thirty-year history, and every time, Seattleites put up a fuss about it, as though the chewed-up hunks of Bubblicious are as much a part of the city as the Space Needle or a Mariners' losing streak.

It's weird and it's gross and I absolutely love it.

"Will you take our photo?" asks a man with a heavy accent I can't place. His family, including a trio of small children, are posing in front of the wall.

"Oh—sure," I say, holding in a laugh because this happens every time I go here. They squeeze together, blowing bubbles as I snap a few photos.

They add their gum to the sticky mosaic, and I take a photo on my own phone. *A tourist doing something a local would be ashamed of doing.* Another green check mark from the juniors.

Two down, thirteen more to go.

I'm examining the clues again, assuming I can grab *something local, organic, and sustainable* at any number of produce vendors in the market, when someone bolts past me, startling me so much that I nearly drop my phone. I turn just in time to catch a reddish blur.

"Neil?" I call out, jogging after him.

He skids to a stop halfway down the alley. "Savannah," he pants, bending over to place his hands on his knees. "She spotted me. I only narrowly escaped. I have to—" He gestures vaguely toward the opposite end of the alley.

"Savannah ran track."

The glare he gives me could melt a glacier. "Yeah. I *know*."

Panic twists through me. We don't have a lot of time. Savannah could be headed down the bricked path right now.

"So you can't outrun her. But you could hide from her." I point at the Market Theater, tucked away inside Post Alley. Ghost Alley, some call it, a nod to the rumors that Pike Place is haunted. They even offer ghost tours.

For the most part, the tourists ignore us, too focused on taking the perfect gum wall photo. I cross the alley and try the theater door. Unlocked.

McNair lifts his eyebrows, as though wondering whether it's safe to trust me. His chest is still rapidly rising and falling, and the wind has tossed his hair out of place. It would be fun to see him so frazzled if I weren't so distraught about his potentially impending death.

"In here," I say, waving him over, and after a few seconds of deliberation, he follows.

"If you lock me in here just so you can give the valedictorian speech, please tell everyone I died exactly as I lived—"

"A giant pain in the ass? Got it."

He disappears into darkness, and I shut the door behind him only a few seconds before Savannah comes barreling down the alley. Tourists clutch their belongings and jump out of her way.

"Did you see him?" she asks, barely breaking a sweat. "Neil?"

I point down the alley. "He ran right by."

She flashes me a smile that I return easily, though my heart is banging against my rib cage. It doesn't slow down until she's out of sight.

I wait another minute before opening the door. "Come on," I tell McNair, and he follows without protest.

We race out of the alley together, away from the tourists and the gum and the ghosts.

WESTVIEW HIGH SCHOOL
INCIDENT REPORT FORM

Date and time of incident: January 15, 11:20 a.m.
Location: Room #B208, science lab
Report submitted by: Todd O'Brien, chemistry teacher

Name of person(s) involved in incident: Rowan Roth, Neil McNair

Description of incident: Made Roth and McNair chemistry partners at beginning of year to encourage them to more peacefully work together. Students immediately asked for new partners, informed them assignments were final. After a few arguments early in the school year, had hoped they'd gotten it out of their systems. Was wrong. During experiment on exothermic reactions, their lab station burst into flames. Immediately grabbed extinguisher to put it out. Students could not pinpoint what went wrong in experiment, each intent on blaming the other.

Illness or injury involved: <u>No</u>

How was incident handled: <u>Students sent to principal's office, said they were happy to serve detention as long as incident wouldn't go on their permanent records. Incident appears to have been an accident, and as students are first-time offenders and top ranked in their grade, no further disciplinary action recommended.
Roth and McNair will be assigned new partners.</u>

Signed:

Karen Meadows

Principal Karen Meadows, M.Ed.

2:02 p.m.

WE END UP in the market's basement, in a shop I can only describe as a punk-rock five-and-dime. Orange Dracula sells all kinds of retro goth novelties, from buttons and patches to vampire incense and shrunken heads. They hold live tarot card readings, and a sign in the window reads YES, WE SELL GUM. As a kid, I thought it was the coolest place in the world. Seattle has no shortage of kitschy weird shit, and this is among the kitschiest and weirdest.

"You saved my life." McNair says it almost with a question mark at the end, like he's not convinced it actually happened. Frankly, I'm surprised too.

I turn down an aisle of magnets made from old pulp paperbacks with titles like *Half Past Danger* and *Sin Street*, most of them with half-nude women on the cover. We figured we'd be safe from Savannah in here, since she'd likely assume McNair fled Pike Place.

"It's not fun for me if you're eliminated this early," I say, which is the semi-truth.

He's acting fidgety, jamming his hands into his pockets, then immediately drawing them back out. I'm not sure if it's the near-death experience or if he's just a fidgety guy and I've never noticed.

"Ah. Now everything makes sense." McNair flips through an assortment of off-color postcards. An animatronic witch cackles at us, and a few giggling preteens pile into the shop's photo booth, the one that uses real film, not digital.

His back is to me, and without my permission, my gaze maps the terrain of his shoulders, the way they curve and slope before dipping into his arm muscles. It's a nice pair of shoulders, I decide. A shame they're wasted on someone like him.

"And let's be real," I say to his shoulder blades, "who else stands a chance against us?"

He turns around, shifting the straps of his backpack, drawing my attention to the flex of his biceps. He's been hiding these muscles for at least a year and a half, and they're more distracting than they have any right to be. I've got to figure out a casual way to ask about his exercise routine. Surely, if I solve this mystery, then I'll stop staring.

"Accurate," he says.

Then both our phones buzz at the same time.

> HELLO, SENIOR WOLF PACK
> WE HOPE YOU'RE HAVING FUN
> YOU HAVE 20 MINUTES
> TO GET TO SAFE ZONE ONE

An attachment links to a map of Hilltop Bowl, a bowling alley in Capitol Hill.

"Already?" McNair says, and though his phone has the time, he checks his watch. "Wow. We didn't have our first safe zone until at least five o'clock."

Safe zone means Kirby and Mara and talking about the vacation they're taking without me. And, inevitably, thinking about the life I'll have without them next year. As much as I'd like to delay all of that, the safe zones aren't optional.

"Well," I say as we make our way out of the store. It's always hot in the market basement, even on the coldest days. And it feels entirely too bizarre to have spent ten minutes inside Orange Dracula with Neil McNair. "See you in twenty minutes, I guess?" If I bus back to my car and drive to Hilltop Bowl, I'll be able to make a speedier getaway when our safe-zone time is up.

"Right. See you there," he echoes, but he falls in step with me.

"Are you following me?"

He stops. "We're going to the same place. Except I don't have a car, so I'm taking the bus. I'd hate for it to get delayed, which would mean I'd risk getting kicked out of the game . . . and now I know you want me to stay in it so badly."

I cross my arms over my chest. "No," I say emphatically. The idea of Neil McNair in my car is unacceptable. There's so much he could judge: my music, my cleanliness, the mangled front bumper. "I'm not giving you a ride."

"Nice car," McNair says, fidgeting with the air-conditioner dials and then rolling down the window when he notices the AC doesn't work. I'm back in my cardigan, self-conscious about the stain on my dress again. It's not that hot anyway—McNair must run warm.

"Please don't touch anything." I'm boxed in, so I have to wiggle out of the parking spot inch by agonizing inch. The car in front of me has a parking ticket, which we both crossed off our Howl lists.

He examines the parking stickers stuffed in the passenger-side door pocket, a few stray receipts on the floor. I wonder what he's thinking. It's so clearly not a nice car, even if I love it. We approached from behind, so at least he didn't see the damage. I hope he doesn't say anything about the weird smell. It's not *bad*, exactly, just mildly unpleasant.

McNair scratches at some parking-sticker residue, then finds the adjustment bar beneath the passenger seat. He moves it back—too far back—and then too far forward. Then—

"Are you always this twitchy?" I ask.

He returns the seat to its normal position and drops his hands in his lap. "Sorry. Still anxious from the Savannah chase, I guess."

"This is a onetime thing," I say as I turn onto Pike Street. While I've never driven him anywhere, we've ridden on buses and carpooled with other kids to school events. "Only because it would have taken you too long by bus. And if you even think about criticizing my driving, you can get out right now."

"I actually don't drive," he says, "so I can't really criticize you."

I . . . didn't know that. I can't imagine McNair not acing a test. "Foiled by the written test?"

"I never took it."

"Oh."

"And I'll be in New York in the fall, so there's no point taking it now."

"Right."

We drive in silence for a few minutes, and it's not a comfortable one. Apparently, we've both forgotten how to sustain a conversation. I have never felt so awkward in my own car.

"This is the trip home from quiz bowl regionals all over again," I say.

No one said a word on the ride home from the Tri-Cities after we lost last year. Darius Vogel and Lily Gulati were in the front seat, leaving Neil and me in the back. Somehow, even a quiet McNair annoyed me. He claimed he got motion sick, but I assumed he was miserable (rightfully so) over losing.

"Except we still have a shot at winning," he says.

"Because now you know the final battle of the Revolutionary War was Yorktown, not Bunker Hill?"

He groans. "Trust me. It's burned into my memory forever."

I'm a little surprised he isn't defending himself, but then, plenty of this day hasn't made sense. He shifts in the seat again as though trying to get comfortable, something that may not be possible in his rival's car, and when we're at a red light, I notice one corner of his yearbook peeking out of his backpack. It's enough to make me grip the steering wheel tighter. I should have just signed it.

Then he picks up his phone, scrutinizing the Howl list. I wonder if he knows any I don't.

"Did you know the world 'clue' comes from Greek mythology?"

he says. "A *clew*, C-L-E-W, was a ball of yarn. Ariadne gave Theseus a *clew* to help him out of the Minotaur's labyrinth. He unraveled it as he went so he could find his way back."

I vaguely remember the myth from world history. "So it used to be literal, and now we're metaphorically unraveling a ball of yarn when we try to solve something?"

"Exactly," he says, nodding vigorously.

"Huh," I say, because while it's not unlike McNair to spout an etymology fun fact, this is maybe the first time I've noticed how excited it makes him.

At last we pull into a parking spot a few blocks from Hilltop Bowl.

"Thank God," he mutters, and I'm not sure if he's glad we had an easy time finding parking or relieved to be getting out of my car. Getting away from me. Probably both.

"Well . . . good luck, I guess," I say when we reach the bowling alley entrance, slightly unsettled but not entirely sure why.

He sticks his hands into his pockets. "Yeah. Same."

After Logan Perez checks our names off a list and announces that we have forty-five minutes of safe-zone time, we go our separate ways. I've never been so excited to put on a pair of shoes that have been on hundreds of other people's feet.

Kirby and Mara are waiting for me in a lane at the end.

"You want bumpers, baby Ro?" Kirby asks.

My bowling skills are about on par with my left eyeliner skills. It's a miracle if I break fifty. "Ha ha. Maybe."

"Let her have bumpers if she wants," Mara says, fiddling with the controls.

A few lanes down, McNair bowls a seven-ten split, that trickiest of bowling shots, and his friends let out a chorus of groans. McNair just laughs and shakes his head. The four of them have an ease to their interactions that makes me wonder again what's happening to all of them after graduation. If they'll spend this summer together before autumn obliterates them, and if they'll stay in touch after that.

"Mara and I decided to team up for the rest of the game," Kirby says after she throws a gutter ball. "We don't have each other, so we figure we're safe for now."

"Team up with us too!" Mara says, a little too eagerly. "The three of us! That would be fun."

Kirby bowls another gutter ball in her second frame. "Maybe I need bumpers too."

"Says the girl who mocked the bumpers." Ordinarily, I'd love to team up with them. But . . . "I'm not sure. About teaming up." And it's not just because I'm intent on destroying McNair by myself.

Kirby slides into the plastic seat across from me. "Is this about the vacation?"

There it is. "Yeah, Kirb, you know what? It is. It's about the two-week vacation you two are taking without me when you're going to have an entire year of college to be together."

"I'm sorry," Mara says, more to Kirby than to me. She wipes

her palms on her khakis before picking up the purple ball. "I really didn't think she'd be this upset."

She bowls a strike, but she doesn't look happy about it.

"I guess it feels like there are so many Mara-and-Kirby things I can't be part of," I say, trying to keep my voice level. "You're in love, and I'm happy for you both, truly. But it's like sometimes you forget I'm here too."

They exchange an odd look. Mara puts a hand on the back of Kirby's seat. "Rowan," she says softly, "that's how we feel about *you*."

I scrunch up my face in confusion. "What?"

"You've been so wrapped up in Neil this year," Mara says, slowly gaining volume. "You had to spend all weekend on your physics project to make sure it was better than his. You had to attend every single school event so you had more face time with the voting public or whatever. Even this morning, when I asked if you were okay after the fender bender in the parking lot, you thought I was asking you about him. And . . . did you two get here together? Maybe this isn't easy to hear, but . . . I think you're a little obsessed with him."

"*Obsessed?*" I throw the word back at her. "I'm not obsessed. McNair—he's not my friend. You two are. There's no comparison." I look to Kirby, hoping she'll be on my side.

Kirby sighs. "We thought for a while that you liked him, and that would have made more sense. You know you can tell us if you do, right? We could talk about it, maybe help you—"

"We're not in third grade." I nearly yell it, but I can't help it—Kirby's theory is that absurd. A cluster of kids at the next lane over swivel their heads in our direction, and I lower my voice. "We're not taunting each other because we secretly like each other. And that shouldn't be a thing, anyway."

"Fine. You're not obsessed with McNair," Kirby says flatly. "Can you remember the last time the three of us hung out?"

"I—" I break off when nothing comes to mind right away. Last weekend, McNair and I had to meet up with Logan to hand over some student council responsibilities. And the weekend before that, Mara was at a dance competition. Then we were studying for AP tests, and Mara and Kirby were at prom, and even farther back, I was with Spencer. . . .

"The senior auction," I say. It was back in early May, but it still counts.

"A *month* ago," Mara says. "And even then, you had to solve a crisis with him, and you abandoned us for most of the night."

I rake my fingers through my bangs. "I'm sorry. It's—you know how hectic the end of the year has been. . . ."

But I'm thinking about how I used to tell them everything, and yet they don't know I'm writing a book. Mara's pursuing an artistic career too, but we all know she's a great dancer. There's plenty of video evidence. All I could do to back myself up would be a tiny whispered confession: *I think I could be good at this.* A confession I'm now wishing I spilled the first time I closed a Delilah Park book and thought, *Maybe I could do this one day too. Maybe I could write a book like that.* Then there would be the need to convince them romance novels aren't the garbage they think they are.

I think about my phone background again, the photo I've had there for nine whole months.

Have the three of us taken any photos since then?

"You talk about the three of us having this great last summer," Mara continues, "and I'm sorry—you know we love you—but it's a little hard to believe."

Her words weigh me down, dragging my shoulders nearly to the floor. Our lane goes wobbly. My friends and I don't ever argue like this. In my head, our relationship was rock solid. It can't be true that in reality, it was crumbling.

"You guys keep playing," I say, slipping off the bowling shoes. "I need to get some air."

Several Occasions on Which I May Have (Inadvertently) Abandoned My Friends for Neil McNair

NOVEMBER, JUNIOR YEAR

Kirby and I were in the same AP US History class, and Ms. Benson let us pick partners for an end-of-semester project. Kirby assumed we'd work together, but because I knew Ms. Benson did not buy into the bullshit "everyone in the group gets the same grade" philosophy, I locked eyes with McNair instead. We traded a nod that meant we were on the same page: we'd try to sabotage each other by working together. We each got a 98.

MARCH, JUNIOR YEAR

McNair and I stayed late after quiz bowl practice. We argued for so long about one of the answers that we got hungry and wound up continuing our debate at a hole-in-the-wall Mexican place down the block from school. He was so annoying that I could barely enjoy my veggie burrito. I was supposed to be at Mara and Kirby's dance recital, but I lost track of time and only caught the second half.

SEPTEMBER, SENIOR YEAR

Kirby and Mara and I planned to go to the opening night of Kirby's favorite Marvel franchise sequel, but I had to help student council tally the votes for president because it just wasn't possible they were split exactly down the middle. By the time we finished counting and recounting at one a.m., it became clear that it *was* possible. And I had missed the movie.

MAY, SENIOR YEAR

It's tradition for seniors to hold a silent auction every year to raise money for the school. Everyone in the senior class and their parents are invited to offer something—an item, an experience—and we make the rounds of the room to scribble down their bids. It's pretty posh for public school. Kirby, Mara, and I dressed up and ate fancy food together most of the night—until a basket of high-end cheeses disappeared, and as copresidents, McNair and I had to track it down. Turned out, a little kid had wandered off with it, but it took us the better part of an hour to find it tucked into a stroller.

TODAY

. . . Oh.

2:49 p.m.

THE ARCADE'S PINBALL machines devour my quarters. Obsessed with Neil McNair—it's laughable, really. We've had nearly all the same extracurriculars, the same classes. That's not obsession: that's both of us working toward a singular goal only one of us could ever get.

What would the alternative have been? I had to get inside his head, figure out how to take him down, solve problems only the two of us could. I never fully cracked him, though. That's the strangest part. All these years without dark secrets or embarrassing confessions. With us, it's strictly business.

Still, I can't get my friends' words out of my mind.

I think you're a little obsessed with him.

God, even now I'm thinking about McNair instead of my friends, the people I've all but abandoned this year.

We're not allowed to leave the safe zone until three, and pinball is easier than self-reflection. It reminds me of one of my favorite romance-novel first dates. In *Lucky in Lust*, Annabel and Grayson spend hours in a run-down arcade, drawing a crowd as she grows closer and closer to beating a pinball machine's high score. The whole time, she's *almost* fully focused on the game. She can feel adorable history teacher Grayson's presence next to her, the heat of his body, the scent of his cologne. And when she claims the high score, he wraps her in this incredible victory hug that she feels down to her toes. I didn't know hugs could be that hot.

I don't have Annabel's luck in lust or in pinball. After I lose a few more dollars in quarters, I check the time on my phone. Somehow it's been only five minutes, but I'm not ready to go back quite yet.

Distantly, I hear someone say my name. I turn my head, but the given way the conversation continues in hushed tones, I'm not sure anyone was actually calling me. I'm not being beckoned—I'm being talked about. The arcade is on the top floor, above the lanes, and it's tough to make out the conversation amid the sounds of pins clattering and people talking, laughing. I'm alone in here, probably because everything looks like it hasn't been cleaned in the last twenty years, including the carpet, which is the saddest shade of greige.

But then I hear my name again, and this time I'm sure it's coming from the food court across from the arcade.

There's no door separating the arcade from the hall or the food court—but there's a potted plant at the arcade's entrance that's roughly my height.

What I'm doing is ridiculous. I'm aware of that. And yet here I am, creeping toward the plant, hoping its leaves can hide most of my body. When I peek between them, I spot about a dozen

Westviewers huddled in the food court, the kind that serves plastic pizza and one-dollar sodas. Savannah Bell is at the head of the table, and she looks about as thrilled as I did when I learned the votes for student council president were split right down the middle.

"Aren't you sick of Rowan and Neil winning everything?" she's saying, waving a cup for emphasis. "Every test, every competition, it's Neil and Rowan, Rowan and Neil. If I never hear their names together again, it'll be too soon."

You and me both.

"It's the last day of school, Sav," says Trang Chau, Savannah's boyfriend. "Why does it matter?"

"Because if one of them wins today," Savannah continues, her earrings trembling with the indignity of it all, "then they win high school. They get to go off to college all smug, thinking they're better than the rest of us. Think how satisfying it would be to take them down a peg. Valedictorian and salutatorian, beaten at their very last game."

This conversation feels *sinister*, somehow. McNair and I earned every accolade, every win.

"I always assumed they were hooking up," says Iris Zhou, and I fight the urge to gag myself with a plant leaf.

"No. No way," Brady Becker says. Bless him. "I did a group project with them last year, and they nearly killed each other. It was fucking brutal."

"I don't know." Meg Lazarski taps her chin. "Amelia Yoon said she saw them go into the supply closet together during leadership last month, and when they came out, Neil's hair was a mess and Rowan was totally blushing."

I muffle a laugh. The closet was tiny, and I'd accidentally brushed against him while reaching for a jar of paint. Simple proximity to another human being in an enclosed space would make anyone feel flushed. As for his hair: well, it was AP test week, and some people play with their hair when they're anxious. Guess we have that in common.

"I don't care if they're hooking up or not," Savannah says. "All I want to do is take them down."

"Isn't this a little . . . unsportsmanlike?" Brady asks before shoving half a slice of pizza into his mouth.

"We're not doing anything that breaks the Howl rules," Savannah says. "I tried to kill Neil earlier, but Rowan swept in to save him."

"Hooking up," Iris singsongs, like this explains everything.

Savannah fixes Iris with a death glare.

"Besides," Savannah continues, "it's not like Rowan needs the money."

"What do you mean?" Meg asks.

"Jewish?" Savannah says as she taps her nose.

She taps. Her *nose*.

I can't hear what anyone says next—if anyone laughs or if anyone agrees with her or if anyone calls her out. I can't hear. I can't see. I can barely *think*. A panic I haven't felt in years flares through me, red-hot.

I curl one hand around the plant's fake bark in an attempt to anchor myself. In bluest-blue Seattle, a place everyone claims to be *so open*, this still happens: the jabs people think are harmless, the stereotypes they accept as truth. There aren't many Jews here. In fact, I can name every other Jewish kid at Westview—all four of us. Kylie Lerner, Cameron Pereira, and Belle Greenberg.

When you're Jewish, you learn from a young age that you can either go along with the jokes or fight back and risk much worse, because you don't have the words yet to tell anyone why those jokes aren't funny. I chose option A. It makes me sick sometimes, thinking about how I egged people on in elementary school, because if you can't beat 'em, join 'em, right?

I run my index finger along the bump of bone in the middle of my nose. In fourth grade, I failed an eye exam on purpose, hoping glasses would detract from the monstrosity in the middle of my face, but I felt so guilty about it that I ultimately confessed to my parents. Even now, it's not my favorite feature. One comment, and it drags me all the way back to that place where I hated looking at myself.

"If you're here," Savannah's saying, and I force myself to refocus on the conversation, "it's because you want to take them down too. Anyone who doesn't can feel free to leave."

At first no one moves. Then Brady gets to his feet.

"I'm out. Rowan and Neil are cool, and I don't want to ruin anyone's fun."

"And I was just here for the pizza," says Lily Gulati. "Which was wonderfully mediocre. Good luck with your revenge, I guess."

No one else stands up.

I'm not naive enough to assume everyone in high school liked me, but I figured at the very least they didn't hate me quite this much. This harsh reality makes me unsteady. Maybe I underestimated Savannah. She's clearly someone who can summon power when she wants to, given the group she's established here. And after what she said, the way she tapped her nose—she's never been my favorite person, but now she's gone full villain.

My neck is starting to cramp. I'm so desperate to twist the other way for some relief, but I can't risk drawing attention to my hiding spot.

"Now that that's settled," Savannah says, "let's talk strategy. I still have Neil's name." She waves the paper for everyone else to see. "But he knows I have it." This last part, she lets hang in the air, as though waiting for her followers to grasp the hidden meaning.

"I think I get what you're saying," Trang says. "Have one of us kill you, then take Neil's name, so he doesn't see it coming?"

A wicked smile from Savannah. "Exactly."

"Artoo? What are you doing?"

The voice startles me so much that I let out a gasp, then immediately clap a hand over my mouth.

"Shit, shit, *shit*," I hiss, whirling around to find McNair staring down at me with a very confused expression on his face.

Heart hammering, I grab his shirtsleeve and drag him into a crouch behind the unoccupied shoe-rental booth. He stumbles but quickly rights himself, following my lead and ducking his head. Our knees meet the greige carpet a little more harshly than I hoped. Bowling shoes are stacked in neat rows in front of our faces. I'm positive we're out of sight, but I can't hear anything Savannah's saying.

"You can let go of me now," McNair whispers.

Oh. It's only then that I realize how close we are, and I'm still holding on to his sleeve. While I feel like I haven't taken a normal breath in hours, his chest rises and falls in the steadiest way, that mysterious Latin phrase moving up and down.

I release my grip on him, trying as best I can to avoid contact with his skin as I sit back on my heels and busy myself with readjusting my sweater. I started sweating when I was spying, and being this physically close to someone else—even if it is McNair—isn't exactly helping.

My mind is reeling. Savannah wants her army to go after McNair and me. As what, some kind of twisted revenge for being good at school?

McNair opens his mouth to say something, but I hold a finger to my lips. Slowly, slowly I creep to the left until I can just barely see the food court. The group looks like they're wrapping up, heading back to their lanes. Whatever else they decided to do, I completely missed it.

I crawl back to Neil, who, much to his credit, is being both very still and very quiet.

"I'm lost," he says. "Is this part of the game?"

"I'll tell you what's going on. I promise." I check my phone. Our safe-zone time is almost up. "But not here."

He claps his hands together and grins in this over-the-top way. "Does this mean I get to ride in your car again? Oh, Artoo, say it isn't so!"

I roll my eyes. "Meet me back at my car as soon as they let us out. And make sure no one follows you." I don't want anyone to see us together.

A flicker of amusement crosses his face, but he nods. He has to be able to tell how serious I am about this. I can trust him.

I think.

"I would make a really excellent spy," McNair says as I approach my car. He's already leaning against it, one foot propped against the back tire. If he were anyone else, he might look cool. "In case you were wondering."

I ignore him and inspect our surroundings to make sure no one followed us. After I left the arcade, Mara said I could still join her and Kirby, but I shook my head and told them I'd see them later. A heavy silence passed between the three of us, as though we were unsure how to navigate this new stage of our friendship where all our problems—*my* problems—were out in the open.

All I know is that McNair and I aren't safe.

Now that he's seeing another angle of my car, he notices my front bumper and draws in a sharp breath.

"Oh," I say, wincing. "Yeah. I, um. Hit someone. This morning."

"That's why you were late?" He bends down to examine it.

"I was too embarrassed to say anything."

Something unexpected happens then: his voice turns soft, his eyes full of something that, if I didn't know any better, might be concern. "Are you okay?"

"I'm fine." I pull my sweater tighter around myself. "I wasn't going very fast. My dress is the one that really suffered."

"Still, I'm sorry. I was in the passenger seat when my mom got rear-ended last year, and the car was fine, but it rattled me. I didn't realize, or I wouldn't have given you such a hard time this morning."

"It's—thank you," I manage, recognizing that this is maybe a normal conversation between two people with one who cares that the other didn't die this morning. "I don't see anyone. Get in."

We shut the doors, but we're too close to the bowling alley for comfort. I drive for a couple minutes in silence, weaving through residential streets until I find a parking spot deeper in Capitol Hill.

"You're starting to freak me out," McNair says when I kill the engine.

I let out a long sigh. "I know this is weird . . . but I heard Savannah Bell talking in the food court about us. She had a group of ten or twelve people, and they were planning to team up to take us out of the game."

His face twists. "What? Why?"

"To be assholes? To get us back for being the best in school?"

"Technically, you're second best," he says, and I'm too anxious to be annoyed by it.

"The way Savannah phrased it, it was like getting back at us after all these years. They sounded pretty serious about it. And Savannah said—" But then I break off, realizing I was about to tell him how she tapped her nose. I'm not sure I can explain to someone who isn't Jewish, who's never experienced this, how equating Judaism with wealth is anti-Semitic. Centuries ago, Jews weren't allowed to own land and could only make a living as merchants and bankers. It evolved into a stereotype that we're not just rich, but greedy, too. "That she, um. Has you now."

McNair nods, tugging at a loose thread on his backpack.

"But from what I could tell," I continue, "they were going to have someone kill her just to take your name."

"Who?"

"I didn't get to hear. That was when you interrupted me."

"And—you don't know who has you, either?"

"I do not. As I said, that was when you interrupted me. Keep up," I say. "They're all going to be out to get us. And they don't care about sacrificing themselves for the cause, either. It's clearly not about the money for them."

A brief silence falls over us. McNair's brow is furrowed, as though trying to make sense of Savannah's plan.

I don't know how to explain to him that the longer I stay in the game, the longer I remain in high school, the longer I don't have to face the reality that I didn't turn into the person my fourteen-year-old self wanted to be. On Monday morning, I want to walk right back into homeroom with Mrs. Kozlowski, debate with McNair during AP Government, joke with Mara and Kirby at lunch. I'm not ready for the world beyond Westview yet.

Or maybe I don't need to explain. Maybe he feels exactly the same way.

"Well . . . shit," he says finally, and despite everything, it almost makes me laugh. It's such a resigned thing to say, and McNair has never been resigned about anything, not as long as I've known him. "What do we do?"

It's weird he asks this. Not just because he uses "we" as though we're a unit, but because it's exactly what I've been wondering: How are *we* going to deal with it?

I summon all my strength to utter this next sentence. Given every time we've been tied together throughout high school, maybe my suggestion is fitting. I've been going over it in my head since I heard them talking, and I'm pretty sure it's the only solution. My jaw is tight, my throat rough as the words climb up it, fighting every urge for self-preservation.

"I think we should team up."

HOWL STANDINGS
TOP 5

Neil McNair: 3
Rowan Roth: 3
Brady Becker: 2
Savannah Bell: 2
Mara Pompetti: 2

PLAYERS REMAINING: 38

MOST RUTHLESS KILL: Alexis Torres 🔪 Aiden Gallagher, by way of breaking up with him 😱 💔

3:07 p.m.

MCNAIR IS QUIET for a few seconds. He's been clutching his backpack in his lap, and he lets it drop down into the space near his feet. At first I'm convinced he's going to tell me I'm being ridiculous, that teaming up is absurd. He frowns, then flattens his mouth into a straight line, then frowns again. It's like he's carefully weighing the options, the pros and cons marching along his face, messing with his features.

"I really hoped there'd be another way," I say. "But if we both want to win, which I think we do, then . . ." I let him fill in the blank.

It's not an easy suggestion to make. When we've worked together in the past, it's usually been forced. In student council, on group projects, we were working toward the same general goals with completely different plans of attack. The *White Man in Peril* incident on infinite repeat. Savannah's plot made it clear this is bigger than a rivalry, bigger than number ten on my list.

"What exactly would it entail, teaming up?" he asks, ever logical.

In the soft afternoon light, his freckles seem almost lit from within. He never looks like this beneath Westview's eco-friendly

LED lights. His eyelashes are glowing amber, and the effect is so startling that I have to look away.

"Help each other with the clues. Have each other's backs." It hits me that I have no idea who McNair's target is, and that makes me uneasy. "Wait, who do you have?"

"Oh Carolyn Gao." Drama club president. She was incredible in last year's production of *Little Shop of Horrors*. "And I know you don't have me, but—"

"Madison Winters."

He nods. "So if we do this, if we team up, what happens at the end? I assume this means we'd be finishing the scavenger hunt at the same time, right?"

"Once we get the last clue, it's an all-out war. Whoever makes it back to the gym first wins. One-two, the way it always is." We team up now, and I destroy him later. That's the gist of it.

I refrain from mentioning Delilah Park's signing. That's more than four hours from now. If we haven't irritated each other to death by then, I'll make up an excuse to slip away.

He pulls at another loose thread on his backpack, where the FREE PUPPIES! pin clings to fraying nylon. "I'm just wondering . . . what's in all of this for you? If you want to win this badly, it can't just be to beat me."

"That's . . . a good part of it," I admit. It wouldn't cancel out valedictorian, but I just know it would feel amazing to win our very last competition. I don't want to be stuck in time, second best. "And I'd love the money for school." Then I fire the question back at him.

"School," he agrees, a little too quickly. "New York is expensive."

"Right," I say, unable to avoid feeling like he's only partially telling the truth.

"Hypothetically, if I agree to this scheme of yours, let's say you win the whole game. You get the glory. What do I get? Seems like a shit deal for me at that point."

I consider this. "We split the money. Fifty-fifty. Regardless of outcome."

A grin spreads across his face and dread churns in my stomach. This cannot be good. "What if we upped the stakes?"

"I'm listening."

"A bet," he proposes. "You and me. A bet to cap off our epic four years of academic bloodshed."

"What, like the loser has to go naked under their gown at graduation?"

He snorts. "Seriously? Are you twelve? I was thinking something far more personal."

I rack my brain. There are probably plenty of things McNair wouldn't enjoy doing, but I don't know him well enough on a personal level to guess what any of them would be.

Then I gasp, covering my mouth to conceal a grin when the idea hits me. "The loser has to write the winner a book report on a book of the winner's choosing."

"How many paragraphs?"

"Five, at least. Double-spaced, no fewer than three pages." I cross my arms over my chest, aware this is the nerdiest bet in history. But *wow*, the books I could have him read . . . "Are you in or not?"

For a beat, neither of us blinks. In all our competitions, we've never placed a bet. There was always plenty at stake.

"As weird as it is to talk about book reports on the last day of school, it's kind of perfect," he says. "The only question is, should it be *The Old Man and the Sea* or *Great Expectations*? Or wait, I'd love to see what you do with *War and Peace*. Unabridged, naturally."

"So many mediocre white men to choose from."

"And yet there's a reason they're called classics." McNair turns in the seat and sticks out his hand. "To mutually assured destruction," he says, and we shake on it.

Despite our matching height, our hands aren't the same size, which I had no reason to notice until now. His hands are slightly larger, his skin warm, freckled fingers woven between my pale ones.

"You really do have a lot of freckles."

He withdraws his hand from mine and glances down at it in mock astonishment. "Oh, *that's* what these are." Then he drops his hands to his lap. "I've always hated them."

"Why?" I know he gets embarrassed when I tease him about them, but I don't think they're unattractive or anything, though of course I'd never say that to his face. They're just plentiful. "They're . . . interesting. I like them."

A pause. A lifted eyebrow. "You . . . like my freckles?"

I roll my eyes and decide to play along. "Yeah I do. I've always wondered if you have freckles *everywhere*."

It's nearly automatic now, the way I can make him blush like this. He really is so sensitive about them. Still, he clucks his tongue and says, "Some things are better left a mystery." He runs a hand up and down his bare arm. "Get ahold of yourself, Artoo. We're teammates now. If you can't handle all these hot, hot freckles, then we might be doomed."

It must be talking about them that makes me stare at his face a moment longer than I normally would. Because the thing is, I *have* wondered if he has freckles everywhere. In a purely scientific way, the same way you'd wonder when the next big earthquake will hit Seattle or how long it takes chewing gum to decompose. Given they're just as densely dotted on his arms as they are on his face, he must, right?

He has to know I'm not being serious. I don't want him to think I'm calculating his ratio of freckled to unfreckled skin. Even if it's in a purely scientific way.

"Your glasses are crooked," I say, hoping this will return us to normal, and he adjusts them.

There. Except *normal* isn't Rowan versus Neil; it's Rowan and Neil versus the rest of the senior class.

This is probably a really bad idea.

Over a slice of what McNair declares is Seattle's best pizza, we strategize. Well—first we argue. I start to pay for my food, but he insists on doing it since I'm the one driving us around. Then I begrudgingly agree to share my photo of the gum wall as long as he shares his photo of an umbrella. Until this point, we'd been equal. And I suppose we still are.

I'd love to decipher every clue right now, but McNair thinks it's a waste of time. He wants to focus on what we know and figure out the rest along the way.

"There's such a thing as planning too much," he says, shaking red pepper flakes onto his pizza. Upper Crust is not the best pizza in Seattle, in my opinion. My slice has too much gooey mozzarella, not enough sauce. "Need I remind you of the summer reading incident?"

I grimace. Our junior English teacher had sent out a list of titles the week school let out, and I decided to read all five as quickly as I could so I could read what I wanted the rest of the summer. The day I finished, she emailed to let everyone know she'd sent the wrong list and "surely" no one had started yet.

"That was an anomaly." I play the car card: if he wants to walk, he's welcome to take off as soon as we finish eating, but I'm staying here until I figure out a few more. He relents.

At least we agree on a few of the more specific clues. *Ice cream fit for Sasquatch* is probably the yeti flavor at Molly Moon's, Seattle's most popular ice cream shop. And we're pretty sure *a place you can find Chiroptera*, the scientific name for a bat, is the Woodland Park Zoo's nocturnal exhibit.

"Do you have any idea what 'a tribute to the mysterious Mr. Cooper' could be?" he says. "It's so vague. I googled 'Seattle Cooper' and only came up with a towing company, a car dealership, and a bunch of doctors. Or this one—'a place that's red from floor to ceiling'?"

"The Red Hall in the Seattle Public Library downtown," I say without missing a beat. My parents have regular story times at the library, and I've explored nearly every inch of it. The hall is eerie but fascinating, a quirk in a building full of quirks. The Mr. Cooper clue, though, is as much a mystery as he apparently is. "Now I know why you were so eager to team up," I say, shoving some of the excess cheese off my pizza. "You don't know any of the hard ones."

"Not true." He points to *something local, organic, and sustainable*. "The compost system you introduced to Westview."

Despite myself, I snort-laugh. "Please, I'm eating."

It's odd, though, eating pizza with Neil McNair. The window of the pizza place is semi-reflective, letting me almost see what it looks like, the two of us in public together. His red hair is slightly windblown, while my bun left windblown and leaped to natural disaster a couple hours ago.

After a few more minutes of bickering, we're still stumped on the mysterious Mr. Cooper, but we'll deal with that later. Our first stop as a team will be nearby Doo Wop Records for Nirvana's first album.

We drop our plates into the compost bin (naturally) before leaving Upper Crust. Neil pulls out his phone to map the record store. In addition to all the regular social media and messaging icons, there are more than a few dictionary apps on his home screen.

"*Merriam-Webster* fanboy?" I ask.

"I'm more of an *OED* guy." When I give him a blank look,

he continues: "*Oxford English Dictionary*? It's only the definitive record of the English language."

"I know what the *Oxford English Dictionary* is," I snap. "I just wasn't familiar with the acronym. How often does that come up in daily life, anyway? When you need to whip out a dictionary . . . or five?"

He shrugs. "Somewhat often, if you want to become a lexicographer."

"Oh," I say, nodding like I know exactly what that is.

The corner of his mouth quirks up. "You don't know what that is either, do you?"

"I'm trying really hard to not find you infuriating right now."

"It's someone who compiles dictionaries," he says, and it kind of suits him. "I love words, and that's what I want to do. There's no better satisfaction than using precisely the right word in a conversation. I love the challenge of learning a new language, and I love discovering patterns. And I find it fascinating that words in other languages have crept into our vocabulary. 'Cul-de-sac,' 'aficionado,' 'tattoo . . .'"

As he's explaining this, his eyes light up, and he gestures with his hands. I don't know if I've ever seen him this animated, this clearly enamored with something.

"That's kind of cool," I finally concede. Because honestly, it is. "How many languages do you know?"

"Let's see . . ." He ticks them off his fingers. "Fives on AP Spanish, French, and Latin. Would have taken Japanese, but they didn't offer it, so that'll have to wait until college. The romance languages, those are easy enough to learn once you have a foundation in one of them, so I've been teaching myself Italian in my spare time." His lips curve into a smile. "You can say you're impressed. It's okay."

I refuse to, but it's hard not to be impressed when my knowledge of my mother's first language ends at Spanish III.

Since the record store isn't far, we decide to walk instead of hoping we'll get lucky twice with Capitol Hill parking. We fall in step, passing a dry cleaner and a shoe store and a sushi place. Because we're exactly the same height, our shoes smack the pavement in tandem. I bet we'd easily win a three-legged race.

Broadway is Capitol Hill's main drag, a street where hole-in-the-wall restaurants and boutiques have slowly been replaced by Paneras and cat cafés. A few pieces of Seattle history remain, like the bronze Jimi Hendrix statue on Broadway and Pine, frozen mid–guitar solo, and Dick's Drive-In. I don't eat the burgers, but their chocolate milkshakes are perfection in a compostable cup. It's also the center of queer culture in Seattle, hence the rainbow crosswalks, which we snap photos of and receive our green check marks.

"Can I ask you something?" he suddenly says. He looks uncomfortable, and I panic, worried he's going to bring up his yearbook again. I'll sign it right now if he does. I won't make any sarcastic comments. "Why do you hate me so much?" It comes out so easily, no buildup. He doesn't stumble over it, but it catches me off guard, makes me pause in the middle of the sidewalk.

"I—" I was ready to fire back a response, but now I'm not sure what it was. "I don't hate you."

"I find that hard to believe. You've been scoffing nonstop for the past half hour."

"'Hate' is a really strong word. I don't hate you. You"—I wave my hand in the air as though the right word is something I can wrap a fist around—"frustrate me."

"Because you want to be the best."

I grimace. The way he says it makes me feel immature about this whole thing. "Well—okay, yes . . . but it's more than that. Most of what we talk about is completely harmless, but you've never been able to stop with the snide remarks about romance novels, and that's not teasing to me. It just . . . hurts."

His grip on his backpack straps loosens, and he ducks his head as though in shame. "Artoo," he says softly. "I'm so sorry. I really thought . . . I really thought we were just teasing each other." He genuinely sounds sorry.

"It doesn't feel like teasing when you go out of your way to make me feel like garbage for liking what I like. I already have to defend it enough with my parents, and with my friends. Like, I get it, ha ha, sometimes there are shirtless men on the covers. But what I'll never understand is why people are so quick to trash this *one thing* that's always been for women first. They won't let us have this one thing that isn't hurting anyone and makes us *happy*. Nope, if you like romance novels, you have zero taste or you're a lonely spinster."

When I finally stop talking (thank *God* I stop talking), I'm breathing hard, and I'm a little warm. I hadn't expected to get so worked up about it, not on the day I'm meeting literary goddess Delilah Park, and not in front of Neil McNair.

He's staring at me, eyes wide and unblinking behind his glasses. He's going to laugh at me in three, two one. . . .

But he doesn't.

"Artoo . . . ," he says again, even quieter this time. "Rowan. I really am sorry. I—I guess I don't know much about them." He changes course, using my real name. Then he lifts a hand until it's hovering above my shoulder. I wonder what it would take for him to lower it. I remember the Most Likely to Succeed photo shoot, how he was so opposed to touching me. As though it would convey some kind of fondness we have never had for each other. Mutual respect, sure. But fondness? Never.

He drops his hand before I can contemplate it anymore.

"Apology . . . accepted, I guess." I was all ready to fight back. I'm not used to peace talks. "Can I ask *you* something?"

"No. You can't." Maybe this is meant to lighten the mood, by the way his mouth quirks up as he says it.

I push at his shoulder, gently. It's the way I'd touch a closer friend, and it feels so strange that my stomach flips over. I'm not even sure if McNair and I are capable of being friends, or if it even matters. We're leaving in a couple months anyway. I don't exactly have time for new friends.

"Why do you hate them so much? Romance novels?"

He gives me another odd look. "I don't."

```
------------------------------------
          UPPER CRUST PIZZA
------------------------------------


   June 12, 20 2003:18 PM
   ORDER #: 0102
   SERVER:JENNIFER  GUESTS:2  TABLE:9


   DINE IN


   1 VEGGIE VENGEANCE          $2.99
   1 PEPPERONI PIZZAZZ         $3.49


   SUBTOTAL                    $6.48
   TAX                         $0.65


   TOTAL                       $7.13


   TIP                         $2.50


   VISA CARD XXXXXXXXXXXX1519
   MCNAIR, NEIL A


            THANK YOU!
```

3:40 p.m.

THE TEMPTATIONS ARE playing inside Doo Wop Records, one of a handful of things that makes me feel as though I've stepped back in time. The whole place is a tribute to the 1960s, with vintage concert posters on the walls and private listening booths in the back.

"You fit right in," McNair says, gesturing to my dress.

"I—oh." It's such an un-McNair-like thing to say that it takes me a while to form a sentence. "I guess so. I like old clothes and old music. Are you . . . into music?" It seems like a basic fact to know about a person: brown hair, brown eyes, would do questionable things to have been able to see the Smiths play live.

"Am I into music?" He scoffs at the question as we head down an aisle marked ROCK J–N. "Was Hemingway the greatest writer of the twentieth century? Yes, I'm into music. Mostly local bands, some that made it big and some that haven't yet. Death Cab, Modest Mouse, Fleet Foxes, Tacocat, Car Seat Headrest . . ."

"Did you see Fleet Foxes at Bumbershoot a few years ago?" I ask, ignoring the Hemingway comment. Just for that, I'll pick an extra steamy book for him to read when I win.

His eyes light up. "Yes! Such a great show."

And though we've been at the same school for four years, there's something strange about this: McNair and I having been at the same concert, clapping for the same band in a sea of sweaty Seattle hipsters.

He finds the *N* section first, flips through it as I open my group chat with Kirby and Mara. It's not impossible Savannah's recruited more people since Hilltop Bowl, and even if we're on shaky ground, I don't want to be scared of my own friends.

> I'm sure the answer is no, but you guys didn't by any chance team up with savannah bell to kill mcnair and me, did you?

MARA
> We definitely did not.

KIRBY
> WTF???

> overheard her organizing an army at the safe zone

KIRBY
> I repeat: WTF???

> yeah 🙁

> so I may have kind of joined forces with mcnair

I slip my phone into my pocket, not quite ready for their responses yet.

"They don't have it," McNair says, and I nudge him out of the way to take a look for myself.

"Can I help you find anything?" asks a woman with a Doo Woop lanyard around her neck. She's probably midtwenties, with a platinum-blond pixie cut, wearing long overalls and combat boots. Her name tag reads VIOLET.

"We're looking for Nirvana's first album," I say, and because I looked it up earlier: "I think it's *Bleach*?"

"It is indeed!" Violet chirps. "Old-school Nirvana. I love it. You're actually not the first people who've asked about it today. Are you playing some kind of game?"

"Sort of like a scavenger hunt," McNair says.

"Hmm, I know we have it. It should be right here." We shift out of the way so she can take a look at the *N* section.

Whoever came here before us—what if they hid it? There are thousands of records in here. They could have slipped it in anywhere.

McNair must come to the same conclusion, because he says, "Would you guys have a copy of it anywhere else?"

"We have *Nevermind*—overrated, in my opinion—*In Utero*, and *MTV Unplugged in New York*. Now, that's a good album." She pulls it out, strokes it fondly. "Best live album I've ever heard."

Violet's gaze lingers on McNair, and at first I assume it's because he has something on his face. I let myself stare for a moment too, but there's nothing there. I—I think she might be flirting with him.

I am so embarrassed for her.

"Definitely," McNair agrees. Is he flirting back?

Violet beams at him. "Unfortunately, I don't see *Bleach* here. Someone might have misplaced it, or taken it back to a listening booth."

"Or bought it," I put in. There are other record stores in Seattle, but we'd lose time getting there, and they may not have the album either.

"Let me take a look in the back, okay?" Violet slides *MTV Unplugged* back into the *N* section. "It's always possible someone brought in a copy to sell."

"Thank you so much." McNair's politeness is at an eleven. When Violet clomps away in her boots, I lift my eyebrows at him. "What?" he asks.

"'Definitely. Best live album ever recorded in the history of mankind.'"

He stares. "Is that . . . supposed to be an imitation of me?"

"Depends. Were you flirting with Violet?" I won't give him the satisfaction of my assumption that Violet was flirting with him first. Maybe she was trying to count his freckles too.

"She was deep in some kind of Nirvana reverie. I didn't want to completely lose her to it."

"You've never listened to Nirvana, have you?"

"Not a single song. While we're waiting"—McNair jerks his head toward the listening booths in the back—"I've always kind of wanted to listen to something back there."

"You really think we can agree on something to listen to?" I ask, though I've been gazing longingly at the listening booths since we walked in.

He taps his chin. "What if we each pick one album, and the other person has to listen to one song in its entirety before passing judgment?"

I can't deny it sounds fun. "Fine, but make it quick."

> **KIRBY**
> oh DID YOU NOW?? 👀
> you teamed up with the guy you're definitely not obsessed with?
>
> **MARA**
> Be nice.
> But actually: 👀 👀 👀

I roll my own eyes, though I'm relieved our friendship hasn't been strained past the point of conversations like this.

I think you're a little obsessed with him.

Obsessed with winning, yes. And he happens to be the only person who can help me get there.

I make it back to the listening booth a moment before McNair, and my heart leaps into my throat as I hide my phone, though of course he can't see our group chat. He's clutching an album so close to his chest, he might as well be hugging it. On the small table are a record player and twin pairs of headphones, with two chairs tucked in. McNair snaps the curtain shut, closing us inside the tiny space.

"You can go first," I say as we pull out the chairs and reach for the headphones.

I used to imagine coming here with someone I liked, spending hours browsing records, bumping knees as we listened to them in a booth like this one. It's where the perfect high school boyfriend and I would have hung out. I'd lie awake at night, marking a mental map of Seattle for me and this mystery guy, and listening to records together was one of the most romantic things I could imagine. I dreamed up entire playlists for us. The Cure's "Close to Me," with those breathy pauses and suggestive lyrics, was the sexiest song I'd ever heard. The universe must find it hilarious that the first time I'm in here, it's with McNair.

McNair's song is upbeat, bouncy, with high-pitched male vocals. Fifteen seconds in, he pulls the headphones off one ear and asks, "What do you think?" He's bouncing his leg up and down, impatient for my response.

"It's . . . fun," I admit, but I don't want him to get an ego about choosing something not-terrible, so I add: "It's almost in your face about how fun it is."

"Didn't realize you were so offended by fun." He holds out the album cover, which features the five band members dressed in bright colors and playing Twister.

"Free Puppies?" I say. "That's seriously the name of the band?"

"No. It's Free Puppies! Exclamation point!" He taps the pin on his backpack. "You can't talk about Free Puppies! without an exclamation point. They're local, and I've seen them a few times. They're starting to get national airplay, but I don't think they'll sell out."

"Your favorite band is called Free Puppies!?" I give the exclamation mark as much emphasis as I can, and he shakes his head at me.

"One day you'll go to a Free Puppies! show and see the magic for yourself."

It's gotten too warm in my cardigan, probably because it's still sunny outside. Or maybe the thermostat in here is set too high. Regardless, I take it off, accidentally whacking him with an empty sleeve in the process.

"Sorry," I say as I drape it across the back of the chair.

"Kind of cramped in here," he says with an apologetic shrug, as though it's his fault.

"You're in luck!" Violet's voice. McNair pulls back the curtain, revealing Violet waving a black album with a negative photo graphic on the front. "We had a copy in a stack of donated records waiting to be processed."

"Thank you," I say as McNair accepts the record from her.

"No problem." She sort of lingers for a while, bouncing on her toes, and for a horrifying moment I wonder if she really was flirting. Then she blurts: "Track three. 'About a Girl.' That was the first sign that maybe Nirvana was going to be more than grunge. Even if you're not buying it, you gotta listen to it on vinyl. That's the way it was always meant to be heard."

"Will do," Neil says, and Violet gives us one more smile before closing the curtain.

McNair turns over the album.

"Did she write her number on the back?" I ask. "I hope she's ready for a lot of texts with proper punctuation and capitalization."

"Artoo. I was checking the track listing. And I think she just really loves Nirvana."

He lays the record on the table, and we each snap a photo.

"I guess we're good, then," I say, but he frowns.

"We still have to listen to your song."

"Not Nirvana?"

He shakes his head. "I might get kicked out of Seattle for saying this, but I've never been a big fan."

I present my record of choice: The Smiths' *Louder Than Bombs*. "Is It Really So Strange?" is the first track, and Neil is annoyingly silent the entire three minutes it's playing.

"It's catchy, but . . . it seems melancholy, too," he says.

"What's wrong with that?"

"There's too much bad shit in the world to listen to depressing music all the time." He taps the FP album. "Hence, Free Puppies!"

When we fling back the curtain to leave, it's almost too perfect: Madison Winters, she of the seven shape-shifting foxes, is browsing records with a couple other Westview kids. She doesn't see me until after I've sneaked up behind her, swiping the blue bandanna from her arm.

"That was stealthy," her friend Pranav Acharya says to me, holding out his hand for a high five. "I respect that."

"Wow, where's your loyalty?" Madison asks, mock-offended, and she's so good-natured about the whole thing that I feel a little bad about making fun of her shape-shifting foxes. I mean, she has a brand at least.

McNair and I linger in front of the store while I pull out my phone to log the kill. Strangely, this has been fun. Maybe I romanticized coming here with a boyfriend, but it wasn't actually that bad with McNair.

"You killed someone!" McNair is practically giddy. He says this in such a jovial way, his eyes bright behind his glasses—like he's proud, which I guess makes sense since we're technically on the same team. For now.

Instead of my messaging app, a helpful blue bubble pops up:

Installing software update 1 of 312 . . .

Sure, now's a great time to do that.

"One second. My phone decided to install an update."

Installing software update 2 of 312 . . .

Suddenly, the screen goes black. I hold down the power button—nothing.

"Shit," I mutter. "Now it won't turn on."

"Let me see it."

I glare at him. "I don't think you pressing the button is going to do anything different from me pressing the button." And I don't want him to accidentally see my group chat with Kirby and Mara and somehow get the wrong idea. Still, I hand it over. I'll just grab it back really fast if it turns on.

"It won't turn on," he agrees after holding down every button for a more-than-acceptable length of time and thoroughly aggravating me in the process. "Did you charge it?"

"It's been plugged into my car." I hold out my palm, since there's something very strange about my phone, with the geometric patterned case Mara gave me for Hanukkah last year, in Neil's hands. I try the power button yet again. "I can't exactly play without my phone."

"Wait. Wait. We can fix this." McNair swipes around on his own phone, tapping Sean Yee's contact photo. "Sean can fix anything. He brought a twelve-year-old MacBook back to life last year."

"And why would he help me?"

"He'd be helping both of us." He types out a message I can't see. "And he got killed pretty quickly earlier, so he doesn't have skin in the game." His phone pings. "Sean's free, and he's at home. He lives right off I-5, Forty-Third and Latona. It'll only take us ten minutes to get there."

"Wasn't he at the safe zone? With you and Adrian and Cyrus?" This is too weird. McNair's friend helping me, out of the goodness of his heart?

A smile curves one side of his mouth. "He just came to hang out. Were you . . . looking out for me?"

"I'm just perceptive."

"You were looking out for me," he concludes. "I'm touched."

HOWL CLUES

- ☾ *A place you can buy Nirvana's first album*
- ☾ *A place that's red from floor to ceiling*
- ☾ *A place you can find Chiroptera*
- ☾ *~~A rainbow crosswalk~~*
- ☾ *Ice cream fit for Sasquatch*
- ☾ *The big guy at the center of the universe*
- ☾ *Something local, organic, and sustainable*
- ☾ *A floppy disk*
- ☾ *~~A coffee cup with someone else's name (or your own name, wildly misspelled)~~*
- ☾ *~~A car with a parking ticket~~*
- ☾ *A view from up high*
- ☾ *~~The best pizza in the city (your choice)~~*
- ☾ *~~A tourist doing something a local would be ashamed of doing~~*
- ☾ *~~An umbrella (we all know real Seattleites don't use them)~~*
- ☾ *A tribute to the mysterious Mr. Cooper*

4:15 p.m.

"WELCOME TO MY laboratory," Sean says in a voice that makes him sound like a villain in a spy movie that definitely doesn't pass the Bechdel Test. He ushers us into the tiny basement of his Wallingford bungalow. And wow, it really does look like a laboratory down here. There's a worktable with four monitors, a rack of tools, and countless wires and electronic gadgets strewn about. The lighting gives everything a vaguely greenish tint.

It's cold in the basement, and when I rub my bare arms, I remember where I left my sweater: on a chair in the listening booth.

"I hope we're not interrupting," I say. "Seriously, thank you so much for doing this. Or for trying to."

Sean and I have never had a reason to talk much. Frankly, he has no reason to be this nice to me. Savannah has me suspicious of everyone who used to seem harmless.

"*Trying*," Sean says under his breath with a glance at McNair, and the two of them snicker, as though the idea of Sean not succeeding is ludicrous. "Nah, I was just playing the new *Assassin's Creed*."

"Why would you put yourself through that after getting killed so early in Howl?" McNair asks innocently.

"Thanks so much for the emotional support."

I tap my dead phone. "I can Venmo you some—"

Sean's eyebrows shoot up. "What? No, no, you definitely don't have to do that. I'd have failed my French final without Neil. I owe him one. Or seven." I don't have a chance to point out that him helping me isn't the same thing as helping McNair before Sean swipes a pair of thick glasses from the worktable and puts them on. "May I see the patient?"

Biting back a laugh, I surrender my phone. Neil said he explained the whole situation when we were driving over, but if it's odd for Sean to see the two of us together, he doesn't say anything.

"So what exactly happened?" Sean asks, gently placing my phone on the table and rummaging through a drawer before extracting a cable and plugging it in. He plugs the other end into his main computer.

"It died while installing an update. And then it wouldn't turn on."

"Hmm." Sean hits a few keys, and the phone's screen turns blue. "This shouldn't be too hard."

I let out a sigh of relief. "Great."

"Thank you," Neil says, and flashes me an encouraging smile.

My fingers are twitchy. I kind of hate that I'm so married to my phone that even ten minutes without it sends me into withdrawal. Madison's target, though—I have that. *Brady Becker.* Guess he's still alive.

"I can't imagine what all of this is worth," I say, gazing around the lab.

"Most of the tech, I found used and restored it." Sean hunches over my phone, black hair falling into his face. "I made Neil a new computer for his birthday last year."

I gape at him. "That's . . . incredible."

Neil makes a vaguely nonhuman sound next to me. "You should probably let him work."

"I can multitask."

"Actually," Neil says, "multitasking is a myth. Our brains can only focus on one high-level task at a time. It's why you can drive and listen to music at the same time but you couldn't take a test and listen to a podcast simultaneously."

"No mansplaining in my lab, please," Sean says.

"I wasn't—" Neil starts, but then he goes silent, as though realizing that's exactly what he was doing. When I peek at him, he's staring at his shoes.

After that, we let Sean work in silence. Every so often, he mutters a curse or takes a swig from an energy drink on his table.

"I *think* I've got it," Sean says fifteen minutes later, unplugging my phone and swiping through a couple more settings. "None of your data should have been impacted. Now we cross our fingers, and . . ." All three of us peer at it, waiting for the home screen to appear. And there it is, the photo of Kirby, Mara, and me and the pattern of familiar icons. "Voilà! Good as new."

"You're a genius," I say. "Thank you, thank you!"

"I also changed the settings so it won't continue the update until next week, so you can finish the game without it interrupting you."

"Oh my God, I love you," I say, and Sean blushes. "Thank you so much. Again. You know Two Birds One Scone? Come in next week and I'll give you a free cinnamon roll."

Sean takes off his glasses. "She isn't that bad," he stage-whispers to McNair.

"Not all the time," he admits.

I clasp my heart. "I'm touched," I say, imitating McNair.

Neil places a hand on Sean's shoulder. My kingdom for more guys who can express physical affection without needing to justify their masculinity afterward. "Still on for Beth's Café before graduation?"

"Absolutely. I never miss Beth's," he says. "Godspeed to you both."

"Quad life," Neil says.

"Quad life!" Sean replies with a whoop, and I experience such extreme secondhand embarrassment that I might burst into flames. Then the two of them exchange a brief but complex handshake before Sean leads us out into the daylight.

We knock out some of the easy clues as we drive downtown—yeti ice cream at Molly Moon's, a display of Washington-grown apples at a corner market (*something local, organic, and sustainable*).

On our way to the Seattle Public Library, Neil tells me more about the Quad. He and Sean were best friends most of elementary school, and same with Adrian and Cyrus at a private school. Sean and Adrian used to be neighbors, so by middle school, the four of them were spending time together pretty regularly. Neil even goes to Sean's family reunions every year.

The conversation feels weirdly natural. Somehow, Neil and I are getting along, which necessitates a mental reminder that I'm going to destroy him at the end of this. That was the whole reason we teamed up.

I get lucky with downtown parking, and I can't help admiring the building as we head inside the library. It's an architectural marvel, geometric shapes and bright colors and displays of public art. And it's always busy. There's an awkward moment on the main level with Chantal Okafor and the Kristens, where we clutch at our armbands, but when no one lunges for anyone else, we all exhale in relief. Then Chantal lifts her brows and looks pointedly at McNair. All I can do is shrug, since there isn't enough time to explain.

"It's—really red," Neil says when we get to the Red Hall on the fourth floor. The shiny curved walls make it feel like we're inside someone's cardiovascular system.

"Any other insightful observations?"

"That whoever designed this was probably a little sadistic?"

We submit our photos before our phones buzz with another Howl update.

> TOP 5
> Neil McNair: 10
> Rowan Roth: 10
> Iris Zhou: 6
> Mara Pompetti: 5
> Brady Becker: 4

"Wow," I say. "We pulled way ahead."

"Naturally," Neil says, but he's clearly pleased.

With the library clue conquered, I can't get what Sean said earlier out of my head. *He's not the most forthcoming about his personal life.*

"Do you . . . usually go to Sean's house?" I ask, trying to sound casual as we retrace our path through the Red Hall.

"As opposed to . . . ?"

"I, um, saw them earlier, Sean and Adrian and Cyrus, before the game started. They said you'd had a family emergency and that they hadn't been to your house in a while. They're your best friends, so I didn't get it, I guess."

McNair's quiet for a few moments. "Doesn't . . . everyone have their secrets?" he says finally, flatly. His tone isn't cruel, but it's not exactly warm either.

Just when I think we're making some progress, beginning to open up to each other, he shuts it down. Except—something's wrong. His face has gone ashen, and he has a hand against the wall, as though he can't remain steady without it.

"Hey. Are you okay?"

"I'm—not feeling great," he says as he sways, pressing his head into his elbow. "Dizzy."

"All the red?" I ask, and he nods. He looks miserable. Some instinct I wasn't wholly aware of kicks in. "Come on. Let's get you out of here."

Before I can overthink it, I place a hand on his shoulder and guide him out of the Red Hall and into a chair near the elevator.

He may not be my favorite person, but that doesn't mean I want him to feel like this.

He cradles his head in his hands. "I haven't eaten anything today except for that slice of pizza," he says. "I know, I know, bad idea, but I was dealing with my sister, and I ran out of time, and . . ."

"Stay here," I tell him. "I'll be right back."

His sister. The family emergency. One answered question and about a hundred more.

From a scrap of paper wedged between the windshield wipers of Rowan's car

You may have noticed the white lines on the street indicating you are currently taking up two parking spots. I wanted to do you a favor and let you know that your car can actually fit just fine in one spot.

Sincerely,
A concerned citizen

4:46 p.m.

NEIL PICKS UP a packet of saltine crackers. "Did you open this for me?"

"No," I lie.

In a minimart across the street, I found a bottle of water, a can of ginger ale, and the crackers. It's possible I overdid it.

"You didn't have to do all of this," he says, taking a slow sip of water. "Thank you. I've always had kind of a weak stomach. Road trips with me are a real blast."

I nod, remembering. When we took the bus to school events, like last year's field trip to the Gates Foundation, he told teachers he had to sit in the front. Bus law dictates the front is for the painfully uncool among us, and for whatever reason, I felt such extreme secondhand awkwardness on Neil's behalf that I took the seat across the aisle from him (not next to him; everyone knows you take your own seat if there's enough space) and argued with him for the rest of the bus ride.

We've been together for a couple hours now—the most time we've ever spent just the two of us—and McNair's been strangely normal. Dorky and occasionally annoying, sure, but not exactly hateable. I'm not sure if the end of school flipped a switch, or whether we've never been in a situation where we didn't immediately pit ourselves against each other.

I lower myself into the chair next to him in a little alcove on the fourth floor, fiddling with a bottle cap. We sit in silence for a while, the only noise the crunch of the plastic bottle or McNair chewing. He even offers me a cracker. Every so often, he rakes a hand through his hair, messing it up more. We must share that nervous habit.

His hair, though—it doesn't look bad when he does this. And it's there, on the fourth floor of the library, watching my nemesis take slow slips of ginger ale, that I have a horrifying realization.

Neil . . . is *cute*.

Not in an I'm-attracted-to-him way. Just, like, objectively nice-looking. Interesting-looking is maybe more accurate, with his red hair and wild freckles and the way his eyes are sometimes deep brown and sometimes almost golden. The curve of his shoulders in that T-shirt isn't bad either, and neither is the definition in his arms. Even that smirk of his is kind of cute. Lord knows I've seen it enough times to make that assessment.

Cute. Neil. Unexpected but true, and it's not the first time I've thought so.

"I could tell you something to cheer you up." It must be the still-mostly-miserable look on Neil's face that makes me say this.

"Yeah?"

I've never told this to anyone, not even Kirby or Mara, because

I knew they'd never let me forget it. "Do you remember freshman year?"

"I try not to."

"Right. Right." I bury a hand in my bangs. They really are too short. This is probably a terrible idea, but if it'll take his mind off the Red Hall, it's worth it. Maybe. I charge forward before I can reconsider. "Before the essay contest winners were announced and you revealed your true self, I . . . had a crush on you."

Nope, that was definitely a terrible idea. Regret fills me almost instantly, and I squeeze my eyes shut, waiting for the laughter. When it doesn't come, I tentatively open one eye.

Neil meets my gaze, no longer nauseous-looking. Now there's amusement on his face: a deeper curve to his mouth, like he's trapping a laugh in his throat.

"You had a crush on me." He turns it into a declarative sentence. He's not asking for clarification; he's stating a fact.

"For twelve days!" I rush to add. "Four years ago. I was basically a child."

He doesn't need to know what, exactly, I found so appealing about him back then. At first I was mesmerized by the sheer number of freckles he had, thought they were beautiful, really. I nodded along with the insights he shared in class, offering my own and feeling a spark of pride when he agreed with me.

He doesn't need to know that every so often over the course of that year, I found myself wishing he hadn't turned out to be the worst kind of lit snob so I could resume my English-class daydreams, the ones where we lounged beneath an oak tree and read sonnets aloud to each other. I was so disappointed he wasn't the guy I'd dreamed up. He doesn't need to know that a couple times, when our shoulders brushed in the hall, I felt this flip in my belly because I was fourteen and boys were a mysterious new species. Touching one, even by accident, was like passing your hand through a flame. I wasn't proud of it, but my body hadn't quite caught up with my brain. And my brain had decided twelve days into freshman year that Neil McNair was to be despised, his destruction earning slot number ten on my success guide. By sophomore year, all those belly-flips were gone, and I could barely remember having a crush on him at all.

He also doesn't need to know about the dream I had a few months ago. It wasn't my fault—we'd been texting before bed, and it had screwed with my subconscious. For all I know, his subconscious gave him wacky dreams too. We were at a fancy restaurant eating math tests and lab reports when he took my face in his hands and kissed me. He tasted like printer ink. My logical side intervened and woke me up, but I couldn't look him in the eye for an entire week after that. I'd dream-cheated on Spencer with Neil McNair. It was horrifying.

Neil's full-on grinning now. "But I was like . . . the dorkiest fourteen-year-old."

"And I was so cool?"

"You were," he insists. "Aside from your inability to acknowledge *The Great Gatsby* as the quintessential American novel."

"Ah, yes, *The Great Gatsby*. A feminist text," I say, though my mind stumbles over his profession of my coolness. "Nick is a piece of white bread. Daisy deserved better than that ending."

He snorts at this. But I can't deny he seems to be feeling much better. His complexion has gone from ashen back to his regular shade of pale. Debating books in a library—this is our natural state, perhaps.

"So like. This crush," he continues. "Did you write poems about me? Did you doodle my name in your notebook with a heart on the *i*? Or—*oh!* Did you imagine me as the hero of a romance novel? Please say yes. Please say I was a cowboy."

"It sounds like you're feeling a lot better." I stretch out my legs, eager to get moving again.

He glances down at his arms. "I didn't even realize—am I exposing too much skin? I don't want to be parading myself in front of you, taunting you with what you can't have. I have a hoodie in my backpack. I can put it on if you're—"

"You're definitely better. We're leaving."

My mom calls when we get to the main floor of the library.

"We made it!" she announces. Her phone's on speaker, and my dad is cheering in the background. "The book is done!"

"Congratulations!" I motion for Neil to follow me around the corner so we won't disturb anyone. "Is it going to come out the same time as the next Excavated book?"

"A few months before. Next summer."

"And most importantly, is this going to be the one that finally gets made into a movie?"

"Ha ha," she says dryly. She and my dad are still salty about the Riley movie getting stalled years ago. "We'll see about that."

"How was your last day, Ro-Ro?" my dad asks. "Did you make valedictorian?"

His words peel the Band-Aid off the wound. "No," I say, glancing at Neil. "I'm salutatorian."

"That's great. Congratulations!" my mom says. "Where are you? It's almost sundown. Are you coming home for Shabbat dinner?"

Neil is watching me with an odd expression. "I don't know if I can. We're—I'm in the middle of Howl. Is the power still out?"

"Unfortunately. But we can do takeout from your favorite Italian place. It'll take an hour. Please. Your last Shabbat dinner of high school?"

This is what gets me. Plus, Neil and I are solidly in the lead, and it would be a chance to change my clothes. "I'll be there as soon as I can."

When I end the call and the background photo of Kirby, Mara, and me reappears, my stomach twists. I switch off the screen to find McNair gaping at me.

"Your parents," he says, his tone full of reverence, "are Jared Roth and Ilana García Roth."

"Yeah . . . ?"

"I read their books. All of them. I was *obsessed*."

Now it's my turn to gape back at him. This happens on occasion, sure, but I never suspected Neil McNair was a fan of my parents' books.

"Which book is your favorite?" I ask, testing him.

He responds without missing a beat. "The Excavated series, hands down."

"Riley's pretty great," I agree. I used to dress up as her for my parents' events, in her red cardigan and trademark pterodactyl stockings they had custom made, my hair in two messy little buns.

Neil gets nostalgic. "The one where she had her bat mitzvah, and her abuela and abuelo visited from Mexico City and learned all about Jewish traditions . . . Artoo, I *bawled*."

"Number twelve, *Mi Maravillosa Bat Mitzvah*?" It was based on my own bat mitzvah, although it wasn't quite the ideal exchange of cultures presented in the book. Rather, my mom's family from Mexico was convinced that my dad's family was avoiding them, and my dad's family complained about the food and that they hadn't been able to hear the rabbi. I wished, not for the first time, that I knew more Spanish, even as I read the Hebrew.

"Yes. I read that one all the time." He says it in present tense.

"Wait. You *still* read them?"

Pink spots appear on his cheeks. "Maybe."

If we'd been closer to friends than rivals, I wonder if he'd have told me this sooner. All this time, he's only been half the lit snob I thought he was. It's unnerving, realizing how much I have in common with someone I spent so much time plotting to destroy.

"I'm not judging. I'm just surprised. Why haven't you been to any of their signings?"

"I didn't want to be the creepy guy in the back who's clearly too old for the books."

"You're never too anything for books," I say. "We like what we like. My parents have plenty of adult fans, and yet they hate romance novels."

The pink on his cheeks deepens. "Once again, I'm sorry. Your parents really don't approve of what you read? Shouldn't they be, I don't know, glad that you're reading at all?"

"That's never been an issue with me," I say. "Children's books, those are fine, but romance novels?" If they knew about Delilah's book signing, they'd shake their heads and purse their lips and I'd know, before they even said anything, that they were judging not just me but Delilah and her fans. "I've sort of started hiding my books from them. I couldn't take it anymore."

"My mom likes them," Neil offers. "If that helps at all."

"I hope you don't ever give her shit for them."

He grimaces. "Not anymore."

I slip my phone back into my pocket. "I have to go home for Shabbat dinner," I explain. "It's the Jewish Sabbath. We're not, like, the best Jews, but we try to have Shabbat dinner every Friday, and—"

"I know what Shabbat is," he says, and points to himself. "Also Jewish."

"Wait. What?"

How has he blown my mind twice in the span of a single minute?

"I'm Jewish. My mom is Jewish, and I was raised Jewish."

"Where do you go to temple?" I ask, still unconvinced.

"I had my bar mitzvah at Temple Beth Am. 'Vezot Hab'rachah' was my Torah portion."

"I go to Temple De Hirsch Sinai," I say. That's the only other Reform synagogue in Seattle. In our city of nearly eight hundred thousand people, we get two. Within three blocks of my house, there are five churches.

I examine him, as though looking for some obvious Jewishness I missed. Of course, there isn't any—just his objectively cute face. I usually have this instant connection with other Jews. It's happened my entire life, despite how few Jews I know.

Neil McNair is Jewish, and there's that tug in my chest, the one I feel when I learn I share a religion with someone.

"Faulty Jewdar?" he asks.

"Guess so. It's the last name, too."

He makes an odd face. "My dad's. I was planning to change it when I turned eighteen. My mom's maiden name is Perlman. But then I . . . didn't." His voice falls flat.

"Oh," I say, sensing some awkwardness there but unsure how to deal with it. "So . . . I do have to go home for this." But it doesn't feel right to split up yet, not when an entire army of seniors is out there plotting our demise.

He glances at his watch and then back at me. "Would it be okay if I stopped by for a minute? Just to like . . . say hi to your parents and tell them that I think they're literary geniuses?" With his teeth, he tugs on his lower lip. "No, that would be weird. It would be weird, right? You've already done a hundred nice things for me today. You don't have to," he adds quickly. He's babbling, oh my God.

It's such a relief to hear he doesn't want to split up—or at least that he doesn't mention it—that I have to force my face not to react. And then I'm wondering why I'm feeling *relief*, of all things. I would have assumed I'd be desperate for a break by now, but I guess my McNair tolerance levels are higher than I thought.

"Do you . . . um . . . want to have dinner with us?" I ask. "You can meet them if you promise to be normal."

I just asked Neil McNair to Shabbat dinner with me and my parents. At my house. Any other time, I'd text Kirby and Mara about it, but I'm not sure how I'd explain it. I can barely explain it to myself.

Neil's eyes grow wide. "You're sure?"

"Of course," I say. "They love having people over."

"Would it—" He breaks off, shoving his glasses up, which have once again slid down his nose. "Would it be okay if we stopped at my house on the way there? I want to get some books for them to sign. It'll only take a few minutes."

It hits me again what his friends said earlier, about him not having people over. He'll probably run inside and run right back out. I'm not actually going *to* his house.

I tell him yes, and on the way back to my car, I text my parents that he's coming. Then I pepper Neil with more questions about the books. He's an Excavated expert, recalling details like the name of Riley's pet gerbil (Megalosaurus), the location of her first dig in book one (a small town just south of Santa Cruz, where her family was vacationing), and what she found there (a Pliocene-era sand dollar). Consider me impressed.

"You're going to have to give me directions," I say as I turn the key in the ignition.

"Turn left after the Forty-Fifth Street exit." He buckles his seat belt. "This is weird, huh? You going to my house, and then the two of us having dinner with your parents?"

I let out a laugh that's a little more high-pitched than usual. "Yeah. It is."

"And just so you know, we might be having dinner together, but this isn't a date," Neil says, completely straight-faced. "I just don't want you to get too excited. I mean, your parents are going to be there, so it would be really awkward if you were fawning over me the whole time."

NEIL MCNAIR'S PERSONAL LIFE: WHAT I KNOW

- He lives somewhere north of Lake Union but south of Whole Foods.
- He has a closet full of suits.
- He's Jewish.
- He has a sister. Maybe more than one? Maybe a brother, too?
- He had some kind of emergency earlier today.
- um

5:33 p.m.

NEIL UNBUCKLES HIS seat belt. When I don't budge, he asks, "Are you coming?"

"Oh—I didn't think—okay," I say, unable to decide which sentence to finish.

"We'll be fast," he assures me. But I don't ask the question I so desperately want to: *Why?* Neil McNair wants me in his house, or he's not even thinking about it, or . . . ?

Before he opens the door, he pauses. "It might—" he starts, and then breaks off. He rakes a hand through his hair, and my fingers itch to smooth the strands back into place. Neil McNair is not Neil McNair if every piece of him isn't in perfect order. "It might be messy," he finally settles on, turning the key and letting me into the McLair for the very first time.

Neil's house is in an older part of Wallingford. The houses on this block are all single-story, yards overgrown with weeds. Neil's is a bit tidier than the others, but the lawn still looks like it could use an hour with a mower. Inside, it's clean—and *cold*. Sparsely decorated, but nothing out of the ordinary. I'm completely mystified by his warning.

"I hope you're okay with dogs," Neil says as a golden retriever jumps on me, tail wagging.

"I love them," I say, scratching the golden behind the ears. My dad's allergic, but I used to beg for one for Hanukkah every year. "Golden retrievers always look so happy."

"She seems to be. She's going blind, but she's a good old girl," he says, kneeling down so she can lick his face. "Aren't you, Lucy?"

"Lucy," I echo, continuing to pet her. "You're so beautiful."

"She's going to shed all over you."

"Have you seen my dress today?"

He gets to his feet, and Lucy follows him. He must notice I'm clutching my arms because he says, "We don't turn the heat on in the summer. Even when our summers are, well, like this."

"That's good," I say quickly. "Smart. To, um, save money and everything."

My family is comfortably upper-middle-class. There's some poverty in Seattle, but the neighborhoods surrounding Westview are generally middle- to upper-middle-class, with a few clusters of mega-wealth.

I never realized money was an issue for Neil's family.

A girl with wild red hair bounds out of a room down the hall. "I thought you weren't coming home until later." She looks eleven or twelve, and she's adorable: high ponytail, a lavender skirt over black leggings, freckles dotted across her face.

"I'm just stopping here for a second," Neil says. "Don't worry. I'm not crashing your sleepover."

"That's disappointing. We had so much fun giving you a makeover last time," she says, and he groans. There's something about the idea of kids giving Neil McNair a makeover that's too precious for words. She turns to me. "I'm Natalie, and if he's told you anything about me, it's a complete lie. Wait, are you Rowan?" she asks, and all of Neil's exposed skin goes red. "I love your dress."

"I am," I say. "Thank you. I like your skirt."

Neil puts a hand on his sister's shoulder. "Are you . . . okay?" he asks in a low voice, as though he doesn't want me to hear. "About earlier?"

She touches a Band-Aid on her knuckle. "I'm fine."

Family emergency. Oh God—did someone hurt her?

I shrink back a few steps, suddenly very, very wary of what I've walked into.

"If they ever bother you about him again, you swear you'll tell me? You won't use your fists?"

"But they're so effective," she says, and Neil shakes his head. "Fine, fine. I promise."

"Neil, baby, is that you?" a voice calls from the kitchen.

Baby? I mouth at him, and if possible, he flushes an even deeper crimson.

"Yeah, Mom," he says. "I'm just grabbing something."

Lucy follows us into the small kitchen. Neil's mom is sitting at the table, huddled over a laptop. Her short hair is a darker auburn than Neil's, and she's wearing what I assume are her work clothes: gray slacks, black blazer, sensible shoes.

"I'm Rowan," I say, and somehow feel the need to explain why I'm here. "I'm helping Neil with a—a project."

"Rowan!" she says warmly, springing to her feet to shake my hand. "Of course. It's so good to finally meet you! I'm Joelle."

"Finally?" I echo, glancing at Neil, grinning at him. "Horrified" doesn't even begin to describe his expression. Oh my God, this is too good. He talks about me to his family. I decide to torture him some more. "It's great to finally meet you, too! Neil talks about you all the time. It's so nice when guys aren't embarrassed to talk about their moms, you know?"

"That's very sweet. You've made these past few years challenging for Neil in the best possible way." She places a hand on his shoulder. He quietly disintegrates beneath it. "He loves a good challenge. He told us you're going to Boston for school next year?"

This is all kinds of amazing.

"Emerson, yes. It's a small liberal arts school in Boston."

"Are you going to be okay handling Natalie and her friends tonight?" Neil asks, finally joining the conversation. His face is a charming shade of scarlet.

"She's a breeze. Christopher's coming over later, anyway."

"Tell him I'm sorry I missed him."

I decide to point out the obvious: "You're all redheads."

"We're part of less than two percent of the world's population with red hair," Joelle says. "I tell them they're special when they complain about it." She bumps Neil's shoulder. "Baby, don't forget your manners. You know how to treat a guest."

The puddle of embarrassment formerly known as Neil McNair mutters, "Uh, do you want anything to drink?"

"I'm good. Do you want to get those books?" I ask, to save him from human combustion. He nods.

"Before you go—did you find out today?" his mom asks. "About valedictorian?"

"Oh"—Neil's gaze darts to the floor—"yeah. I, um, I got it."

"I am so proud of you," she says, drawing him in for a hug.

And all of a sudden, I don't feel like making fun of him anymore.

His mom releases him, and I hear him murmur a thank-you.

I follow him down the brown-carpeted hall to his room. Once we're inside, he shuts the door and leans against it, closing his eyes. It's clear he needs a moment to decompress, though I don't fully understand why. Truthfully, it puts me a little on edge. His mom is a sweetheart. His sister is cute. . . . I'm inclined to think his home-life is pretty normal.

Still, I take this opportunity to examine his room. The paint is peeling off the walls in some places. There's a *Star Wars* poster, one of the new ones, I think, and a Free Puppies! concert flyer. Above his desk is the framed Torah portion from his bar mitzvah. His bookshelf is filled with titles like *Learn Japanese the Easy Way* and *So You Want to Speak Modern Hebrew*. His desk is cluttered with calligraphy pens, and off to one side, two eight-pound dumbbells. One McMystery solved. I try to picture it,

McNair lifting weights while reciting the Hebrew alphabet.

And there's his bed, a blanket haphazardly thrown across it. I assumed it would be perfectly neat. His suits, peeking out of the closet, are the nicest thing in this room. Being in his room feels too personal—like reading someone's journal when you're not supposed to.

"Sorry about all that," he says when he opens his eyes.

"It's cool. You talk to your family about me. I'm flattered." Now that his eyes are on me, I'm suddenly not sure where to look. Clearly, looking at him is the safest. I don't want him to think I'm staring at the weights on his desk or, God forbid, his bed. "Is everything okay with your sister?"

"It will be," he says, and then waits a long, long time before speaking again. "My dad . . . is in prison."

Oh. My heart drops to the floor.

That is not even remotely within the realm of what I was expecting, but now that he's said it, I have no idea what I expected to hear. *Prison*. It sounds cold and distant and terrifying. I can barely wrap my mind around it, barely force words out.

"Neil, I—I'm so sorry." It's not nearly enough, but my voice has turned to chalk.

His shoulders tighten. "Don't be sorry. He fucked up. That's on him. He fucked up his life, and he fucked up ours, and that's *all* on him."

I've never seen him like this. There's an intensity in his gaze that makes me back up a few paces. I have so many questions—what did he do and when did it happen and how is Neil dealing with it, because I don't know how I would. And his sister, and his mom, and . . . holy shit. Neil's dad is in prison. This is a lot.

"I had no idea" is what I say instead.

"I don't talk to anyone about it. Ever. I don't really have people over, either, because it's easier not to answer questions about it." He stares at the floor. "It happened in sixth grade. The fall of sixth grade, after I started middle school. Money's always been tight. My dad owned a hardware store in Ballard, but it wasn't doing great, and he had some anger issues. One night he caught a couple kids stealing. He was so furious . . . he beat one of them unconscious. The kid—he was in a coma for a month."

I'm struck silent. Because truly—what can you say to that? Nothing I could say would make it okay.

When he speaks, his voice is scratchy. "I didn't know he was capable of something like that. Of that kind of violence. My father . . . he nearly *killed* someone."

"Neil," I say quietly, but he's not finished.

"I was old enough to understand what was happening, lucky me, but Natalie wasn't. All she knew was that our dad was gone," he says. "Kids in middle school found out, and it was horrible. The jokes, the insults, people trying to pick fights with me. To see if I'd lash out like he did. Most days, I didn't even want to go to school. We couldn't afford private school, and because of zoning, I couldn't switch schools, so I came up with my own plan. I distracted everyone by doing the opposite of what I wanted to do, which was disappear. I threw myself into school, became consumed by being the best. If I could have that label, I figured, then I could shake the 'dad in prison' label. And . . . it worked. If anyone at Westview even remembers, they don't say anything about it.

"Some kids at Natalie's school found out and were bullying her about it, so she fought back. Despite how many times I tell her that's *not* okay, that we don't want to turn into our father . . ."

"That's not going to happen," I insist. I can't imagine that sweet girl being violent.

"So that was the family emergency you were asking about. I had to pick her up from school before Howl started." His shoulders sag. "At least she's having her friends over tonight. That'll be good."

All these years, he's been wearing armor. His plan to hide so many pieces of himself clearly worked, and I'm not sure if that's a good thing or a bad thing.

"It will. Thank you . . . for telling me this." I hope I'm not saying all the wrong things. I hope he knows I'll keep this as safe as if it were my own secret. No—safer.

"I—I haven't told anyone in a while," he says. "Please don't act weird around me now. That's why I stopped talking to people about it. Of course my friends know, and I used to talk to Sean about it all the time . . . but not as much anymore. Everyone would act like they wanted to ask questions but didn't know a tactful way to go about it. So. If you have questions, go ahead and ask them."

God, I have a million, but I manage to pick one. "Do you visit him?"

"Natalie and my mom do, but I haven't seen him since I was sixteen. That was when my mom said I could decide for myself whether I wanted to see him, and I just . . . don't. That's why I want to change my name, too." He continues messing with the blanket. "But it costs money, and it was a legal mess when my mom looked into it for Natalie and me. There was always something else that felt more important.

"I hate having his name sometimes. Even when he was here, we were never really close. It was clear I didn't exactly fit his description of what a man should be. In his mind, there were 'boy hobbies' and there were 'girl hobbies,' and most of what I liked fit into the latter category. It was a crime that I wasn't interested in sports, and if he knew I was getting emotional about this—" He breaks off, as though the weight of it all is just too heavy. He tries to take a deep breath, but all he gets is a shallow little puff.

I despise Neil's father with every fiber of my being.

"You have every right to be emotional. About anything."

He sits on the edge of his bed, gripping the blanket. His shoulders rise and fall with his labored breaths, and all I want is to sit down next to him, drape an arm around him, *something*.

"It's okay," I tell him in what I hope is a soothing voice. I hope that's something I'm capable of when talking to Neil McNair. But it's not okay. What his dad did was horrendous.

"That's why I wanted to win so badly," he says, voice breaking. "He—he wants to see me before I go to college, but the prison is on the other side of the state, and I'd have to stay overnight, and my mom's already working overtime, and . . . I won't be coming home that much in the next four years, and when I do, my mom and Natalie will be my priority. So . . . I almost feel like I need to say goodbye and close the book on that whole situation. And—and if I won the money, I wouldn't have to feel guilty about dipping into what I've saved for school."

This is what breaks my heart most of all: that he thinks he needs to use the prize money for someone who's been so awful to him.

He's crying. Not full-on sobs, just soft little hiccups that make the bandanna on his arm bob up and down. Neil McNair is *crying*.

And that's what does it. The bed creaks as I sit down next to him, a good several inches of space between us. Still, I can feel the heat from his body.

Slowly, I lift one hand and place it on his shoulder, waiting for his reaction. It's an odd boundary to cross. I'm even more aware of his breaths, their erratic rhythm. But then he relaxes into my touch, as though it feels good, and it's such a huge relief that I haven't misstepped, that I've reacted to this like a friend would. So I run my palm back and forth across the fabric of his T-shirt, his skin warm underneath. Then it's not just my palm, but my fingertips, too, my thumb tracing circles on his shoulder. A hug would have been too much, too out of character, but this—this, I can do.

The entire time, I'm radically aware I am *sitting on Neil McNair's bed*. This is where he sleeps, where he dreams, where he texts me every morning.

Texted me every morning.

This close, I can tell his freckles aren't just one color, but a whole spectrum of reddish brown. Long lashes brush the lenses of his glasses. They're a shade lighter than his hair, and I'm mesmerized by them for a moment—how delicate they are, a hundred tiny crescent moons.

When his eyes flick open to meet mine, I immediately drop my hand from his shoulder, as though I've been caught doing something I shouldn't be. Something my fourteen-year-old self with "destroy Neil McNair" as her ultimate goal would be very, very disappointed by.

Besides, an average amount of shoulder-comforting time has passed.

"I'm sorry," he says, and we've been quiet for so long that his words jolt me. He has nothing to apologize for. I should stand up. It's strange sitting on his bed like this, but even though I'm no longer touching him, I can't seem to make myself move. "I didn't know I was still so messed up about this. My parents, they got divorced a couple years ago," he continues, swiping at the tear tracks on his face. "We've all been in therapy, which has helped a lot. And my mom's started dating again. Christopher, that's her boyfriend. It's extremely weird that my mom has a boyfriend, but I'm happy for her. And I'm not ashamed of not having money," he adds. "I'm ashamed of what he did to us."

"Thank you for telling me," I say again. Softly. "Truly."

"It's the last day," he says. "It's not anything you can use against me now." He gives what sounds like a forced laugh. "Or the crying."

"Never," I say emphatically. I want him to know it is okay to cry around me, that it's not a sign of weakness. "I swear. I wouldn't have. Even if we were going to school on Monday." I wait for him to meet my eyes again. "Neil. You have to believe I'd never have done something like that."

Slowly, he nods. "No, you're right."

"We can change the subject," I say, and he lets out an audible exhale.

"Please."

I spring to my feet, unable to handle the reality of being on Neil McNair's bed any longer. It feels warm in here, despite the low thermostat setting. The bookshelves feel like a much safer part of the room.

"When you said you were a fan . . . wow. You might have more copies than my parents."

He kneels next to me, examining the books. "Don't laugh, but—they were like this adventure I felt like I'd never get to have," he says. "We've gone on every car trip imaginable in the Pacific Northwest, but I've never been on a plane. The Excavated books were a way for me to experience it all. It used to make me sad that I didn't have that . . . but I knew I would someday."

"Next year," I say softly. "I hear college is something of an adventure."

He spends a lot of time assessing the bookshelves, pulling a few books out, glancing at the covers, chuckling. If it weren't Neil McNair, it would be adorable. Maybe it still kind of is.

Everything that happened to me in elementary school and middle school made it into a book somehow. The book where Riley gets her first period, the one that got some pushback from parents because apparently basic functions of the human body are taboo, is based on my own experience. I got mine on a sixth-grade field trip to a museum, and I told a teacher I thought I must have injured myself because I was bleeding—which in hindsight is strange because I knew what periods were. When she asked where I was bleeding, I pointed in between my legs, and she quickly found me a pad. I spent the rest of the day hoping no one would notice the bulge in my pants, which I was positive everyone could see.

Now that I'm thinking about it, I hope Neil doesn't bring that one. As much as this kind of thing doesn't usually faze me, I would really like to not discuss my period or Riley's in Neil McNair's bedroom.

"There's this word in Japanese: *tsundoku*," Neil says suddenly. "It's my favorite word in any language."

"What does it mean?"

He grins. "It means acquiring more books than you could ever realistically read. There's no direct translation."

"I love that," I say. "Wait. What's that in the back?"

"Nothing," Neil says quickly, but I'm reaching for the familiar cover, the woman in a wedding dress. *Vision in White* by Nora Roberts. The romance novel I wrote about freshman year.

"Huh. Isn't this interesting." My grin cannot be contained.

He fists a hand in his hair. "I—uh—got it used. Later in freshman year. I thought maybe I'd been . . . a bit of a dick about it? I figured, maybe you were onto something, maybe I should read it if I was going to pass such harsh judgment on it. It's the way so many people talk about romance novels, right? I was young, and I guess I thought it was cool to make fun of things I didn't really understand? I wanted to give it a chance."

"And what did you think?"

"I . . . liked it," he admits. "It was well written, and it was funny. It was easy to get invested in the characters. I could see why you loved it."

He is surprising me in so many ways.

"I'll take it off my list of potential book reports. There are three more books in the series, though," I say. "Wow. My head is just reeling. From everything." I open it up, freezing when I land on the copyright page. "Wait. This is a *first edition*? Are you serious?"

He peers over at it. "Wow, guess it is. I never looked."

I'm gaping. Neil has a first-edition Nora Roberts.

"Take it," he says.

"What? No. I couldn't," I say, though I'm hugging it to my chest.

"It means more to you. You should have it."

"Thank you. Thank you so much." I unzip my backpack, and in my rush to reshuffle and make room for the book, a small foil packet plummets to the floor between us.

I have never before experienced the silence that comes over us. "Red" doesn't even begin to describe the color of his face.

"Did . . . you have plans later?"

I am deceased.

"Oh my God. No. *No*," I say, snatching the condom and stuffing it into my backpack. "It was a joke. Kirby was cleaning out her locker—she'd gotten it in health class—and I'll just go die now. Leave me here with your books."

If this had happened to any of Delilah Park's heroines, they'd breezily laugh it off and crack jokes about it later. I can do that with Kirby and Mara, but not with Neil McNair. In the back of my mind—okay, maybe somewhere closer to the middle of my mind—I wonder if he's had sex. Earlier today, I would have said absolutely not because of how he and his girlfriend were so cold at school. But after all that happened here in his house . . . anything is possible. I'm only just now realizing how little I knew about him.

"Please don't die. I have to tease you about this later."

"We have to go," I urge, shouldering my saucy little minx of a backpack. "Shabbat."

Before he opens the door, he glances back once, as though the image of me in his room is too strange for words. Honestly, everything that happened here is too strange for words.

Stranger, though, is the new kind of determination pulsing through me.

I was wrong earlier. Howl is bigger than Neil and me, but it's bigger than Westview, too. Destroying Neil to accomplish some freshman-year dream sounds so trivial when this money could change his life. God, he could even change his name. While I can't erase what's happened to him, it's clear now that I can't take a cut of the prize money. I can't keep playing Howl just for myself. When we win Howl—*if* we win Howl—we're winning it for him.

Excavated #8: A Haunted Hanukkah

by Jared Roth and Ilana García Roth

Riley tightened one of the little buns coiled on top of her head, and then the other. She wasn't about to let her hair get in the way of this mission. Not again.

She wasn't scared. She hadn't been scared since she was ten, maybe eleven. Roxy was the one who got scared, who begged Riley to check inside her closet and beneath her bed for monsters. Riley had always taken her role as monster vanquisher very seriously, and after poking her head into every shadowy space, she declared in her most official voice that her sister's room was officially beast-free.

No, she wasn't scared, not as she crept up the familiar steps to her favorite place in the world at half past midnight. Being in the museum after hours was a privilege; Riley knew that. As she swiped her badge and waved hello to Alfred, the overnight security guard, she reminded herself she had to see the stone up close. She needed silence to allow her mind to fully process it.

The museum's senior curator, Mrs. Graves, said it had been found on a dig in Jordan, and the image carved into it was unmistakably a menorah. It was, in fact, perhaps the oldest depiction of a menorah that had ever been found.

And yet there was something about the stone carving that

hadn't felt quite right to her, something that pulled her back to the museum when her parents thought she was asleep.

Riley drew closer, her lucky sneakers tip-tapping the tiled floor. It should be up ahead, near the other religious relics housed as part of the museum's permanent collection.

But just as she turned the corner, she heard someone scream.

And suddenly, Riley was very, very scared. . . .

6:22 p.m.

NEIL MCNAIR IS ogling my parents like he can't quite believe they're real.

"Do you want to lead the kiddush?" my mom asks him after lighting the candles with a hand over her eyes. Maybe she sensed he wanted to by the way he was staring at them.

"I'd love to," he says after a pause.

In the car, he lamented not having changed into something nicer, but I insisted my parents wouldn't care that he's wearing a shirt with an obscure Latin phrase on it. Downside: the whole Neil's arms situation is back.

It's not quite sundown—read: not the best Jews—so there's still light coming in from outside. When we got here, he took off his shoes in the hallway and shook my parents' hands, but he could barely speak. They know the basics about him: longtime rival, infuriating, mediocre taste in literature. And Jewish, which I included in my message letting them know Westview's valedictorian would be making an appearance at Shabbat dinner. My parents love opening our home to other Jews, and it happens much too infrequently.

My mom passes him the kiddush cup.

"*Baruch atah Adonai Eloheinu melech ha'olam borei p'ri hagafen,*" he says in this low, honeyed voice. The blessing over wine.

His pronunciation, his inflection—flawless. Of course they are, with his affinity for words and languages. There is so much I love about Judaism, the history and the food and the sound of the prayers, but it isolates me too. Yet here's someone I labeled as an enemy who was maybe feeling isolated in the same way.

After what happened at his house, I'm not quite sure how to act around him. It's clear things have changed between us; we've shared more about ourselves than we do with most other people. But I don't know how to tell him that if we win, I want him to take the Howl money without it sounding like it's coming from a place of pity.

We pass around the kiddush cup that belonged to my dad's grandparents, silver and ornately designed. Neil takes a small sip, then hands it to me. My sip is tiny too. I wonder if he thinks I purposefully sipped from a place he didn't. Then I pass it to my dad and try to act a little less neurotic.

After that, we recite the blessing over the challah, and then it's time to eat. True to their word, my parents picked up mushroom ravioli and threw together a salad with my dad's secret vinaigrette recipe.

"Do you observe Shabbat with your family, Neil?" my mom asks.

"Not very often, no. But I have a good memory, and we used to do it when my sister and I were younger." It's slight, but I notice his jaw tense for a split second. "You do this every week?"

"We try to have Shabbat dinner together every Friday," my dad says. "I suppose it'll be different when Rowan's in college."

"It's strange being one of only a few Jewish kids in class," Neil says, and it's odd to hear him vocalize something I've only ever thought to myself. Odd and a bit of a relief to hear someone else say something you thought was the way only you felt.

Most of the year, you don't notice it makes you different. It's just what your family does every Friday, and we don't completely unplug like some more-observant Jews. But during the entire months of November and December, you're a complete outsider. So many people never realize that someone doesn't, by default, celebrate Christmas.

"In fifth grade, one of my teachers put up a Christmas tree before remembering that I was the only Jew in her class," I say. "So she announced to the entire class that because she didn't want to offend me, she was taking it down. And everyone was mad at me for, like, a whole week. She didn't even ask what I thought, or if she should add a menorah to balance it out. It was almost like she wanted people to know I was the reason they couldn't have a tree."

The table is quiet for a few moments. I didn't realize I'd been holding on to this for so long.

"You never told us!" my mom exclaims. "What teacher was that?"

"I didn't want to make it a thing," I say. But maybe I should have. "Mrs. Garrison?"

"We donated a set of books to her class," my dad says with a grumble.

"That's terrible," Neil says. He gestures around the room. "This is nice, though. To be around other Jewish people."

And simply put, it really is.

My mom shines a smile on our unexpected guest. "Rowan said you're a fan of our books?"

Neil's mouth opens and closes, but no human sounds come out. His Excavated books are underneath the table. Fanboy Neil: definitely not someone I ever thought I'd meet.

I kick him under the table. *Please remember how to word*, I try to telepath to him. My parents' egos are going to be unmanageable after this.

"Huge fan," he finally says. "I started reading Excavated back in third grade, and then I couldn't stop. Those books actually got me into reading."

My parents are utterly charmed. "That's the best compliment you could give us," my dad says. "Have you read the entire series?"

"Too many times to count." He gestures to the table. "And you both are vegan, right? Just like Riley!"

"We are," my dad says. "Rowan's a vegetarian, though. She just can't get enough dairy." My parents became vegans in college, and they wanted me to decide for myself when I was old enough. In kindergarten, I declared myself a vegetarian, and I've never gone back. I loved animals too much to imagine eating them. As a result, keeping kosher, as least its most basic rules, is pretty easy at our house.

"Rowan *loves* cheese," my mom says. "Sometimes when she

wants a snack, she'll take a spoon and a tub of cream cheese up to her room."

Neil lifts his eyebrows at me, clearly trying not to laugh.

"Mother." Yes, cream cheese is the food of the gods—specifically Chris Hemsworth circa *Thor: Ragnarok*—but I've only done that a few times. Definitely fewer than ten. "Let's maybe tone down the cheese talk?"

Besides, it's not just cheese. I couldn't survive without Two Birds cinnamon rolls.

"Fine, fine. How's Howl going?"

They're rapt as Neil and I explain our strategy, this year's clues, and the grand prize. Now that they're not on deadline, they're much more relaxed.

"We should put that in a book," my dad says. "That would be fun, huh?"

My mom shrugs. "I don't know. It might be a little hard to follow. A little too niche."

"I think it would be great!" Neil says, a little too enthusiastically. "What was the book you just finished?"

Once he gets them going, they won't be able to stop. I sneak a look at my phone. An hour and a half until Delilah's signing. Since it's unlikely we'll get all five remaining clues by then, I'll have to leave Neil alone for a bit. I wonder if I can do it without telling him why.

"This one's the start of a spin-off series about Riley's younger sister—"

"Roxy!" Neil blurts. "She's hilarious. I love the way she uses foods she doesn't like in place of exclamations, like *Oh my grapefruit* or *What the fig?* Always cracks me up in the Riley books."

"Our editor loves her too," my mom says. "And the publisher thought we could reach a whole new audience of kids with this series. So it follows Roxy on her quest to become a pastry chef, and each book is going to have recipes in the back that are easy for kids to make."

"What a cool idea," Neil breathes. "My sister would love those. She's eleven and just starting to get into the books. You know, I always thought *Excavated* would make a great movie."

"So did we!" my dad says. "The rights sold, but nothing happened with them."

"Knowing Hollywood, they probably would have whitewashed it anyway," my mom says. "Turned Riley Rodriguez into Riley Johnson or something like that, and made the Hanukkah books revolve around Christmas."

Neil shudders. "I actually brought a couple books with me, if you don't mind . . ."

"Of course we don't mind!" my dad says. I swear he already has a signing pen ready. "Is Neil *E-A* or *E-I*?"

He gives them the correct spelling, and they swoop their signatures over the title page.

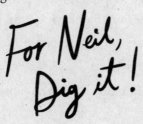

Neil reads it over and over, lips forming the words. He looks like he might faint. "Could you make the other one out to my sister, Natalie?" he asks, and they oblige. "Thank you. Thank you so much. I can't tell you how much this means to me."

All these years, I've been waging war against a Riley Rodriguez superfan. I can't deny that it's a little endearing.

"Anytime, Neil," my mom says. "If you want to come over later this summer, we can show you some drafts of sketches for our next picture book."

"That would be amazing," he says, and I swear he sits up straighter, seeming to gain more confidence. "You know what other kinds of books I love? Romance novels."

And then he shovels more salad into his mouth, all casual.

Pardon me while I reattach the lower half of my jaw.

My mom lifts her eyebrows. "Huh," she says in this perplexed tone. "Is that so?"

"You and Rowan have that in common," my dad says. "I guess they're not just for bored housewives anymore." He places an emphasis on "bored housewives," as though it's not a phrase he likes, necessarily, but couldn't come up with a better one. Dad, your misogyny is showing.

"And not just for women, either," Neil says, after a pause that maybe indicates he was bothered by my dad's comment too. "Though they center women's experiences in a way little other media does."

His voice is solid, steady. There's no hint of sarcasm there, and

I'm no longer convinced he's teasing me. When his eyes meet mine, one edge of his mouth pulls up into a smile that's more reassuring than conspiratorial. Almost like he's trying to help my parents understand this thing that I love.

But that's bananas.

"Well, I don't know if that's necessarily true," my dad says, and rattles off the names of a few Netflix shows because, of course, three recent examples are incontrovertible proof that an entire art form isn't still majorly skewed toward the male gaze.

What would they say if I told them right now? If I said when I take creative writing classes at Emerson, it's because I want to write the kind of books they think are worthless? Would they try to change my mind, or would they learn to accept it? Part of me is hopeful they'd understand if I wanted to semi-follow in their footsteps, but I want a guarantee their reaction won't flatten me.

My lungs are too tight, and suddenly there's not enough air in here. In one swift movement, I get to my feet.

"Excuse me for a moment," I say before escaping into the kitchen.

I revel in my solitude for a few minutes, trying to figure out how this day went from Neil McNair winning valedictorian to defending romance novels to my parents. The laughter from the dining room is dimmed, but I can still hear it.

"Rowan?" My mom's voice.

I turn from where I've been staring out the window at our

backyard. My mom whips off her glasses, wipes the lenses on her sweater. Her hair is in the same kind of bun as mine, though hers looks professional-author sloppy somehow. It's probably the pair of pencils sticking out of it.

"This can't be the same boy you've been competing with for four years," she says, motioning to the dining room. "Because he's very nice. Very polite."

"Same boy." I lean against the kitchen counter. "And he is. Shockingly so."

She gives me a warm smile and cups my shoulder. "Rowan Luisa Roth. Are you sure you're doing okay? I know this last day must have been rough."

Rowan Luisa. My middle name belonged to her father's mother, a grandmother who lived and died in Mexico before I was born.

I only notice my mother's accent on occasion, when she pronounces certain words or when she gets a paper cut or stubs a toe, mutters "Dios mío" so fast, I used to think it was all one word. When she's reading aloud to herself—instructions, a recipe, counting—she does it in Spanish. Once I pointed it out to her, just because I thought it was interesting and I love hearing my mom speak Spanish. She wasn't even aware of it, and I was so worried that now that she knew she was doing it, she'd stop. Fortunately, she never did.

"I . . . don't know."

I've always been able to be honest with my parents. I even told my mom when I lost my virginity. Romance novels made me so eager to talk about it.

The thing is, I'm afraid.

Afraid of saying I want what they have.

Afraid they'll dismiss it as a hobby.

Afraid that if they read my work, they'll tell me I'm not good enough.

Afraid they'll tell me I'll never make it.

Her hand brushes my cheek. "Endings are so hard," she says, and then laughs at the double meaning. "I should know. We spent all day trying to get ours just right."

"Yours are always perfect." And I mean it. I was my parents' first reader, their first fan. "Did you ever—" I break off, wondering how to phrase this. "Did you ever have people who looked down on you and Dad for writing children's books?"

She gives me this look over her glasses, as if to say, *obviously*. "All the time. We told you what his parents said when the third Riley book hit the *New York Times* list, right?" When I shake my head, she continues: "His father asked when we were going to start writing real books."

"Grandpa does only read World War II novels."

"And that's fine. Not my cup of tea, but I understand why he enjoys them. We've always loved writing for kids. They're so full of hope and wonder, and everything feels big and new and exciting. And we love meeting the kids who read our books. Even if they're not kids anymore," she says with a nod toward the dining room.

"Have you ever thought . . . ?" I chew the inside of my cheek.

"What Grandpa said about your books. That's—that's sort of how I feel sometimes."

"About romance novels? I'd never argue that they're not real books, Rowan. We each have our preferences. We can agree to disagree."

I try to keep my heart from sinking. It's not progress, not exactly, but at least it doesn't feel like a step backward. It's going to have to be enough until I meet Delilah.

"Speaking of romance," my mom says. "Is there something going on between you and Neil?"

My hands fly to my mouth, and I'm sure there's an expression of abject horror on my face. "Oh my God, Mom, no, no, no, no, no. No."

"Sorry, I didn't quite catch that."

I roll my eyes. "*No*. We teamed up for the game. Completely platonically."

But my mind trips over the way he said the kiddush, the sound of those words I knew so well in a voice I thought I did. My fingers tingle at the memory of sitting on his bed, touching his shoulder. An unusual moment of physical contact between us. Then the pointillism of freckles across his face and down his neck, the dots that wrap around his fingers and crawl up his arms. And his *arms*—the way they look in that T-shirt.

It's probably just that I'm really into arms.

"Well. I hope you enjoy the rest of your *game*," my mom says with a smirk before she heads back into the dining room.

HOWL CLUES

- A place you can buy Nirvana's first album
- A place that's red from floor to ceiling
- A place you can find Chiroptera
- ~~A rainbow crosswalk~~
- ~~Ice cream fit for Sasquatch~~
- The big guy at the center of the universe
- ~~Something local, organic, and sustainable~~
- A floppy disk
- ~~A coffee cup with someone else's name (or your own name, wildly misspelled)~~
- ~~A car with a parking ticket~~
- A view from up high
- ~~The best pizza in the city (your choice)~~
- ~~A tourist doing something a local would be ashamed of doing~~
- ~~An umbrella (we all know real Seattleites don't use them)~~
- A tribute to the mysterious Mr. Cooper

7:03 p.m.

"EATING CREAM CHEESE straight out of the tub," Neil says with a shake of his head as we drive down Fremont Avenue. "You barbarian."

"No one has manners when they're eating alone," I say as I pull into a parking spot. "I'm sure you have plenty of terrible habits."

"I'm actually quite sophisticated. I put things on plates before I eat them. You've heard of them, yeah? Plates? See also: bowls."

Toward the end of dinner, we strategized: the Fremont Troll (*the big guy at the center of the universe*) and then *a view from up high*. When I suggested Gas Works Park, made famous by the paintball scene in *10 Things I Hate about You*, he scoffed. "Is that really the best view in Seattle?" he asked. "It's *a* view of Seattle," I said. "It doesn't need to be the best one."

Fremont is busy on Friday nights. It's not dark yet, and voices spill from bars and restaurants. Next week, during the summer solstice, Fremont will celebrate with a parade and a naked bike ride. The troll, which is nearly twenty feet tall, has a hand wrapped around an actual Volkswagen Beetle and a hubcap for an eye.

I check the time on my car's dash for about the tenth time in the past minute. Delilah Park's signing is in an hour, and I am now officially panicking.

She'll be elegant, of course, like she is in all her photos. And kind. I'm sure she'll be kind. I've met my parents' author friends, but it's not quite the same. Delilah is someone I discovered for myself, not someone my parents have over for late-night drinks whenever they're in town. Horrified, I realized I forgot to swap my stained dress for something clean. I pray it'll be dark in the bookstore. I don't want to sit in the front row, but I don't want to sit in the very back, either. What do normal people do when they go to events alone? Maybe I'll leave my backpack on the seat next to me, pretend I'm saving it for someone.

"You have somewhere else to be?" Neil asks as we search for parking. "You keep looking at the clock."

"Yes. I mean, no. I just—there's something I want to do at eight."

"Oh. Okay. Were you . . . planning on telling me?"

"Yes. Now."

Even after his mini romance-novel spiel at dinner, this signing is something I have to experience on my own. If he's there, I won't feel like I can fully be myself, though I'm unsure who that person is, the one who's able to love what she loves without shame.

"Okay," he says slowly. "Where is it?"

"Greenwood. It'll only take ten minutes to get there, and I'll only be gone about an hour. And we're already so far ahead," I say, aware I sound like I'm trying to defend it. "We can meet back up and finish the game then. Unless you think you'll be too tired?"

"I'm in it for the long haul."

"Good. Me too."

A bit of an awkward silence follows. I have to change the subject before I dissolve in a puddle of nerves.

"You and your sister seemed close."

"We are," he says before biting back a smile. "Except for the six months I convinced her she was an alien when she was eight."

"What?" I sputter, laughing.

"She's left-handed, and the rest of our family is right-handed, and she's the only one who has an outie belly button, so I convinced her that meant she was an alien. She was so freaked out about it, and she was determined to try to get home to her home planet, which I told her was called Blorgon Seven. Every so often, I'll ask her how things are going on Blorgon Seven."

I can tell there's genuine affection there. That he's a good brother, though as an only child, I've never been able to completely understand the depths of sibling relationships. It tugs at my heart in more ways than one.

"Your poor sister."

"And you, with your parents—you're close," he says, more a statement than a question.

I nod. "That was nice, what you said to them. Thank you."

"I figured I was wrong. They are too," he says. "But really, your parents are pretty cool. You're lucky."

His words feel weighty. I know I'm lucky. I really do. And I love my parents, but I don't know how to make them understand what I want when they don't understand what I love.

"Thank you" is all I can manage. "Again." Politeness with Neil McNair. That's new.

We find a parking spot a ten-minute walk from the troll. I lock my car while Neil mimes stretching, like he's getting ready for a big race. He raises his arms skyward, his T-shirt riding up and exposing a sliver of his stomach. He's wearing a simple brown belt, and the navy band of his boxers peeks out above his jeans.

My face grows warm. The command to look away gets lost between the part of my brain that makes good choices and the part that doesn't. It's as though Neil McNair's stomach somehow does not compute in my mind. Obviously he has a stomach, and naturally it's covered with freckles. . . .

Objectively, it's an attractive stomach. That's all this is—an appreciation of the male form. His shoulders, his arms, his stomach.

And the ring of freckles around his navel.

And the reddish hair directly beneath it that disappears into his boxers.

His arms flop back down, as does the hem of his shirt, safely concealing his stomach from view. He meets my eyes before I can avert my gaze, and one corner of his mouth quirks up.

Oh no, no, no. Does he think I was staring?

"I haven't had a Shabbat dinner in a while," he says, and I'm relieved because Judaism is something I can talk about. Reasons I was staring at Neil's freckled stomach, not so much. "Thank you for that. Really. What you said, about that teacher you had . . ." He shakes his head. "I've had too many experiences like that to count. People tell you to lighten up, that you're overreacting. Or they seem that way at first, and then it's one 'joke' after another and you start wondering if you really are lesser because of it. That's why I stopped telling people, and with my last name . . . no one assumed." We fall in step, passing a frame shop and a gluten-free bakery. "But the holidays are hard. Every year, I think they won't be, and then they are."

"Don't you love when people call it the holidays, or a holiday party, but everything's red and green and there's a fucking Santa?" I say. "It's like they think calling it 'holiday' makes them automatically inclusive, but they don't want to put in the actual work of inclusion."

"Yes!" He nearly shouts this, so loudly that a family leaving a Thai restaurant stares at us. Neil's laughing a little, but not because it's funny. "I had a teacher straight-up tell me I couldn't participate in an Easter-egg hunt, even though I wanted to."

"When people learn I'm Jewish, I swear sometimes they nod, like, 'Yep, makes sense.' I've . . . been told I look very Jewish."

"I had a friend in elementary school who stopped coming over to my house," he says, his voice low. "This kid Jake. When I asked him about it, he told me his parents wouldn't let him. I came home crying to my mom about it because I didn't understand, and she called his dad. When she got off the phone . . . I'd never seen her look like that. And some part of me just *knew*, before she even said it, why he wasn't allowed over anymore."

He just keeps breaking my heart.

"That is fucking terrible." I scan our surroundings before uttering the next part. "Earlier, when I overheard Savannah at the safe zone. She said I obviously didn't need the Howl money. And then—and then she tapped her nose." At this, I do the same with mine, realizing I'm drawing attention to it and wondering if Neil thinks it's too bumpy or too big for my face, the way I used to. He stops abruptly, his eyebrows slashed.

"Are you serious?" A loud exhale. "The fuck, Rowan. That's messed up. That's so messed up. I'm sorry."

His reaction helps me relax a little. Like I could be justified in how I felt about it because I wasn't alone in thinking it was shitty, but . . . my reaction was enough, wasn't it? If I felt like crap about it, that was enough.

Neil steps forward and grazes my forearm with a couple fingertips, a small gesture to match his expression of empathy. The way he touches me, it's soft and tentative. It's the way I touched him back in his room, on his bed. "I'm sorry," he repeats, his eyes not leaving mine, and there's something so foreign about those words combined with his fingertips on my skin that I have to look away, which makes him drop his hand.

"People think it's harmless. They think it's funny. That's why they do it," I say, trying to ignore the strange shiver where he touched my arm. Must be static electricity. "And sure. I guess it's harmless until something bad happens. It's harmless, and then there are security guards at your synagogue because someone called in a bomb threat. It's harmless, and you're terrified to get out of bed Saturday morning and go to services."

"Did that—" he asks in a quiet voice.

"Right before my bat mitzvah."

The police found the guy who did it. It had been a prank, apparently. I'm not sure what happened to him, if he went to jail or if a cop simply patted his shoulder and asked him not to do it again, the way they do when white men do something atrocious. But I was so scared, I wailed and begged my parents not to make me go to synagogue for weeks afterward. And eventually we stopped going altogether, except on holidays.

That fear took something I loved away from me.

Obviously not harmless.

Neil and I are both a little breathless. His cheeks are flushed, like this conversation has been a physical effort as much as an emotional one. We fall in step again.

"But it's weird sometimes, with my last name, and then with the hair and the freckles, the assumption is that I'm fully Irish. I pass as non-Jewish until someone learns I'm Jewish, and then they refer to it all the time. People here go out of their way to try to make you feel comfortable, and by doing that, they sometimes alienate you even more. Some of them mean well, but others . . ."

Yes. Exactly that. "When you learn about the Holocaust, you assume anti-Semitism is something historical. But . . . it's really not."

"When did you learn about it?" he asks. I have to think for a moment. "My mom told me after what happened with Jake."

"As a class, we learned about it in fourth grade. But I already knew about it at that point. The thing is . . ." I trail off, searching my memory, but only one devastating answer comes to mind. "I can't remember ever learning about it. I'm sure my parents told me at some point, but I can't recall ever *not* knowing."

I wish I could remember. I want to know if I cried. I want to know what questions I asked, what questions they couldn't possibly answer.

"We're going to fucking destroy Savannah, okay?" Neil says.

His casual use of profanity is a mix of amusing and something else I can't quite name. He's serious. He's enraged on my behalf, out for revenge. Like we really are allies in more than the game.

This conversation makes me regret, just a little, that we weren't friends. Kylie Lerner, Cameron Pereira, and Belle Greenberg ran in different circles, but I wanted Jewish friends so badly. I was convinced they'd understand me on this deep level that no one else could. I'm not blameless—I never made an effort to know him on a level beyond competitor. I messed up, treating him as a rival when he could have been so much more than that. What would we be now, if I hadn't sought revenge after that essay contest, if he hadn't retaliated?

That alternate timeline sounds so, so lovely.

"I almost—" I start, and then I catch myself.

He stops walking. "What?"

"I—I don't know. I almost wish we could have talked about

this kind of thing earlier," I say quickly, all in one breath, before I can regret it. Fuck it, we've already shared plenty tonight. "I've never had anyone to talk to about it."

The few moments he waits before responding are torture.

"Me too," he says quietly.

We take our photo of the troll—*with* the troll, Neil insists, handing his phone to a tourist. I'm positive I'm scowling, but when we peek at the picture afterward, I'm surprised to find us both smiling. A little awkwardly, sure, but it's a step above the Most Likely to Succeed photo.

"We don't have time to go to Gas Works before your thing," Neil says as we head back to my car. "We should do the zoo first."

I nod. "Okay. Fine. Wait, why are you stopping?"

He twists his mouth far to one side, as though considering whether he wants to say what he's about to. "This might sound ridiculous, but . . . I've heard that exhibit while high is a really wild experience." With raised eyebrows, he points at the shop to our left. HASH TAG says the sign in the window, with a marijuana leaf drawn below.

Neil McNair, Westview valedictorian, just suggested we go to the zoo while *high*.

"Excuse me," I say, fighting the urge to laugh, "I think you just suggested we buy some weed?"

"I have layers, Artoo."

"We have"—I check my phone—"thirty-five minutes before I have to leave for my, um, thing. Not to mention, neither of us is twenty-one."

"We have plenty of time for your thing and the zoo," he says. "We're right here. And Adrian's brother works here. He's always saying we should come by and pick something out."

"Employee of the month right there." But I have to admit, I'm curious. I'm not opposed to weed, and it's been readily available at parties. I worried I wouldn't know what to do with it, though, which stopped me from asking to try it.

"Wasn't there anything you wanted to do in high school but never got a chance?"

That's what gets me.

"Actually," I say, because we've shared so much today already. Might as well show him more of my weird brain. "I had this list. This success guide I made four years ago that mapped out everything I should do before graduating. I'd forgotten about it for a while, until today. And I'm realizing I missed out on some quintessential rites of passage. Not pot, necessarily, but—other things."

It's a bit cathartic to mention the guide out loud. But what I'm wondering is how a friendship with Neil McNair fits into that list—because I'm pretty sure it doesn't.

"Like what?"

"Prom, for one. I didn't go." Part of me wondered if it would have been fun without a date, without that perfect high school boyfriend, but in my head, the perfect prom was with a date who was deeply in love with me. Instead I wallowed in my FOMO all night, scrolling through social media while rereading my favorite Delilah Park, trying to ignore the twinge that felt like regret.

"You didn't miss much. Brady Becker was prom king, Chantal Okafor was prom queen, and Malina Jovanovic and Austin Hart were nearly asked to leave because they were, uh, dancing too suggestively, according to Principal Meadows." He rubs the back of his neck. "And . . . Bailey was really quiet the whole time, so it made sense when she said she wanted to break up a few days later."

I knew they'd broken up somewhat recently. I had a couple classes with her, but she was always pretty quiet.

As though anticipating I might apologize, Neil adds, "It's okay. Really. We didn't have much in common. We've even been able to stay friends."

"Spencer wanted to stay friends too, but we barely had fun even when we were together." I heave a sigh, digging my feet into the pavement. It's strange to tell him all of this, and yet I find myself wanting to. "In hindsight, the relationship was mostly physical. Which was fun, but I wanted more than that."

Neil gives a little cough. "You two seemed . . . happy? You were together for a while."

"Not the same as *being* happy."

If there's anything I'm learning today, it's that every kind of relationship is complicated. Which explains why I'm here with Neil and not with my best friends. Their words hit me again. I'm not here because I'm obsessed with him—I'm here to finally end this between us. Only then will I be able to move on from it all. At least, I hope so.

"So many relationships are ending," I continue, not wanting to linger on Spencer. "Darius Vogel and Nate Zellinsky broke up last week, and they've been together since sophomore year. I guess it's tough to stay with someone who's going hundreds of miles away."

"Is that really what you think?"

I shrug, unsure of the answer, wanting another subject change. "Let's go in." Today's already been filled with plenty the two of us never would have done. If I want to make it a real send-off, we might as well cross something off Neil's list. That's what Howl is becoming: a goodbye to high school and the boy who drove me bonkers for most of it.

Neil grins.

The guy behind the counter looks like a typical Seattle hipster, plaid shirt and thick-framed glasses, well-groomed facial hair. The lights are bright, and the counter is stocked with all sorts of edibles. Pipes in all colors and designs line the walls.

"Neil, my man!"

"Hey, Henry," Neil says, and as both of us register that Adrian is there with him—"Hey!"

The Quinlan brothers are holding twin containers of food. Adrian waves us over.

"Our mom doesn't love that he works here, but she still wants to keep him well fed," he says by way of explanation. "And I'm dead, so. You guys still alive?"

Neil nods and tells him our plan.

"Sick!" Adrian exclaims. To Adrian's credit, he doesn't send any odd looks my way.

"Let me know if you need any help," Henry says cheerfully, evidently not worried about selling pot to minors.

We browse the edibles and the selection of pipes, many of which look like works of art. There are caramels and cookies and lollipops, pie and gummies and even lip balm.

I am in a pot shop with Neil McNair. What is my life?

"Do you want me to ask if they have pot-laced cream cheese and a big ol' spoon?" Neil whispers.

"Shut up," I say around a laugh, though that does sound like it could be good smeared onto a bagel.

Neil taps his fingers on the glass case. "What would you recommend to two people who are relatively new to the world of marijuana?" He could not sound like more of a dork if he tried, oh my God.

"Are you looking for edibles, or something to smoke?"

"Edibles," I say. Much less conspicuous.

He reaches inside the glass case. "A good starter dose for beginners is five milligrams of THC. These cookies are our best sellers, and we have them in both five- and ten-milligram servings. Chocolate, peanut butter, and mint."

"What does it feel like?" I ask, not wanting to seem like an amateur. I don't want to take anything that will make me too much not like myself.

"Relaxing," Henry says. "It doesn't completely turn off your brain, but a serving this small, it'll just mellow you out."

My ears perk up at that. Maybe that's what I need to meet Delilah. "That sounds perfect." We'll go to the zoo, and then I'll go to Delilah. I'll be normal and cool and mellow.

We buy two five-milligram cookies.

Adrian wishes us luck and raises his fist. "Quad life!" This time I'm not quite as embarrassed when Neil says it back.

Outside, Neil bumps my weed cookie with his. "Cheers to questionable choices," he says before we take a bite.

HOWL STANDINGS

TOP 5
Neil McNair: 11
Rowan Roth: 11
Mara Pompetti: 8
Iris Zhou: 8
Brady Becker: 7

PLAYERS REMAINING: 21

HOWL HISTORY: The shortest game of Howl lasted 3 hours and 27 minutes. The longest game lasted 4 days and 10 hours, causing future game makers to implement the Sunday graduation deadline.

7:34 p.m.

I CAN'T SEE anything. It takes a while for my eyes to adjust, for my other senses to balance me out. It's warm in the nocturnal exhibit. Darker than dark. Something rustles, something scurries, something hoots. Shapes of trees, maybe a pond, slowly come into focus. This has always been my favorite exhibit, its eerie peacefulness able to turn even the wildest kids calm and reverent.

I'm a little far from peaceful at the moment, since we just barely missed a kill on our way into the zoo. Carolyn Gao was about twenty feet in front of us, exiting the nocturnal house with Iris Zhou.

"Neil!" I hissed, but he didn't react. I had to poke his arm. There was his freckled arm and unimpressive but still pleasantly surprising bicep again. "Seriously? Carolyn!"

"Carolyn . . . ?"

"Carolyn *Gao*. Your target?"

"Oh." He blinked as though waking up, though I doubted the weed had kicked in yet. "*Oh*. Shit. You're right."

Carolyn and Iris turned in the opposite direction, toward the zoo's exit.

"We don't have time," he said, heading for the exhibit, and I reluctantly followed him.

We took a photo at the entrance to the nocturnal house, but instead of a green check mark, the juniors sent back a red *X*. "We probably have to go inside," Neil said, which I guess was the whole point of those edibles in the first place. He insisted we'd be fast. That I wouldn't miss my mystery appointment. He'd better be right.

A bat swoops by my head, and I stop so suddenly that Neil bumps into me.

"Sorry," he whispers, but I can still sense him right behind me, the tips of his fingers brushing my shoulder as he regains his balance. Not knowing exactly where he is makes my heart jackrabbit in my chest. "Do you feel anything yet?"

"Not really," I say, but even as the words leave my mouth, I'm aware something has changed. A laugh bubbles out of me, though nothing's funny. "I—wait. I might be feeling something."

My annoyance with him seems to float away, and suddenly Delilah's signing doesn't seem as terrifying. Thank you, Henry.

Delilah. I check my phone again—ten more minutes until I have to leave.

Indistinct chatter fills the exhibit as another group of people enters.

"What do you think you'll do if you win?" someone says, not whispering the way we're supposed to.

"Five grand is enough for a used car, and I'm so sick of the bus," another voice says. "I know Savannah said killing them was more important, but damn if I don't want that money."

As slowly as I can, I turn around, and though I can't see the expression on Neil's face, I swear I can feel him tense next to me.

"Trang was camped out here all afternoon and didn't see them. They have to be headed here soon."

"I thought he'd be easier to spot, with the red hair."

"Apparently not. Did Savannah mention who had Rowan?"

"Nope. Must not be someone in the group."

We crouch down, and Neil leans in so he can say directly into my ear, "We'll stay here until they leave?" His breath is hot on my skin.

I swallow hard. "Okay," I whisper back.

This close to Neil, I can feel his body heat, smell what must have been the soap he used this morning, or maybe his deodorant. It must be the edible taking over my brain, warping this experience.

Savannah's emissaries continue making their way through the exhibit, stopping every so often to take a closer look at something. I try my best to keep my breathing under control, aware that at any moment, they could find and kill Neil.

And then I don't know what I'd be playing for.

Without access to my phone, I can't tell how much time has passed. Two minutes? Ten? I have to get out of here, have to see Delilah, but the more pressing issue is this: we've been crouching for far longer than crouching is reasonably comfortable, and my muscles are not happy with me.

I stretch forward until I'm pretty sure my mouth is right up against his ear.

"I don't know if I can keep balancing," I whisper. I'm so close that my nose grazes—the side of his face? The shell of his ear? I'm not entirely sure.

He's quiet for a moment. "Okay. As slowly as you can, come forward onto your knees," he says, "and then slide your legs to the side."

"Could you, um—"

"Help you?"

I nod before realizing he can't see me. "Please," I whisper.

A warm hand lands on my shoulder, steadying me, and slowly, *slowly*, I maneuver into a more comfortable position. He's stronger, more solid than I ever expected him to be. Definitely no longer a twig in a T-shirt.

"Good?" he asks once I'm settled.

I try to exhale. "Mm-hmm," I mumble. His hand leaves my shoulder.

We are extremely close, and that fact plus the drug plus the fear of being caught combine to send a unique kind of panic through me.

"I don't think there's anyone else here," one of the seniors finally says. "Let's go. Savannah can be an asshole, anyway. I want to win this for myself."

I wait a little longer than is probably necessary to make sure they're not only gone but far enough away from the exhibit not to notice us when we leave. Then I get to my feet, eager to stretch my legs.

"I think we're safe," I tell him, and when I don't get a response, I interpret it as tacit agreement.

By the time I make it outside, the sky has turned a dusky blue, and the clouds are heavier than they've been all day. It's beautiful, really, and I can't help staring up at it for a while, waiting for my eyes to readjust to the light. Ah, yes, there's the mellow Henry was talking about.

Then two things hit me like an electric shock, one right after the other.

Delilah's signing started ten minutes ago, and Neil is nowhere in sight.

The zoo is closing soon, and I'm frozen in between the nocturnal exhibit and the main pavilion. I don't want to send him a frantic text, so I try to sound casual. Hey, did you make it out okay?

I don't think he'd ditch me. Would he? Maybe he's still in the exhibit—but what if he got out before I did and one of those seniors with his name killed him?

I need an answer before I see Delilah. I can't bring myself to leave without touching base with him. I'll make sure he's okay, race to the bookstore, and sneak into a seat in the very back. This is fine. This is all going to be—

"Rowan?"

I whirl around to find Mara lifting her hand in a wave.

"Hey," I say, wary, but she shakes her head.

"I don't have your name."

"Oh. Good." I sort of shuffle awkwardly from foot to foot. "Neil and I are still working together. I'm . . . waiting for him." At least, I hope I am.

"He's Neil now?" One corner of her mouth pulls into a half smile.

"It *is* his name."

"You always call him McNair, or McNightmare, or something like that."

Oh. I guess I do. I must have made the mental switch at some point without even thinking about it.

"It's been a weird day," I finally concede, but she's full-on grinning now. "Where's Kirby?"

"Dead," Mara says, as flat as if she were informing me she got a B on a paper. "I couldn't save her."

"You really do get a little too into this."

"Ahem, look who's talking," she says. "It was pretty wild. Meg Lazarski spotted her at Seattle Center, and for some reason, Kirby thought she could hide in the fountain and Meg wouldn't go after her. She was wrong. So she got totally drenched, and she went home to clean up. We're meeting back up at the next safe zone."

It splits something open inside me, imagining the two of them having this completely different last day. But I made my choice—I'm sticking with Neil. If I can find him.

It doesn't mean I can't try to make things right with my friends, though.

"Mara," I start, and because apologizing is hard, my teeth worry my lower lip before I speak again. "You and Kirby were right. I've been really selfish this year. I want to make things better between the three of us. I'm so sorry I haven't been putting in the effort. I think maybe I was so focused on the idea of us I had in my head that I didn't realize I actually had to, you know, *try*. I've . . . been a shitty friend."

I think of that photo on my phone again. I don't know when we lost that, but we have some time to get it back. Not trying is the only thing that guarantees we won't.

Mara's quiet for a few moments, toeing a straw wrapper on the ground with her sandal. "You're being hard on yourself," she says. "I mean, yes, you've been a bit of a ghost this year, but we've all had a lot going on."

"You're letting me off the hook that easily?" I say, and she smirks.

"I'm a lot harder to get rid of than you think." She leans in, places a hand on my shoulder. "And we still have the summer. We have breaks from school. We have social media. We're not going to suddenly turn into strangers. I can't promise that we'll be as close forever, but . . . we can try."

"I want to make it up to you both. We'll talk more after the game? After graduation?"

"I'd love that. And who knows . . . maybe *Neil* can come too."

I lift my eyebrows at this, not entirely understanding. I'm not sure if Neil and I will hang out after today, but Mara's being her usual optimistic self: assuming that because Neil and I teamed up tonight, we're magically friends now.

"If I have any hope of catching you guys, I have to hustle," she says.

"Good luck," I tell her, and she jogs off toward the zoo's exit.

AP Literature Group Chat
(Junior year)
Tuesday, January 15, 8:36 p.m.

Brady Becker

SWEET got the two smartest kids in my group

so are we getting an A or A+?

Lily Gulati

Brady, you may actually have to *gasp* put in some work to get an A.

so I already have a bunch of project ideas

I love ms. grable

Neil McNair

Sure, if you don't mind reading books that won't even be on the AP exam.

Brady Becker

@lily ur killin my buzz!!!

you don't have to be a dick just because we're not reading your bro mark twain

Neil McNair

He's not my bro. And every other sophomore English class is reading Huck Finn this year. Forgive me if I was looking forward to it.

Brady Becker has changed his profile photo.
Brady Becker liked this.

I can't imagine looking forward to blatant racism and misogyny, but you do you.

Lily Gulati

Is . . . every conversation going to be like this?

Neil McNair

No.

yes

Neil McNair has left the chat.

8:28 p.m.

HE'S STILL NOT answering his phone. Delilah Park is probably making a room full of romantics laugh and laugh, and Neil McNair is not answering his phone.

My group chat starts lighting up again, and while I know we have work to do, I'm relieved we're okay.

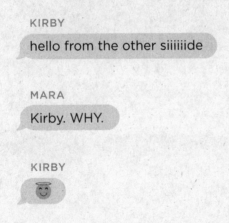

But Neil is silent. I'm about to lose my nerve completely when he exits a small brick building across the square.

"Where the hell were you?" I ask, aware I sound like a parent furious their child has come home after curfew.

All around us, parents haul their kids toward the zoo exit.

He gives me an odd look. "I was in the bathroom. I whispered to you in the exhibit. I told you that you should go to your thing and text me when you're done."

"I didn't hear. I was—worried," I say, stilted, because it sounds so ridiculous. "We have to stick together. I thought you'd—" I break off, suddenly embarrassed by my reaction.

"Abandoned you?" he asks, but he doesn't say it meanly.

"Well . . . yeah," I concede. "Or that you'd been killed."

"I wouldn't abandon you. I swear." He clears his throat, looks at his watch. "Shit, it's almost eight thirty."

"Yeah. I know." The anger I forgot in my panic that he was gone makes its way back to the surface. I picture stacks and stacks of *Scandal at Sunset*, all waiting to be signed. I bet no one there feels guilty about buying them. I bet they don't turn the covers over to make sure no one else can see them as they leave the store.

"Can you show up late?" His eyes are large behind his glasses. Hopeful.

At this point, it's too late for late. "No thanks. I don't need to draw more attention to myself." Even as I say this, there's a tiny part of me that relaxes at the idea of missing the signing. No anxiety over figuring out where to sit or what to say to her. The opposite of FOMO. I'm not entirely happy with this tiny part of me, but still—it's there. "I shouldn't have taken that edible. I completely lost track of time in the exhibit." That must be what's messing with my brain too.

"Well, it would be great if you told me what it is so I can at least attempt a helpful suggestion."

"It's a book signing," I say with a sigh, trying to make that tiny relaxed part even smaller. It's easier to be upset with him, so I focus on that instead. "My favorite author, Delilah Park, is—*was*—doing a book signing, and thanks to Henry 'it'll just mellow you out' Quinlan and your supremely well-timed disappearance, it's practically almost over."

He doesn't say the obvious: that I didn't have to wait for him.

"You didn't want to tell me about a book signing?" he asks, further igniting my frustration. He says it like it would have been so simple. "Didn't we talk about romance novels earlier? Didn't you see one on my shelf? I don't know why you felt you had to keep this a secret."

"Because I'm writing a book, okay?" It just slides out, and after a moment of shock, I realize I like the way it sounds out loud. Admitting it sends a shot of adrenaline through me. "A romance novel. I'm writing a romance novel. I'm not ready to show it to anyone yet, and it's probably terrible anyway—I mean, some parts of it are okay? I think? And I haven't told anyone because you know how people treat romance novels, and I just thought, this event, seeing her, being around other people who love these books . . . I thought I'd feel like I belonged there."

I'm not sure why my brain picks the moment I declare myself a writer to prove I'm completely inarticulate. I brace myself for the taunts, but they don't come.

"That's . . . extremely cool," he says.

I wasn't expecting the relief to feel quite like this: my shoulders relaxing, a long exhale. I assumed he wouldn't understand the weight of a secret kept for so many years—except maybe he can.

"You really think so?"

He nods. "You writing a book? Yes, absolutely. I don't think I've ever written something longer than ten pages."

"I want—" I break off, collect myself. There's no going back now. "I want to be a writer. And not in the sense that I'm writing and that, by definition, makes me a writer—it's what I want to do with my life. And it feels . . . really lonely sometimes. Not the actual writing—of course that's mostly solitary. But feeling like I can't tell anyone, it almost makes me think it doesn't really exist. This book signing felt like some validation of that."

"I've read your papers," he says. "None of that was fiction, of course, but you're a good writer."

"Sure didn't stop you from nitpicking my grammar and punctuation," I say, but I want to relish the compliment. I want to embrace what I love all the time, not just with Neil on the last day of school, when the stakes are pretty much non-existent. I want to be fearless about it even when people judge it. "I guess it's like, in my head, my writing can be as great as I want it to be. But as soon as I declare I'm a writer, I'll have something to prove. It's hard to admit that you think you're good at something creative. And then it's so much worse for women. We're told to shrug off compliments, to scoff when someone tells us we're good at something. We shrink ourselves, convince ourselves what we're creating doesn't actually matter."

"But you can't believe that. That it doesn't matter."

"It's just as valid as becoming a lexicographer," I say, zero sarcasm in my voice.

"Maybe it's the whole concept of a guilty pleasure," Neil says gently. "Why should we feel guilty about something that brings us—pleasure?"

He stutters a bit before uttering that word, the tips of his ears turning pink.

I point at him. "Yes! Exactly. And it's usually things that women and teens or kids like."

"Not everything."

I raise an eyebrow. "Boy bands, fan fiction, soap operas, reality TV, most shows and movies with female main characters . . . We're still so rarely front and center, even rarer when you consider race and sexuality, and then when we do get something that's just for us, we're made to feel bad for liking it. We can't win."

His expression turns sheepish. "I've . . . never thought about it that way." Neil McNair admitting I'm right: another surreal moment.

Still, his agreement doesn't feel as validating as it should. If we'd talked about this one, two, three years ago . . . we could have had a Westview romance-novel revolution.

Neil swipes around on his phone. "Look at this." He's pulled up Delilah's Twitter. Her most recent tweet is from a few minutes ago.

Delilah Park @delilahshouldbewriting
AMAZING event tonight at Books & More! Thanks to everyone who showed up. I might read some pages from my next book at an open mic. Is Bernadette's any good?

"Do you know what she's talking about?"

"Oh. It's something she does sometimes. She always talks about the importance of reading writing out loud to really get the rhythm of it right, and she likes doing it with an audience."

"So why don't we go to that?"

I know he's trying to be helpful, and I appreciate that, I really do, but . . . "It's not the same," I say, feeling myself deflate. The whole point was to be around people who love what I love. "And we shouldn't waste any more time. Let's just move on."

He slips his phone back into his pocket. "If that's what you want."

I force it to be. We make a plan to return to my car and drive to Gas Works for the view clue. When we reach the bus stop along Phinney Avenue, hoping for a shortcut, the numbers on the digital sign inform us the 5 isn't coming for another twenty minutes. Though the sky looks ominous, we decide to walk. It's all downhill from here. Literally.

"It's weird no one's come after me," I say, my hands shoved deep in my pockets to guard against the cold, trying my best to banish Delilah from my mind. "I mean, we don't know how many of them teamed up. But it seems like everyone's been going for you, not for me."

Neil straightens. "Well, I *am* the valedictorian."

Ignoring him, I say, "It's making me uneasy, not knowing who it could be."

"We'll just continue to be careful," he says. "Three more clues. We can make it."

The first raindrop hits my cheek when we're a few blocks from the zoo.

"Okay, so what's on your shirt?" I ask. "It's been bothering me all day."

He grins. "It means 'anything sounds profound in Latin.' The literal translation is 'everything said in Latin seems deep.' But that sounds like Yoda-speak."

"Who?"

He staggers backward, clutching his heart. "*What* did you say? I might have to take back that nickname."

"No—" I start to protest before catching myself.

This makes him smile. "You like it," he says. There's a glint in his eyes, like he understands something I don't. "You like that nickname."

And . . . I kind of do. It hasn't felt irritating in a while. It's a language only we have, even if it's a reference I don't understand.

"It's original. And it's better than Ro-Ro, which is what my dad calls me."

The smile deepens. "Okay, Artoo. *Yoda*," he continues, as though informing me how a peanut butter and jelly sandwich is made, "is a Jedi master of an unknown species who trains Luke to use the Force."

"The little green guy?"

He groans, rubbing his eyes behind his glasses. "The little green guy," he confirms, resigned.

The street we're on is mostly residential, pastel-painted houses with progressive political signs in their front yards. The drizzle turns into a steady rain, making me miss my cardigan.

"So . . . if we're going to keep going, there's something I need to tell you," Neil says.

"Okay," I say, hesitant.

"Do you remember when we compared college acceptances?" I nod, and he continues. "I applied early decision to NYU's linguistics program. I was going to have to scrape for the application fees if I didn't get in, and then I held my breath, knowing I'd be relying on loans or financial aid or both. I sort of let you believe that I got lucky, and I did, but . . ." He turns sheepish. "I don't really talk about it with my friends, but I get . . . embarrassed sometimes. About money. And not having very much." He steals a glance at my face. "And this is exactly why I don't. Because it always gets this reaction, this sympathy. I don't want you to feel sorry for me, Artoo."

"I—I don't," I say quickly, though he's 100 percent right. I try to make my face look less sympathetic. "I just didn't know."

"I do a good job disguising it. The suits help. I scoured Goodwill until I found what I wanted. I learned to tailor them myself with my mom's old sewing machine, though I never did a perfect job. I worked overtime to save up for regional quiz bowl competitions. It's all about projecting an image. I feel like I've spent all of high school maintaining this image because I don't want people's pity. And when I get out of here, I just want to start fresh. I don't want to be Neil McNair, valedictorian, or Neil McNair, whose dad is in prison, or Neil McNair, the guy who never has enough money. I want to see who I am without all of that attached to me."

I sink my foot into a puddle that splashes muddy water up my knee socks. "I want you to have all of that," I say, meaning it. "Though if you don't want my sympathy, I'm not quite sure what else to say." Now it's my turn to be sheepish.

"Just . . . be normal. Don't change how you act because you know this about me. Don't let up on me." Rain soaks his hair, drips down his glasses. "I'd hope that you of all people wouldn't treat me differently."

"Okay. I won't. I still find you quite insufferable." Though I'm stuck on something else he said: *Don't let up on me.* After today, when will I have a chance not to?

However fun this is, however much I've enjoyed our conversations, I can't let myself forget that this—our rivalry, our partnership, even potentially our budding friendship—ends after tonight. Is there a word for what happens after your sworn nemesis lets you into their room and tells you their secrets?

"Good. I'd hate to disrupt the balance of the universe."

I want to roll my eyes at this, but despite the frustrations of the past hour, my face decides to pull my mouth into a smile.

And—I let it.

By the time we reach the car, we're soaked and shivering. I hurl myself inside. Neil is much more meticulous than I am, drying his glasses and the face of his watch with a few delicate swipes against the seat cushion.

When he sits down next to me, his hair is slicked with water, his T-shirt pasted to his skin. If I thought his T-shirt was revealing, his wet T-shirt is downright indecent.

I grope under the seat for my cardigan before remembering where it is. "I left my sweater at the record store." My teeth are chattering.

He removes a dry gray hoodie from his backpack. "Here," he says, holding it out to me. "Take this."

"Are you sure? We're both pretty soaked."

"Yeah, but you're wearing less." His face twists, brows coming together to form a pained expression. "I hope that didn't sound gross. I meant, you're not wearing anything underneath the dress except, uh, you know. Like, you don't have pants or tights or leggings under it. To be honest, I've never understood the difference between tights and leggings. I'm making it worse, aren't I? You're wearing a completely normal amount of clothing. Are you seriously going to let me keep talking?"

"Yes." Flustered Neil is never not funny. "I knew what you meant. Thanks." I zip the hoodie over my rain- and coffee-splattered dress. Then I blast the heat and retie the armband to his hoodie sleeve. "Leggings are footless and usually much thicker than tights."

It's not until I lean back in the seat, waiting for my car to warm up, that the scent of his hoodie hits me. It smells good, and I wonder if it's detergent or just the natural scent of Neil, one I've never really paid attention to before. I guess I've never been close enough to notice. I'm stunned by how much I don't hate it, so much so that it makes me light-headed for a split second.

It might also be the weed cookie warping my brain again.

He shoves his hands toward the vents.

"It'll heat up soon," I say. I'm afraid of the mythological beast I'll see in the mirror, but I sneak a glance anyway. My eyeliner has mostly faded, and mascara has migrated down my cheeks. I swipe it away, then tug the elastic out of my hair and open the car door so I can wring out the water as best I can. With the extra bobby pins in my cup holders, I pin it back up. My bangs, though . . .

"You're always messing with your hair."

I withdraw a hand from my bangs like I've been caught doing something I shouldn't be. It's strange when someone else notices your nervous habits. "My stupid bangs," I say with a sigh. "I can never decide what to do with them."

He studies me for a long moment, as though I am a sentence he's trying to translate into another language. "I like them the way they are," he says finally, which isn't helpful and somehow makes me more self-conscious.

I vow to cut them before graduation. I am not taking hair advice from Neil McNair.

I plug in my phone and put on the Smiths. Back to rainy-day music.

Neil groans. "Seriously, do you not have any happy music?"

"The Smiths are happy."

"No, this is mopey and depressing. What's this song called?"

"I don't want to say."

He grabs for my phone. I try to snatch it back, but he's quicker than I am. "'Heaven Knows I'm Miserable Now'?"

"It's a good song!"

He scrolls through my phone as we wait for the car to heat up. I'm gripped with that itchy someone's-messing-with-my-phone feeling. He selects a song by Depeche Mode and places the phone back in the cup holder. My shoulders relax.

"Gas Works?" I say, and Neil lets out a long-suffering sigh.

"It's not the best view, but fine. And we have to figure out this Cooper clue or we're fucked. I'm going to do some more sleuthing online, see if Sean or Adrian or Cyrus have any ideas."

With Neil on his phone, we drive in relative quiet for a few minutes, except for Dave Gahan singing about not being able to get enough. When I make a left turn, something in the back seat thuds to the floor.

Neil twists around to look. "You always carry around that many books with you?"

"Oh *shit*," I say, banging the steering wheel. "I was supposed to return those today!" It completely slipped my mind this morning with the power outage. "Do you think there's any chance school is still open?"

"Yeah, given that it's almost nine o'clock—no, Artoo. It's definitely closed."

"How much do you think the fine would be?"

"Per book? You have, what, five back there, so . . . a lot." He clucks his tongue. "I hear they don't let you walk if you have overdue books. It could be an urban legend, though. I haven't heard of it happening to anyone. Hey, you could be the first!" He glances at the books again and then back at me. "Well, I guess there's only one thing to do."

I blink at him, waiting for some magic solution.

"We have to break in."

I snort-laugh. "Right. The valedictorian and salutatorian breaking in to the school library. Not to mention, we can't keep taking detours like this."

"We're pretty solidly in the lead," he says, and he's right. "What other option is there if you don't want a fine? And if you want to walk on Sunday?"

I bite down on the inside of my cheek. Damn it, he's right. I don't want to risk not walking. I mean, I definitely don't believe him, but just in case.

"We'll be safe in there," he continues. "And we'll be fast. In and out."

I stop at an intersection before making the turn that will take us back to school. "Then I guess we're doing it. We're breaking in to the library."

Text conversation between Rowan Roth and Neil McNair
April of junior year

McNIGHTMARE

Mr. Kepler accidentally hinted at a pop quiz in 3rd period today.

I know you have him for 4th period, so I wanted to let you know,

So we're on equal footing and all.

that was . . . oddly nice?

are you broken?

8:51 p.m.

"PETRICHOR," NEIL SAYS as we creep toward the library. We parked a few blocks from the school to make sure no one would recognize my car. We're in a residential neighborhood, half the homes already shut down for the night. A man tugs his dog away from a row of flowers, while across the street a trio of girls in fancy dresses piles into a Lyft.

"What?" I ask, lugging the books in a canvas grocery bag.

"The smell of the earth after the rain," he says. "It's a great word, isn't it?"

I tug his hoodie closer. We're not soaking wet anymore, just a little damp. Now that we're outside again, I'm convinced the scent of his hoodie had to be the rain. I'm not still thinking about it, but if I were, it's just . . . petrichor.

"So you know the plan?" he says as we head down the sidewalk.

We discussed it in the car after googling "how to break in to a library" because we are nothing if not resourceful.

"Yep." I hold up the backpack filled with books. "We find a window and see if it's unlocked. Then we get in and drop off the books."

"And then we get the hell out," Neil says.

"You're sure there's no security system?"

"Not for the library."

We match each other's steps, and I try my best to ignore the scent of his hoodie.

"I can add this to the list of my sentimental late-night Westview memories," I say. "Right after hooking up with Luke Barrows for the first time in his car, parked right around . . . there." I point across the street.

He mock-gasps. "Rowan Roth, I thought you were a good girl."

That stops me in my tracks.

"I am," I say, extremely aware of the thud of my heartbeat, "but . . . that doesn't mean I'm a virgin."

"Oh—I didn't mean—"

"Because you assumed good girls—girls like me who get straight A's—don't have sex?" My voice is a little too hard-edged, but I can't help it. He fell right into something I happen to feel particularly strongly about. I don't know what's messing with my head more, wondering what Neil might have meant or that we're now officially talking about sex. "You realize how wrong and outdated that is, right? Good girls aren't supposed to have sex, but if they don't, they're prudes, and if they do, they're sluts. And of course, none of that takes the spectrum of gender or sexuality into account. Things are starting to change *slowly*, but the fact is, it's still completely different for guys."

Neil chokes on what I assume is his tongue, his wide eyes

indicating he had no idea this was where the conversation was going. "I wouldn't know," he says, clearly making every effort not to meet my gaze, "seeing as I've never . . . you know."

Oh my God, he can't even say the word.

"Had sex?" I say, and he nods.

"I've done other things," he adds quickly. "I've done . . . everything else, just about. Everything except . . ." He waves his hand.

Other things. My mind goes a bit wild with that, wondering if *other things* means the same for him as it does for me. And here's my answer to the question I had earlier: Neil is a virgin.

"Sex."

"Yeah."

"It's not a bad word," I say.

"I know that."

We start walking again. A few years ago, I'd have been utterly embarrassed by this conversation. While my friends and I have had these kinds of discussions—Kirby won't miss an opportunity to rail on the patriarchy—I've never talked like this with a guy. Not Luke, not Spencer. Romance novels should have made me less afraid. I've read the words so many times. I should be able to say them out loud, but it hasn't been easy when I can't even admit I love those books in the first place. And here I am, finally saying what I want, and it's with Neil of all people.

"You've . . . ?" he says, letting me fill in the blank.

"Yeah, with Spencer. And Luke," I say, and I appreciate that he doesn't have a dramatic reaction to this. "I don't know why it should be embarrassing when so many of us think about it so often. And yet it's especially taboo for girls to talk about it." This is another reason I love romance novels: the way they attempt to normalize these conversations. Not saying the world would be better if more people read romance novels, but . . . well, yeah. I am. "Masturbation is the worst double standard."

The sky is nearly black, but a streetlamp slashes light across his extremely red face.

"I'm . . . familiar with the topic."

I snort. "I'm sure you are. It's just assumed that guys do it, so much so that guys can even joke about it. But for girls, it sometimes still feels like this dirty thing we're not supposed to talk about, even though it's perfectly healthy and plenty of us do it."

"So you . . ."

"I mean, I'm not going to give you a play-by-play."

He coughs again, and it turns into a choking fit. This is it. I have murdered Neil McNair.

He holds up a hand as though to assure me he's okay. "I've learned a lot tonight."

We've reached the senior parking lot on the edge of the library. I'm grateful to refocus on the reason we're here, because truthfully, the conversation was making me a little feverish. And my brain won't quit with the *other things* spiral, summoning a variety of helpful images to fill in the many, many options.

More likely, though, I'm anxious about the break-in. That would account for my increased heart rate.

"I'll go check these windows," McNair says, jogging several yards away, and once he leaves my general bubble, I let out a long, shaky breath and rearrange my bangs.

First I try the back library door. It doesn't budge. "Back door's locked," I call to Neil. I push at a window. "Damn it. If anyone spots us here, do you think they'd rob us of our titles? I mean . . . we're breaking and entering to return books. They wouldn't call the police, would they? Since we go here? Or went here? All of these are stuck. There's supposed to be something you can do with a credit card, right?"

I unearth a card from my backpack and locate a very helpful wikiHow. "It says to wedge the card into the gap between the door and the frame, and—Neil?"

I turn to Neil, who's suddenly struggling to muffle a laugh. He fantastically fails, the laughter sputtering out.

"What? What's so funny?"

He shakes his head, doubling over as he clutches his stomach. I get the sense he's laughing at *me*.

"Neil McNair. I demand you explain yourself."

He holds up a finger and digs into his pocket, revealing a key ring. "I—I work here," he manages to say around a laugh. "Or—worked here. I should probably turn this thing in while we're here."

"Seriously? This whole time?" I reach for them, but he holds them out of my grasp. "Why didn't you tell me you still had a key?" But I'm laughing too. A little bit.

"I wanted to see if you'd actually try to do it. I didn't think it would go this far. I thought you'd give up sooner."

"You are the worst," I say, shoving his shoulder.

Still howling with laughter, he turns the key in the lock, and then we're in.

We use the light from our phones to guide us to the circulation desk.

"It's kind of eerie in here," I say.

He must sense I'm nervous, because he says in a soft voice, "It's just us, Artoo."

"You know, I've never seen *Star Wars*."

"You haven't seen the originals," he corrects, but I shake my head. "Wait. What." He shines his phone light on my face, making me squint.

"I told you I didn't know who Yoda was!"

"Yoda is barely in the new ones. I assumed you'd at least seen one of those!"

"I think I saw a few minutes of one at a party? All I remember is a really moody guy all in black."

"You *think*? You'd know, Rowan. You'd know," he says. "We have to watch them."

Now I turn my phone light on him. And I stare. "*We* have to watch them?"

He flushes, using a hand to shield his face from my phone's

light. "*You* have to watch them. Not with me. Why would we do that?"

"I have no idea," I say, lifting my shoulders in an exaggerated shrug. "You're the one who suggested it. And now you're blushing."

"Because you're interrogating me!" He whips off his glasses to rub at his eyes. "It was a slip of the tongue. And I hate that too, almost as much as the freckles. It always gives away how I'm feeling. I've never been able to talk to a cute girl without turning into a fucking tomato."

"Would I fall into that category?"

His deepening blush says it all. Huh. Neil McNair thinks I am a cute girl.

"You know you're not unattractive," he says after a few seconds of silence. "You don't need me to validate that."

True, I don't, but that doesn't mean it's not nice to hear. I must really be starved for compliments if "not unattractive" makes me feel this great about myself, if the warmth in my chest is any indication.

"Should I just leave them here?" I ask, taking the books out of my backpack. "Or should I write a note or something?"

"As much as I'd love to write in calligraphy 'Rowan Roth's overdue library books,' you should probably just drop them in the slot."

One by one, I feed each book to the return. They land with increasingly loud thumps.

I've been at Westview after hours plenty of times. I know this school so well: best locker locations, which vending machines are always out of order, quickest route to the gym for assemblies. But tonight . . . it really is spooky. It doesn't feel like my school."

I guess it isn't anymore.

We should go, I try to say, because I want so badly to win that money for him, but instead, I find myself drifting toward the stacks. Neil follows me. The library may be eerie, but it's also peaceful.

"I really will miss all of this," I say, running my fingers along the spines.

"I think they have libraries in Boston. Big ones."

I nudge his shoulder. "You know what I mean. This might actually be our last time in here."

"Isn't that kind of a good thing?"

I lean against the stack of books opposite him. "I'm not sure." I reach into my backpack, pull out the success guide. We've already shared so much today. After you've cried on your nemesis's shoulder, what boundaries are left? "I was so wrapped up in having this perfect high school experience, and I can't help feeling disappointed that the reality isn't what I thought it would be. You're going to make fun of me, but . . . here's that success guide."

He accepts the wrinkled sheet of paper and scans it, one corner of his mouth tilting upward. I wonder what he's smiling at: figuring out my bangs or making out with someone under the bleachers.

"I guess I thought I'd be this very specific person by now," I continue. "And I'm just—not."

When he gets to the end, he taps number ten in this matter-of-fact way. "'Destroy Neil McNair,'" he reads. "I can't say destroying you wouldn't have been on my own hypothetical success guide."

"Obviously, I failed. At everything."

He's still staring at it, and it's killing me not knowing what's going through his head. "You wanted to be an English teacher? 'Mold young minds'?"

"What, you don't think I'd be a good mind molder?"

"I actually think you would be. If you could get over your distaste for the classics." He passes it back to me, and I'm both relieved and disappointed he didn't say anything about the perfect boyfriend thing, if only because I'm curious what he would have said. "It's not a bad list. I don't know if it's realistic, but . . . do you still want any of these things?"

The thought has crossed my mind a couple times today—before I've soundly dismissed it.

"Some of the ones it's still possible to achieve, yes. It's not something I think about very often, but I'd love to be fluent in Spanish," I say. "My mom is, and her whole family is, and I've always wished I learned it when I was younger."

"It isn't too late, you know."

I groan with the knowledge of him being right.

"And there was a reason you stopped taking Spanish." When I shrug, he says, "Because your interests changed. Other things became more important for a while. It's the same reason you don't want to be a teacher anymore. You can't tie yourself to this list you made when you were fourteen. Who still wants the same things they did at fourteen?"

"Some people do."

"Sure," he says. "But plenty don't. People *change*, Rowan. Thank God they do. We both know I was an arrogant little shit at fourteen, though it didn't stop you from crushing on me."

"Twelve. Days."

He smirks—funny he thinks the arrogance is a thing of the past. "Maybe this version of you would have been cool," he says, tapping the paper again. "But . . . you're kind of great now, too."

Kind of great.

The compliment turns my heart wild. I slide down the bookshelf, settling onto the carpet, and he mirrors me, so we're facing each other.

"I just wish it didn't have to end right now," I say, though part of me would love for him to elaborate on all the specific ways in which I'm *kind of great*. "I wish I had more time."

It's not until I say it out loud that I realize it's true. *Time.* That's what I've been chasing all day, this notion that after tonight, after graduation, none of us will be in the same city again. The things that mattered to us for the past four years will shift and evolve, and I imagine they'll keep doing that forever. It's terrifying.

"Artoo. Maybe you didn't do everything on this list, but you did a *lot*. You were president of three clubs, editor of the yearbook, copresident of student council . . ." The smirk returns as he adds: ". . . salutatorian."

But it doesn't bother me anymore. I tug up my knee socks, which are damp and muddy. Howl has wreaked havoc on my perfect last-day outfit.

"It's strange, though, isn't it?" I say. "Thinking about our specific group of seniors all spread out next year? Most of us will only be home for breaks, and then less and less after that. We won't see each other every day. Like, if I see you on the street—"

"On the street? What exactly am I doing 'on the street'? Am I okay?"

"You're probably selling your signed collection of Riley Rodriguez books for pizza money."

"A whole signed collection? Sounds like I'm doing great, then."

I stretch across the aisle to swat his arm with my hoodie sleeve, which is, well, his hoodie sleeve. "Fine, if I *run into you*, how are we supposed to act? What are we to each other when we're not fighting to be the best?"

"I think it would be kind of like how we are tonight," he says softly. He taps my ballet flat with his sneaker, and while my brain tells my foot to shift away from his, for some reason, the message doesn't quite get there, and my shoe stays put. "Kind of like . . . friends."

Friends. I've competed with Neil McNair as long as I've known him. I've spent so much time wondering how to beat him, but I've never considered him a friend.

The truth is, I'm having more fun with him than I've had in a while. Here he is, this secret source of deep conversations and adventures and *fun*. I was so sure I'd be sick of him by now, but the opposite is true. We only have three clues left. Finishing the game means severing whatever connection we've forged. It means graduation and summer and getting on two different planes at the end of it. Maybe that's why I'm reluctant to leave the library—because, of all the things I've learned about him today, at the top of the list is that I genuinely enjoy spending time with him. I thought beating him would feel incredible, but all of this feels so much better.

It makes me wish, again, that I'd realized sooner that we could have been more than rivals. I wonder if he feels it too, this desire to have had more talks like this over mediocre pizza. And whether that makes us friends or just two people who were supposed to meet somewhere but got lost along the way.

"Yeah," I say, ignoring this weird flip my stomach does that must be caused by this after-hours heart-to-heart. I should move my shoe away from his. Rowan Roth and Neil McNair, even as friends, don't do shoe-to-shoe contact. I don't know what they do. "I guess we could be that."

I lean back against my stack of books, feeling less comforted by the biographies of incredible women quite literally backing me up than I thought I might. Neil and I have been in close proximity in too many dark places tonight. It's rearranged my molecules, made me unsure of things I thought I was certain about.

Example: how much I like not just his arms or his stomach but *him*, and the way he looked at me when he told me I was "kind of great."

But that's absurd. Isn't it? Of all the things on my success guide that I got wrong, Neil is definitely not the perfect high school boyfriend. It's just that it's hard to remember that when our shoes are touching or when a streetlamp outside catches the softest angles of his face.

"Now that we're friends," he says, "can you tell me more about your book?"

His words remind me how close I was to meeting Delilah Park. She's probably back at her hotel at this point. Off to her next tour stop tomorrow.

If I can't be brave there, maybe I can be brave here.

"You really want to know?" When he nods, I take a deep breath. Anything to take my mind off whatever's happening with our shoes and what I may or may not want to happen with the rest of our bodies. "It's . . . sort of a workplace romance. Between two coworkers."

Hannah and Hayden. Two made-up people who've lived in my head since the summer before junior year. Hannah came to me first, a free-spirited, smart-mouthed lawyer with a mix of traits from my favorite heroines. Then Hayden, the uptight attorney with a hidden soft side, challenging her for a promotion. Opposites attract is my favorite trope, so it made sense to start there. Because, of course, the thing about opposites: they always have a lot more in common than they think.

Sometimes I think about them before I go to sleep, then dream about them. Telling Neil about them feels like I'm telling him about my imaginary friends. In a way, I kind of am.

"Was that so hard to say?"

"Yes! It was," I say, but now that it's out there, it doesn't feel nearly as terrifying.

"Isn't the whole point of being a writer for someone to read your stuff?"

"I mean—yes, ugh, but I haven't gotten there yet," I protest. "It's . . . complicated. No one's ever read anything I've written that wasn't for school."

Theoretically, I *want* to share my work. I want to fully own this thing I want to spend my life doing. I want to not care when people call it a guilty pleasure, or have the courage to convince them why they're wrong. Or even better, the confidence not to care what they think.

"You want to, though," he says.

I nod.

"Let's say you're not instantly perfect at this. You keep trying. You get better."

"I don't know, that sounds like a lot of work," I say, and he rolls his eyes.

"I have an idea. But you might hate it." When I lift my eyebrows at him, he continues: "What if . . . you let me read it? Just a page or two? What could be scarier than me reading it, right?"

Surprisingly, I don't hate his suggestion. His expression is soft, and I'm convinced he wouldn't laugh at it. What's more surprising is that I want to show him. He loves words as much as I do—I want to know what he thinks.

"You wrote a fucking *book*. Do you know how many people wish they could do that, or how many people talk about doing it and never do?" He shakes his head, as though he's impressed by me, and I want so badly to be that impressed with myself. "You saw *Vision in White* in my room. I'm not the guy I was freshman year. And you can tell me to stop whenever you want, okay? I'll put it down as soon as you say the word."

He's being so sweet about this. I want to tell him how much this lack of judgment means to me, but maybe it's easier to show him.

"I—I know." With trembling hands, I find the file on my phone and pass it to him. I shut my eyes, my heart pounding. I can't see him, but I can sense him right next to me, hear the softest swipe of his thumb on the phone screen.

"Chapter one," he starts.

"Oh my God. Please don't read it out loud."

"Fine, fine." He goes quiet, and I last only a few seconds before I lose it.

"I take it back. The silence is worse."

He laughs. "Do you want me to just not read it?"

I let out a shaky breath, wiggling my shoulders to release the tension there. "No. This is good for me. Keep going, and I'll tell you when to stop."

"Okay," he says. *"Chapter one. Hannah had despised Hayden for two years, one month, four days, and fifteen—no, sixteen—minutes...."*

Chapter 1

Hannah had despised Hayden for two years, one month, four days, and fifteen—no, sixteen—minutes.

She remembered the exact moment he'd walked into the office, his suit impeccable, not a hair on his head out of place. She knew because she'd been glancing—okay, staring—at the clock that hung above her desk, counting down the minutes until her boss's next meltdown.

She'd already heard more than she wanted to about this new hire, a graduate from Yale Law who also held an MBA from Penn. No one else at the firm had multiple advanced degrees, and Hannah knew this thrilled the partners; the trio of salt-and-pepper-haired men in the swanky corner office.

Hannah, however, was a little less thrilled. She was on track to be made partner, and she wasn't about to let this multiple-degreed hotshot get in her way. Not when she'd given the firm sixty, seventy, eighty hours a week for the past five years of her life. She hadn't gone on a vacation or a second date since law school, but it would all be worth it when she had a swanky corner office too.

If Hayden Walker didn't get in her way.

So she watched as he flicked raindrops off his jacket and made his way toward his desk, which happened to be right across from hers.

He gazed down at her with electric-blue eyes. "Are you my secretary?" he'd asked.

Of course he had a British accent.

9:20 p.m.

"You can stop there," I say softly.

Without missing a beat, he passes my phone back to me. He doesn't try to read ahead or hang on to it any longer—he listens. He didn't put on a voice, not even when he was reading the dialogue. He read it like he was in front of the classroom, giving a presentation. When I finally regain enough composure to look at him, his cheeks are flushed.

I liked how my words sounded in his voice.

"That was . . ."

"Horrible? Should I quit? I'll quit."

"No. God, no. Not at all. Artoo, that was really, really good. You should have used a comma in that third paragraph, not a semicolon—"

"I sincerely despise you."

He offers a sheepish smile. "You're a great writer. I mean it. That was so . . . *tense*."

Now I'm blushing too. Neil McNair likes my writing. More than that, hearing him read it made me realize how much I like this story and these characters.

"Nothing even happened between them," I say.

"It's the anticipation, though. The reader *knows* something will happen."

"The anticipation is great, don't get me wrong. I love it. But I love the happily-ever-after that a romance novel almost always guarantees. Even if it's not realistic."

"Happiness is, though," Neil says. "Or it can be. Maybe not ever-after kind of happiness, but that doesn't make it any less real. My mom and Christopher have gone through a lot. Shouldn't you want that other person to help you through difficult stuff?"

"That kind of stuff doesn't happen after the epilogue," I admit. "Most of Delilah's books end with a marriage or a proposal and the assumption that everything's going to be perfect. I know sometimes it really is just a fantasy. Obviously, Spencer and I weren't perfect."

Spencer, the boy I tried to force into the role I'd dreamed up. What would the past semester have looked like if I'd broken up with him, given myself permission not to have a PHSB by the end of it? I could have had more fun, I'm sure. I could have spent more time with Kirby and Mara instead of trying to interpret Spencer's latest cryptic text.

"I've never felt that way about anyone either," he says, and I sit a little straighter, ready for more Neil McNair Relationship History. "The relationships I had . . . They were nice, but not earth-shattering. I don't know. Are relationships supposed to feel that way?"

"Earth-shattering?"

"Yeah. Like every moment you're with them, your head is spinning and you can't catch your breath and you just know that this person is changing your life for the better. Someone who challenges *you* to be better."

"I—I think so," I say, because he's caught me off guard, and I really am unsure. Spencer didn't challenge me—he wasn't a question on an AP exam. What I don't tell Neil is that I've been looking for that earth-shattering love too, and sometimes I want it so badly, I'm convinced I could wish it into existence.

"You're going to think this is bonkers, but Bailey and I . . . We broke up because she thought I had a thing for you."

I snort. Loudly. It's so ludicrous. "Oh my God. Kirby and Mara—they think I'm obsessed with you."

"My friends think I'm obsessed with *you*!"

This sends us into a fit of laughter for a solid couple minutes.

Neil recovers first. "I really thought romance novels were just . . ." He waves his hand. "Sex." Though he says it a little less awkwardly this time, he still leaves plenty of space around the word.

"Well. That's often part of it, but not all the time. And . . . I definitely don't hate that part. But they're so much more than that. They're about the characters and their relationships. How they complement and challenge each other, how they overcome something together." I break off, then add: "Although they did lead me to believe my first kiss would be more magical than it actually was."

"Now I'm curious."

"Gavin Hawley. Seventh grade. We both had braces. We were doomed."

"I'll do you one better. You know how I get nosebleeds in the winter?"

"Oh. Oh no."

"Oh yes," he says. "Chloe Lim, eighth grade. In the cafeteria, which in hindsight was absolutely the worst idea I've ever had. Everyone called it the Red Necking." This makes me snort-laugh, and he shakes his head. "I was traumatized. I didn't kiss another girl for two years after that."

But he's laughing too. I love the sound of his laugh, and the way he looks when he's laughing. It's like he lets himself go, forgets that he's supposed to be stiff and smug. I don't think I'd ever really seen it until today.

"Will you finally sign my yearbook now?" he asks when we quiet down. "I have to have a Rowan Roth autograph for when you get famous."

A waterfall of relief. "I've been feeling like garbage ever since I said no."

I write the nicest message I can muster, one that recounts some of our past rivalries and wishes him all the best next year. Neil takes his time. The pen stops and starts, and he taps it on his chin, smudges his hand with ink.

When we swap back, I make a move to open mine up, but he lunges for it.

"Don't read it until tomorrow," he says.

"It's almost tomorrow."

He rolls his eyes. "Just don't read it while I'm here, okay?"

Naturally, it makes me more curious, but given that I only just let someone read my writing, I can't blame him. It can be awkward to read a yearbook message in front of the person who wrote it.

"Fine. Then don't read mine, either." I tuck the yearbook into my backpack. "We should go. Unless there are any clues we could find here?"

"Oh—a floppy disk!" I'm positive it's the most enthusiastic anyone's been about a floppy disk in at least two decades. "This is exactly where we'd find one, right? I'll check the resource room." He jumps to his feet, but before he leaves our aisle, he kneels back down as though he forgot something. "The one down the hall. Next to the science wing. I just want to be really clear about where I'm going this time. I know you get freaked out when I leave."

When he comes back five minutes later, he's holding a floppy disk, a roll of streamers, and a pack of Skittles.

"I assume that doesn't have anything to do with the mysterious Mr. Cooper," I say, gesturing to the streamers and the Skittles.

"I had this idea." He places everything on the circulation desk, spending an inordinate amount of time arranging each object, as though mulling what he's going to say next. "You didn't go to prom. We've been talking so much about high school ending, and it seems to be this quintessential high school experience, at least if movies and TV are to be believed."

"Right..."

"Well, the food was pretty mediocre." He holds up the Skittles. "And here's an appropriately cheesy song." He scrolls through his phone, then hits play on an old song from *High School Musical*, and I snort because it really is cheesy. "My sister just discovered it. I will graciously accept your condolences." Then he makes his face serious, sliding his phone onto the circulation desk and holding out his hand. "It won't be the perfect prom from your success guide, but... will you go to prom with me?"

I stop laughing because while part of me finds this corny as hell, it's also incredibly sweet. My heart is in my throat. I can't remember the last time someone did something this nice for me.

Behind his glasses, his gaze is steady. Unwavering. It makes me even more aware of how wobbly I've suddenly become.

"We should leave" is what comes out instead of *yes*. Clearly, my brain-to-mouth connection is broken when it comes to him.

His expression doesn't falter. "One dance?"

And God, he looks so earnest in the darkness that I have no idea why I didn't give him my hand immediately.

"Fine," I relent, "but not this one."

I find something else on my own phone, something soft and lovely by Smokey Robinson and the Miracles.

"Much better," he agrees.

I slide one hand into his and bring my other up to his shoulder, while his free hand settles on my waist. I've danced with people before—Spencer, Luke, a couple awkward guys in middle school—but we'd already been dating. This is uncharted territory. Because we're the same height, we're staring directly into each other's eyes, my right hand clasped in his left.

"We don't have to leave room for Jesus," he says. "Or whatever the Jewish equivalent is. If there is one. Leave room for Moses?"

"Leave the door open for Elijah," I say, and he snorts.

"Yes. That's the Jewish version."

"And we're the worst Jews." Still, I inch closer. "But it's awkward, staring at you like this. I'm going to spend this whole thing trying not to laugh."

He shifts so his hand on my lower back gently pushes me closer to him, so I can rest my head in the space where his neck meets his shoulder. Oh. Wow. We are . . . much closer than we were a second ago, and he is solid and confident and *warm*, which I don't understand, since he's been in a T-shirt most of the day. God. That dorky T-shirt. QUIDQUID LATINE DICTUM, ALTUM VIDETUR. It might as well mean "look at these sick biceps."

"Better?" he asks, his breath hot on my cheek, my ear. That single word travels down my spine and into my toes, an electric current. I'm reminded of my freshman-year crush, when for twelve days I fantasized about the two of us going to homecoming together. Is this what it would have been like? How he would have held me?

Probably not, I decide. I towered over him back then, before his growth spurt brought him up to my height. And he was scrawny, and now he is decidedly . . . not.

"Mm-hmm," I manage to say, but I'm not actually sure it is. It's both better and worse because Neil McNair is a fucking paradox. That good hoodie smell from earlier—it wasn't the rain. It was just *him*. If my face is flushed from being this close, at least he can't see it.

"Good."

As we sway back and forth to the music, one thing becomes apparent right away:

"I'm not great at this," I say after apologizing for stepping on his feet.

It transports me to this scene in *Sweet as Sugar Lake*, where diner owner Emma closed the place early so she could teach her best friend (and longtime crush) Charlie how to dance before his brother's wedding. It still stings, missing my chance to take a photo with the replica of the Sugar Lake gazebo Delilah was bringing on tour.

"It's okay. I make up for it."

It's arrogant but true. He's *good*, while my dancing style draws inspiration from those floppy things at car dealerships. "You are, like, absurdly good."

"I took dance as a kid. Ballet and jazz, mostly. A couple tap classes here and there."

"That is really cool," I say, and it is. "My cousin Sophie is a choreographer. Or, she's studying it in college. She and Kirby and Mara have tried to teach me, but I am a total lost cause. Do you have any sick moves? I want to see some sick moves."

"I'm afraid this is the extent of my sick moves these days," he says, and at that, he guides me through a gentle spin, and when I wind up exactly where I started, my level of impressed is officially off the charts. His limbs are more confident moving to a rhythm than they are the rest of the time. I can't believe this is the same boy who wore a suit with too-long sleeves earlier today.

Neil being this good a dancer—it's kind of hot.

The realization turns me inside out, as though my traitorous heart and brain are on display for him to see.

"What made you stop dancing?" I ask his shoulder, no longer able to make eye contact. If I don't keep talking, I'm going to spiral. *Neil. Hot.* My brain has gone rogue, and with it my trembling hands, which he tries his best to keep steady. *Because he's a good dancer. Which I find hot.* Damn it. Spiraling. I try to summon memories of the past few years, the times he made me so furious I couldn't see straight.

It doesn't work.

"School got too busy," he says. There's some sadness there that only increases my tenderness for him. "And my dad never liked that I was interested in it."

"Maybe you could take some classes in college."

"Maybe," he echoes as the song changes. *One dance*, he said. I'm certain he'll let go, but he doesn't, and I remain firmly in his arms. "I've missed it. This is . . . nice."

It is. It's so fucking nice, but it's fleeting, like everything else about tonight. I can't get too attached. All of it is about five kinds of concerning. Neil isn't my PHSB. He's not the guy who would make out underneath the bleachers or hold my hand during a movie. He wouldn't take ridiculous selfies with me and post them with ironic hashtags I kind of unironically like, or declare his love with a bouquet of roses. He is not a romance-novel hero.

"It's probably nicer if you're actually into the person you're dancing with."

Immediately, I realize it was the wrong thing to say. *Shit.* He stiffens. It lasts only a second, but it's enough to drop us out of time with the song.

"Yeah. I'm sure it is."

I bite down hard on the inside of my cheek. I wanted to stop the current of emotions threatening to pull me under, but clearly I went too far. I should tell him I'm not imagining anyone else at all. That I've grown dizzy with the scent of him. That it would be impossible to think of anyone but him when we are touching like his, when his hand is spread across my back, when my lashes brush against his neck every time I blink.

"I mean," I backtrack, stepping on his toes and muttering an apology. "Not that I don't like dancing with you. I just—"

"I get it." Without warning, he lets go of my hand. "You were right earlier. We should get going."

"We—um—right." I stumble over the words, over my feet, which struggle to move on their own. The mood changed so quickly it gave me whiplash, the temperature in the room dropping from balmy to subzero. I grab for my phone to anchor me. "There's another Howl update."

We're still in the lead: 13 for Neil and me, 9 for both Brady and Mara, and 8 for Carolyn Gao.

"Good job, Brady," Neil says with a low whistle.

I've also missed about a dozen notifications in my Two Birds group chat.

> **COLLEEN**
>
> Can anyone close for me tonight?? My kid threw up at a sleepover, and I have to go get him ☹
>
> Anyone?? I'll give you all my tips from today.

All the other employees have responded that they can't do it, that they already have Friday plans they can't get out of. The most recent message is from Colleen again, just my name with three question marks.

"After the floppy disk, we're down to two. The view and Mr. Cooper. For the view, we should really do Kerry Park. It's my favorite spot in Seattle," Neil is saying as I debate how to reply to the message. He must notice I'm distracted. "What is it?"

"It's work," I say. "Two Birds One Scone. My boss needs someone to close up the café tonight, and I'm the only one who's available. Do you mind if we make a quick stop there? It'll take ten minutes, I swear."

"Oh. Sure, okay." There's a chilliness in his voice I'm pretty sure isn't entirely related to this detour.

I shouldn't have implied I wished he were someone else. No one would be thrilled to hear that while dancing with someone, even if that person is their sworn enemy. I'm cursed to never say the right thing around him—but I'm starting to wonder if I have any idea what that right thing is.

It's the yearbook incident all over again. Was I so worried about the kind of friendliness a "yes" would connote that I leaped to "no"? Is my subconscious trying to protect me from getting too close, or am I really that scared of what acknowledging these feelings would mean? Because it's clear now—they mean something. If I've learned anything from romance novels, it's that the heart is an unflappable muscle. You can ignore it for only so long.

Neil picks up his backpack. All of a sudden, I can't bear the thought of leaving this place. Not the school or the library itself, but this moment. With him.

But I force my feet to follow his as we creep back outside, the door locking automatically behind us. We don't talk as we make our way to my car, and it's only once we're in the semi-light of the streetlamps that I open my mouth to speak.

"Thank you," I say, reaching out to graze his bare arm with my fingertips. He's cold too. "For all of that. Though I doubt the actual prom was quite as extravagant. They probably had the generic brand of Skittles."

What I don't say is that somehow I'm positive this was better than prom. I can barely remember how I imagined it. Sure, the PHSB and I would have danced, but we would have been dating for a while. Would it have been as exciting as dancing with Neil for the first time? Would I have shivered when his hand dipped to my lower back or when his breath whispered across my ear?

Thank God, he half smiles at that. "Only the best for Rowan Roth," he says, and then I'm spiraling again.

In the light, his freckles are almost glowing, his hair a golden amber. Everything about him is softer nearly to the point of appearing blurry, like I can't quite tell who this new version of Neil McNair is, leaving me more uncertain than ever.

AN INCOMPLETE LIST OF NEIL MCNAIR'S FAVORITE WORDS

- petrichor: the scent of the earth after it rains (English)
- tsundoku: acquiring more books than you could ever read (Japanese)
- hygge: a warm, cozy feeling associated with relaxing, eating, and drinking with loved ones (Danish)
- Fernweh: a feeling of homesickness for a place you've never been (German)
- Fremdschämen: the feeling of shame on someone else's behalf; secondhand embarrassment (German)
- davka: the opposite of what is expected (Hebrew)

10:09 p.m.

"THANK YOU SO much," Colleen says as she unties her apron. "I would have closed up early, but we had a last-minute rush." She lists the remaining tasks: wiping tables, washing dishes, and wrapping up any remaining pastries for tomorrow's day-old bin.

"It's no problem. You know I love this place."

Neil leans against the pastry case, scoping out the goods. If Colleen wonders why he's here, she blessedly doesn't ask.

Colleen grabs her purse. "We'll miss you next year."

"I'll be back on breaks," I insist. "You know I can't resist those cinnamon rolls."

"That's what all the college kids say. But then they get busy, or they want to spend time with their friends, or they move away for good. It happens. Whether you come back to work or not, there will always be a cinnamon roll with your name on it."

I want to tell her I won't be one of those people, but the truth is, there's no way to know.

Colleen leaves us alone in this small café. During the car ride, I couldn't stop thinking about the dance. I was so wrapped up in it that I relinquished music privileges, letting him play a Free

Puppies! song he claimed was their best. But I could barely hear it.

Being that close to him in the library muddied my feelings. I tried to rationalize it: I'm exhausted, and the game has turned me delirious. My mind is playing tricks on me, convincing me I feel something for him I'm positive I didn't feel yesterday. Or my body was craving closeness to another person's. I'm a writer—I can make up a hundred different reasons.

The things I said, though, about wishing he were someone else—they hurt his ego. They must have. But I don't like us like this. I didn't like it after the assembly this morning, when I refused to sign his yearbook, and I don't like it now. Or maybe it's that I like this too much, and that's even scarier. Neil is softer than I realized, and I'm a barbed-wire fence. Every time he gets too close, I make myself sharper.

"What should we do first?" he asks.

I reach into the pastry case. "Well, *I* am having a cinnamon roll. And you should too."

It's not a perfect spiral, because as Colleen is fond of telling us, imperfect-looking food tastes the best. I hold the plate near Neil's face, letting him inhale the sweet cinnamon sugar. Before he can take a bite, I snatch it away.

"Icing first," I say, heading back into the kitchen.

All I want is for us to be normal after what happened in the library, and my brilliant plan is to ignore it. I cannot like him this way. It's the opposite of destroying him, and even if that's no longer my goal, until about seven hours ago, he was my enemy. He's Neil

McNair, and I'm Rowan Roth, and that used to mean something.

I open the refrigerator, the cold a welcome blast against my face, but it doesn't slow my wild heart.

"Cream cheese icing?" he asks, a teasing lilt to his voice.

"I'm never going to forgive my parents."

"I for one appreciated the Rowan Roth Fun Facts." He leans against the counter, and it looks so casual. Maybe the dance loosened him up, which is ironic because it only tied me into knots. I haven't felt this tense since my AP Calculus test, and maybe not even then. "Like Kevin fever. That was gold."

I groan. After I rejoined the dinner table, my parents told him all he could ever hope to know about the Riley books and their lives as writers, including how they used to complain they had cabin fever when they holed up in the house on deadline. When I was younger, I thought they were saying "Kevin fever," and one day I asked, thoroughly worried, if Kevin was okay.

"I'm not afraid to use this as a weapon," I say, holding up the tub of icing. "And hey. If you want to talk embarrassing parents, we should talk about how your mom knew exactly where I'm going to school."

"The school sent out a list. My mom is very invested in my education." He nods toward the icing. "And I think you're bluffing."

Only because I'll rinse out this tub afterward, I dip my index finger inside, and before I can overthink it, I dab icing onto his freckled cheek.

For a moment, he's frozen. And then: "I can't believe you just did that," he says, but he's laughing. He reaches into the container and swipes an icing-coated finger across my eyebrow. It's cold but not unpleasant. "There. We're even."

Our gazes lock for a few seconds, a staring contest. His eyes are still bright with laughter. I'm not about to turn this into an all-out food fight, not when the library dance is still so fresh in my mind. That just sounds dangerous.

Then something frightening happens: I get the strangest urge to *lick the icing off his face*.

This is *fun*. I'm having fun with Neil McNair, whose face I want to lick icing off of.

Thor help me.

"Somehow I get the feeling this is the opposite of what we were supposed to do here," he says, reaching for the roll of paper towels behind him.

With the back of my hand, I wipe icing off my eyebrow, trying to ignore the hammering of my heart. In one swift motion, I grab a palette knife and spread icing on a much safer place: the cinnamon roll. I slice it in half, the sugary cinnamon oozing out the sides.

His eyes flutter closed as he takes a bite. "Exquisite," he says, and I feel a little thrill, as though I baked it myself. I don't even have the urge to make fun of his word choice.

"You eat. I'll wash these dishes."

He frowns, setting his plate down on the counter. "I'll help you."

"No, no. It's my job. This is why they pay me the big bucks."

"Artoo. I'm not going to sit here watching you do the dishes."

I polish off my half of the cinnamon roll. I guess we'd get done faster, and it *would* be weird for him to just stand there watching. So he turns on some Free Puppies!, insisting this is their best song, but that's what he said about their last three songs. And then together, we wash dishes.

He even sings along in this unselfconscious way. He has to change registers to get all the notes, which sometimes happens in the middle of a line, and it cracks me up every time. Most people wouldn't feel this confident singing around someone else. I can admit the band has one good song. Fine, maybe two. And maybe I join in when "Pawing at Your Door" comes on, and we belt out the chorus together.

This is officially the weirdest day of my life.

"Seriously, thank you," I say for the tenth time, hanging a frying pan on the drying rack. "Is this what being friends would have been like?"

"Washing dishes and eating cinnamon rolls and talking about being Jewish? One hundred percent," he says. Soapsuds climb up his caramel-dotted arms. "Think about all the movies we could have seen, all the Shabbat dinners we could have had together."

Something about the way he says that last one tugs at my heart. The feeling is similar to the nostalgia I've felt all day, except this is a nostalgia for something that never actually happened. There has to be a word for that specific brand of wistfulness.

Regret.

Maybe that's what it is.

We could have had this. Four years of sparring when we could have had *this*: his awful singing voice, his hip bumping mine to encourage me to sing along, the scarlet on his cheeks when I attacked him with icing. While I was so focused on destroying him, I missed so much.

"It turns out I'm a bad friend, so maybe you're better off," I say, and immediately wish I could take it back.

I pass him a plate, but he just holds it under the water.

"Is that . . . something you want to talk about?"

"I've been holding on to the idea of my friendship with Kirby and Mara, but I haven't really been there for them lately. I'm going to try to be better, but—I might do this with a lot of things, actually. I idealize." I let out a long breath. "Am I not realistic enough? Am I too . . . dreamy?" I cringe when the word comes out. "Not dreamy as in hot, dreamy as in . . . dreaming too much."

He considers this. "You're . . . optimistic. Maybe overly so, sometimes, like with that success guide. I don't think it's a bad thing, though. Especially if you're aware of it."

"I've been aware of it for a whole three hours."

One side of his mouth quirks into a smile. "It's a start." He makes a move to point, but since his hands are buried in soap bubbles, he gestures to me with his elbow instead. "But are you aware you have icing, like, all over your eyebrow?"

My face flames. His eyes pierce mine, and there's an intensity there that pins me in place.

If we were in a romance novel, he'd run his thumb along my eyebrow, dip it into his mouth, and give me a come-hither look. He'd back me up against the kitchen counter with his hips before kissing me, and he would taste like sugar and cinnamon.

I'll give my brain points for creativity. This shouldn't be a romantic moment. We are scrubbing other people's crumbs and chewed-up bits of food off plates. Still, the thought of kissing him hits me like an earthquake, the tremor nearly making me lose my balance.

"Are you . . . going to clean it off or wait until it gets all crusty?"

Ding, ding, ding, we have a winner for the word most likely to kill the romance. Congratulations, crusty.

"Right," I say, swiping my wrist across my eyebrow. The moment is gone—because that's how it always is, isn't it? What happens in my head is better than the reality. "Hand me that towel?"

Once I lock the doors, Neil makes a strange clicking sound with his tongue.

"You know," he says. "We're actually not far from that open mic. We have time to make it, if you still want to see Delilah."

The air bites at my cheeks. "We shouldn't," I say. But we have only two clues left, and the thought of this night ending, being done with Neil . . . it makes me unreasonably sad. The open mic would at least increase our time together.

"Okay." He jams his hands into his pockets and turns down the street where my car is parked.

"Okay?" I have to jog to keep up with him. "I thought you'd put up more of a fight."

He shrugs. "If you don't want to see her, don't see her."

"Is this some kind of reverse-psychology bullshit?"

"Depends. Is it working?"

"I really hate you."

"You don't have to do it. We can get in the car right now. But you love her, don't you? If not today, when will you get another chance? What excuse will you make the next time your favorite author is in town, or when someone wants to know what kind of book you're writing?" He leans in, plants one hand on my shoulder. It's meant to be encouraging, I think, but it's incredibly distracting. "I know you can do this. You're the person who revolutionized garbage collection at Westview, remember?"

Despite myself, I crack a smile at that.

"So hear me out," he continues. "If you don't just do it and rip the Band-Aid off—"

"Two clichés in one sentence?" I say, and he shoots daggers at me.

"—you might wish you had. All that regret you were talking about earlier, with the success guide—here's a goal you can accomplish now, even if you can't cross it off some list."

I try to visualize it—but I've never been to Bernadette's, so I can't. Maybe I'll stumble over my words, make a fool of myself in front of Delilah. But today was supposed to be about owning this thing that I love, and I've already made so much progress with Neil of all people. It felt so great to finally talk about it. *Freeing.*

And I don't think I'm done yet.

"You win," I say.

When he grins, it's bright enough to light up the night sky.

It's kind of beautiful.

SIX THINGS ABOUT NEIL MCNAIR THAT ARE NOT ACTUALLY TERRIBLE

- He occasionally wears T-shirts.
- His knowledge of words and languages is somewhat impressive.
- He's a decent listener—when he's not being combative.
- He read Nora Roberts.
- He knew, somehow, that I could do that open mic, even if I didn't.
- His freckles. All seven thousand of them.

10:42 p.m.

BERNADETTE'S IS DESIGNED to look like an old speakeasy, dimly lit, black-and-white photographs of old Seattle lining the walls. Tables and chairs point toward a small stage in the back, where a girl maybe a few years older than we are is onstage, sawing back and forth across a violin. No—a viola.

"She probably already left," I whisper to Neil. "Or she'll think it's stalker-y that a fan tracked her down to get some books signed."

"Or she'll be flattered," he says.

I run my fingers through my bangs, pushing them to the left where they're supposed to sit after years of combing to teach them to lie flat that way. I'm growing them out, and that's final.

I like them the way they are, Neil said about my bangs earlier. It ricochets off the inside of my skull until it's *I like I like I like I like* over and over and over again. When I catch him looking, he quickly glances away, and I feel myself flush.

Naturally, that's when I spot her, sitting with another woman at a table a few feet away.

She's flawless, laughing at something the other woman is saying in this full but quiet way. Her black hair is cut in a sleek bob, and she's wearing a navy jumpsuit with white hearts all over it. Little heart decals even adorn her nails.

And of course I have what looks like shit staining the front of my dress.

"Say hi," Neil whispers, placing a hand on the small of my back.

Somehow, I propel myself forward. "Sorry, but—are you, um, Delilah Park?"

Delilah and her tablemate turn to us. Her berry lips curve into a warm smile. "I am." Ever polite, she gestures to the woman next to her, dressed in a fitted blazer and ignoring how often her phone lights up on the table in front of her. "This is my publicist, Grace. I'm so sorry, I just performed about twenty minutes ago."

Cool, cool, I'll just disappear now. I'm ready to turn and run when Neil taps my backpack.

Courage. I can do this.

"I love your books," I blurt. "I mean, I'm sure you get that a lot. Because obviously if someone is going to one of your events, it's because they love your books, unless they're being dragged there by someone else, in which case they should still, like, be respectful and not outright tell you they don't love your books? Not that I'm saying a bunch of the people who go to your events don't love your books. I'm sure nearly all of them do. And I definitely do. Love your books, that is."

Grace tries to suppress a grin.

"Thank you," Delilah says, and she sounds genuine. "Did we meet at the bookstore earlier?"

I shake my head. "I missed the signing. It's a long story that involves the zoo and a pot cookie and a really complicated game."

"Um, that sounds like the best story," she says, like we're friends.

My shoulders dip with relief. Somehow, I am speaking to her. I'm having a conversation with Delilah Park, whose words I've admired for so many years.

"Is this the person who doesn't love my books who you dragged with you?" she asks, gesturing to Neil.

I feel myself flush hotter, but there's kindness in her voice. She isn't making fun of me.

"I haven't read any yet," Neil admits, and then locks eyes with me before adding, "but I want to."

I am floating. "I have some books with me, if you don't mind signing them?"

"Absolutely," she says. Grace is already handing her a pen. "Who should I sign them to?"

I spell my name for her. Grace has Delilah's lip stamp, too, and when she presses it into the ink pad and then onto the page, I am shocked I'm still standing. It gives me a sense of déjà vu after what happened with Neil and my parents. I guess we can't help it—we're both book nerds.

"It was so great to meet you, Rowan," she says, passing the books back to me. She gestures toward the stage. "Are you performing something?"

"Actually," someone says, and with horror I realize that someone is me, "I was just going to sign up."

Maybe she tells me good luck or that she's looking forward to it or that I'm about to make the worst mistake of my life. This is when my brain temporarily shuts off, and Neil has to guide me to a table.

"You're trying really hard not to smile, aren't you?" he says.

I nod before letting my face split open. "Oh my *God*. She was so nice? I love her? Did I sound too ridiculous, or just a normal amount of ridiculous?"

"You were *fine*," he says, grinning. "And you're going to perform?"

Oh. Right. "I got caught up in the moment."

"I think it's a great idea."

And maybe it is, or at the very least, not a terrible one, because I, human-cloud Rowan Roth, am suddenly making my way over to the hipster at the counter holding a clipboard.

"It's a light night," the guy says when I ask if there are any open slots. He's wearing Seattle's official flag, a plaid flannel shirt. "You could go up next, if you want."

Voice trembling, I tell him my name before meeting Neil back at our table. He asks if he can get me water or a soda or anything, but I'm not sure my stomach would be able to handle it. As I remove my notebook from my backpack, my fingers graze my new signed books. I wrote the first few chapters by hand before typing them up, and I'd rather read off paper than a phone.

I can't picture the best-case scenario, and so I don't let myself brace for the worst, either. This doesn't have to be scary. I let Neil read. Neil, my rival and nemesis, who used to tease me relentlessly about the books I love. And I'm *proud* of what I wrote. Why is that so hard to admit, even to myself?

"Give it up for Adina," the emcee says, his boots making the floorboards bounce and squeak. "Always a treat to have her back here."

The room applauds for the violist. I was so in my head, I hadn't realized she'd finished. I clap along with everyone else, my stomach performing an impressive gymnastics routine.

Adina and I cross paths as she leaves the stage, long dark hair tumbling down her back, a swipe of red across her lips. Her cheeks are flushed from the performance. She might be the most beautiful person I've seen up close.

"That was amazing," I tell her.

She does something strange then. Instead of brushing off the compliment the way someone else might, she gives me a half-smile, as though she knows exactly how amazing she was.

"Thank you. Have I seen you here before?"

"First time," I say.

Her smile gets wider. There's an ease to her, an effortlessness. "I've been coming here for a few years, mostly on breaks from school. It's a good crowd." She glances behind me toward the audience. "Your boyfriend seems really excited for you."

"Oh, he's not—" I start, but I'm not about to recite our history to this stranger, and the word "boyfriend" is doing strange things to my heart that I don't want to think about before I get up on that stage.

"You'll do great," she assures me.

The emcee's voice: "Next up, we have a newcomer, so let's give an extra-special Bernadette's welcome to Rowan!"

I make my way up to the stage, watching as Adina joins a short-haired girl at a table in the back.

"Hi," I say into the microphone. "Thank you." The lights are too bright. It takes me a few seconds to spot Neil, and then I wonder why he didn't stand out to me right away because he's grinning that genuine grin, the one that crinkles the corners of his eyes in this adorable way. And damn it if it doesn't soothe some of the nerves in my stomach.

And there's Delilah, giving me her full attention, as though she's truly interested in what I'm about to read.

"This is coffee, by the way," I say, gesturing to my dress, realizing under the lights just how brown the stain must look. "A hazelnut latte, to be exact. Not, um. Something else. It's been a very weird day."

At this, the audience laughs.

"I'm going to read from the opening of a novel I've been working on. It's short, and all you really need to know about it is that it's . . . a romance novel." A couple people whoop at this, and one person whistles. Maybe it's Delilah. Maybe it's Neil.

"Here it goes," I say, and then it becomes easy.

Neil's waiting for me outside, leaning against the brick building across the alley. When I finished, he held up his watch and stuck a thumb in the direction of the door. My heart is still pounding, my head buzzing. Woof, the adrenaline is *wild*.

"I fucking did it," I say as I race over to him.

He's beaming. "Yes you fucking did," he says, matching my enthusiasm. "You were *amazing*."

When I reach him, I fling my arms around his neck in a hug that clearly surprises him, given how his body jerks back at first. But then he relaxes, as though his body needed a moment to process what was happening, and his arms come around me, his hands resting against the small of my back. I'm grateful for the hoodie—I'm sweating like mad underneath it.

My face fits in the space below his ear, where his jaw meets his neck. Have we hugged before? This might actually be our first one. I move my hands to his shoulders, lingering on the soft fabric of his T-shirt. I wonder if he's cold. If I should return his hoodie, the one I'm still wearing. He smells like a combination of rain and boy sweat—not entirely a bad thing—and underneath, something clean and comforting. I fight the urge to inhale deeply, to avoid sounding as though I am literally breathing him in.

"They didn't hate it."

His pulse shudders against my skin. "Because it was *good*."

Slowly, we pull back from the hug, and I can't believe I just did that, and I can't believe Neil McNair was here to see it and that he's *happy* for me. If we'd been friends instead of competitors, I wonder how many more hugs we'd have had.

It was a rush unlike anything I've experienced, getting to read my words in front of people. It might have been even better than hearing Delilah read. She listened to *me*, a complete nobody hoping to one day become a somebody.

"And Delilah's following me on Twitter now," I say, in part to distract myself from how badly I want to hug him again. "She flagged me down before I left, and she just took out her phone and asked for my handle, and oh my God, what am I supposed to tweet? She's going to see everything. Maybe I should delete my account."

He lifts his eyebrows. "Is this what I was like when I met your parents?"

"No. You were worse." I grab his arm to look at his watch. "What time is it?"

I have a phone I am perfectly capable of removing from my pocket, but there's something adorable about the anachronistic way Neil checks his watch.

"Just past eleven," he says. "We got the next safe zone message while you were up there."

We read it together.

> SENIOR WOLF PACK, LISTEN UP
> HOW'RE YOU FEELING? HAD ENOUGH?
> IT'S TIME FOR US TO GOLF WITH YOU
> SEE YOU AT SAFE ZONE NUMBER TWO

The message links to a mini-golf course that isn't too far away and asks us to meet there at 11:30.

"I need to sit down first," I say, still shaky with adrenaline.

Since we have some extra time, we make our way over to a

bench in the adjacent park. The cold seems to hit me all at once.

"Do you want your hoodie back?" I ask.

"You keep it." He shifts until his hip is a couple inches from mine. I could fit two paperbacks in the space between his jeans and my dress. "It's only fair, given that coffee stain."

I'm not sure even a dry cleaner could save my dress after all the suffering it's been through today, but I don't know if I could throw it out. It'll be a trophy from this night, a reminder of all the things I did but thought I couldn't.

"Thank you so much," I tell him. "For—for helping me realize I could do it."

Ever so slightly, I scoot closer to him on the bench. I tell myself it's because of the cold.

I am a big fucking liar.

In the moonlight, his hair looks bronze, as though he's the bust I teased him about earlier today. I can't quite believe that was only hours ago.

"I . . . don't know if you realize how much you've helped me." He says it to the frayed knees of his jeans instead of to me. "All of these years. I couldn't afford not to step up my game. It wasn't just that you kept me on my toes or made me better. Competing with you, *you* in general . . . You helped me stay focused. Helped keep me from letting everything with my dad get too overwhelming. I just . . . I could have so easily drowned in that. And you did it without even trying."

It breaks my heart all over again.

"Neil," I say quietly. "I don't even know what to say to that."

"You're welcome?" he suggests, and I laugh, nudging him with my elbow. There's barely any space between us now, and when he tilts his head to look at me, his eyes pull me into something thrilling, something intense. I don't know how I missed it before.

"You're welcome. And thank you. Again," I say, then charge forward with the secret I've been keeping since his house. "So I've been thinking. If we win, you should keep the money."

"Rowan—"

I knew he'd protest, so I cut him off immediately. "And you should one hundred percent not use it for your dad. He did something horrible not just to that kid, but to your whole family. To you." The words tumble out smoothly now. "You should use it for yourself. For some nice things. Change your last name, and maybe you could study abroad, or you could get a suit at . . . wherever they sell nice suits."

He's quiet for a few moments. I'd be positive I said completely the wrong thing if he weren't still nearly touching me, a whisper of space between his hip and mine.

"Now I don't know what to say," he says, and forces a laugh. "Which, as you know, is unusual for me. I don't know if I could accept all of it, but thank you. That . . . sounds really wonderful." He heaves a sigh, and then speaks again. "I'm scared," he says, and the words are so soft. I could tuck myself in with a blanket made of *I'm scared.* "I've never said that to anyone before, but I'm really fucking scared of what happens when I leave. I want to leave so badly, and yet . . . I get worried that I'm not as independent as I think I am. I'll get to school and I won't know how to work the laundry machine, even though I've been doing my own laundry for years. Or I won't know how to get around the city, and I'll get lost. My mom seems happy with Christopher, but I'm worried she'll overwork herself. I'm worried my sister won't be able to outrun it all. Or that wherever I am, I won't be able to get away from my father.

"Sometimes I worry I'll turn out like him. I wonder if that kind of thing is genetic. If I'm doomed to fuck up as much as he did, if there's this violent streak inside me."

"That's fucking terrifying," I say, tapping his shoe with mine, letting him know he's wrong, that he's not doomed. "And you are *nothing* like that."

This boy is gentle to his core. He spars with his words, not his fists. He is so close that I could use the tip of my nose to connect each freckle on his cheeks. Forget counting. His mouth looks soft, and I wonder how he'd kiss—slow and deliberate or hard and desperate, if he'd grip my waist or my hips. Would he be measured, each motion of his lips plotted out beforehand? Or would he turn off his mind, let his body take over?

The thought of him losing control like that is almost too much for my poor brain to handle.

"You don't have to talk about it," I say. "If you don't want to."

"That's the thing. I think I do. I've not talked about it for so long, and with you . . . for some reason, it's not as hard as I thought it would be."

"I want to make a dirty joke right now, but I don't want to embarrass you."

He nudges my shoulder with his. It's a friendly teasing kind of gesture that makes me think thoroughly unfriendly thoughts. And our legs—still almost touching. It feels somehow more intimate than our dance in the library. I have never been so aware of every nerve on my outer thigh.

A car honks a few streets away, and when I turn my head on instinct, I realize a bit of my hair is stuck between the slats of the bench. Just in case I wasn't enough of a mess tonight. I reach up to my messy bun that is more mess than bun at this point and tug-tug-tug it out of its elastic and pins.

"It might be a lost cause," I say by way of explanation. "I sealed its fate when I showered in the dark this morning and couldn't dry it, and it's been getting exponentially worse by the hour."

Neil watches me comb my fingers through it. "It, uh. It doesn't look bad, you know. You've been playing with it all day, but. It always looks nice."

And then he does something that maybe shocks us both: he reaches for one of my curls loosed by the pins, grazing it with a fingertip. As though to say, *This. This is the hair that always looks nice*. It's so light, that touch. The gentleness decimates me, the way he's uncertain but brave at the same time. The fingertip is gone before I can lean into him, even as I'm imagining what it would feel like for him to slide both of his hands into my hair.

It always looks nice.

"And I don't actually hate your suits," I tell him. "I mean, don't get cocky about it or anything. It's still a supremely dorky thing to wear in high school, but . . . you don't look terrible in them."

"We're not the best at compliments, are we?"

"I'm better," I say, and he laughs. His laugh sounds like that first gooey indie pop song he played for me in Doo Wop Records, the Free Puppies! one. Behind his glasses, his dark eyes light up, turning amber. Again I'm convinced I've never paid enough attention to him when he laughs. Maybe he hasn't done it enough in my presence. Maybe he has looked at me only through narrowed eyes, his brows slashed in annoyance. But tonight I want to make him laugh again and again.

Heart hammering, I shift my leg until it's finally right up against his, closing the distance between us. I couldn't take it anymore, not touching him.

His breath catches in his throat. God, that is a great sound. "You cold?" he asks, and it makes me feel slightly guilty, given I'm wearing his hoodie.

"A little," I say, surprised by the sudden scratchiness of my voice. If being cold makes him inch closer, then I am fucking Antarctica.

Then I hear, feel the rustle of fabric as he moves his leg against mine too, this pressure that confirms what's happening is absolutely deliberate, and we are hip to hip and thigh to thigh and knee to knee. He brushes my knee once with his thumb, a quick little swipe.

That swipe deserves its own romance novel.

"Okay?" he asks, and I don't know if he's asking if I'm okay, if what we're doing is okay, or okay as in am I ready to go, and I'm not. I'm not. It's cold, but I could light a fire with how it feels to be this close to him. Yes, this is okay, but it's also not nearly enough.

All I can do is nod. Suddenly his hoodie feels too warm. I've mourned what we lost by not being friends, but what if we'd become friends and then something else? Maybe we'd have shared all our firsts. Learned together, explored together, and beyond the physical, we'd have helped each other on those rough days. This entire night, I've been defending my emotions because I couldn't admit the reality: that I have real feelings for this boy. There are so many things I didn't know about him, like that he is a fan of children's books and his favorite word is 'tsundoku' and he alters his suits himself. He cares about his mother and his sister. He cares about me, Rowan Roth, the girl he's been trying to destroy for four years.

I've never experienced something earth-shattering, like Neil said. But I have a feeling that if something happened with us . . . it might be.

And that possibility is what pulls me like a magnet toward my former nemesis, Neil McNair, who is looking at my mouth like he has just discovered the perfect synonym for a word that doesn't have any.

And maybe it's what pulls him to me too.

"Rowan, right?"

A voice shatters the darkness, and Neil and I spring apart before our lips meet.

"Hey, girl, was that you onstage at Bernadette's?" A girl who looks to be in her midtwenties is standing a few feet from us, a beanie hiding her hair, the lamplight glinting off a septum piercing.

"H-hey," I croak out. "Yes. Yeah. That was me."

My cheeks are ablaze, as though I've been caught doing something I wanted to be private. If she saw what we were maybe about to do, she didn't notice or isn't letting on. I can't even look at Neil, who's frozen next to me.

A foot of space has suddenly materialized between us on the bench. Like he was worried about getting caught too.

She breaks into a grin. "I loved your piece. I'm addicted to romance novels, but none of my friends really get it. And there you were, reading a romance novel at an open mic and owning it."

Wow, I'd love to have this conversation literally any other time.

"Thank you. Thank you so much." *Thank you for ruining what might have been the most romantic moment of my life.*

"I just had to tell you," she says. "Hope I see you at the next one!"

"Yeah. Hope so."

She waves and skips off into the night.

The left side of my body is cold, and I'm shivering again. I want that Neil softness from five minutes ago, but now he's a statue, iron spine and concrete shoulders. We were about to kiss. I didn't just imagine it.

Finally, Neil comes to life. "We should go," he says, leaping to his feet, dusting off his pants. "We have to be at mini golf by eleven thirty."

"Right," I manage. I stand on wobbly legs.

Neither of us says a word the entire walk to my car.

HOWL CLUES

- *A place you can buy Nirvana's first album*
- *A place that's red from floor to ceiling*
- *A place you can find Chiroptera*
- *A rainbow crosswalk*
- *Ice cream fit for Sasquatch*
- *The big guy at the center of the universe*
- *Something local, organic, and sustainable*
- *A floppy disk*
- *A coffee cup with someone else's name (or your own name, wildly misspelled)*
- *A car with a parking ticket*
- *A view from up high*
- *A tourist doing something a local would be ashamed of doing*
- *An umbrella (we all know real Seattleites don't use them)*
- *The best pizza in the city (your choice, but you will be judged)*
- *A tribute to the mysterious Mr. Cooper*

11:26 p.m.

WE'VE HAD A lot of awkward car rides today, but this one is *silent*. Neil is staring out the window, chin propped on one hand. I want to play my melancholy music. I want him to tell me the etymology of the word "heartbreak."

The ache in my chest has only intensified since we left the bench. He learned to hide so much of himself after what happened to his dad, and based on the way he's turned stoic, he's still excelling at it. And *fuck*, it's crushing. I don't like it at all, not the tightness in my chest or the pressure building behind my eyes.

I swear he was leaning toward me too. Unless, now that we have distance from the open-mic adrenaline, he's realized what a colossal mistake we nearly made. Maybe he's glad we were interrupted. Regrets what almost happened. Six hours ago, I would have been horrified by it too—or would I have been? When did this really start for me? Because I'm pretty sure it wasn't today. When I dreamed about him? Has it been dormant since that short-lived freshman-year crush? No, it couldn't have been. This is something new, the way I feel about him, but it's old and familiar too. I tease him about his suits, but I love them, don't I? And the freckles. God, the freckles. I am trash for his freckles.

He keeps glancing between his watch and the clock on my dashboard.

"It's three minutes fast," I say.

"We're going to be cutting it close."

What he doesn't say: if we hadn't gone to the open mic, if we hadn't lingered on that bench, if we hadn't almost kissed, then we wouldn't be threatening our Howl status.

"There was a spot back there," he says as I make a loop around.

"It was too small."

My driving is safe but frantic, especially after the fender bender this morning, but I swear, we get hit with every red light, which blesses us with more time to sit in silence. Neil sighs, then coughs, then sighs again, seeming to prepare himself to say something he never finds the words for.

"Late," he says under his breath when I put my car in park near the downtown mini-golf course.

Don't cry. "We can't be."

"You can't exactly argue with time. If we're late, we're late. It's just a fact."

This snippiness catches me off guard. This isn't even how we spoke to each other the past four years. There was always a respect there. I don't know what this is, but it makes a hard pit settle in my stomach. He regrets what almost happened. I'm sure of it.

Logan Perez is at the door, armed with her clipboard. "You two are late," she says, shaking her head.

"Only two minutes," I say feebly, but I'm a rule-follower to my core. Late is late, whether it's two minutes or two hours.

"Logan." Neil stands up straighter. "It's my fault. I made us take this weird route, even though Rowan didn't want to. Eliminate me, if you have to. But let her stay."

My face immediately heats up, and that pit in my stomach softens. I'm not exactly sure what he's trying to pull here. He didn't outright say he'd take the money if we win, but if I were the only one left, we'd be reducing our chances pretty significantly.

Logan's gaze flicks between the two of us. "I shouldn't do this," she says, "but as the incoming president, I imagine I have some kind of executive power. In general, I consider myself pretty hard-hearted. But what you're doing, Neil, is really sweet. It makes me feel something right in this general vicinity." She holds a hand over her heart and grins. "You can both stay in the game, but you speak *nothing* of this to anyone else." We nod, and she steps aside to let us through. "Enjoy your safety."

Once inside, he's suddenly fascinated with the straps of his backpack.

"You didn't have to do that," I say, still not entirely sure how to interpret it.

He shrugs. "You were right. We shouldn't have taken so many detours."

That makes me feel about two feet tall. "I guess I'll see you in half an hour?"

He nods back his agreement and once again disappears with his friends. I have never been so relieved to see mine. Mara waves, and Kirby, a little more tentative, offers a smile.

"Hi," I say, unsteady on my feet. If I'm going to cry, at least my friends are here. "I think I need to talk."

In a darkened corner of an indoor miniature-golf course, after I apologize a hundred more times for being sour about the Chelan trip, I confess to my friends what they've suspected for all these years: that my feelings for Neil McNair go deeper than rivalry.

I tell them everything else, too, about the books I read and the book I'm writing and Delilah Park.

"Go ahead," I say, pressing my back against the wall, bracing myself. "Make fun of me."

"You're writing a romance novel," Kirby says slowly. "You showed it to Neil."

Miserably, I nod, waiting for them to insist I could have shown them. But I feel better now, knowing I'm not hiding anymore.

"You didn't think we'd be supportive?" she asks. There's no amusement on her face. I think she might be hurt.

"It's a romance novel. You've made it pretty clear what you think about them."

"Yeah, but . . ." Kirby shakes her head. "I didn't realize you *loved* them, loved them. I was always joking. It wasn't meant to be mean. You never gave the impression that you were that into them, just that you had them lying around."

"Because I was afraid," I say in a small voice. "And I don't want to be. Maybe I'm not the most amazing writer yet, but I think I'm okay. And I have plenty of time to get better. I don't want to be ashamed of what I like."

Mara's been quiet the whole conversation, which isn't entirely unusual for her. "I like Harry Styles," she finally says, which surprises both of us.

Kirby turns to her. "Really? You've never told me that. I mean, I can admit he's a good-looking guy."

A blush creeps onto her cheeks. "No. I like his *music*."

"Oh," Kirby says. "I've never heard it."

"It's good," Mara insists. "I'll send you some songs."

Then Mara and I both stare at Kirby, as though waiting for her confession.

"Okay, okay," she says. "I love reality TV. But not even the shows that require talent, like singing or fashion design. The *really* bad stuff that's just hot rich people yelling at each other. I started watching it ironically with my sister a few years ago before she went to college, but then I sort of started liking it for real."

"I love Harry Styles!" Mara shouts, in a move that's completely out of character for her, and then giggles as a few classmates glance our way with raised eyebrows. "And I don't care who knows about it!"

I adore her.

"Maybe you could recommend a couple books to us," Kirby says, and my heart tugs.

"I can definitely do that."

Recovered from her outburst, Mara places a hand on my knee. "So . . . Neil."

Even his name brings heat to my face.

"For a while, I thought you guys just needed to hook up and get it out of your system," Kirby says. "You really like him, though."

"God. I really do. But it was like what happened on the bench flipped some kind of switch with him, and now he's acting even weirder than usual."

"It sounds like maybe he got scared," Mara says. "I felt like that with Kirby at the beginning. That if we were going to do this, we couldn't go back to how things were before. That it would change our friendship forever, for better or for worse."

"Fortunately, for better," Kirby interjects.

Mara threads her fingers with Kirby's. "And school might be over, but you'd have to figure out what happens this summer, and in college, assuming you haven't murdered each other by then. That's terrifying. We're going to the same place, and I'm still terrified."

Kirby blinks at her. "You are?"

"Well . . . yeah. We'll have new classes and will meet new people, and we'll be halfway living on our own. We're going to change."

"But I like myself," Kirby says with a small whine, and Mara swats at her arm.

I love them. I love them both so much, and maybe I don't deserve them, but I am so fucking glad I have them right now.

"I am so sorry," I say again. "About everything with Neil, and for abandoning you."

"You can't erase all our history in just a few months," Mara says. "But if you really want to make it up to me, you could share a few of your Howl photos."

"Not a chance."

"And I'm not going to tell you 'good riddance' because we had one fight." Kirby smiles sadly. "All I wish is that it would have happened earlier. The four of us could have hung out, double-dated."

There's that pang of regret again, the one that makes me wish the past few years had been different. I can imagine it: late nights in Capitol Hill, taking up an entire booth at Hot Cakes, Mara taking ridiculous photos. I have to press a hand to my chest, as though the regret is a physical pain.

"I don't know what it's going to look like, if anything happens with us." It's bizarre to acknowledge it as a possibility. *Something might happen with us.* "But I know I want you both to be part of it. Well, not all of it."

"I want all the McNasty details," Kirby says, batting her lashes.

I roll my eyes. "How do you tell the person you've spent four years trying to destroy that you have a crush on them?"

"I would guess there's a book about that," Mara says. "And that you've probably read it."

"Make sure he knows that you're serious and genuine. No sarcasm," Kirby says. "You're an overachiever. I have full confidence you can overachieve the shit out of this."

"I'll try." I'm so overwhelmed with emotion in this moment—for this entire night and for them. Then I get an idea. "Hey—could we take a picture? It's been a while."

Mara's already reaching for her phone. "I thought you'd never ask."

And I don't care that my eyes are puffy and my makeup's faded and my dress is, well, you know. Mara stretches out her practiced selfie arm, and we lean our heads together, and without even looking, I already know it's perfectly imperfect.

In the distance, a whistle blows, and then there's Logan's voice over the intercom: "Wolf Pack! You have three minutes until your safe-zone time expires. Everyone please proceed to the exit in an orderly fashion."

"Okay." I get to my feet, renewed and reenergized. "I'm going to do it. I'm going to tell him."

I'm still feeling a bit like a newborn giraffe learning how to walk, but after I hug my friends, I'm more solid. Grounded.

"Can you be proud of someone who's the same age as you? Because I'm proud of you," Mara says, and that makes tears back up behind my eyes for an entirely different reason.

When I spot Neil, my stomach stages a revolt. If possible, he looks even cuter than before. All I want is to wrap my arms around him again, for him to tug me close, the way we hugged after Bernadette's. I want to go back to that bench and climb into his lap. I want to kiss him like I've never kissed anyone else. I want him to lose himself in me the way I've never been able to imagine—or maybe it's that I can't imagine it happening with anyone except me.

Hi. I might like you. Do you want to eat another cinnamon roll with me?

So you know how I hate you? Turns out, I don't!

You. Me. Back seat of my Honda Accord. Now.

"You ready?" he asks.

I'm so stuck in my thoughts that what comes out is "Huh?" which makes him raise an eyebrow at me. I shake myself out of it. "Yes. Let's grab the view clue at the place you insist is the best view in Seattle, then see if we can figure out who this mysterious Mr. Cooper is."

Logan blows another whistle, which means we have five minutes to get as far away from this place as possible before we can start making kills again. Someone opens the door, and Neil and I run for it, racing toward my car in the murky darkness.

We zigzag through the streets, ensuring no one who has our names can follow us. It's gotten a lot colder, and I jam my hands into the hoodie pockets. I should give it back, I know I should, but I like it too much.

We're almost to my car when my fingertips close around a small slip of paper in the pocket.

I skid to a stop and pull it out, my heart plummeting as I read and reread the name written on it. *No.* No, no, no. With my thumb, I trace the ink of the letters, trying to get them to make sense.

Rowan Roth.

12:05 a.m.

NEIL HAS MY name.

Neil has my *name*.

Neil hasn't killed anyone, which means he's had my name since the beginning of the game.

"Rowan?" he's saying. Not "Artoo." Because we're not friends. We're not whatever we almost became on that bench. "I keep wondering if Cooper was involved in the founding of Seattle somehow, or something else in Seattle history, maybe. I found this article about Frank B. Cooper, this guy who oversaw the building of new schools in Seattle neighborhoods. Could it be leading us to the first school in Seattle, or is that too circuitous? What do you think?"

My heart is pounding and oh my God, oh my God, oh my God. I cannot think about Frank B. Cooper or Seattle schools right now. I rock back and forth on my heels, tugging at the straps of my backpack, my face on fire.

It is all of a sudden so obvious: when he acted fidgety after I saved him, how he didn't pursue Carolyn Gao. He did this just so he could best me one last time. He played me, letting me into his house and his room, telling me his secrets and listening to mine.

Just to rub it in when he kills me, even after we allied ourselves.

I can't believe I was about to tell him that I had feelings for him.

I close my fist around the slip of paper. Slowly, I turn to face him, unclenching my hand, revealing my name.

We hover in that space for a few seconds, frozen.

The color drains from his face. "Oh. Shit," he mutters. "I can explain that."

"I'd really love to hear it."

He rubs at his eyes, jostling his glasses. "I'm so sorry. I—I didn't mean for you to find out."

"Obviously," I choke out. "Have you had me the whole time?"

With a miserable nod, he says, "Since Cinerama. Yeah. I should have told you. I just thought—I thought you wouldn't trust me if you knew."

Irony of ironies.

"So what was your plan? Keep it secret until the end, then surprise me because I already trusted you? Soften me up, get me to let my guard down?" I shake my head. More than anything, it's about the loss of trust, not the grand prize. "You know it's not about the money for me anymore. Why wouldn't you just tell me?"

He doesn't say anything.

"Well, congratufuckinglations. You got me. So go ahead. Kill me."

I hold out my arm for him, indicating he should swipe the blue armband.

"That's not what I—"

"Just do it, okay?" I grit out. We both stare at it. Lightly, I nudge his shoulder, but he doesn't budge, like he is made of metal instead of skin and bones. "Stop talking to your shoes! At least look me in the eye."

When he finally wrenches his eyes up to mine, my stomach drops. He looks more pained than he has all night.

"Rowan," he says, voice quaking, clearly trying so hard to sound gentle. He swallows hard. "Okay. You're right. I wasn't going to wait until the end at first. When we were in the record store, I had a moment where I thought, 'This is it. I'm going to do it.' But I couldn't. I don't know. We were getting along, and it was—forgive me—*nice*. It was *nice*. I *liked* spending time with you."

"You say that like it's such a shock," I say, though I can't deny how good it feels to hear it. "Like it's so impossible to have enjoyed my company."

He crosses his arms. "We both know your self-esteem isn't that low. I'm sorry I wanted to spend more time with you. I'm sorry I wanted to keep you in the game—which, I might point out, was exactly what you did for me at Pike Place—so we could go up against each other at the end and so you could ultimately beat me, since that's apparently the only thing that matters to you."

"It isn't." It hasn't been for hours.

Beneath his freckles, his face is a mess of angry red splotches. It isn't cute. It's fucking infuriating. This close to him, I can see all his freckles, plus a scar on his chin I've never noticed before. And I've never seen him with facial hair, but now that he's been out all night, a dusting of auburn is beginning to grow in, and it doesn't look terrible. Except that it's Neil, and I despise him—don't I?—and therefore it does.

"Up until today," he says, "we only sort of knew each other. I knew you hate it when you don't get enough votes for a measure in student council and that you like romance novels. But I didn't know why. I didn't know about your family or your writing. I didn't know how much you like sad songs or why you love reading the books you do. And"—he sucks in a breath—"you didn't know about me either. You didn't know about my family. Do you know how many people I've voluntarily told about my dad?" He shakes his head. "Maybe five? And I trusted you with that. I haven't trusted anyone with that, not for a long time."

He's apologizing. He clearly feels bad about it. Maybe it isn't so awful that he kept this from me. Maybe we can move past it, keep playing.

The moonlight catches his face, and I can't deny how lovely it looks.

"We shared some really personal shit," he says. "Does that not matter at all?"

I'm blushing too. I can feel it. I'm thinking about what we talked about in the library. How it felt safe to have those conversations around him. How I liked playing with him, but more than that . . .

I wanted to kiss him, and I wanted him to kiss me back. That's what I wanted.

What I *want*.

"It does matter," I say, stepping closer. I don't want to be at odds with him. The day flashes through my mind: the assembly, my Pike Place Market rescue, arguing over pizza. The record store and Sean Yee's lab and Neil's house, the place no one ever goes. My house, then, and the zoo and the library. *The library*. That dance. Then Two Birds, and singing while scrubbing dishes, and the open mic and how incredible I felt afterward.

The bench.

How much of it was real? What happened at his house, yes, and what happened at mine. But everything else? Before I forgive him, I have to know for sure.

"I just need to know," I say. "How much of today was real? Because what happened on the bench—we almost kissed, Neil." That last part, I whisper it.

I didn't want it to be an almost, I will myself to say. I wanted his mouth on mine and his hands in my hair. It wasn't something I'd been imagining for months and months. I had no preconceived notions of what it would be like, and for once I wanted to turn off my brain and simply *feel*.

I don't know how to explain to him how unusual that is for me.

He turns even redder. "I guess it's good we didn't. We just . . . got caught up in the moment. It would have been a mistake."

A mistake.

He hunches his shoulders, turning slightly away from me. The shock of learning this was one-sided sends me backward a few paces. A boulder shoved into my chest. So I was played, then.

After all these hours, I am still merely a game to him.

Hours. It's only been hours. A mind can't change that quickly—and yet mine did. I was so sure his did too.

I force my face not to fall, force my hands not to tremble. My heart, though—that's the one I can't control. When I was younger, I never understood it when someone's "heart sank" in a book. *It's not physically possible*, I told anyone who'd listen. Now I know more than ever before exactly what it feels like for a heart to sink. Except it's not just my heart; it's my entire body that wants to crumble.

He's so embarrassed about what happened on the bench that he won't even look at me, instead immersed in what must be a fascinating dip in the sidewalk.

"Rowan?" he says, as though he wants to make sure I heard him break me.

"Right. Right," I say with more conviction than I feel. It's too cold outside, and I hug my arms tight around myself. It doesn't stop that sinking feeling. It doesn't stop the pressure building behind my eyes or the way my voice sounds strained and high-pitched. "A huge mistake. Got it."

"Glad we're on the same page," he says, but his words are clipped, and he sounds anything but glad.

"Good thing we came to our senses. I mean, you and me? In what universe would that have made sense?" If I force myself to say it out loud, maybe I'll believe it. It has to make this hurt less. "The rest of the senior class would have had a field day with it."

I think about all the moments I was too cruel, the times I

pushed him away. If I'd done the opposite, would we be having this conversation? Or would it only be more painful?

"Can we—can we just drop it?" he asks. Stammering. "Please?"

"Sure. Fine." I kneel down to open my backpack, searching for my keys. I can't look at him right now. I don't want him to see that I'm on the verge of crying. He doesn't need more ammunition.

God, what is wrong with me? Neil McNair wouldn't have been my perfect boyfriend. Under no circumstances is he the person I should have been with.

My fingers close around cool metal, and I make a tight fist around the keys to anchor myself. Maybe he deserves to win the game after all. He tricked me into thinking I had feelings for him, then somehow turned them real. He's the true champion of Westview, ensuring this final competition would end with me utterly sunk.

"We only have two more clues," he says, softly this time. He turns to face me. *Fuck.* I hope he doesn't think he needs to treat me delicately now. I'm not sure what would be worse, the teasing when I confessed my ninth-grade crush, or this. "Let's finish them up, and then we can figure this whole thing out."

This is worse. Definitely this.

"There's—there's nothing to figure out." I spring to my feet so quickly my head spins. I clutch the keys tighter. "We can go our separate ways now or at the end of the game or after graduation. Why drag it out? You and I don't know how to be friends." Vengeance fills me up, the way it has all these years. It has to replace the sinking feeling. The drowning. I want to hurt him back. And I know exactly where to jab right between his ribs so he'll feel it the most. "The worst part is—I liked the person you were today! I liked spending time with you too. And that's why it's so upsetting you were holding something back the entire day. You could have told me so many times, but you didn't. I thought you were different, but maybe you're more like your dad than you thought."

Regret hits me immediately. Again with this stellar ability I have to tear him down. It made me strong the past four years, but tonight it only makes me feel small. This isn't me. At least—I don't want it to be.

I watch his face as the remark hits him. His eyes grow dark, and his mouth opens slightly, like he might say something, but nothing comes out.

"That's a shitty low blow, and you know it," he says. "If we're talking personal flaws, what about you?"

I take a step back. "What about me?"

He throws his hands up. "Rowan! You're sabotaging yourself. You've been doing it for years. That high school success guide?"

"I hadn't thought about that in forever," I say quietly, wondering why I suddenly feel on the defensive yet again.

"You made that list when you were fourteen. Of course you're going to want different things now. You're a different person. You've grown and changed and that's a *good thing*," he says. "When we were at the zoo, were you actually high, or were you using that as an excuse because you were anxious about meeting Delilah?"

"No," I insist, but suddenly I'm not sure. That tiny slice of relief I felt—is that what it was?

"Spencer? Kirby and Mara? Your *writing*, the thing you want to devote your entire life to? You said it yourself. You're so worried the reality won't measure up to what's in your head that you don't even *try* things that scare you, and you don't realize there's a problem with your relationships. Because if you don't have to confront it, then it doesn't exist. Right?"

I'm shaking my head. "I—no. No." I got onstage tonight at the open mic. And Kirby and Mara, we're okay. We're going to work things out. Neil doesn't know that, but I'm not about to tell him. I don't owe him anything. I don't have to convince him that he's got me all wrong.

He straightens to his full posture. Exactly my height, and yet somehow he seems so much taller right now. "You're standing in your own fucking way, and until you realize that, you won't ever be happy with your reality."

I only have one more comeback.

"If we're not friends," I say, my voice this horrible choked sound, "then why are you still here?"

His face is a mix of pained emotions. Hurt, confusion—regret? Maybe that's wishful thinking on my part.

"Good question."

With that, he puts his back to me, shoulders hunched against the wind, and walks away.

And then I'm on my own in the cold, dark night.

HOWL STANDINGS
TOP 5

Neil McNair: 14
Rowan Roth: 13
Brady Becker: 12
Mara Pompetti: 10
Iris Zhou: 8

PLAYERS REMAINING: 13

12:27 a.m.

IF PIKE PLACE Market really is haunted, the ghosts would be out right now. I feel a little ghoulish myself as I slump through downtown, past the commercial district and along the waterfront. It's colder out here. Windier.

I hug Neil's hoodie tighter around me, wishing it belonged to anyone but him. It's annoying that it still smells good. Curse you, good-smelling hoodie I can't take off without freezing.

My feet ache from all the walking. I parked at the market, which was empty, the shops long closed, but then I needed to clear my head and figure out what the hell happened and what the hell I'm supposed to do now.

I must be obsessed with Neil McNair because even with him gone, he's all I can think about. The worst part of it is this: he wasn't wrong.

That success guide is four years old. Just because I'm not 100 percent who I wanted to be at that age doesn't mean I'm not successful. Deep down, maybe I've known that all day, but the guide was such a comfort to me, the idea that I still had a chance to cross something off.

Nothing about today, about tonight, went as planned, and

until our fight, it was okay. *Great*, even. I've clung to my fantasies and convinced myself the reality can't measure up.

I allow myself to think something I never have before: What if the reality is *better*?

I just . . . don't know how to fix this about myself. This *flaw*, Neil called it. If I manage to finish Howl by myself, then we're done competing forever. He goes off to New York and I go off to Boston, and if we see each other in Seattle when we're home on breaks, maybe we'll have a moment of sustained eye contact, a nod, and then a quick glance in the opposite direction. If something happened between us, he would be just another thing that ends after high school. Our schools are more than four hours away from each other. (I looked it up earlier.)

I want to tell Kirby and Mara, but I don't know if I can put what happened into words yet. And despite everything else, I'm glad I got onstage and read my writing. Another thing Neil McNair is inexorably tied to.

Fuck it.

I whip out my phone and hit the familiar icon on the home screen.

"Rowan?" My mom picks up after the third ring. They always celebrate deadlines the same way: getting incredibly wasted. They keep a bottle of twelve-year-old scotch in their office for these occasions. "It's late. Is everything okay? We just opened the scotch—"

"I'm writing a book," I blurt out.

"At this very moment?"

"No—I mean, I've been working on it for a while." I chew the inside of my cheek, waiting for her reaction. There's some shuffling in the background, and I can tell she's put me on speaker. "It's a romance novel."

Silence on the other end of the line.

"And I know they're not your favorite, but I really love them, okay? They're fun, and they're emotional, and they have better character development than most other books out there."

"Ro-Ro," my dad says. "You're writing a book?"

I nod before realizing they can't see me. Ugh, talking is hard. "I am. I—might want to do that. Professionally. Or at least I'd like to try."

"That's incredible," my mom says. "You have no idea how cool it is to hear that."

"Yeah?"

She laughs. "*Yes*, the fact that having us as parents hasn't ruined the writing magic for you? That's kind of awesome, if you think about it."

And maybe it is.

"It's a romance novel," I say again, in case they didn't hear me the first time.

"We heard you," my dad says. "Rowan, that's"—a pause, and some exchanged murmurs between them—"I'm sorry if we ever gave you the impression we thought it was . . . a lesser genre. Maybe it was because you started reading them so young, and we thought it was this cute, funny phase you were going through."

"It wasn't."

"We know that now," my dad says.

"I love what you do, and I love those books," I say. "And I know I have a lot to learn, but that's what college is for, right?"

Predictably, my dad laughs at this non-joke.

"Full disclosure," my mom says. "We're both a little tipsy. But we're so glad you told us. If you ever want either of us to read it, we're more than happy to."

"Thank you. I don't know if I'm there quite yet, but I'll let you know."

"Are you doing all right? You won't be out too late, will you?"

"We'll probably be asleep by the time she gets home," my dad says, "if the scotch does its job."

My mom lets out a low whistle. "This is almost as bad as what happened after that D. B. Cooper book. I think that was whiskey, though."

"The what?" I ask.

"Riley tried to solve the D. B. Cooper case in one of the Excavated books," my mom says. "Do you remember? We were so upset when our editor didn't want to publish it. She didn't think it was kid-friendly."

"D. B. Cooper . . . That was a Seattle thing, right?"

"You don't know the story?" And when I tell her no, she explains it to me.

This is the legend of D. B. Cooper: In 1971 a man hijacked a Boeing plane somewhere in the air between Portland and Seattle. He asked for $200,000 in ransom and parachuted out of the plane . . . but was never found, even after an FBI manhunt. It's the only unsolved case of its kind.

I'd read the book in manuscript form, but must have forgotten about it when they had to shelve it. And Neil wouldn't have known about it either.

"We even worked with the staff at the Museum of the Mysteries," my mom says. "That creepy old building downtown?"

"It's just as creepy on the inside," my dad says. "And *weird*, too. It's half museum, half bar. So they keep it open late."

Suddenly, everything clicks into place. God, I love my parents.

"Rowan?" my mom says, with enough urgency that makes me think I must have zoned out. "Rowan Luisa, when do you think you'll be home?"

"I probably won't be too much longer."

"Have fun," my mom says, and they start giggling again as we hang up.

The Museum of the Mysteries. If I still cared about Howl, I'd get this view clue and then go there. Good to know, I guess.

I blow out a breath. They know, and Kirby and Mara know, and when I start classes in the fall, this could be what I tell my new friends too. *I'm writing a romance novel.*

The Great Wheel glimmers against the night sky. I've never actually been on this Ferris wheel. The name is no joke. When it was built, it was the tallest Ferris wheel on the West Coast, and the idea of being so high up scared me. But tonight its lights draw me closer, and I wonder why I was ever afraid of it.

"Last ride of the night," the guy at the ticket booth says after I hand over my five dollars. "You're just in time."

A minute later, my feet are off the ground.

The air is cool against my face, and down below, the water is black and serene. A couple cars above me, two teens are laughing and taking selfies. A couple cars below me, a father is trying to calm a too-rowdy child.

"Don't you dare rock this seat, Liam," he says. "Liam . . . LIAM!"

I am on a Ferris wheel at midnight. It would be extremely romantic if I weren't alone.

This whole day, I've felt on the edge of so many things. In high school, I knew how to do everything and how it should all make me feel. There's a comfort in challenging Neil because there are only ever two outcomes: he wins, or I win. A routine. A security blanket.

I've lived here my whole life, but I'd never been on the Great Wheel. I'd never almost broken into a library. I'd never experienced Seattle the way I did tonight, but it's not just the setting. Bit by bit, today forced me out of my comfort zone. The end of the game means the end of high school, and while there's plenty I romanticized, there's so much I'll miss. Kirby and Mara. My classes, my teachers.

Neil.

"Oh my God," someone says, breaking my concentration. A woman's voice. "Oh my God!"

The voices are coming from the other side of the wheel. It's not a scared-sounding *oh my God*. It's the good kind.

"She said yes!" Another woman's voice.

Everyone on the wheel breaks into cheers as the couple embraces. If that's not romance-novel-worthy, I don't know what is.

I want to leap fearlessly into whatever is next for me. I really do. And it's not like I have a choice—I'm not going to sit on top of this Ferris wheel for the rest of my life. I mean, the guy said I'm the last ride of the night, so quite literally, it's not an option. I'm just terrified of falling, of failing, of not being able to catch myself.

My car stops at the top. It's so fucking beautiful, my lit-up city, that I'm going to be a tourist and take a picture. I unzip my backpack and reach for my phone, my fingers grazing a familiar hardcover.

My yearbook.

Slowly, I pull it out of my backpack, hands trembling as I turn to the back pages. He didn't want me to read it until tomorrow, but fuck it, it's tomorrow, and I'm desperate to know what it says.

I have to flip around to find it. Two pages in the back were stuck together, and that's how he managed to find some space. There's my nickname in calligraphy, and—woof, it's long. My eyes dart around at first, struggling to focus on any single word. What I'm hoping is for some reassurance that I haven't fucked things up beyond repair, though of course he wrote this before our fight. Still, it feels like a life preserver.

So I inhale the cold night air, and then I start reading.

Artoo,

I'm switching back to regular handwriting. Calligraphy is hard, and I didn't bring my good pens. Or I need more practice.

Right now you're sitting across from me, probably writing HAGS 30 times in a row. I know a little bit of a lot of languages, but even so, I struggle to put this into words. Okay. I'm just going to do it.

First of all, I need you to know I'm not putting this out there with any hope of reciprocation. This is something I have to get off my chest (cliché, sorry) before we go our separate ways (cliché). It's the last day of school, and therefore my last chance.

"Crush" is too weak a word to describe how I feel. It doesn't do you justice, but maybe it works for me. I am the one who is crushed. I'm crushed that we have only ever regarded each other as enemies. I'm crushed when the day ends and I haven't said anything to you that isn't cloaked in five layers of sarcasm. I'm crushed, concluding this year without having known that you like melancholy music or eat cream cheese straight from the tub in the middle of the night or play with your bangs when you're nervous, as though you're worried they look bad. (They never do.)

You're ambitious, clever, interesting, and beautiful. I put "beautiful" last because for some reason, I have a feeling you'd roll your eyes if I wrote it first. But you are. You're beautiful and adorable and so fucking charming. And you have this energy that radiates off you, a shimmering optimism I wish I could borrow for myself sometimes.

You're looking at me like you can't believe I'm not done yet, so let me wrap this up before I turn it into a five-paragraph essay. But if it were an essay, here's the thesis statement:

I am in love with you, Rowan Roth.

Please don't make too much fun of me at graduation?

Yours,
Neil P. McNair

12:43 a.m.

AT FIRST THE words don't sink in. It doesn't make sense. This has to be some elaborate joke, one final, twisted way for Neil to win by making a fool of me. So I read it again, lingering on the fourth paragraph, and the sixth paragraph, and the way my nickname looks in his handwriting. And then the seventh paragraph, the single-sentence confession:

I am in love with you, Rowan Roth.

There is too much care and sincerity in those words for it to be a joke. My pulse is roaring in my ears, my heart a wild animal.

Neil McNair is in love with me. Neil McNair. Is in love. With *me*.

I'm not sure how many times I read it. Each time, different words jump out at me, "crush" and "beautiful" and "in love," "in love," "in love."

Something catches in my throat—a laugh? A sob? Valedictorian Neil McNair wrote "fuck" in my yearbook. I read it again. I can't stop. "Shimmering optimism"—not head-in-the-clouds-ism. He likes that about me, enough to tell me when I'm so extreme about it that I'm standing in my own way.

Except. *It would have been a mistake*, he said when I asked about what happened on the bench.

He was bluffing. He had to be. This note is so heartfelt, he couldn't have switched off those feelings in a matter of hours. I may not know much about love that I haven't read in a book, but I'm sure it lingers longer than that. A simmer, not a spark.

This message, it's sweeter than any romance novel.

It's *real*.

Neil loves me.

Earlier today, I couldn't picture him kissing anyone. Is it because I can only picture this happening with me, that Rowan plus Neil is this inevitability everyone has known except us? Kirby and Mara, Chantal Okafor in student council, Logan Perez who let us into the safe zone, my parents . . .

Do I love Neil McNair?

Even if I'm not entirely certain, the reality is that I really think I *could*.

I have to get off this fucking Ferris wheel.

Life is funny, though: the most romantic moment of my life, and I'm at the top of a Ferris wheel with a yearbook instead of the boy who wrote in it that he's in love with me.

The Museum of the Mysteries, located in a downtown Seattle basement, is Seattle's only museum dedicated to the paranormal. I'm not sure why they need to explain it or why the city would ever need more than one museum dedicated to the paranormal, but there it is on the sign in front.

Can we talk? I texted Neil once the Ferris wheel touched down. I feel really awful about what happened. And I think I figured out the last clue. No one's won Howl yet, or we'd have received a message blast. I'm determined to make things up to him.

He replied ok without any punctuation, very un-Neil-like. He was clearly upset if he wouldn't spell out the word, but maybe it's proof he still feels the way he did when he wrote in my yearbook that he agreed to meet back up. Or he wants to win this game and be done with tonight.

He's waiting on a bricked street with a rickety staircase that leads to the museum. His hair is mussed, his posture slightly hunched. Why did I ever tease him about those freckles? I love them. I love every single one of them. I love his freckles and his red hair and the too-short legs of his suit pants and the too-long sleeves, the way he laughs, the way he pushes up his glasses to rub his eyes.

I am in love with you, Rowan Roth.

He lifts one hand in a wave, and I melt.

I am in so much trouble.

"Hi," I say in a small voice.

"Hey."

"Eerie that it's—" I say, at the same time he says, "Should we—"

"What was that?" he asks.

"Oh. Um. I was going to say, it's eerie that it's open so late."

"It *is* Seattle's only museum dedicated entirely to the paranormal," he says, pointing to the sign.

He's not quite as stiff as I thought he'd be. We both reach for the door at the same time, our hands brushing. Then we yank them away like we've touched fire.

The woman working here is reading a book behind the counter. She has white-blond hair down to her hips and large purple glasses.

"Evening," she says, barely glancing at us.

We pay the cheap entry fee, thank her, and venture farther into the museum. A strange soundtrack is playing, a classical piece punctuated by screams. It feels like we're in a haunted house. We keep bumping into each other, like our feet have forgotten how to walk.

"I, um, got the 'view from up high clue,'" I say.

"Me too." But he doesn't ask where I went, so I don't either.

We pause in front of a display about the Maury Island UFO Incident.

I read off the plaque: "'The Maury Island UFO Incident occurred in June 1947. Following sightings of unidentified flying objects over Maury Island in Puget Sound, Fred Crisman and Harold Dahl claimed to witness falling debris and threats by men in black. Dahl later took back his claims and stated it was a hoax . . . BUT WAS IT?'" I tap my chin. "A little bit of editorializing, I think."

He just grunts.

None of our silences have been this awkward.

"You could take your sister here," I suggest, trying to lighten the mood.

He shrugs. "She might get scared. She's not really into creepy stuff, especially after the whole Blorgon Seven thing."

"Oh. Right." I round a corner and point to a sign that says THE D. B. COOPER ROOM. "He's got an entire room to himself, lucky guy."

One wall lists all the facts known about him:

> *Ordered a bourbon and soda*
> *Midforties*
> *Dark-brown eyes*
> *Wore a mother-of-pearl tie pin and a black necktie*
> *Receding hairline*
> *Had some level of aviation knowledge*

The FBI retired his case in 2016, but clearly Pacific Northwesterners are still fascinated by it, as demonstrated by this exhibit.

"He's got to be dead," Neil says. "There's no way he survived that jump."

"I don't know. It's cool to imagine that he's still out there somewhere. He'd be ancient at this point, but he could've had kids. Maybe he got away with it and outsmarted all of us." We pause in front of a wax bust of his head. "Kind of a hottie," I say, trying to lighten the mood again.

"Middle-aged and balding is your type?"

No, freckled redheads who alter their own suits are my type. "Oh yeah," I say, and it feels, for a split second, like we're back to normal. But then Neil walks around the room, snaps a photo.

"I guess that's it," he says. "We're done. We can go to the gym and divide up the prize and go our separate ways, like you wanted. You don't have to give me your share as some kind of pity money."

And if that isn't a gut-punch.

He turns to go, but I reach for his arm.

"Neil. Wait."

"I can't, Rowan." He shuts his eyes and shakes his head, as though wishing he could pull a D. B. Cooper and disappear. "This was a ridiculous idea, the two of us teaming up. If we tried to destroy each other for four years, why would we suddenly get along tonight?"

I bite down hard on the inside of my cheek. "I'm sorry for what I said about your dad. I didn't mean it. You shared so much personal stuff with me today, and I should have treated that with more respect."

"You should have. I agree."

I take a step back, trying to give him space. "I want to be friends."

He snorts. "Why the hell would you want that? You made it pretty clear earlier that's not what we are."

"You're right. I did." I take a deep breath. "Look . . . you've been a huge pain in my ass for the past four years, but you're also all these things I didn't know until today. You're an excellent dancer.

You love children's books. You care about your family. And you're Jewish, and, well . . . it's nice to know another one."

"You'll meet plenty of other Jewish kids in Boston."

"You're making it really hard for me to compliment you."

He gives me a sheepish smile, and at that I finally feel myself relax. We can be okay. We have to be. "I'm sorry about what I said, too," he says. "About you sabotaging yourself. That was . . . completely out of line. You were incredible at that open mic, and—and I should have given you more credit for that."

"You weren't entirely wrong, though." I lean against the railing, a couple feet from him, testing our boundaries. "I'm a bit of a dreamer, and I stand in my own way. Sometimes it feels like competing with you is the only thing that's grounded me." I pause, then: "I called my parents. I told them about my book."

His eyes light up. It's a crime that I've never noticed how lovely they are. "And? How did it feel?"

"Terrifying. Fantastic," I say. But I'm not done apologizing yet. I haven't been fully honest with him tonight. Every time I said something wrong, I was trying to stick to a plan that no longer feels like mine. I wonder how it would feel to let go of that completely. "Neil. I keep saying these horrible things to you, these things I don't mean. Not just what I said about your dad, either. Like when you asked me to sign your yearbook. It's like my natural instinct is to fight with you, and I'm trying really hard to override it, but I've messed up a few times. And I'm so sorry."

He's quiet for a moment. "My instinct is to brush it off and tell you it's fine, but . . . thank you for saying that."

"What I said in the library, when we were dancing . . ." When I exhale, it's shaky. The way he spilled his heart on my yearbook page, he might be braver than I've ever been. He makes me want to try harder. "I wasn't imagining anyone else."

This drags a smile out of him. "Yeah?" he says, and I nod.

"I really did have fun with you today." Slowly, I inch closer to him, watching his face carefully. His brows twitch, and if I didn't know any better, I'd say he's swaying slightly in my direction. One and a half more steps and we'd be chest to chest, hip to hip.

"Was that so hard to admit?" he asks, his smile deepening into a smirk.

I am in love with you, Rowan Roth.

I fist a hand in my hair and let out a strangled, frustrated sound. "God, you are so infuriating." It doesn't come out cruel, though. Teasing, maybe, but not cruel.

"But you like it." It's possibly the boldest thing he's said all day, and when he takes a step forward, I can feel the heat radiating off him. No wonder he was fine parting with his hoodie—the boy is a human sauna. "You like being infuriated. By me."

I do. I like it so much.

My breath hitches. He must be able to hear it, because one side of his mouth slants up, and he runs his hand along the railing until it almost but not quite touches mine. There's so little space between our bodies now. His scent is earthy and heady, making me ache for something I didn't know I wanted.

The fantasy: that my perfect high school boyfriend would be the epitome of romance.

The reality: Neil McNair has been here all along.

"Passive voice?" I challenge, sounding much huskier than I'm used to hearing. "Westview taught you better than that."

It doesn't make him laugh the way I hoped. Instead, he gives me this look that's half amused and half serious, one that turns me electric. His gaze is steady, and I have a view of the gorgeous angles of his throat as he swallows hard.

"No," he says, so close to me that I can almost hear his heart beat in time with mine. "You did."

And that's what pushes me over the edge. Before I can overthink it, before I spend forever dreaming up the perfect moment, I lunge forward, pinning him against the railing and covering his mouth with mine.

HOWL STANDINGS
TOP 5

Neil McNair: 14
Rowan Roth: 14
Brady Becker: 14
Mara Pompetti: 13
Carolyn Gao: 10

PLAYERS REMAINING: 11

ARE WE CLOSE TO A WINNER? HURRY AND GOOD LUCK!

1:21 a.m.

NEIL MCNAIR IS kissing me back. There's no hesitation, not like when we hugged earlier with shy, uncertain limbs. This time, he lets himself fall.

His lips press hard against mine as I wrap my arms around his neck, sinking into him. It's a fast, desperate kind of kiss, and *God*, he feels good. His hands get lost in my hair, and that plus his mouth plus this sound he makes deep in his throat turn my blood to fire. I part my lips, tasting a lingering sweetness from the cinnamon roll we shared. My imagination wouldn't have been able to do him justice.

When he smiles against my mouth, I can feel it.

"Rowan?" he says as he pulls back, his voice a mix of surprise and awe. He's breathing hard. His eyes are beautiful and heavy-lidded, those long lashes fluttering against the lenses of his glasses. Maybe it's drowsiness, or maybe he's just as drunk on this feeling as I am. "What's . . . happening?"

"I'm kissing you." I move one hand from the collar of his shirt to the back of his neck and into his hair. I want to burn every texture into my fingertips. "Should I stop?"

He skates his thumb along my cheekbone. Despite how light

his touch is, I feel like I might detonate. "No. Absolutely not," he says. He traces my nose. My lips. "I just wanted to make sure—I don't know. That you realized it's me."

The uncertainty in his voice unstitches me. All the books in the world couldn't have prepared me for this moment. There aren't enough words.

"That's the best part," I tell him.

No, this is the best part: when we lean in again and it turns wilder. With one hand in my hair and one on my hip, he spins us so I'm pressed against the railing. Our mouths clash together, teeth and tongues arguing with each other. Trying to win whatever new competition this is. I run my hands over his chest, up the arms I've been staring at all day, overwhelmed by how much of him I want to touch. I underline and then scribble over that dorky Latin phrase with my fingertips. He's so solid beneath my palms, and I can't help gripping the fabric of his T-shirt a little.

His hands find their way back to my hair. And his lips, beckoning, taunting, *daring* me. Because *fuck*, Neil is hot. It's absurd, and it's true.

"You like my hair," I tease between kisses.

"God. So much. It's fucking phenomenal hair."

Now I'm even more certain why I couldn't picture him kissing anyone else: because it was always supposed to be like this. With us.

He keeps me pinned to the railing, kissing my jaw, my neck, beneath my ear. I shiver when he lingers there.

"Is this okay?" he asks against my skin.

"Yes," I say, and he stamps my collarbone with his mouth. I'm addicted to the way he asks me that. How he wants to be sure.

This has to be the earth-shattering feeling he was talking about. This: his hands sliding down the sides of my body. This: his teeth grazing my clavicle. And this: the way, when he moves back to my lips, he kisses like I'm alternately something he can't get enough of and something he wants to savor. Fast, then slow. I love it all.

Since we're the same height, our bodies line up perfectly, and—*oh*. The proof of how much he's enjoying this makes me feverish. I rock my hips against his because the pressure feels amazing, and the way he groans when I do this sounds amazing too.

I drop my hands lower, to his belt. My fingertips graze the soft skin of his stomach, and he lets out a quiet, involuntary laugh. Ticklish. Distantly, I'm aware that we're in public. That we have to stop before we go too far. But I've never felt this wanted, and it's an intoxicating, powerful feeling. I've never lost myself in someone like this.

With every molecule in my body, I force myself to pull away.

"That was . . . wow," I say, breathless.

He leans his forehead against mine, still holding me around my waist. "'Wow' is not an adjective."

In four years, I have never heard his voice like this. This ragged, this spent.

I'm not sure how long we stand there, breathing each other in, breaking the relative silence every so often to laugh like the lovedrunk loons we are. His cheeks are flushed. I'm sure mine are too.

"I was so sure I'd ruined everything," he says after a while. He reaches for my hand, and it's so easy to thread my fingers with his. "I wanted to kiss you on that bench so badly. But then we were interrupted, and I got . . . scared, I guess. Scared you didn't feel the same way."

It's a relief to hear him say it. "So that's why you said it would have been a mistake." I trace his knuckles with my thumb.

He nods. "I thought, I don't know, that you regretted it, and the best way for me to get over it was to pretend it was a mistake. I didn't want it to make you uncomfortable."

"A defense mechanism."

"Yeah," he says, bringing up his other hand to cup my face.

"I guess I have a few of those too."

When we kiss again, it's softer. Sweeter.

Out of the corner of my eye, I can see D. B. Cooper watching us, reminding me why we came here in the first place.

"The game." I use all my willpower to stop kissing him. We're so close to that five grand, to Neil potentially being able to change his name. To some freedom from his old life—whether I'm part of that new life or not. "We should go."

"I, um. Need a moment," he says, glancing down sheepishly. Heat rushes to my cheeks, and I can't help grinning again.

With some effort, we untangle ourselves and reach for our phones. No Howl updates, meaning no one's won yet. Slowly, I feel myself slide back into competitive mode. Westview is less than fifteen minutes away. Howl is nearly ours.

We weave our way out of the museum, hiding our flushed faces from the woman at the front desk. When I glance back, I swear I see her smile.

I'm not sure if I reach for his hand first or if he reaches for mine, but it immediately feels natural. He brushes his thumb across my knuckles on the way to my car, and when we get there, he pushes me up against the driver's side door like a bad boy in a teen movie.

"We have a whole summer to do this," I say, even as I'm grabbing his T-shirt and tugging his mouth to mine. "I mean—if you want to."

And although his yearbook confession is stamped behind my lids whenever I blink, his response sends sparks down to my toes.

"Do I want to kiss you all summer?" He raises his eyebrows, mouth quirking to one side. "Is Nora Roberts prolific?"

"More than two hundred books," I say. Then, with some reluctance: "But we're so close. We'll come back to this."

One long kiss, and then he groans. "Fine, fine. You win."

"Can you say that again? I like the way it sounds."

"Shameless," he says, but there's that lazy-sweet-sly smile again, the one I'd never seen before tonight. The one I know now is solely mine.

But something tightens in my throat. *A whole summer.* Suddenly, it doesn't sound very long at all.

"Hey, lovebirds. You guys finally figured it out, huh?"

Across the street, Brady Becker is unlocking a little white Toyota, pausing to wave at us. The paper with his name on it burns hot in my pocket.

Stronger than the shock of star quarterback Brady Becker realizing we're together is the sense of dread creeping up my spine.

Neil blinks a few times, as though trying to process what Brady's doing here. "Hey," he says quietly, voice laced with uncertainty. We haven't talked about how to announce ourselves to the rest of our graduating class, if that's something we even want to do. I twine my fingers through Neil's, showing him exactly how I feel about that. His features relax, and he wraps his fingers around mine again. "Yeah, we, um . . . yeah. We did."

His nerves are too adorable.

"Cool museum," Brady says, and I force my oxytocin-addled brain to remember where Brady was in the most recent blast of Howl standings.

Fourteen.

He had fourteen, just like we did. And if he's leaving the museum, that must mean—

"See you back at school," he says. "I'll be the one with the five-thousand-dollar check."

DRAFT: (no subject)

Rowan Roth <rowanluisaroth@gmail.com>
to: jared@garciarothbooks.com,
ilana@garciarothbooks.com
Saved Saturday, June 13, at 12:32 a.m.

Dearest Mom and Dad,

This is scary, but here are the first few chapters. Be gentle with me.

Love,
Your favorite daughter, cream cheese enthusiast, and potential one-day romance author

Attachment: chapters 1–3 for mom and dad.docx

2:04 a.m.

I DIDN'T THINK Howl would end with a car chase, but I've been wrong about a lot of things today. To be fair, it's a chase between two used cars with decent fuel economies and five-star safety ratings. *The Fast and the Furious: Sensible Sedans.*

The streets are deserted, nighttime lights smudging the skyline with gold, and my heart bangs against the seat belt as we trail Brady to the freeway.

"I didn't realize he was so close to us," I say, changing lanes and hitting the gas. We remain parallel with the Toyota, even as I accelerate up to 70 mph.

Neil stares down at his phone. "D. B. Cooper must have been his last one too. I guess we were . . . distracted."

"Right," I say, my stomach dropping. If he regrets what happened at the museum . . .

"Even if he wins," he says, as though he can detect the insecurity in my voice, "I wouldn't have done anything differently. I want you to know that." He sounds more solid than he has all night, and it fills me with a fierce determination.

"Don't worry. We're not going to let him."

We're neck and neck until we approach the exit, where I have to switch back into his lane. Behind him.

"A for effort!" Brady yells out his window as he sneaks through a yellow light the moment before it turns red.

I hit the brakes. "Shit. What now?"

"Turn right," Neil says. "He's probably taking Forty-Fifth all the way. If we take the backstreets, we won't hit any more lights."

"You sure?"

"No," he admits. "But it's our only chance."

I flip on my blinker and swerve right, taking us into a residential neighborhood. I circle a few roundabouts, white-knuckling the steering wheel the whole time.

The school parking lot is just up ahead, and Brady's white Toyota is approaching it from the other side of the street. There's Logan Perez, standing at the entrance to the gym with Nisha and Olivia, holding two black-and-white checkered flags. There's a grassy field between the parking lot and the gym. We can get close, but we'll still have to make a run for it.

This is it.

"There's two of us, and only one of him. You have to go for Logan," I say. "I'll park as close as I can and try to stop Brady. All I have to do is grab his bandanna." A laugh tumbles out. "It sounds easy when I say it like that."

He reaches over to brush my wrist with a few fingertips. Even his lightest touches feel impossibly intense. "Okay. We've got this. Then—then we'll figure everything out later?"

Our bet. Splitting the prize.

I've already conquered more tonight than I ever thought I would. Second place has never sounded so great.

"Yes," I say, following Brady to a parking spot at the edge of the lot and throwing the car into park. *"Go!"*

Summoning any latent athletic ability I left on that soccer field in middle school and any strength gained from carrying a massive backpack for the past four years, I throw open the door, launching myself at Brady. On the other side of the car, Neil leaps onto the grassy field and heads for Logan.

"Rowan—what the—" Brady asks, but I'm clawing my way toward his bandanna, capturing it in my fist, ripping it off. "Oh, *shit*."

We tumble to the pavement, legs tangling. Brady cushions me to some degree, no doubt experienced when it comes to tackles, but I still manage to smack my knee on the way down. I'm too amped on adrenaline to care, especially not when I hear the whoops and cheers from a few yards away. The blow of a whistle. Neil's stunned laughter.

Breathing hard, I thrust Brady's bandanna into the air like a victory flag.

We did it.

"Fuuuuck," Brady groans from beneath me, and I'm not sure if it's pain or the agony of losing.

I scramble to a sitting position, then try to stand—*ow*. Not bleeding, but that's definitely going to bruise.

"I'm so sorry," I say to Brady. "Are you okay?"

"Gonna have a bruise on my ass the size of Jupiter, but yeah. You?"

"Yes," I say with a wince, hobbling toward the gym.

When he spots me, Neil rushes forward, and I practically topple into his arms.

"Your knee," he says, but I wave it off. He clutches me tighter, his lips brushing my ear when he speaks. "You are amazing. I can't believe we did it. We *won*."

"You did." I slide one hand around to the back of his neck and into his hair, not caring what Logan or Nisha or Olivia thinks about us embracing like this.

He pulls back and lifts an eyebrow. "Seriously? There's no way I could have done any of this alone. Guess we make a pretty good team after all."

And I honestly can't not kiss him after that.

I believe it now, that this is how we were always meant to be, and yet I can't quite wrap my mind around everything that's happened. We won, and I don't think it would feel nearly as good if I'd done this by myself.

The trio of juniors descends on us.

"Congratulations again," Logan says, eyes darting back and forth between us as though she knows exactly what was going on with us back at that safe zone. It's scary how good a politician she might make someday. She turns and opens the door to the gym. "Your party awaits. Well—as soon as we tell everyone it's happening." She motions to Nisha and Olivia, who pull out their phones, presumably to send another text blast.

"Our what?" Neil says.

The gym is bright and festive, decked out in Westview blue and white—streamers, banners, lights. There are rows of carnival games and food vendors, a small stage at one end. A few juniors are still finishing the setup.

"We had some money left over, and we wanted to give all the seniors one more thing to celebrate," Logan says. "We were going to launch it when the game ended, so we've just been waiting—"

"—and hoping we can get sleep at some point," Olivia puts in.

"But it was worth it!" Nisha says.

I can't stop gaping at the scene in front of us. Maybe I'm delirious, but I've never seen the gym look this beautiful. "Thank you. All of you."

Neil appears mesmerized by the band unpacking a drum kit and loading their amps onto the stage.

"Oh my God," he says. "Free Puppies!"

It's the best party I've ever been to. Nearly all the seniors are here, plus Neil's favorite band, and he's just won five thousand dollars, half of which I'll refuse to accept if he offers it to me. A few teachers show up to chaperone, but we're not rowdy. Maybe we're all too tired to cause much trouble.

When they see us together, Mara gasps, and Kirby immediately races over to crush us into a bear hug. "I knew it, I knew it, I knew it," she yelps. Most reactions fall solidly within that range. Neil and I can't stop grinning, can't stop touching: hands linked, his palm on my back, a stealthy kiss when we think no one's looking. Turns out, someone always is.

The walls are covered with posters for events that have already happened, and there's a sense of nostalgia in the air, but for the first time tonight, it doesn't feel sad. Howl has always been a farewell to Westview and to Seattle. A last-day tradition that's about so much more than winners and losers.

Savannah approaches us while we're waiting for Free Puppies! to start playing. The sight of her makes me tense up.

"Congratulations, I guess," she says flatly.

"Thank you," Neil says, ever polite. Always earnest, beneath all that smirking.

But I'm all out of politeness when it comes to Savannah Bell.

"Hey, you know what I'm craving?" I say to Neil. "Bowling-alley pizza. Like at Hilltop. Do you think they have any pizza here?"

"You . . . had the pizza at Hilltop Bowl?" Savannah asks, brows drawing together in an expression of concern.

"No. But I know you did." With that, I meet her gaze, unblinking, and I bring up my right index finger to tap my nose once, twice. Her face flushes, and it immediately becomes clear she knows what I'm talking about.

Neil catches on. "I'm Jewish too." His hand drifts to my back.

"And this might sound odd to you, but that money's actually going to make a big difference for me."

I really, really like him.

"That's—great," Savannah manages, and she steps backward until she disappears into the crowd.

Kirby and Mara wind up on one side of us, sharing a gigantic sugary pretzel, and Neil's friends on the other. They seem about as surprised by our romantic development as Kirby as Mara—which is to say, not at all.

"What are you gonna do with the money?" Adrian asks. "And don't tell me something responsible like putting it in savings. You have to have a *little* fun."

Neil glances at me, and I become putty. "Oh, we will. And I already have some ideas."

McNasty, Kirby mouths to me.

"What was that?" Neil asks.

"Kirby's being inappropriate."

"Did you think that would make me less curious?"

"Oh, we're going to have fun this summer," Kirby says.

Mara, though, is a bit of a sore loser. "I only had two more clues left," she laments, half joking.

Still, the three of us and sometimes the seven of us take selfies and make plans to go to the Capitol Hill Block Party in a couple weeks. I don't know if we're going to be okay in college. But we have the summer, and after that, we'll try our best. I can be content with that for now.

A squawk of feedback drags our attention to the stage.

"Good morning, Westview!" shouts the neon-haired lead singer, earning a whoop from the audience. "We're so glad you stayed up all night for us. This first song is called 'Stray,' and if we don't see you dancing, we're packing up and leaving."

They're pretty fantastic live, like Neil said. He brushes back my hair to plant a kiss below my ear, and as I'm wondering whether he knows exactly how sensitive I am there, he gives me this wicked grin that proves he does.

I didn't know it could feel this way.

When the band takes a break, Neil and I wander through the crowd, accepting congratulations and playing a few games, though after about ten minutes, we're a little gamed out. My knee is starting to ache, and I'm not sure I can stand for much longer.

"I'm trying to think of a clever way to say this, but . . . do you want to get out of here?" I ask him.

"I do," he says, "and I actually have somewhere in mind, if you're up for one more adventure."

I give him an emphatic yes before following him through the crush of our almost-former classmates. There will be more parties over the next week. I'm sure of it. But there is so much out there beyond high school, so much that I cannot possibly begin to wrap my mind around. I'm trying my best to keep it that way. This summer, I will say plenty of goodbyes—to my friends, to my parents, to the gum wall and the Fremont Troll and cinnamon rolls as big as my face. They won't be forever goodbyes. I'll be back, Seattle. I promise.

So when we get outside, I take one last look at the school. Later, Neil and I will talk about what this means, about what we've done tonight and what happens tomorrow. But right now I want to savor this moment with him, both the quiet and the way he looks at me like he's counting the seconds until we can kiss like we did in the museum.

Maybe this is how I'm supposed to say goodbye to high school: not with an arbitrary list or a preconceived notion of the way things are supposed to be, but by realizing we're actually better together.

Neil squeezes my hand. "Ready?" he asks.

"I think I am."

Then I take a deep breath . . . and I let it all go.

THE TOP 5 FREE PUPPIES! SONGS,
ACCORDING TO NEIL MCNAIR

1. "Pawing at Your Door"
2. "Enough (Is Never Enough)"
3. "Stray"
4. "Darling, Darling, Darling"
5. "Little Houses"

2:49 a.m.

"THE BEST VIEW in Seattle," Neil says as we get out of my car on the south side of Queen Anne Hill.

Kerry Park isn't big, a narrow strip of grass with a fountain and a couple sculptures. The view of the Space Needle completely sneaks up on you. It looks unreal from here, huge and bright and glorious, especially at night. He's right: it's the best view in Seattle.

"This is where you went earlier?" I ask, and he nods.

I limp along with him to the edge of the lookout.

"I cannot believe you did that." He gestures to my leg. "Are you sure you don't need some ice or something?"

I shake my head. "Sacrifices had to be made."

We position ourselves on the ledge, our legs dangling onto the grassy hill below. Again I'm struck by how normal this feels. He's been part of my life for so long that there's a comfort mixed with the newness, and I can't wait to know him in all the ways we missed out on.

"When did you know?" I rest my head on his shoulder. "That you didn't despise me."

"It wasn't one singular event," he says, his arm settling around my waist. "Early junior year was when I started having feelings for you, but I figured it was pointless. You couldn't stand me, and I seemingly couldn't stand you."

"You hid it so well."

"I had to. If I suddenly acted differently, you'd get suspicious."

"So you liked me even during that student council meeting that lasted until midnight, that *White Man in Peril* incident?"

"The what?"

"Oh—*A White Man in Peril*. It's what I call your classics, since they're all about, well—"

"White men in peril," he finishes, laughing. "And yes. Yes I did. What about you?"

"Three hours ago?" I say, and with his free hand, he clutches his heart as if in pain. "Fifteen hours ago, when I saw your arms in that T-shirt?"

"God bless my rigorous workout routine."

"Is that what you call those eight-pound weights on your desk?"

"I—um—I keep the bigger ones in my closet," he says. "Really massive ones. Fifty, sixty pounds. I don't want anyone to get too intimidated, you know."

"That's very thoughtful." I snuggle closer. "If I'm being honest, though . . . I'm not sure. I realized it today, but I think I've liked you for a while."

After a few moments of quiet, he asks, "Do you remember that election for freshman-class rep?"

"Of course. It was a landslide victory for me."

"As I recall, you won by a pretty narrow margin." He twirls a strand of my hair. "I won that essay contest, and you won the election. And then we kept at it, trying to one-up each other."

"All these years, we were fighting when we could have been . . . not fighting."

He pulls back, and when I lift my head, he's eyeing me strangely. "I was actually thinking the opposite. That I'm not sure we were ready for it. I definitely wasn't."

"Maybe not," I admit. Still, it's shattering, thinking of what we could have shared. Visions of an alternate timeline pass through my mind—football games and homecoming dances and awkward photos and—

I force it away. That's not our reality.

"It's kind of poetic that it's happening tonight, though," he says. Then, with a thread of worry in his voice: "It's not just tonight for you, is it? Because I'm really in this, if you are."

"I am. This . . . this feels real. I want to be with you." I'm aware, again, of all the conversations we haven't had yet. The conversations I'm suddenly afraid to have when he feels so *right* next to me.

He traces the outline of my eyebrow with his fingertip. One, and then the other, as though he is trying to memorize what I look like. "I wanted to tell you. I decided I'm not going to see my dad this summer. Maybe one day I'll change my mind about it and want some kind of relationship with him, but it's still too raw. I'm not ready."

"You feel good about that?"

He nods. "I do. And—I made an appointment online. To change my last name. It's time."

"Neil," I say, placing my hand on his knee. "That's . . . wow."

"It's the right decision for me. For a lot of reasons."

"I'll have to change your nicknames." When he makes an odd face, I add: "I look forward to it."

I lean in and kiss him. It's so easy to get caught up in the moment with him, for the outside world to dissolve away.

"I also, um, got something for you," he says after a few moments, shifting so he can get to his backpack. "After we split up, I passed by a QFC, and I thought it might at least make you smile if you decided you wanted to talk to me again. And that maybe you'd be hungry." With that, he reveals the gift: a tub of Philadelphia with a red ribbon around it, and a compostable bag with two bagels inside. "I also have a spoon, if you prefer it that way."

"You're never going to let me forget that, huh?" I say, though my heart trips over this unexpected gift. It's ridiculous, yes, but it's also so damn sweet.

"No. I love it. I—" He breaks off, as though realizing he might reveal something he's not sure I'm ready for.

"I love you too," I say, and the horror on his face eases back into calm. It's so easy to say, and it gives me such a rush that I immediately want to say it again. "I, um, I read what you wrote in my yearbook. In my defense, it was tomorrow, and I thought you hated me. But I'm in love with you, Neil McNair—Neil Perlman—and I think maybe I've been in love with you for a long time. It just took my brain a while to catch up to my heart. I don't know how I missed it, but you are pretty fucking great."

It's incredible to watch someone melt in front of you. His face softens and his lips part, and he pulls me so close that I can feel our hearts thudding against each other.

"I know I wrote it down, but I have to say it out loud now too," he says. I brace myself for it. I've wanted to hear those words ever since I found that first romance novel at a garage sale. "I'm in love with you. You are the most interesting person I know, and I've never been able to talk to anyone the way I can talk to you. I've devoted the past four years to leaving Seattle, but you . . . You are the best thing about this city. You are going to be the hardest to leave. I love you so much."

From all the books I've read, I thought I understood the concept of love, but *wow*, I knew nothing. I fold myself into him, not because I want his body heat but because I can't seem to get as close as I want to be. I thought I was prepared to hear it. After all, I'd already seen it in writing. But it fills me up completely, to the point where my chest nearly aches. I've given this boy the messiest parts of me, and he's done nothing but convince me he'll be careful with them.

With starry eyes, we kiss and we watch the sky and we dip bagels into cream cheese. When we finish eating, I reach into my backpack and pull out Rowan Roth's Guide to High School Success.

"So this was kind of bullshit, huh?"

"Not bullshit," he says. "But possibly not the most encouraging or inspiring thing?"

"I don't know if I want to tear it up." I flip it over on the railing, smooth out the wrinkles. "But maybe we could write a new one?"

Rowan Roth's Guide to College Success.... and Beyond!

By Rowan Luisa Roth, age 18
and Neil (Perlman) McNair, age 18

1. Abandon the idea of "perfect" because it doesn't exist. No one wants a perfect cinnamon roll; they want one that's wonky and misshapen and slathered with icing. Cream cheese icing, of course.

2. Finish my book. Write another one.

3. Take as many classes that sound interesting as I can. Creative writing, and maybe Spanish, and maybe some other things too. Keep an OPEN MIND!

4. Listen to more happy music, though melancholy music has its time and place too.

5. Enjoy as many nights like this as possible.

3:28 a.m.

THE POWER IS still out, and Neil McNair is in my room, and that is somehow not the strangest thing that's happened today.

After we finished our list, I asked if he wanted to come back to my house, since he never got a chance to see my room. It's the right ending to this day: letting him into my little piece of the world, the way he let me into his.

I am extremely grateful my parents are downstairs and heavy sleepers. I'm sure they won't be up until after noon, but I don't want to take any chances, so we tiptoe inside, and I have to force myself to whisper.

My phone has some juice from my car charger, so I find a soft but not too mopey Smiths song and hit play.

"So this is Rowan Roth's room," he says, trailing a hand along my desk. I love the way he looks in my room, softly lit from a flashlight. He glances from the photo collages and academic awards on my walls to the books stacked on my nightstand to the dresses spilling out of my closet.

"Yep. All the magic happens right here."

"I like it. It's very you." He turns so his back is to the desk. "What do you feel like doing?"

"Hmm . . . I was thinking Monopoly."

"Monopoly?" There's that lazy grin. "Okay, but I'm really good at Monopoly, and it's going to be embarrassing if I beat you aga—"

My lips are already on his. This kiss feels heavier than what happened at the museum, in the gym, at Kerry Park. Like someone stuck us in an electric socket or lit us on fire. He buries his hands in my hair, propelling me backward. When the backs of my knees hit the bed, he whispers, "Sorry," and I have to hold in a laugh as I tug him down next to me. Climb into his lap. Then we're kissing again, and his glasses keep falling down, so he whips them off and places them on the nightstand. He is so adorable and so hot and so *sweet*, always so sweet.

"I want to see you," I say, my fingers flirting with the hem of his T-shirt.

"I'm warning you, it's a lot of freckles." But he pulls it off, revealing, to my delight, the wonderfully freckled stomach I got a glimpse of earlier.

"I love your freckles. Really and truly."

I leave invisible handprints all over his chest, learning exactly where he's ticklish. He skims his hands up to my knees, my hips, beneath the dress that has suddenly become a straitjacket. I twist on his lap, trying to reach the zipper. He has to help me with it, and together we tug it off.

Once I'm in just my bra and underwear, he stares.

"I'm not unattractive, right?" I say, because teasing him will never stop being fun.

"Now you know why I was wholly incapable of paying you a

compliment. You are spectacular," he says, leaning in to kiss down my neck. "And stunning. And—sexy." There's a beat before he says that last one, and the word makes me shudder. *God.*

"You are going to destroy me," I whisper.

Losing my dress makes me kiss him with even more urgency. I run my hand over the front of his jeans, and he sucks in a breath through his teeth. It's maybe the best sound I've ever heard, at least until I unzip and unbuckle and cast his jeans aside completely, pressing him deeper into the bed, and he releases another breathy groan again. Yep, I'm destroyed.

For a while we dissolve into a blur of lips and sighs and touches. The occasional mattress squeak when we reposition, a thin layer of fabric separating us. With every new touch, he's timid at first, and it fucking kills me.

His hand slips between my legs, stroking the inside of my thigh and up, up. "Would this . . . be okay?"

"Yes. *Yes.*" What I really mean is *please.*

It took me long enough to figure it out for myself, so I give him some guidance. It turns out, he is an excellent listener. He whispers my name into my ear, slowly undoing me, and then I'm at the edge and falling, falling. . . .

I'm still recovering when the power suddenly returns and the house flashes to life, every light in my room blinking on at once.

He does have freckles everywhere.

I absolutely love it.

We've spent so much of tonight in the dark that I can't help laughing, and he joins in, squinting at the bright lights. "Shhh," I say, but it's no use.

"Too bright," he groans. "There's plenty of natural light coming in from outside."

And he's right, so I peel myself out of bed to turn everything off and then wait a minute to make sure my parents aren't moving around downstairs. When I'm confident they're still safely ensconced in scotch comas, I crawl back to him.

He reaches for me, but I place a gentle hand on his chest.

"Hold on," I say. "How far are we going here, exactly? We should talk about . . . whatever it is that we're doing. Or not doing." Anxiously, I tug at my bangs. "Because I'm kind of on board with all of it, but I know you haven't, you know. Had sex."

The weight of it hovers between us. Neil pushes into a sitting position, the sheets pooled around our ankles. This isn't like with Spencer, where, because I'd already done it with Luke, I figured, why not. I want this, with Neil. I want to talk about it, and I want him to feel comfortable talking about it with me. The idea of being with him in that way makes me dizzy with desire. I want more than this one night, but I can't think about the future right now.

"Trust me," he says, his hand settling on my waist like it's the most natural thing in the world, "there is literally nothing I want more than you. Not even valedictorian."

"I don't know if having sex is better than being valedictorian.

And I'm also not sure that's the correct usage of 'literally.' You should know that."

"With you, it might be." Worry flickers across his face. "I have to be honest. I'm a little nervous. That I'll, like, mess up or something, or make it horrible for you. And then you'll never want to do this again, which would be devastating, given how much I like you."

His nerves endear him to me even more. I like that he doesn't immediately become this smooth, overconfident guy.

"I'm nervous too," I admit. "Excited, but nervous, and that's normal. That's why we'll talk to each other. We've always been good at that, right?" I say, and he nods. "The first time with someone is usually imperfect. That's part of what makes it fun: figuring out together how to make it good."

"It's not going to be romance-novel perfect," he says, but he's not admonishing me.

"No. Not the first time, and probably not the second or third either. Maybe not ever, honestly, but it'll be *ours*. And . . . that might be better."

His thumb draws circles on my hip. "Are you sure you want this too? We haven't—I mean, we've known each other awhile, but we only just kissed tonight, and . . ." A rambly Neil McNair is almost too adorable.

It's an easy decision. "I'm sure."

"And hey, you still have a condom in your backpack."

I groan. "Oh my God. I was so mortified."

"Chekhov's condom," he says, and then I'm laughing along with him.

"I do, in fact, have some that haven't been sitting in Kirby's locker for God knows how long."

It takes only a moment to slip out of bed and grab them, a moment to shed our underwear. Another few moments to help him put one on before realizing it's inside out. Into the trash it goes, and then we try again.

Once we get it right, it doesn't last extremely long, because we're tired or because it's his first time or some combination of both. Every so often, he checks in with me, asking if it's still good, if *I'm* still good. And yes. *Yes.* We try our best to be quiet, but we can't stop whispering to each other. We've only just become friends, real friends, and there's so much we want to say.

He finishes first, and then his fingers drift down between us and he gets me there for the second time tonight. Another thing I've learned: Neil McNair is exceedingly generous.

Then we're quiet, quieter than my sleeping, darkened house. It's a peaceful, appreciative kind of quiet. I burrow close to him, resting my cheek against his heartbeat while he plays with my hair.

"Earth-shattering," he says.

"What just happened? Agreed."

He kisses the top of my head. "Well, yes, but I meant *you*."

ROWAN

good morning 🎧

this is a friendly reminder that you have one (1) minute and counting before I wake you up

5:31 a.m.

WHEN I WAKE up, I'm immediately hit with that panicky feeling you get on weekends sometimes when you're convinced you're late for school.

Only I'm not late, I no longer have school, and Neil McNair is in my bed.

He's on his side next to me, one arm thrown across the pillow, the other around my waist. The early morning sunlight slants across his face, turning his hair fiery. He is beautiful. The sky is a clear cobalt canvas, yesterday's storm forgotten.

It finally feels like summer.

As though sensing I'm awake, he pulls me closer, presses a kiss to the back of my neck. The reality drips back in. Neil and I had sex last night. Well—an hour ago, technically this morning. And it was *good*.

"Did that really happen?" I say aloud.

"Yes, unless you and I both had the same intensely erotic dream."

"I prefer the reality." I snuggle closer. "Was it okay for you? Do you feel different?"

"We'll have to do it a few more times to know for sure," he says with that wonderful smirk of his. "Yes. It was incredible. I'm not sure if I feel different, exactly. Mostly, I think I'm just happy. And . . . it wasn't terrible for you?"

I answer by pressing myself into him, dropping kisses down his jaw, onto his neck. "You make me really, really happy too. I hope you know that."

He holds me tighter. "I love you, Rowan Roth," he says. "I can't believe that's a thing I get to say."

I don't think I'll ever get tired of hearing it. I whisper it back, into his skin. I run my hand down his freckled arm, then pull on it to peer at his watch. "As horrible as it sounds, we should get up before my parents do."

He kisses my bare shoulder as I force myself to a sitting position. "Don't think I don't expect your book report on my desk by tomorrow just because we had sex."

"What book?"

"Hmm. *The Age of Innocence*? *Moby Dick*? *The Turn of the Screw*?" He thinks for another moment, that lazy-sly smile appearing again. "*Hard Times*?"

"Is that an autobiography?"

"No, it's Dickens. At least three pages, please," he says before I push him back down on the bed.

About ten minutes later, he grabs his T-shirt, pulls it on. "So what do you think? Should I be all cool and sneak out the window?"

"I think you might have to."

"I guess I'll see you at KeyArena for graduation. Which is now tomorrow. Wow. I should really work on my valedictorian speech."

"And the next day," I say, "we can have a *Star Wars* marathon. Or go on a real date."

"And this?" he says, gesturing to my sheets. "We should definitely do this again."

"We should definitely do this a lot. At least until August." That sudden heaviness pins me to the bed. "So . . . that's a thing we're going to have to deal with."

Neil must notice the change on my face because he stops halfway through buckling his belt and comes closer. "Artoo. Hey. We'll figure it out."

The nickname melts me.

"I just . . . I'm not ready to say goodbye," I say, surprised by the unexpected break in my voice. "I can say goodbye to the rest of it, to school and to our teachers and to everyone else—but I can't say goodbye to you."

"You don't have to." He cups my face, running a thumb along my cheekbone. "This isn't the end. Far from it, hopefully. If we haven't annoyed each other to death by the end of the summer, then why can't we keep going? New York and Boston aren't that far apart."

"A little over four hours, by train." Exploring other cities with Neil—it sounds too wonderful.

"And we'll be back here on breaks," he says. "You and I have to always be the best, right? So we'll be the best at long distance, if that's what we decide to do. But right now . . ." He gestures to the room around us. "Right now, we have this."

I let it sink in, trying to be okay with that uncertainty. As much as I've idealized the happily-ever-after, I can't deny that he's right. Today isn't my epilogue with Neil—it's a beginning.

I'll leave the happily-ever-afters in the books.

"I think I can do that," I say, and reach for him again.

The love that I wanted so desperately: this isn't what I thought it would feel like. It's made me dizzy and it's grounded me. It's made me laugh when nothing is funny. It shimmers and it sparks, but it can be comfortable, too, a sleepy smile and a soft touch and a quiet, steady breath. Of course this boy—my rival, my alarm clock, my unexpected ally—is at the center of it.

And somehow, it's even better than I imagined.

Author's Note

SEATTLE DIDN'T ALWAYS have my heart.

A city built on Duwamish land, Seattle has been inhabited for thousands of years. It was incorporated in 1869, after pioneers noted a lack of "marriageable women" and recruited about a hundred from the East Coast to serve as brides for the city's early residents. The city flourished after a gold rush but lost its business district to the Great Seattle Fire of 1889, then quickly rebuilt. Two twentieth-century world's fairs were instrumental in the city's progress: first the Alaska-Yukon-Pacific Exposition in 1909, and then the Century 21 Exposition in 1962, which gave us the Space Needle. Today, Seattle is a hub for both start-ups and big tech.

I've lived here my whole life, first in a suburb known for its connection to Microsoft, then in a college neighborhood, and now on a hill in North Seattle not unlike where Rowan lives. As a teen, I was captivated by the idea of reinventing myself on the other side of the country, and I was eager to escape. I was sick of trees and clouds and gloom. When it became clear I'd be attending college in Seattle, I focused my energy on applying for internships and later jobs outside the state.

It wasn't that I resigned myself to loving Seattle when nothing came to fruition. I didn't feel stuck. Rather, it was a gradual appreciation of the sights and culture and people. The music, too—I have yet to meet someone who's more of a music snob than someone who's grown up in Seattle. I like to think Seattle and I have a relationship where I'm able to poke fun and the city doesn't mind. I'm doing it out of love.

When we see Seattle in pop culture, we usually only get a piece of it: rain, the Space Needle, flannel. I wanted to dig deeper—and so the game of Howl was born. While this book takes place in a very real city, it's a patchwork of present-day Seattle and the Seattle I grew up in. Many of the landmarks are presently intact: Cinerama, Pike Place Market and the gum wall, the Great Wheel, the Seattle Public Library, the Fremont Troll, Kerry Park. Some of them I took fictional liberties with. Sadly, the Woodland Park Zoo's nocturnal exhibit is no longer open. It was shut down during the recession, and though there were plans to rebuild, a fire in the building put those plans on hold. The Museum of the Mysteries was once a real place in Capitol Hill, but now exists online only at nwlegendsmuseum.com. I should also mention that Rowan and Neil really have quite incredible luck finding parking spots.

When I began writing *Today Tonight Tomorrow*, it was important to me that Rowan love Seattle, even if she was committed to leaving it behind for college. This book is a love letter to love, but it was a love letter to Seattle first.

Cities are perennial works in progress, and it's possible some of the setting details have changed by the time you're reading this. More and more of my favorite holes-in-the-wall are becoming condos and townhomes, and before they were my favorite holes-in-the-wall, they were someone else's favorite something else.

This is my third book that takes place in Seattle, but there is still so much I don't know about the place that's always been my home. If and when I leave this setting behind, it will always be in my veins and in my storyteller's soul.

Seattle, you are weird and wonderful, and I wouldn't have it any other way.

Acknowledgments

THIS BOOK IS a happy one, but I began writing it during a difficult time. While I have always been drawn to dark and heavy books, for months after the 2016 election, I couldn't bring myself to open one of the many guaranteed heartbreakers waiting on my shelf. I wanted to read—I don't know who I am if I'm not in the middle of three books at once—but nothing was calling to me. And that's when I found romance novels.

I've always loved romantic subplots, but I was largely unfamiliar with romance as a genre, and the more I read, the more I realized this was what I wanted to do next. My first two books had bittersweet endings and plenty of levity, but there was also a lot of despair. I didn't know if I could write a fun book—even all my shelved manuscripts are dark dark dark—and yet suddenly, it was all I wanted to write. Rowan wasn't actually a romance novelist in my first draft, but after I'd spent so much time learning the genre, it felt right to turn her into one. Nora Roberts, Meg Cabot, Christina Lauren, Alyssa Cole, Tessa Dare, Alisha Rai, Sally Thorne, Courtney Milan—without their books, I wouldn't have been able to write a romance about romance.

I'm ashamed to admit that my younger self was a lot like Neil, a lot like the people who judge an entire piece of pop culture before reading, watching, listening. The truth is that romance novels made me really and truly *happy* in a way books had never made me feel before. I'll always love dark books, and darkness finds its way into romance novels too, but there is such a comfort in knowing an HEA is waiting for you. And yet it still manages to feel earth-shattering every single time.

There aren't enough adjectives for my phenomenal editor, Jennifer Ung. Thank you for being immediately on board with a book so tonally different from my first two. Somehow you understand exactly what I'm trying to do, even when my intentions get lost between my brain and the page. My books are infinitely better because of you.

Thank you to Mara Anastas and the brilliant team at Simon Pulse: Chriscynethia Floyd, Liesa Abrams, Michelle Leo, Amy Beaudoin, Sarah Woodruff, Ana Perez, Amanda Livingston, Christine Foye, Christina Pecorale, Emily Hutton, Lauren Hoffman, Caitlin Sweeny, Alissa Nigro, Savannah Breckenridge, Nicole Russo, Lauren Carr, Anna Jarzab, Chelsea Morgan, Sara Berko, Rebecca Vitkus, and Penina Lopez. Laura Eckes, thank you for designing the cover of my dreams, and Laura Breiling, thank you for the perfect, perfect illustrations. To complete the Laura trifecta, thank you to my agent, Laura Bradford, for soothing my author anxiety and making the business side of writing run so smoothly.

Kelsey Rodkey, maybe it's fitting that this book begins and

ends with you. The insightful notes, the pep talks, the flailing, the memes . . . thank you for all of it. I adore you, and your friendship is so dear to me. HAGS! I'm immensely grateful to the friends who offered feedback in various stages of this book's life: Sonia Hartl, Carlyn Greenwald, Tara Tsai, Marisa Kanter, Rachel Griffin, Rachel Simon, Heather Ezell, Annette Christie, Monica Gomez-Hira, and Auriane Desombre. Thank you to my publishing confidantes Joy McCullough, Gloria Chao, Kit Frick, and Rosiee Thor, and thank you to my favorite coffee shop coworker, Tori Sharp. I am never letting any of you go!

I shared the earliest version of this book at a Djerassi workshop in June 2017, helmed by the spectacular Nova Ren Suma. Thank you, Nova, and thank you to Alison Cherry, Tamara Mahmood Hayes, Cass Frances, Imani Josey, Nora Revenaugh, Sara Ingle, Randy Ribay, and Kim Graff. That week in the mountains was one of the highlights of my career.

Ivan: these are the first acknowledgments where I can call you my husband! I'm so glad you're my person, and thank you for making the best deadline food.

It's always a little terrifying sending a book out into the world, and the support from readers, bloggers, booksellers, librarians, and teachers has made that experience much less terrifying. You all are INCREDIBLE, and I'm grateful beyond words for the posts, tweets, emails, and word of mouth that have helped make it possible for me to keep doing my dream job. With all of my heart, thank you.

Read the beginning of
Today Tonight Tomorrow
from Neil's point of view!
Turn the page for a sneak peek.

koi no yokan: *the feeling upon first meeting someone that you will inevitably fall in love with them (Japanese)*

I wake up before her.

It isn't my first thought when my alarm nudges me from sleep, but it's close.

My first thought is more of a feeling, this anticipatory nostalgia that ignites all my nerve endings, erases the dreams clinging to the edges of my mind. It's the way I've felt all week, and while we don't have a word for it in English, another language must—I'm sure of it. I'll have to look it up later.

My hand stumbles along my nightstand before finding my phone and dismissing the 5:45 alarm. No new messages, meaning she's either still asleep or decided not to text me. I'm certain there's about a zero percent chance of the latter.

I roll onto my side, propping myself up on one elbow while I swipe over to our text conversation. And even though I should be firing off a victorious "good morning," instead I scroll back, back, back, through days and weeks and months of taunts and jabs. Sometimes she wins this competition and sometimes I do, but it's been a while since the losing bothered me.

All this talking without saying anything. All these words that don't come close to conveying how I really feel.

Neil McNair

> Good morning!
> This is a friendly reminder that you have three (3) hours and counting before suffering a humiliating defeat at the hands of your future valedictorian.
> Bring tissues. I know you're a crier.

The anticipatory nostalgia strikes again. This is the last morning I will wake up as a high schooler with this precise view: a *Force Awakens* poster, a Free Puppies! concert flyer, the framed Torah portion from my bar mitzvah. The bookshelves, overstuffed, because if there is any other way to have a bookshelf, I haven't discovered it yet.

Eight minutes to six. I have to get moving.

I fight with the blanket for a moment before tossing it haphazardly across the bed. It isn't just the last day of senior year making me an anticipatory nostalgic mess. It's the letter that arrived last week from my dad, the one I've been trying my best not to think about. *Hope to see you before you go off to your fancy New York school*, he said, and somehow the adjective managed to feel like an insult. I shouldn't be surprised—he could attach malice to just about anything.

My phone buzzes, two soft pulses that immediately relieve some of the tension in my shoulders.

Rowan Roth

> oh, I didn't realize we still thought crying was a sign of weakness

> in the interest of accuracy, I'd like to point out that you've only seen me cry once, and I'm not sure that necessarily makes me "a crier"

I'm already grinning as I type back, because that is the magic of this rivalry we have. No matter what else is going on, Rowan Roth has this stunning ability to make me forget, to make me focus on only her.

She is a wonderful, terrible distraction.

> Over a book!

> You were inconsolable.

> it's called an emotion

> I highly recommend feeling one (1) sometime

A familiar white spine jumps out at me from my overstuffed bookshelves. I could probably pick out that Nora Roberts book with my eyes closed, given how often I've debated telling her that I read it. That I enjoyed it.

How many times have my fingers hovered over my phone's keyboard, wondering if I should text her exactly that? It would be casual—the kind of casual that comes with spending hours meticulously crafting a single sentence. Manufactured casual, but if there's one thing I'm good at doing around Rowan Roth, it's acting.

Other times, braver times, I've written out entire questions. *Do you want to meet up and study together? Do you and your friends want to check out a concert this weekend with the Quad and me?*

Theoretically, so simple. Subject, predicate, object. They're just words, after all. But words have power, and the words that make up a question like that could send us spiraling out of orbit. Or that's what I've been telling myself, because losing her as a rival is too depressing to fathom.

Our world has rules, and I've never wanted to break them as badly as I do today.

kopfkino: *the act of playing out a scenario in your mind (German)*

My mom is in the kitchen, locked in a staring contest with the sink. Our golden retriever, Lucy, is sitting next to her, tail swishing back and forth.

"You do know you have to actually turn on the water, right?"

She turns around. "Wow. Who is this handsome man, and what have you done with my son?"

Here's the thing. I love my mom. Genuinely and purely. My dad's crime must have shattered her more than it shattered me. It hasn't been easy for her since his imprisonment, but she's worked overtime, sometimes odd hours, to ensure she can spend as much time as possible with my sister and me.

That doesn't mean she isn't extremely embarrassing sometimes.

I drop my hand to Lucy's head, scratching behind her ears. "Is it too much?"

I have a few suits, all of which I've bought at Goodwill and altered myself using Mom's old sewing machine. She taught me years ago so I could help out with mending and hemming, and I liked it a lot more than I expected to.

Rowan loves to tease me for wearing suits on assembly days, and that might be part of the reason I keep doing it.

"Not at all," Mom says. "You look snazzy. Are the kids still saying that these days?"

"I'm not sure the kids have ever said that." I gesture to the sink. "What's going on here?"

Mom sighs, dragging the back of her hand across her forehead. She's in her work clothes, business casual, her auburn hair that's two shades darker than mine pulled back into a stub of a ponytail. "This ancient garbage disposal couldn't handle the tiny bit of sugary cereal milk I poured down it."

The sink is half full of murky water. I try the disposal, and it emits a low hum.

"I should have been out the door ten minutes ago," Mom continues, "but I didn't want to leave this for you or Natalie to deal with. And clearly mind control didn't work."

I'm already unbuttoning the suit jacket and rolling up my shirtsleeves. "I have time. Let me take a look."

I kneel on the cracked linoleum and peer underneath the sink, using my phone for some extra light. Our kitchen is small and dark, especially after a storm like the one we had last night. Not unusual for Seattle, but hopefully not auspicious for this last day of school.

"Good morning, good mooooorning!" my sister sings as she glides into the kitchen. She treats every day like the opening act of a Broadway musical. It must be good to be twelve.

"Morning, Nat," Mom says as she rummages in the pantry. I call out a hello from under the sink, grabbing the wrench we store down here for this exact reason and jamming it into the bottom of the disposal. "There's one last Pop-Tart, if you want it."

"I don't think we're legally allowed to call them Pop-Tarts if they're the generic kind," Natalie says.

"Right, what are those, Sucrose Squares?" I ask, teeth gritted as I work the wrench back and forth.

"Toaster Pies?" Mom tosses the box to Natalie before heading for her work bag, open on the kitchen table, and flipping through some file folders. Our morning routine is always a special kind of choreographed chaos.

"U-Toast-Ems. And they're delicious." Some shuffling as Natalie pops one in the toaster. "That's a nice suit. What do you think *Rowan*'s going to wear today? Is *Rowan* dressing up?"

Really, the younger generation is far too perceptive. Sure, I've talked about Rowan with my family, but I've never so much as alluded to the crush I've had on her for the past year, and yet Mom and Natalie are convinced I'm going to come home from school one day and declare I've asked my longtime enemy for her hand in marriage.

"Crush" doesn't feel like the right word, though. It never has.

I twist from my sitting position to look up at my sister, innocently munching her off-brand Pop-Tart at the kitchen table while Mom races back to her bedroom for "one last thing."

"If I had to guess, I'd say clothes. She'll probably be wearing clothes."

As soon as I say it, my face flames, and I have to turn back to the sink so my mother and sister don't think I'm imagining the opposite of Rowan Roth "probably wearing clothes."

Which I'm not.

For the love of Hemingway, Natalie starting babbling about the sleepover she's having tonight, saving me from any further Rowan discourse.

"We're just about—*there*," I say with a swell of satisfaction as the wrench starts moving more freely. I turn on the faucet and hit the switch for the disposal, and there it is, its usual soft gurgle.

Natalie thrusts her U-Toast-Em into the air. "Hooray, we can dispose of garbage again!"

"One of these days, we'll get a new one." Mom arrives back in the kitchen, shrugging into a blazer, her expression morphing to horror when she sees me. "Oh no, Neil. Your suit."

Sure enough, there's grayish water running down my shirt and onto my pants.

I only barely have time to shower again. My jacket's unharmed, but it doesn't match the pants of my next best suit, and unfortunately my next best suit is . . . imperfect. I was still getting the hang of the sewing machine, and the pants are slightly too short, the jacket sleeves slightly too long. Given most teens aren't menswear experts, I don't expect anyone to notice—except Rowan. When it comes to me, her level of scrutiny is unparalleled and, frankly, impressive.

A *Seattle Times* update on my phone informs me a few thousand Seattle residents are without power, and when I pull up a map, I realize Rowan might be in one of those neighborhoods. I only have a vague idea of where she lives, since going to each other's houses is not something rivals do.

Hope everything's okay if you lost power, I type. I let the draft marinate while knotting my tie, then erase it. We don't do sympathy.

Neil McNair

> Aren't you in that neighborhood without power?

> I'd hate to mark you late . . . or have you lose the perfect attendance award.

> Have they ever had a student council (co)president win zero awards?

Rowan Roth

> how have you not run out of ways to mock me after four years?

What can I say, you're an endless source of inspiration.

> and you are an endless source of migraines

Excedrin and Kleenex, DON'T FORGET.

As I hit send, I get an idea. I grab a travel pack of Kleenex from our bathroom and tuck it into my pocket. If it annoys her, great. If it makes her laugh, even better. Then I head back to the kitchen, backpack over one shoulder. My Free Puppies! pin, the one I got at the first show of theirs I ever went to, is hanging on for dear life. Once I'm in New York, I'll get a new backpack, I tell myself. Something big enough to carry around my new life.

"Mom! You should really go."

"I know, I know," she says, even as she's loading plates into the dishwasher. "I just couldn't let you leave without saying goodbye. Don't you want something to eat? Some cereal, maybe, or a piece of toast?"

I wave this off. The bus will be here in a few minutes. "I'll be fine. Short day."

Mom seems to allow herself to breathe for the first time this morning. She takes a step back, examining me like she's seeing me for the first time, or maybe in a different light. Her first kid, almost done with high school. I imagine it's a surreal feeling, as evidenced by the almost-too-tight hug she gives me. "Thank you for your help. I love you. Go be valedictorian."

"Love you too," I say, and with that, she disappears into the garage.

"Tell Rowan I say hi!" Natalie calls as I leave, and I call back to her that I most definitely will not.

She's still laughing as I shut the door, this light, bright sound that makes me think everything is going to be okay. We *are* okay, the three of us. Even if for the longest time, I didn't think we ever would be.

saudade: *a profound melancholic yearning for someone (Portuguese)*

The bus drops me off a couple blocks from school, the way it has nearly every weekday for the past four years. My last bus ride—something that shouldn't make nostalgic, especially given my propensity for getting sick if I sit anywhere but the first three rows. Really, it's astounding Rowan hasn't thrown herself at me already.

Sean, Cyrus, and Adrian are waiting at our lockers. When he spots me, Sean gives me a nod of approval that doubles as a way to flick his long bangs out of his eyes. "Looking sharp." If he doesn't notice the imperfections of the suit, maybe there's a chance Rowan won't either. "Okay, now that McNair's here, are we doing this?"

"My Anime Appreciation Society friends nearly took up all my free pages, but I told them they had to leave room for you guys," Cyrus says. "Because, you know, Quad life."

"Quad life!" the rest of us whoop back. Maybe people stare at us sometimes, but these guys are more my family than my dad is these days.

We decided to wait until the last day to sign each other's yearbooks—"it'll be more meaningful that way," Sean said—but we had to promise to save each other enough pages. When Adrian takes my yearbook after Sean and Cyrus have signed, I say, "Make sure you leave a little space, okay?"

"Still psyching yourself up to ask Rowan?" Adrian shakes his head. "Dude. When are you going to admit that you're madly in love with her?"

When there's no fear of her using it against me in some way.

"Signing each other's yearbooks is a perfectly normal thing to do." I force myself to stand up straighter as Adrian rolls his eyes.

The warning bell rings just as we're passing yearbooks back to their original owners. Classes are more of a formality today than anything else. I'm an office assistant during homeroom, a gig I took because, well, I like the people who work in the office, the secretaries and the counselors and the principal and vice principal. When you're a good kid, they treat you like an adult. I'm not sure I have any cool points left—or if I ever had any—but if I did, surely this would plunge me into the negatives.

My hair is still damp from my second shower, and I run a hand through it as I enter the office, hoping I don't look as unkempt as I feel. I was so confident in my first suit, but I left all that confidence wherever my cool points are. I trade hellos with the secretaries and vice principal, then take my seat behind the front desk.

Principal Meadows strolls inside with a large cup of coffee and thank-god-it's-almost-summer sunniness on her face that clashes with the weather outside. "Morning! You hanging in there, Neil?"

"I'll be a lot better after the assembly," I admit, but suddenly, I'm not so certain that's true.

"It's going to be tough to say goodbye to you two. You've really given us quite a show," she says, and there's that familiar warmth that comes with being mentioned in the same breath as Rowan.

Of course I want valedictorian. My entire high school career has been leading up to it. But Rowan's worked hard for it too, with this drive I admired long before my feelings for her changed. Today isn't just my last competition with her—it's my last chance to tell her those feelings go beyond rivalry.

If I don't summon the courage, I'm sure I'd recover from this eventually, this more-than-a-crush that sparks through my veins and makes me choose words more carefully than ever before. Years from now, I could scroll through her social media and not feel a thing except a prickly pang of high school nostalgia. I'd forget the sound of her scoff and the curve of her mouth and the scent of her strawberry shampoo when she sits too close in student council meetings.

But I'd always wonder, *what if*.

It's then, as Principal Meadows disappears into her office and the bell chimes again, that I make a decision: I'm going to tell her. Somehow.

For the next fifteen minutes, I hand out late passes for underclassmen who won't be getting out of school for another two weeks.

When the door opens at 7:21 a.m., though, I have to use every muscle in my face to keep from smiling.

Because there is Rowan Roth, giving off intense *you are the last person I want to see right now* vibes. She's wearing a cute blue dress with a white collar, and oh god—knee socks. I didn't know I was weak for knee socks, but if she's wearing them, I am. She's always messing with her wild, impossible, beautiful hair, tucking wayward strands back into place or smoothing out her bangs, and today is no exception. I wonder if she's even aware she's doing it.

She's half out of breath, electric with a frantic kind of energy, and it looks like she spilled something on the dress. Coffee? This may also be the reason she seems so upset—her brows slashed, a little furrow between them. So maybe it isn't just me, a thought that makes me considerably more hopeful than it should. I fight every urge to ask her what happened. In a parallel universe, I'd offer her a towel or ask if anyone in the office has one of those stain remover pens, although I think she might need a bit more than a single pen. Or maybe I'd offer her a hoodie. The vision of Rowan Roth wearing a hoodie of mine is enough to make my brain short-circuit.

I wish I could see something on her face besides disdain, a flicker of *anything* to indicate she won't laugh or run or just stand there staring once I confess to her that I don't just have a crush on her.

I am in love with her, and I can't bear to think about how much I'm going to miss her next year.

She looks so adorably frazzled that it's an effort to school my expression into the rival I'm supposed to be.

"Rowan Roth," I say, reaching inside my jacket pocket for the pack of tissues. "I got you something."

Turn the page for a sneak peek at the sequel to *Today Tonight Tomorrow*

ROMANCE NOVELS DON'T talk about what happens when the heroine and hero go off to different colleges.

Of course, this is usually because both people are gainfully employed adults. Maybe they're lobbying for the same promotion, or one is an environmental activist trying to protect a park from a real estate developer—and its unfairly charming CEO. Or one is a governess to three wild rascals whose father is a grumpy, dashing rake with a hidden vulnerability at his core.

There aren't many rakes who attend small liberal arts schools on the East Coast.

"I can't believe I'm saying this," Neil starts, surveying my room with a grim expression, eyes narrowed behind his glasses, "but I think you might be bringing too many books."

I glance up from where I've been pleading with my suitcase's stubborn zipper. "If they're not close to me, how will I be inspired by them?"

Except he might be right, a statement I'd never have allowed to cross my mind until three months ago, because the suitcase is too small and too full and there are still too many things I can't take with me. In my defense, most of my stuff is already packed and waiting in the hall downstairs. This is my last suitcase. The one I've been dreading, because of everything it symbolizes.

When the zipper doesn't budge, I dig a hand inside and extricate two pastel Nora Roberts paperbacks, weighing them for a moment before putting one back on my bookshelf.

Neil lifts an eyebrow. His arms are crossed over his chest, giving him the appearance of a stern, extremely cute statue.

With a groan, I add the other one to the shelf too.

"You said you needed help," he reminds me. "In fact, 'I need you to be ruthless' were your exact words when you sent me that SOS text this morning."

"Yeah, but not about *Nora*." I return my attention to the suitcase, and after an initial stutter, the zipper slides shut. "You know, I think I've been demonstrating extraordinary restraint." I walk over to my closet, nudging aside a few dresses to reveal the stack of mass-market paperbacks that don't fit on my bookshelf, most of them collected from garage sales and thrift stores.

Neil doesn't even look surprised. "Ah, yes. That infamous Rowan Roth restraint. She never exaggerates. Never bends the truth. Never romanticizes anything."

I give him an intense side-eye, and his faux seriousness finally cracks, gaze softening and mouth tilting into a grin.

Late August sun arrows through my window, illuminating the freckles on his skin and the lovely golden undertones in his auburn hair. This time of year, it doesn't get dark until after ten o'clock, and we've been taking advantage of those daylight hours as much as we can.

Most people seemed to think we wouldn't last the summer, but the past two and a half months have been the best of my life—and that's not an exaggeration at all. Some days Neil would hole up in the café where I work, sitting in a corner with an iced chai, busy with his own summer job—remote transcription for a local law office—and when Two Birds One Scone closed, we'd take unsold pastries to a park or sneak them into a movie theater. We'd bring his sister to the beach or skate park, double-date with Kirby and Mara, argue about *Star Wars* with his friends. A few days ago, we celebrated my nineteenth birthday with a ferry trip to Whidbey Island. We have eaten too much gelato and squinted too many times into the sun, picked out books for each other to read and mapped the entire city on foot. We've gotten great at pushing curfew, chasing sunsets, "just ten more minutes." And then fifteen more after that.

The whole time, what we've really excelled at is putting off talking about the inevitable: the fact that tomorrow, I fly to Boston while he boards a plane to New York.

I turn away from the closet. "You like telling me what to do," I say, placing the tip of my index finger on his sternum and slowly inching it upward. Teasing, which is still one of my favorite things to do to him.

He's already blushing, long lashes fluttering shut. In the

beginning of our relationship I worried he might stop blushing altogether, and it's been the sweetest surprise that he hasn't, that he wears his emotions so plainly for me. "Only because there's no other circumstance under which you'd allow it."

The spark in my chest when I tug him closer by the collar of his T-shirt is a familiar little thrill. I intend for it to be a quick peck, but the moment my lips meet his, I dissolve.

His hands come up to my hair, deepening the kiss as I propel us backward, shoving at my suitcase to make room for us on the bed. Then I'm in his lap, his earthy scent altering my brain chemistry, each ragged exhale making me crave the next one. His fingertips on the waist of my shirtdress. My mouth on his throat.

There is something about this boy that undoes me every single time, and sometimes I still can't believe all of it is real.

As though perfectly attuned to what's going on behind it, there's a knock on my half-cracked door. Neil and I spring to our feet, smoothing our hair and pretending to be immersed in separate tasks: me, unzipping and rezipping the suitcase, Neil, examining the mug on my desk where I keep my pens and pencils, the one with a watercolor splash of the Seattle skyline.

We've gotten good at that, too, almost as good as my parents are at knowing exactly when we're about to cross the line into PG-13.

It's become something of a joke, albeit a frustrating one: the fact that it's nearly impossible to find some alone time. When we slept together for the first time on the last day of school—or I guess technically, the day after the last day of school, since it happened around four in the morning—neither of us had intended for the relationship to progress that far. I definitely hadn't woken up that day and imagined I'd be kissing my longtime rival Neil McNair, let alone sneaking him into my bedroom. But it had just felt *right*, the two of us being connected in that way. I had this new, persistent ache that I'd never be able to get enough of him; I wanted to have long, sometimes contentious conversations about the world just as much as I wanted to learn all the ways our bodies could fit together. Because even if we went from zero to one hundred in a single night, there's still plenty we haven't done, bases we've skipped that I've been hoping we can find our way back around to.

His sister just hit the age where their mom is comfortable leaving her home alone all day, and my parents work from their downstairs office. A few times, we tangled ourselves in the back seat of my Honda Accord, at least until a police officer banged on the window and it spooked us so much we haven't tried it since.

My dad steps inside my room and greets Neil with a wave before turning to me. "Ro-Ro?" he says, leaning against the doorframe. "You just about ready? We should leave soon if we want to get there by five."

Before answering him, I take a moment to gaze around the room. The bulletin board above my desk, where I've pinned photos of my friends and academic ribbons and a list Neil and I made on the last day of school: ROWAN ROTH'S GUIDE TO COLLEGE

SUCCESS . . . AND BEYOND! My senior yearbook with his love confession in it, an item too precious to transport across the country because I'm not sure I could bear it if an airline lost it.

And Neil, standing there with a sweet, sheepish smile, one stubborn strand of hair refusing to lie flat.

Yes, and no.

Theoretically, I'm ready, but I'm also not sure how fearlessly I can let go.

"As I'll ever be," I say, and when I close the door, it somehow feels like I'm shutting away so much more.

My parents insisted on a send-off before I leave, a picnic at Green Lake with black-bean burgers and roasted corn. Kirby Taing and Mara Pompetti are already there, no doubt ready to gloat about their extra weeks of summer because the University of Washington doesn't start until the end of September.

Eager to have a job, my dad lights the grill while my mom passes out compostable plates. Neil's mom, Joelle, arrives with a Tupperware of cubed watermelon and a wide-brimmed sunhat. A family of redheads means a lot of SPF.

It's only mildly embarrassing for your parents to meet your boyfriend's mom, something I discovered last month when all five of us went out to dinner. It hadn't happened with my past boyfriends, felt too serious for those relationships. A strange kind of *So, how about our kids' raging hormones?* But they clicked instantly, bonding over their opinions about the new Seattle waterfront (mixed) and whether the Seahawks have a chance at the playoffs this year (no).

We take a few minutes to settle in, exchanging hugs and hellos. All around us, people are playing croquet and walking their dogs and rollerblading, the latter two occasionally done at the same time, Seattleites soaking up what might be the last nice day of the season. Because in this city, you just never know.

"If someone doesn't promise me this isn't the end, I might cry," Mara says. Her wavy blond hair is in a loose bun, and a minidress emphasizes her calves, toned from years of dance.

With one eye, I watch Neil and my dad standing semi-awkwardly at the grill, as though they've decided that this is how they Bond as Men, though Joelle is the one to inform them that the burgers are starting to burn.

Next to Mara on the park bench, Kirby gives her shoulder a squeeze. "It'll be okay. Just think, only one hundred and twenty-two more days until we're all reunited."

"That's supposed to make me feel better? That's an eternity."

I reach for a passionfruit La Croix and pop the tab. "Just think about all the times I've annoyed you over the years," I say. "You'll be too busy to miss me. How many credits are you taking again, Mara?"

"Only twenty-two," she says innocently. "I just want to get all my pre-reqs done as soon as I can." Kirby, long known for trying to get as much done with as little effort as possible, is taking the recommended fifteen credits for freshmen, unsure what she'll major in.

"And I still think you should have decided to take Anthropology of Ice Cream with me," Kirby says. "Although if we don't actually get to eat ice cream, I may riot."

Burgers and corn are passed around while we talk more about our fall schedules. My creative writing class is the one I can't wait for, taught by a darling of the literary fiction world whose books I devoured earlier this summer. In college, I will be entirely unashamed of my dream career, and Miranda Everett's class—undeniably full of other aspiring novelists—will be where I take the first step.

Mara bites into her burger. "If your roommate is cooler than we are, please don't tell us."

"Speak for yourself," Kirby says, miming putting on boxing gloves. "Personally, I think it's more advantageous to know your enemies."

"I'm not replacing either of you!"

Neil slides in next to me with his plate of food, our parents immersed in a conversation about the rising cost of textbooks. His knee nudges mine. "Neither am I. Who else could mercilessly torment us about our relationship like you, Kirby?"

It's true: even though my friends knew how I felt about him before I did, they rarely hesitate to joke about our four-year rivalry and the game that made us realize what idiots we'd been. Lovingly, of course.

Kirby beams. "I try my best."

"Seattle's definitely going to feel smaller without both of you," Mara says as Kirby sinks her teeth into her ear of corn, the kernels blackened and buttered, and it's then that I realize something else: I've been so caught up in the logistics of packing, I've barely processed the fact that in twenty-four hours, I will no longer live here.

The place I've spent my whole life, the city that's just as much a part of me as my troublesome bangs or my affinity for vintage clothes. Case in point: the lavender floral shirtdress I'm wearing now, plucked from a rack at Red Light last month.

I wonder if thrift shopping will be as fun in Boston without my best friends.

Just as the black-bean burger starts to turn uncomfortably in my stomach, my mom calls out to get everyone's attention, lifting her can of seltzer in a toast. "Hear, hear," she says. "To Rowan and Neil, and all the adventures you're going to have next year on the other side of the country. We're all going to miss you, but we know you're going to do great things."

Joelle holds her own can high. "That's lovely, Ilana. To having new experiences and meeting new people, and then coming home and telling us all about it."

"To trying a slice of real New York pizza," Neil says.

"To exploring Boston's independent bookstores," I add, even as a lump forms in my throat. "And never being embarrassed to be caught in the romance section."

Everyone toasts. Sips. The fizz settles my stomach, and I try my best to banish my nerves for the rest of the evening. Because in a matter of hours, this—my life in Seattle—is really, truly ending. I thought I'd made peace with it, allowed myself to mourn while leaving space for all the excitement I'm taking with me to the East Coast. But now I'm just not sure.

Maybe that's how you're supposed to feel on the precipice of drastic change.

By the time the sun begins its descent in the sky, Joelle has to leave to pick up Neil's sister from a friend's house and my parents, perpetual early risers, are starting to yawn, a fact we considered when we took separate cars. Kirby and Mara, realizing that Neil and I might want just a little more time to ourselves, hug us tight as I promise to text them the moment I land.

It's gotten chilly, but it's nothing that can't be solved by burrowing closer to Neil on the picnic blanket. I brought his heather-gray hoodie with me, the one I don't plan on ever giving back, but I left it in the car. His body heat is so much better.

"On a scale of one to ten, what do you think is the likelihood that our parents will become best friends while we're gone?" he asks, draping his arm across my shoulders and pulling me against his chest.

"At least a nine. It's cute, though. I don't want any of them to be lonely." When I let out a sigh, it sounds much more agonized than I'm anticipating. I'd hoped we could end the night without a therapy session, but apparently I was wrong.

"You're anxious. Do you want to talk about it?"

"Oh, just the usual fear of the unknown," I say. "I think the worst part is that I don't know *any* of what to expect. Every single part of it will be new. I can visualize the campus, but not my dorm room or my classrooms. I don't know what Boston's transit cards look like or if my professors will like me or where I'll sit when I'm calling you."

"Is it unhelpful if I remind you that you don't have to have it all planned out right now?"

"No, but it doesn't change the fact that I *want* to," I say with a small whine.

For a few thoughtful beats, he lets his fingertips play through my hair. A gentle rhythm. "Do you remember," he says, "sophomore year, when honors English went on that field trip to see a modern reimagining of *Macbeth* and we wound up sitting next to each other?"

"Shhh! The Scottish play," I quickly correct him. As if I don't remember all of it. Every moment of the last four years. "The one where all the characters worked in a McDonald's, and Lady Macbeth kept trying to scrub ketchup off her hands? Of course. I should probably apologize, huh. I think I tried to get Sean to switch seats with me."

His laugh drums against my cheek, that sound I love becoming something almost tangible. "You asked, once, if I remembered when I started having feelings for you. And I think that was it. The whole time we watched, I could hear everyone else making fun of it, but you were so quiet. You paid attention, because it was school, and the fact that it was a field trip didn't change that.

When you laughed, it was genuine. Sincere. The acting was terrible, but you took it seriously. And a couple times, you glanced over at me to see if I was laughing too."

"You were," I say, that seemingly trivial day coming back to me. A dark theater, my nemesis next to me. The pride that comes with getting the humor, obnoxious smart alecks that we were. Are. "At the same time, usually."

"Right. And it made me feel so connected to you, the fact that you were curious if I found the same things funny. Plus . . . you smelled really nice. I went home and thought to myself, 'This is it. This is the girl.' I was done for." His thumb travels down the length of my neck, and it would be so easy to close my eyes and fall asleep like this as the sky turns dark. Then he buries his nose in my hair, takes a deep inhale. "Still just as intoxicating."

I laugh-yelp as he does this, pretending to push him away.

"You've been important to me for years," he continues, as though he knows I need the reassurance, and I tuck those words right next to my heart. "The distance isn't going to change that."

We shift on the blanket, Neil sliding me on top of him while he kisses me, and it isn't long before I'm pressing myself more firmly against his jeans, grateful the park has emptied out. I've given a little thought to missing him like *this*, the abject neediness of his breaths and mine. The groan when my lips settle in the spot where his neck meets his shoulder. His hands on my hips and mine on his face, as though if we just cling tight enough, we can make those weeks go by that much faster.

I never expected to fall so hard, so quickly for someone right before our lives split in different directions. Even if my feelings had been dormant for most of high school, that night in June put the past four years in such sharp, renewed focus. A rose-tinted filter. While I also never thought I'd be starting college with a boyfriend, I can't imagine how I'd feel if we'd given ourselves an expiration date, the way some couples in our graduating class did, determined to go to school with zero attachments. A few times, I wondered if we'd break up before August and wouldn't have to worry about it.

But the thing is, dating Neil McNair isn't actually all that different from sparring with him. We just get to make out afterward.

Being with Neil, I realized a few weeks into our relationship, is *easy*. Which naturally makes me more convinced the universe was playing a trick on us this summer, two and a half months of bliss before catapulting us into a long-distance relationship.

All my years of planning and daydreaming, the times I swore I'd be different and live more in the moment, and the imminence of it takes me completely by surprise. It's nerves and uncertainty and a touch of nausea knotted up in one twisted ball.

It's the fear that once I drive away tonight, we will never again have what we had this summer.

Eventually we have to head back to my car, one of the last ones in the parking lot after we circled and circled to find a spot hours ago. His hair is wonderfully mussed, my body still buzzing with a desperate electricity. As though my bones and muscles cannot bear to let him go.

The drive is too short—we pull up to his house after several detours and "just five more minutes" that somehow last almost thirty. With more effort than it's ever taken, I shut off the engine and engage the parking brake, an ominous silence filling the car.

"We were too spoiled," I say, staring directly ahead because if I look at him, I might not be able to hold it together. "Seeing each other nearly every day for the past four years."

Neil shakes his head; I catch the motion out of the corner of my eye. "No, no, no. I was pining for most of those four years, absolutely tortured because the girl I liked couldn't stand me. You were simply going about your life, vaguely annoyed by some guy with too many freckles."

"Maaaaaybe. But before we got together, I couldn't imagine not seeing you every day. Did I ever tell you that?" I turn to him, and the look on his face tells me that I did not. "The few weeks leading up to graduation, I'd get your texts in the morning and feel a little sad that they were coming to an end."

A patented Neil McNair smirk. "And you, connoisseur of romance novels, didn't realize you were madly in love with me."

"Yeah, well. We all have our flaws."

When he reaches for my hand, there's no trace of humor in his expression. "I miss you already," he says as we thread our fingers together. "Is that weird?"

"We'll text and talk all the time. I already have my train ticket for the end of September."

"And then I'll be in Boston for Thanksgiving."

"Why does that feel so far away?"

Suddenly I'm worried we haven't discussed it enough, that we spent too much time living in the moment this summer when we should have mapped out call schedules with color-coded spreadsheets.

It's what High School Rowan might have done, but I guess that's not who I am anymore.

"We're going to be okay." His voice is solid, and his eyes on me will never not make me feel so wholly *seen*. "I can't wait to show you New York. Assuming, of course, that I know my way around after a month." A soft smile. "I love you, Artoo."

The nickname has its intended effect: to remind me that all our history cannot be undone just because we'll be in two different states.

"I love you too." I hold him close. Inhale deeply. One more kiss, and then another. "Fly safe and don't forget me."

"Impossible."

I try to stop the statistics about long-distance relationships racing through my mind as he opens the passenger door, kisses two fingers, and holds them to his heart. With a grit I honed over four years of trying to best him, I push aside the anxiety and replace it with a fierce resolve.

We're going to be the ones who make it.

After all, overachieving is kind of what we're known for.

Read the "**unequivocally hilarious and delightful**" (*Kirkus Reviews*), "**sweet and funny**" (Kerry Winfrey, author of *Waiting for Tom Hanks*) rom-coms by *New York Times* and *USA Today* bestselling author **LYNN PAINTER**.

PRINT AND EBOOK EDITIONS AVAILABLE FROM SIMON & SCHUSTER BFYR
SIMONANDSCHUSTER.COM/TEEN